THE

BLOOD

CONFESSION

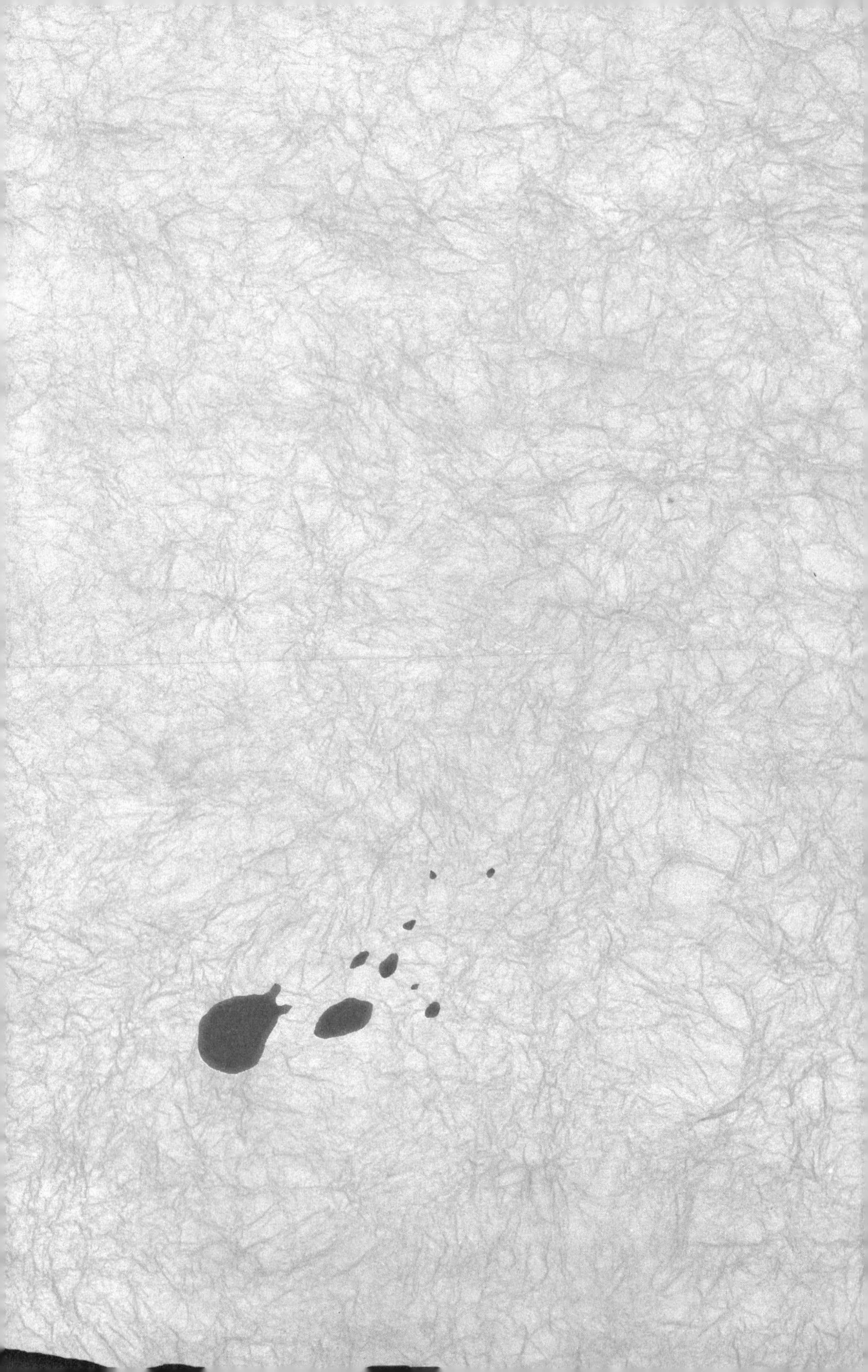

The Blood Confession

Alisa M. Libby

DUTTON
BOOKS

DUTTON BOOKS
A member of Penguin Group (USA) Inc.

PUBLISHED BY THE PENGUIN GROUP

Penguin Group (USA) Inc., 375 Hudson Street, New York, New York 10014, U.S.A.

Penguin Group (Canada), 90 Eglinton Avenue East, Suite 700, Toronto, Ontario, Canada M4P 2Y3
(a division of Pearson Penguin Canada Inc.)

Penguin Books Ltd, 80 Strand, London WC2R 0RL, England

Penguin Ireland, 25 St Stephen's Green, Dublin 2, Ireland (a division of Penguin Books Ltd)

Penguin Group (Australia), 250 Camberwell Road, Camberwell, Victoria 3124, Australia
(a division of Pearson Australia Group Pty Ltd)

Penguin Books India Pvt Ltd, 11 Community Centre, Panchsheel Park, New Delhi–110 017, India

Penguin Group (NZ), Cnr Airborne and Rosedale Roads, Albany, Auckland 1310, New Zealand
(a division of Pearson New Zealand Ltd)

Penguin Books (South Africa) (Pty) Ltd, 24 Sturdee Avenue, Rosebank, Johannesburg 2196, South Africa

Penguin Books Ltd, Registered Offices: 80 Strand, London WC2R 0RL, England

Library of Congress Cataloging-in-Publication Data
Libby, Alisa M.
The blood confession / Alisa M. Libby.—1st ed.
p. cm.
Summary: Cursed at birth, the beautiful and ruthless young Erzebet becomes obsessed with achieving eternal youth and begins to bathe in the blood of virgin girls in order to preserve her beauty. Based on the life of the "Blood Countess," who lived in Hungary in the 1500s.
ISBN 0-525-47732-2
1. Báthory, Erzsébet, 1560–1614—Juvenile fiction. [1. Báthory, Erzsébet, 1560–1614—Fiction. 2. Blood—Fiction. 3. Beauty, Personal—Fiction. 4. Murder—Fiction. 5. Countesses—Fiction. 6. Hungary—History—Turkish occupation, 1526–1699—Fiction.] I. Title.
PZ7.L591177Bl 2006 [Fic]—dc22 2005029781

Published in the United States by Dutton Books,
a member of Penguin Group (USA) Inc.
345 Hudson Street, New York, New York 10014
www.penguin.com/youngreaders

Designed by Heather Wood
Printed in USA / First Edition
1 3 5 7 9 10 8 6 4 2

This book is dedicated

to the memory of my father,

Bertram Moskowitz,

my first reader, critic, and fan.

THE

BLOOD

CONFESSION

Part One

CASTLE

*For the life of the flesh is in the blood:
and I have given it to you upon the altar
to make an atonement for your souls: for
it is the blood that maketh an atonement
for the soul.*

LEVITICUS 17:11

I

Day three, tower, late in day

A small sharp blade is required for sharpening the point of a quill. I sit close to the fire in this dim chamber, honing the point of a feather to ready it for the awaiting page.

"I can do that for you, my lady." A young servant steps into my light, her face flushed and urgent.

"No need," I mutter, but she moves closer and holds out her hand.

"Please, my lady," she repeats. She is a young woman, but there is a deep crease between her eyes. She looks at me steadily with her hand outstretched.

"Does it make you nervous," I ask her, "to see me hold a knife?"

I balance the slim blade between my thumb and forefinger. She does not answer, but all of the servants watch us, their eyes gleaming in the dimness. Obediently, I rest the blade and quill in her open palm.

Settling back in my chair by the fire, I watch the servant work. She struggles to hold the quill steady while paring the edges to a fine point.

"I'm going to write a statement of confession before they bring me to trial." I watch how my words are reflected in their faces. "Don't you think that's wise?"

"I suppose that would be, Countess," one servant ventures cautiously, "unless you would rather wait for the prince to arrive."

"I'm tired of waiting; he takes too long," I inform them restlessly. The five young women sit in a crescent around me upon silk-cushioned sofas and chairs—assembled like an audience, I muse, and I am on the stage. None of them look at me, their noses buried in embroidery in the flickering light of the fire, their eyes creased with strain.

"I can tell you all a story, while we wait. You do like stories, don't you?" I ask them. A few acknowledge my question with a flash of their eyes. Others stare dutifully at the mending upon their laps. One young girl begins to nod, but is cut down by a harsh look from the woman beside her. I smile at this girl especially.

"You've heard this story before, I'm sure. It's the story of the evil queen," I begin, my voice a bit louder than before, "who sees a girl far more beautiful than she, the girl's face appearing in the queen's mirror."

The women say nothing, but I know they are listening. I hear the guard shift nervously outside the door of the tower.

"The evil queen sends a hunter to kill the beautiful child and bring back her heart, so that she may make a feast of it for her dinner. The taste of the girl's blood will give the queen's envious heart peace, for it will make her again the most beautiful. You do know this story, don't you?"

I look again at the girl who nodded and I smile. She begins to smile but blushes and looks back to her mending, fearing any repercussions. It's inappropriate to smile at a madwoman.

"Yes, I remember," she murmurs.

"It teaches a valuable lesson. Beauty can be transferred through the blood, from one woman to another."

A log cracks upon the flames and a shower of sparks fall over the hearth.

"There is danger in beauty, as well as power. Wouldn't you agree?"

No one answers. One servant purses her lips and sighs, setting aside her embroidery. She walks to lift a tapestry from a narrow window, to check the hour. From where I'm seated I can see the pink light of sunset reflected upon her pale face.

When night falls I will remain in this tower, and two guards will stand at my door. The rest of the servants will tramp gratefully down the spiral stairs and sigh into bedchambers on the first floor of the castle. Despite their seeming indifference, these stories will rise in the darkness, while they lie in bed not sleeping. My voice will repeat these words in their heads. When they wake and trudge up the stairs to this tower tomorrow their shoulders will be hunched; their eyes will look bruised.

It is this way in the village, as well, where such stories were born. This castle lies in the distance, sprawled upon the mountains like a great, sleeping lion. In the daytime the peasants of Novoe Mesto will spit angrily in its direction and warn their children to look away. But at night, in the darkness, the image of Castle Bizecka will rise before them and the words of legends will lie upon their bodies like lead.

"Ah!" the servant beside me gasps and a hiss of air escapes her clenched teeth. The quill and knife lie on her white apron as she inspects the cut on her finger: a bead of blood, like a ruby, rises from the wound. The sight of it warms, satisfies me.

The taste of the girl's blood will give the queen's envious heart peace. *Some of those old stories are true.*

Day four, tower, mid-morning

This tower is where the bleedings took place. As soon as the charges made against me became public, I was sequestered here by force, per order of Stephan, Prince of Poland and distant cousin of my father. We are waiting for his arrival, for the prince is eager to have the trial take place under his watchful gaze in the small town of Novoe Mesto, before word of it spreads over the borders of this provincial Hungarian town. I suppose I cannot blame him—he desires to be king someday.

"Are you sure I cannot leave here, with supervision, of course?" I ask, feeling claustrophobic in the circular tower room. A group of female servants arrives every day to keep close watch over me, but none of them bend to my will, as I am accustomed.

"We are under strict orders, my lady. You are not to be released." A girl with round cheeks and mouse-brown hair offers a clipped bow at my feet, then resumes her arrangement of the tea tray.

"Not even for a walk in the garden? You could come with me—the garden is lovely, even in the winter."

"I'm sorry, Countess. We are under orders from the prince." She offers me a teacup. With a wave of my hand I smash the cup to the floor. The servant says nothing. I watch as she carefully picks up each shard, then I move to my dressing table and sit before the oval mirror.

I lift a hand to affix a loose curl with a pin and lean forward to look closely at my face. My skin is still smooth and white as the porcelain pitcher on my nightstand. I must keep a close eye on it, especially during my imprisonment: my beauty rituals are not accessible to me while I'm watched by servants and guards in this tower room. Until my release I can only inspect my face carefully, wary for any blemish, any change.

At my age, many women of beauty are already long past their prime. But my face has not changed since my portrait was painted at the age of sixteen: fair skin, sparkling black eyes, a long narrow nose, and high cheekbones. My face and body are elegantly angular; a long white neck, long thin limbs. I pin up a lock of shining dark auburn hair, enjoying how it shines glossy in the firelight. The light in this chamber reflects off the golden tissue of my grand gown: a rich, lustrous skirt and bodice of red satin overlaid with a delicate lace of gold. I watch my movements in the mirror, the way the dress seems to twinkle like a star in this light, as though it might suddenly blaze forth in vivid glory. The prince will visit me any day now; it's important for me to look my best. I remain wary of the servants' grim, nervous faces reflected in the background.

When I look back at my own reflection in the mirror, it is not my face I see: a flash of dark hazel eyes, a cloud of curly black hair. I gasp and grip the back of a chair, to steady myself. In a moment the vision fades, and I'm relieved to see my own face again. But my face is different, pale as parchment, black eyes wide with fear. I laugh lightly, hoping the twinge of pain in my chest will subside.

My mother was right after all: a mirror remembers every face it has reflected.

Day four, tower, night

I don't like the servants, but when they leave at night, I am lonely. The stone walls of this tower feel like ice against my skin. Wind seeps through the narrow casements, lifting the heavy tapestries and shifting shadows upon the floor.

I have nothing to do in this chamber but remember. Beyond the door to this tower is a stairwell, where two guards remain through the night. At the bottom of those stairs is a wide hallway, where white patches of sunlight shine upon the flagstone floor. At the end of the hallway is the dining hall. This room connects to the main kitchen, where the kettle is boiling over the hearth, the cook is kneading dough for bread, and the eggs are stacked in the larder. I imagine all of this clearly, with my eyes shut to the dark: my daintily slippered feet tapping upon the flagstones, the heavy tapestries pressed beneath my palm, the smells of paprika lifting my nose. No one can see me. My memory moves through the halls of this castle like a ghost.

My memory wanders back to this tower and climbs down the spiral staircase to the dungeon below. I don't want to go here, not even in my head, but memory is stubborn and often brings you places you don't want to go. I walk through the main chamber and into one of the dark, adjoining rooms.

This chamber is where the box of dead girls is kept. I'm so close to them, stuck as I am in the tower all day. These old ghosts pull me to their crypt at night. But tonight something is wrong in this room, something is different; I can feel it.

They found you, didn't they? They know that you're here? *I ask them. Suddenly the splintered box is roiling with move-*

ment from within—jostling, elbowing one another out of the sleep of death. They lift the lid—dozens of pale hands skitter anxiously through the gap like a troop of white spiders. A mess of limbs pushes the lid aside and kicks over the side of the box. In a haphazard, desperate effort, they gradually disentangle from one another and tumble from the box onto the dirt floor below them.

Their eyes are pale and flat and seem to glow with a bright whiteness in the dim of the dream. I am both repulsed and fascinated by their struggle back to life, watching omnisciently, placidly, until I realize again why they have come back—they know that I'm here, imprisoned in this tower. They have come back for me. Their white eyes are blinkless; they recognize their surroundings with resignation and disdain (this, the scene of the crime, the stage of their last act). They lift their noses to the air, not speaking; they sniff the air like dogs.

When I open my eyes, the candles flicker, weakly. Threads of smoke unravel into the darkness. The mirror is watching me, I can feel it; the slick silver surface like a wide-opened eye. Can I trust the mirror to show me my own face? I stand warily and peer into the glass: the same arched brow, full lips, and inky-black eyes I recognize. I lift a hand to touch my own face when suddenly I notice the scene reflected behind me. The room glows with the light of hundreds of candles and this chamber is full of faces, eyes and lips glistening in the warm, golden light. Women lounge on the divan, the thick rug at my feet, the brocade chairs. They are sipping wine from my goblets, their necks and fingers sparkling with my jewels. Laughter crackles like sparks of flame. All of the women in this tower are smiling at me, even though they are dead.

"They found you, didn't they?" I ask them, but they only laugh at me in response, "They found the boxes, in the dungeon."

Your girls showed them where to find us. *They answer as one, many voices melded into a perfect unison.*

"My girls?" I ask, and the words pull the breath from my chest. Mary, Elizabeth, Sarah, Althea . . . my girls revealed where the dead lay buried. The thought makes me feel very lonely, surrounded by ghosts. The faces in the mirror smile at me.

"Don't they know any better," I demand, "than to wake up the angry dead?"

One face slowly emerges from the mirror's shadows, stepping around and over the outstretched legs and arms of lounging girls and approaching where I stand. The sight of her stops my heartbeat, but I dare not look away from the glass. Marianna stands beside me, our faces reflected side by side, just as I had seen the day before, but now startlingly clear. Dark curls frame her face and cascade over her shoulders. A warm blush makes her cheeks vivid with color. When my gaze meets hers I wince; her dark eyes are bright as blades.

Why did you do it? *she asks me. The girls seated behind her rustle upon their silk cushions and lean forward, eager for my answer.*

"You will never understand." A rusty whisper squeezes from my throat, startling me. The warm flames of the reflection fade; the faces recede into darkness. I turn and look behind me: the room is empty, but doesn't feel empty. Distant laughter shivers down my spine.

Why did you do it? *Marianna's voice echoes. She is the first to ask me this. I move to a small table in the center of the room and touch a wooden bowl. It has long been empty; the ruddy stain at the bottom is bone-dry. A Bible rests beneath my palm. The blank pages at the back are petal-smooth beneath my fingertips. The crooked quill lies upon the table beside a small inkhorn. The knife, of course, has been confiscated.*

What were the words I planned to use for the prince, for the trial, to explain? I'm too far away for even God to hear. But your voice, Marianna, echoes off every stone in these walls. This tower remembers you as well as I do.

I offer you my confession. May God have mercy on your soul.

My soul is not your concern.

Part Two

TOWER

But of the fruit of the tree which is in the midst of the garden, God hath said, Ye shall not eat of it, neither shall ye touch it, lest ye die.

And the serpent said unto the woman, Ye shall not surely die: For God doth know that in the day ye eat thereof, then your eyes shall be opened, and ye shall be as gods, knowing good and evil.

GENESIS 3:3

II

I came into this world in the winter of 1572, in a castle constantly prepared for attack. On the night of my birth, a star tore free from the firmament and shot a bright blaze of orange fire across the sky. Stars were believed to be angels, fixed into heaven and burning in the immense darkness. Prophets and astrologers saw this clearly as a sign that the world would soon end. They marked this day on their calendars, charted the stars, and filled rolls of parchment with urgent predictions. As prophets warned of the wrath of God, I rested peacefully in a small oak cradle, the whispers of worried servants a distant current in the background of my dreams.

From infancy, a host of servants crowded my nursery and attended to all of my earthly comforts. There was always a young woman there to dress and feed me, straighten the furs upon my bed, mend my silk nightclothes, and ready me for sleep each night. As years progressed and no more angels came loose from their heavenly throne, fears of the impending Apocalypse were put aside for the more mundane matters of village life. I lay in bed with my eyes closed and was entertained by tales of vile husbands, wayward daughters, and the occasional recipe for mutton stew.

Despite their kind treatments, the attentions of servants were not what I craved. Every day, once I had been properly dressed and my glossy hair perfectly braided, I asked if I could visit my mother. The countess was a tall, willowy woman with long, milky-blond hair and wide blue eyes. Her fingers were long and delicate and her touch, though rare, was gentler than that of my nursemaids. She was often busy tending to her official household duties: selecting fabric for new dresses and creating detailed lists of produce to be purchased at the market in the nearby village. When these tasks could be put aside, I would sit on a small stool before the mirror in her bedchamber, where she would play with my hair and sing songs she had known since her own childhood. As I grew from a plump baby into a pretty child, these visits involved less gentle touching, less singing, and more focus upon my reflection in her newest looking glass.

On one such visit I perched upon a large chair by the fire, watching as a new mirror was installed in her chamber. The old mirror had begun to warp, she explained, though I was not certain she was addressing me directly. I sat quietly, my small feet tucked demurely beneath my gown, my still-pudgy white hands folded serenely upon my lap. Even at the age of five I appreciated fine fabrics and I admired the way the fire reflected golden light upon the rich satin. I hoped that Mother would comment upon the new gown, but she was too distracted with overseeing the hanging of the new mirror—an oval monstrosity with trumpeting cherubs carved into the edges of the frame—to pay me any mind.

Once it was properly placed, we turned to look into the slick surface; it glistened like water. I enjoyed seeing our faces reflected side by side.

"A mirror is a magic thing, Erzebet," she told me that day, tapping an elegant finger against the glass. "It remembers all the faces it has reflected."

"A mirror remembers?" I asked, pushing my face close to the silvery surface.

"Yes, it certainly does," she said, still inspecting her own reflection. finally her eyes broke from their own gaze and locked with mine.

"You've become an awfully pretty little girl, Erzebet," she said to my face in the glass. The mirror seemed to agree: the face reflected back at me was fair-skinned and smooth, with glossy dark auburn hair clasped in a golden circlet. My glistening black eyes reflected the firelight behind me in two flickering golden flames. I smiled at Mother's approval, but the smile she returned was thin, strained. Her face paled and her fingers fluttered nervously with her lace collar. Then she pressed one hand to her forehead and with the other waved a servant near.

I was taken to my own chamber, despite my cries.

"Quiet now, Erzebet, your mother is tired," I was told, "she needs her rest. We must leave her alone."

But I did not want to be alone. No matter how much idle chatter filled my chambers each night, I yearned for my mother's company. I lay in bed and imagined our faces reflected side by side in her oval mirror. I often visited her in dreams.

My father, Count Bizecka, was much older than Mother and no beauty himself, but a collector of beautiful things. When I was three years old he departed to Vienna to serve the newly crowned Emperor Rudolf, and I saw little of him thereafter. When he did return on occasion to Castle Bizecka, I delighted in the beautiful objects he brought with him: paintings, sculptures, sparkling jewels, and fashionably cut clothing. I often marveled at how adept the pale, haggard-looking count was at choosing such marvelous items with which to adorn me, his only child.

As soon as I was old enough to sit up by myself in my crib, the count commissioned my portrait to be painted. The paintings show my progression in age: a grim-faced cherub perched atop a satin cushion; a corseted toddler posing beside a tall painted vase; a miniature countess in a regal gown, a circlet of pearls dripping low on my white forehead.

"Your beauty is the stuff of legend, child," Father told me. At the age of seven, I was being readied for my fourth portrait.

"Thank you, my lord," I said, nodding my head slightly. The artist—a wrinkled old graybeard stooped over his palette—scowled at my slightest movement. A servant moved forward to tilt my head to the artist's liking, arranging the gathers of my rose-colored gown as I posed, my spine stiff as an iron rod. I was aware of the artist's penetrating gaze, but even more I was aware of my father's eyes.

"Such a treasure," Father murmured; his eyes glistened like the sapphire ring glinting on his finger. "I consider myself no artist, of course, but you cannot deny the charms of my one and only creation." The artist nodded obsequiously, then turned back to the mixing of his paints. I felt light-headed with my father's praise and had to fight to keep a smile from spoiling my composed expression.

That afternoon, I listened as a minstrel my father had commissioned sang a ballad about my flawless face. I sat alone at the long dining table, nibbling distractedly at a feast of venison and roasted pheasant. When finished with my meal and tired of the minstrel's endless warbling, I slipped quietly from the dining hall. In the hours not spent in tutoring sessions in the chapel or posing for portraits, I enjoyed wandering the castle halls inspecting the new paintings and sculptures the count had procured on his travels. The chamber where all of my portraits were hung was my favorite room in which to spend my time daydreaming.

Making my way to the portrait chamber that evening, I heard voices echoing in the vast hallway: two voices, one light and one dark. I stopped short and watched them from the safety of the shadowy hall.

"You are pleased with the fair countenance of your young daughter," Mother said, her voice barely audible to my prying ears.

"She is *our* daughter, my dear, or do you so easily forget?"

"Indeed." She sighed vaguely. "You seem happier with the child than with your wife."

"That is simply not true," he said, reaching for her hand. His dark velvet cloak passed like a shadow over her pale blue gown. "It's no wonder that she's such a pretty girl. She has a beautiful mother."

His laugh rumbled low as he pulled her close to him, her light gown and light hair vanishing in a swish of velvet darkness.

"Then you are content with me. With what I have given you."

"Perhaps this will prove my feelings to you as little else will," he told her, stepping back from her embrace. I saw him lift a gloved hand from his vestment pocket: a glistening chain dangled from his fingers, set with a series of blue stones. The necklace sparkled brilliantly in the light of the fire. Mother gasped, unbidden; her hands flew to her mouth as though to snatch the sound away. Father said nothing as he clasped the chain around her neck and pulled her close to him again. For a moment they were silent.

"I've given you something to treasure while I'm gone. Now you must give me something in return."

"What do you want of me," she murmured, but it did not seem to be a question.

"You know what I want, and need—you've always known. Another child. At least one more child—a son, an heir."

"You certainly cannot blame me for the accident of her sex," she said, spinning from his grasp.

"And you cannot blame me for the whims of fate," he said smoothly. "You also cannot deny that you've been remiss in your duties to me." A coldness had crept into his voice and Mother stood very still for a moment, as though she were made of ice. I held my breath and dared not make a sound.

"She is not simply some sculpture you commissioned," my mother hissed, her voice rising. She turned, and the light from the fire made her hair shimmer like gold as she moved. "She is a child—our daughter—whom I harbored in me for months. Just so you could pose her like a painted doll before your fashionable parade of artists."

He hummed meditatively, rocking back on his heels and smiling. "I see. You're jealous of the child. I should have known."

"How dare you—you who treat her as little more than a plaything. She is more than that to me."

"You're right, she is much more: she is the daughter of Count Bizecka, part of one of the most respected families in Hungary."

"Respected," she spat, wringing her hands. "You are all exiled! The Turks have control of most of Hungary, and yet you strut around your castle and talk about respect."

"I should have expected that you would not understand," he said coldly, "the daughter of a mere merchant, after all." I was shocked at the harsh tone of his voice.

"But I am also a countess," she said, gesturing to my portraits on all the walls, "and I'll not have my only child sold to the highest bidder, as though she were chattel!"

"Enough!" He spun on her suddenly and grasped her arms tightly, squeezing them against her rib cage. "Listen to me: one child is not enough for a legacy—especially this child. As you well know, she may not be here for long." She opened her mouth to speak, but he tightened his grip and continued, his voice rising. "It seems you need reminding that you were nothing but a pretty village girl when we met. You and I both know that you are little more than that now: a village girl in a rich satin gown, with an expensive gold chain around her throat!" He shook her brutally with the force of his words. "I made you a countess; this is the least that you can do for me. I am working toward a betrothal, but there is little time and nothing more that I can do with her. I need a son—an heir."

"And I have no choice, do I," she uttered, straining against his grip, "no choice but to give you what you want? Though it may kill me to do so."

"You are correct," he said, his voice lowering but his tone still harsh, "but that is a risk all women take. You are my wife. You made your choice." He stopped shaking her, though he did not slacken his grip on her arms. Instead of fighting, she became listless, like a doll herself.

"What more can I do with her," he hissed, "a girl-child, and cursed?"

So engrossed was I in the scene that I only dimly understood that they were talking about me. Before they could stir again I padded swiftly and silently down the hallway, my slippers in my hand. All the way to my bedchamber the words and the images replayed in my head. I imagined I had caught one last quick glimpse of my mother's eyes in the firelight: they looked darkened, void of life. By the time I reached my room I was gasping for air.

Everywhere I looked, one word hovered before me, obscured my vision, as if it had been burned into every wall with a brand of fire: *cursed*.

III

From the window of my bedchamber that evening, I watched as carriages were prepared for the count's departure. Servants loaded the carriages with heavy rugs, ermine-lined cloaks, woven tapestries, and barrel upon barrel of rich Hungarian wine. At dawn the next day he would travel back to Vienna, to the court of Emperor Rudolf. My recently completed portrait had been swaddled like a baby in soft cloths to accompany him on his voyage.

"The emperor is very ill, and your father must travel swiftly," a servant told me. Three women sat in my chamber by the warmth of the fire, stooped over like hawks on a perch, mending my gowns and embroidering my underclothes. I remained huddled on the cold window seat, partly wishing they would leave but also afraid to be alone. I had sat there since overhearing the argument between my parents. I had conjured and reconjured the word *cursed* in my head so often that it no longer held any meaning for me, like a word in a foreign tongue. I watched the horses snort and stomp as they were harnessed. When the sky turned a rich dark blue and it was too dark to see, I stared at my reflection in the puckered windowpane.

"Am I to travel with the count?" I asked suddenly.

"Not at this time, my lady," one servant said. "Not that the count has told me."

"Do you know of my going anywhere? Leaving here at any time?" I did not turn to face them, but saw their forms outlined vaguely in the dark window.

"Not that I know of, my lady," the servant offered. "I will certainly tell you of any plans the count has for you, as soon as I'm made aware of them."

"See that you do," I told her, mimicking words I had heard the count use. Then I focused on my own face, dimly reflected against the dark blue sky.

Unable to sleep in the oppressive darkness, I crawled from my bed and carefully tiptoed down the chilly hallway to my mother's bedroom. I walked close to the wall, running my hand across the cold stones and tapestries as I passed. Though it was late, I knew that servants would still be bustling through the halls, readying the count's provisions for his journey. I needed to use care in order to make it to my mother's chamber undetected.

I had not been able to visit her since the count's arrival and hadn't seen her at all since earlier that evening, in the portrait chamber. The thought of what I had overheard still lay like a cold stone in my chest. I tried my best not to think about it.

The sound of fervent whispers in a nearby chamber gave me pause. Lingering in the shadows of the doorway, I saw a young woman with a rapt look upon her face. She was staring at something I could not see, as only a slice of the room was visible to me. She stepped forward and gently bent her head. Her neck was encircled by large, dark arms: I recognized immediately the count's rich velvet cloak, this time silvered in the moonlight of a nearby window. When he removed his arms from around the young woman's neck, I saw that something glistened in their place: a golden chain with a dark round stone suspended from the end of it. The count reached out a jeweled finger to touch the stone, which rested upon the woman's full breasts.

Was this as fine as the necklace he had given to Mother? I strained in the darkness to see. The chain was thin and delicate, a mere glimmer in the dimness. I had never imagined that the count would bestow such a gift on a servant. I watched as his hand lifted to gently touch the curls that framed her face, and smooth his finger over her round cheek.

He had never touched my hair in such a way, I thought, though he had helped arrange it the previous evening as the artist perfected my pose. But his touch of the servant's face seemed different—reverent. This girl was petite and softly curved, with tight curls that framed her cherublike face. She did not look at all like me.

This, I now realize, was the moment when I learned the art of jealousy, the frantic comparing and disassembling of parts: her eyes, her neck, her arms, her face . . . how does she compare to me, to my eyes, my neck, my arms—each part of myself I dissected, put on display. How did I compare to her? The way that gold necklace rested upon her soft skin. In comparison I felt, for the first time, somehow diminished. Less than who I had thought I was.

I did not visit my mother, but turned and walked back to my bedchamber.

By the next morning the count and his retinue had departed. The silence in their wake was broken only by a low moan, as if the stone walls were crying. I followed the sound to the south wing of the castle—my mother's chambers. A servant rushed to meet me at the end of the hall.

"Erzebet, you can't see your mother today. She's not well."

"But I need to see her," I demanded, though the noises I heard emanating from her chambers did give me reason to pause. I only knew my mother as a quiet woman, given less to speech and more to humming softly as she played with my hair. But the screams that came from her chamber were animal, guttural cries, wanton in their desperation. Despite the lump rising in my throat, I pushed past the servant and made my way down the hall.

"I need to see her!" I insisted, my voice rising to be heard above the screams. It was as if this was a wild creature in that room, and not my mother at all.

"Erzebet, please—"

A sudden crash followed the servant's words—a violent shattering of glass. We both jumped at the sound, standing in the doorway to Mother's bedchamber. Shards of glass spilled out into the hallway: silver slices of the countess's many mirrors. Another crash followed, obliterating the anxious voices of Mother's handmaidens. The servant took my hand and led me quickly to my bedchamber.

"What's wrong with Mother?" I asked, ashamed of the tears that burned my eyes. *What is wrong with me?* I wanted to ask her, but quickly banished the thought. The servant only cooed sweetly in response to my sniffling and began setting my auburn hair into shining braids.

"Oh, Erzebet, don't you look like a princess?" She sighed, patting my head gently. "Your skin is perfect as a china cup." She smiled eagerly at my reflection in the mirror.

My eyes met my own reflection in the glass. The braids formed an intricate crown upon my head. I blinked back tears and patted the smooth cords of hair with appraising fingers. Before I could request it, the servant had brought a minstrel to my chamber to entertain me, his reedy voice and cheerful lute drowning out the sounds of Mother's screaming. By the time he had exhausted his repertoire later that evening, the cries had silenced. That silence filled me both with relief and fear.

When I asked about my mother again, the servants saw to it that I had new satin ribbons, a handheld mirror, and a new circlet for my hair. My face became my most effective distraction.

Though I tried, I was unable to forget the count's reference to his "cursed" daughter. My lack of understanding served me well at the time, for I became certain that the curse referred to the misfortune of my being female. Though I was the daughter of a count, it still seemed that I had little power in this world.

The winter of my seventh year was a dismal one. A more rigid structure was gradually imposed upon every hour of my day: I was woken early in the morning, fed, and properly dressed by a host of brusque and harshly cheerful women ("Don't you look pretty today, Erzebet? Would you like a red tie in your hair, or gold?").

Then I was to meet with Father Pugrue in the small castle chapel for my daily tutoring session. Each of my lessons concluded with a ritual of confession, which Pugrue assured me was a necessary precaution to keep safe my innocent soul. Perhaps he was right, as my sense of greed, pride, and vanity was exploited on a daily basis by servants eager to placate me; this was not sin, but simply a way of life. Meanwhile, other servants shared with me the pamphlets that were flung like dried leaves in the marketplace, describing in lurid, bloody detail the eternal torments of hell. There were no such pamphlets about the glory of heaven, for the atrocities of hell offered a more compelling reason to seek salvation.

Once Pugrue had assigned the penitence for what measly sins I offered him, I was begrudgingly permitted to leave the chapel. The rest of the day was filled with a variety of mundane tasks: being measured by the mistress of the wardrobe for new clothes, reading Bible verses aloud to the servants (per Pugrue's orders), or suffering through interminable lessons in embroidery. The servants tended to the cooking, the cleaning, the trips to market, and the overall management of the castle and the nearby vineyard owned by the count. Some of the tasks I had always known my mother to control—the purchase of fabrics for gowns, overseeing of the production of wine and honey, the commission and purchase of lush tapestries and thick rugs for our chambers—had now become the complete jurisdiction of the servants. Not least of all of these was me. Though I was nobility in a sea of inferior faces, I began to feel that not only was I completely reliant upon the servants, but that all of the count's affairs at the castle had become their responsibility as well. This seemed a remarkable weakness on the part of my noble parents, and the knowledge of it burned me.

As I knew I was too young yet to manage a ledger, I showed my disapproval of their control in other ways: upsetting my teacup, throwing a dinner plate, even pulling a servant's hair when she did not properly starch the white collar of my gown. In order to calm my temper, all of my demands were met in a hasty manner. Though effective, this was still not entirely satisfying. For all of my histrionics, the boundaries of power and authority in Castle Bizecka had become uncomfortably blurred.

The snow came and made an even more distant island of the castle upon the hill—we would have no trips to market, no dried fruit, no new silk handkerchiefs until after the wind had died and the snow clogging the narrow roads had melted. The morning after a great storm I was distracted in my tutoring session by the sight of the white snow banked against the stained-glass windows of the chapel; a glistening veil of it hung upon the wind, like a shimmering ghost. It was January, and the day of my birth fell in that bleakest week of winter when the world was white, the fire never warm enough, and all the special smells and treats of the holiday season were gone. Turning a year older was always a desolate feeling for me, as though my heart were wrapped in the white-and-gray arms of winter. I shivered: I had just turned eight years old.

Once released from Pugrue's chapel, I dallied in the hallway, not ready to return to my cloistered bedchamber and the servants waiting for me there. In spite of the cold, I wandered down the castle hallways, looking out different windows for various views of the persistent snowfall. I also lingered in doorways, watching servants at work, huddled by the fire; their diligence made me revel all the more in my idleness. I had often been informed that I moved too quietly, like a ghost, and on this day I used it to my advantage. I stood in the narrow passageway between the kitchen and the main dining room.

Two women sat at the table and plucked pheasant fresh from the hunt. The cook tended a full-bellied kettle that sputtered over the crackling fire, the air turning thick with smoke. A third servant sat heavily in a chair at the table and sighed.

"She was quiet last night, fortunately," she said, and rubbed her eyes, "not like nights ago, up late screaming like some banshee."

"She frightens me more when she's quiet," another added nervously. "I never know when she's going to strike—she's smashed so many mirrors it's a wonder there is gold left to keep buying new ones."

This was different talk than I had ever heard the servants share in my company. Part of me wanted to walk away, but I didn't dare move, though the sight of the naked flesh of pheasant piled on the table suddenly sickened me. I watched in disgust as the old woman's hands moved over the lifeless bird, her fingers gnarled like the roots of trees.

"I think it's God's work that woman is mad," the old woman croaked, her voice like stones crumbling. "She was a vain one from the moment she arrived here as a bride—very vain and proud. The mirror that blessed her years ago has cursed her now."

Mad—my mind seized upon the word like a prize. The countess was not simply ill, after all, as I had been repeatedly told. The realization of my own ignorance burned in my chest.

"Pride is an ugly sin to bear." The cook shook her head, a wry smile tugging at the corners of her mouth.

At the sight of that smile, there was no time for the thought in my head to complete itself. In one great stride I stepped from the shadows of the doorway. I approached the cook, who looked at me in blank surprise. Before she could say anything, I leaped forward and scratched her across the face.

The cook staggered back in shock, dropping her wooden spoon. A guttural noise choked from her throat when she looked down at the blood upon her white blouse. Her eyes filled with water at the sight of her own blood.

"How dare you?" I asked, and my voice was surprisingly calm, though my hands were trembling with rage. "How dare you talk about the countess in such a way."

When I stepped toward her again, the servants behind me leaped up from their stupor and grabbed my arms. I turned to the old woman, who was still seated at the table, her face as gray as stone. The sight of her wrinkled face only increased my rage.

"How dare you—any of you!"

"Shall we call Father Pugrue?" the old woman suggested. She watched from a safe distance as I kicked at the legs of the servants who held me, my clawed hands lashing out at their faces. They squeezed my arms tighter and pleaded with me to stop.

"Rage is a sin," the old woman said, as if in warning. "A deadly sin. Perhaps we will need Pugrue to help."

"Do you think she has the devil in her? The child?" a servant asked, straining to control my lashing arms. They were talking about me as if I were no longer in the room, which only filled me with more anger. Is this how they treated my mother?

"She fights more like a beast than a girl," the old woman murmured in a low, secretive tone. I began screaming to drown out their words. The old woman moved closer; I recoiled at the sight of her gnarled hands.

"What are you doing to her?" a voice suddenly called out from across the room. All the servants turned to look, in surprise. I even slowed my kicking in order to see who it was: a young servant stood in the doorway, her thick dark brows knitted over glistening dark eyes.

"Let her go," she said easily, with a shrug of her rounded shoulders.

"What? Rowena, you don't understand. She's—"

"I said, let her go," the young woman insisted. She parted the crowd around me and grabbed my hand, drawing me away from their grasp. Rowena was a pretty, plump young woman with warm hands, I observed, though I noticed that she did not meet my gaze. She looked to the cook, who stood holding her apron to her bleeding cheek.

"Would you help her, please?" she addressed one of the servants who had been attempting to restrain me. "Rinse the wound and affix a clean bandage. I'll look after it tomorrow."

With my hand in hers, Rowena led me to my bedchamber. As soon as the door shut behind us she went to stoke the weak fire flickering in the hearth. I stood there in the middle of the room, watching her. I noticed that my hand, still curled like a claw, had begun to cramp. I went to rub it and noticed the cook's blood caked in my fingernails. Rowena walked over to a small table, where she poured water from a white pitcher into a large bowl.

"It's cold," she murmured, "but it will do. Come here." She extended her hand to mine. I offered her my clean hand, which she tugged close to the bowl.

"Both hands now, my lady. Yes, there we go."

She set to work cleaning the blood from my hand, even scrubbing beneath my fingernails with a stiff brush. She began to hum as she worked, and I was grateful that she did not ask me about what

I had done to the cook. She knew that it was not her place to ask; moreover, she didn't even seem very interested. When she could not find a clean cloth with which to dry my hands, she shrugged and wiped them on a corner of her white apron.

"There you are," she said simply.

For the rest of the day we engaged in familiar activities: I read Scripture aloud as she first tended to her mending, then polished my jewelry. I observed her work approvingly: this is what a servant should be, I thought, a woman who works without comment or judgment.

Rowena became my handmaiden from that day on, which was a welcome change. I preferred her calm demeanor to the meticulous bustle of the other serving women. But another, deeper, less perceptible change had also taken place. From the moment I scratched the cook's face with my own hand, I learned an important lesson about the power my rage could possess. In the gray, quiet days that followed, I carried this knowledge; it kept me safe and warm. Even the sight of the cook's scarred face, days later, did not tarnish the feeling with remorse; indeed, the fear I detected in the woman's eyes made the feeling of power inside of me burn a brighter flame.

In spite of my newfound power, I felt restless, and often lay awake at night replaying the conversation I had heard between the servants. They thought my mother was mad. Was it true? I was still angry with them for saying such things, but most of the anger stemmed from my own ignorance. How had I allowed mere servants to keep me away from her? What was wrong with her? Did she not want to see me? This possibility shamed me most of all. Wide awake in the darkness, I watched the pale moonlight filter into my bedchamber. I crept from my bed like a sleepwalker, then pulled a warm robe over my shoulders. The pale light made the room seem dreamlike, unreal. Blinking in the darkness, I tiptoed down the hallway to my mother's room.

When I entered her bedchamber, I was surprised to find that she was still awake. She was dressed in a pale satin gown trimmed with silver lace and was fluttering around her room, opening drawers and jewelry boxes, as if it were midday. An enormous fire raged in the fireplace, making the room exceedingly warm and casting it in a strange reddish glow.

"Mother?" I uttered awkwardly, taken aback by her demeanor.

"Hello?" she asked, her eyes unfocused in the flickering light. Her gaze seemed to dance over me, as if I were not there at all.

"I'm sorry to disturb you, Countess," I said graciously, showing her my most elegant curtsy.

"Well, that is lovely." She sighed. I noticed her eyes were strangely glassy, like twin mirrors. She did not blink as she looked at me. "And who are you?"

"Who am I?" I responded, as if I suddenly didn't know myself. She looked at me steadily, unsmiling, waiting for a reply. I recognized the look in her eyes from the last time I had glimpsed her, just before the count's departure. They were not my mother's lively eyes; they were flat, expressionless.

"Why, I'm your daughter."

"No, no, no. Silly child." The countess laughed, a loud laugh that startled us both. "No, no, that's not possible, my dear. My daughter is dead."

I said nothing, but formed a question with my eyes.

"Yes," she assured me, returning to her fluttering canvassing of the room. "She died as a baby. We buried her in a tiny casket; she was so small. I don't have any daughter but that one. I don't have any daughter at all."

"No?" I uttered, my throat suddenly hoarse. I watched her flutter around the room, lifting mirrors and necklaces and books and gloves with trembling hands. She seemed to be looking for something, constantly shifting an item, then shifting it back, never content with how it was placed.

"I will tell you this: I will never have another. No matter how much he wants one. Once was enough for me—to grow so big, so useless, like a beast and not a woman. And for what? For nothing. Dead in a day. No, no. Not for me. You know better than that, too, don't you, little girl?"

She turned to me with a strange smile, her dead eyes fixed on my face. She stared at me as if she could detect something no one else was able to see. The fire cast its red light over her pale gown, over her face, over her golden hair. The silver lace glistened red in the light; even her eyes glistened red. When she walked toward me I took a step backward, toward the doorway.

"You must be very careful, little one. Careful with husbands, and with children. But you know that already, don't you?"

"Yes, Countess. Yes, I do." I told her, and curtsied again. Her eyes were still on me as I slipped from the room.

The moonlight slanting into my bedchamber made the room seem cold with metal-hard light. I huddled under the covers, searching for sleep and dreams.

I watched the winter progress from within the chilly castle walls: the hills of black pines dusted with pure white snow, the midday sky pale, bruised with dark wisps of cloud. I never asked again about visiting my mother, and the servants were relieved. Eventually I grew accustomed to thinking of her less and less, as if the very thought of her bordered on impurity of the mind. In my company, not a word was mentioned about her, and in quiet moments this made it easy to forget that she even existed; indeed, I think the servants hoped that I would do exactly that.

In Mother's absence, I thought all the more about my father, and felt neglected when he delayed his return in order to stay at court. Didn't he know that his wife was unwell? Didn't he think it wise to visit his daughter? But when Father did visit, our conversations were restricted to the typical subjects—my studies, my daily devotions, my next portrait—and nothing was mentioned in regard to the wailing woman beyond the wall.

Though we dared not speak about her, Mother had other ways of making her presence known, especially late at night. The disembodied cries I heard seemed to reach out to me with ghostly hands. The wails emanating from her chamber dissuaded me from visiting her more effectively than any gift the servants could bestow. Though it shamed me that the servants knew of her condition, the realization of my mother's insanity became a strange comfort to me, to assuage the fears of our last interaction. Meanwhile, the image of who she had been—the golden hair, the gentle touch, the light voice—slowly disintegrated, as though part of a childhood dream.

Despite Rowena's reassuring presence, I was a lonely child. Until the summer of my twelfth year, the girl I saw reflected in the mirror was my only friend. She was a consistent friend: when I was angry, she was angry; when I was lonely, or tired, she felt the same. Over time I learned how to hide these truths from the glass—anger, loneliness, sadness, and fear—tuck them away in a hidden chamber of my heart where they could not mar the brilliance of my own beautiful reflection.

I woke as dawn filtered through the tapestried casement of my bedchamber, shedding a reddish glow upon the polished flagstone floor.

Spring had just barely begun; sunrise was a quiet hour and I was glad to be awake to revel in it. I rolled over in bed and stretched my long legs, my toes nearly reaching the edge of the bed frame.

Over the years I had grown weary of the oppressive demands suffered by the only child of a well-known noble family. My father, who had visited but a few brief times in the last four years, made it clear to all of those in his employ that he was grooming his daughter for a future at Emperor Rudolf's court. Our brief time together over those years was spent testing my manners, reciting biblical passages from memory, demonstrating my grace and beauty in a variety of fashionable new gowns, and playing the virginals for his entertainment. He assured me that the end result of this perfection was a worthy betrothal. To me this didn't seem enough of a reward for the charms I displayed before him, but I knew better than to voice my own opinions.

When Father returned again to court, my only comfort was the safety offered by Castle Bizecka: secret passageways and hidden doorways I had found over my years of wandering. The servants were too busy with their other duties to notice my disappearance, and Rowena understood my tendencies to hide in dark corners—"as long as you meet with me in your chambers to ready for bed," she would say with a sigh.

Indeed, Rowena was my other comfort, though I was abashed to admit it. She bustled in shortly after sunrise with a breakfast of bread, jam, milk, and cheese. I stretched beneath the covers as she entered, and she greeted me with a sleepy smile. Wordless, she set the breakfast tray upon my bed and stoked the fire in the hearth. Sitting up against the pillows, I sipped my mug of milk as she readied my bath in a large metal tub in the middle of the room.

"I'll wear my pale gray silk today," I told her as I crouched, naked, in the tub. She poured warm water over my head from a white china pitcher.

"It's raining today, dear," she murmured over the trickle of the water. "The silk could be ruined if you go on one of your walks."

"Then I shall wear a cloak," I told her. Rowena knew better than to argue. She laid the moon-pale dress out on the bed, then helped me with my silk stockings and delicate slippers. With gentle, familiar tugging she secured my corset.

"You'll need fitting for a new corset soon," she remarked. "You're more woman and less child every day."

"I just turned twelve years this winter," I told her, a warning tone in my voice. I still preferred my long, lean features to the soft curves of women; but surely the new corset was the sign of another portrait in my near future, the thought of which excited me. I sat before the mirror as she coiled my hair into a snakelike braid.

"Soon enough you'll be thirteen years." She sighed. "Many young ladies are married by thirteen, you know."

"Then why are you not married?" I asked her. She lowered her eyes to the braid in her hands.

Rowena's face often turned wistful, reflected beside my own. She was not unpretty, plump and full of comfort as she was, but I sensed her reverence for my fair skin and slim, supple limbs. I enjoyed the sight of my face all the more for her admiration: the pale, ethereal gown complemented my fair skin and contrasted with the dark auburn waves of my hair. I blinked and admired the dense blackness of my eyes. She patted my head gently and smoothed the collar of my gown. It was like the touch of a mother, I imagined, though the touch of my actual mother was something I remembered only distantly, as if part of a dream.

Every day I carried the vision of my own face with me as I lifted my ample skirt and descended the stone steps. Even seated in the chapel for my tutoring sessions, I was often distracted by the image of my own flawless face, reflected in the gold and crimson panels of stained glass.

"What was the original sin?" Father Pugrue shouted at me, cracking his cane against the stone wall of the chapel tower when he noticed my wandering eyes.

"Eating the forbidden fruit," I answered.

"Correct." Pugrue nodded. "And why did Eve listen to the serpent?" he asked, his eyes glimmering darkly beneath heavily wrinkled lids. *Perhaps she was hungry,* I had the urge to answer, thinking of the dried fruits I might later find in the granary. I licked my lips and swallowed hard.

"It is the weakness of a woman," I answered, in a clear, unwavering voice.

"That also is correct," Pugrue announced with a triumphant crack of his cane. "You must remember it every day, Erzebet," he warned.

Pugrue instructed me in Latin and the Scriptures, as well as offering vehement diatribes against the Heathens (the Turkish invaders, taking over Hungary) and the Heretics (the Protestants). I was a good student and the captive audience he craved, and for this he forgave some of my female deficiencies.

When our lesson was done, he snapped shut his Bible and lit a tall, slim candle that he carried to the altar, where I was to make my confession and receive Communion. I stood and smoothed my palms distractedly over the rich silk of my gown as he readied the sacramental bread and wine. When he nodded at me to kneel before the altar, I hesitated.

"You will not kneel, child, to receive the blessing of God?"

"Of course I will kneel," I assured him.

"But I saw you pause," he said, relishing the moment and leaning upon his cane. I was shocked that my thoughts had been so transparent, but it was true: for the floor of the altar was dirty, and the fabric of my gown so delicate.

"Follow me," Pugrue said grimly, lifting the candle and fumbling in his robes for a key. He walked over to a heavy oak door and I followed cautiously.

"I've been thinking about this for a while. It will be your new altar for confession." With these words, he passed the threshold beyond the oak door and began inching carefully down a dark spiral staircase, the candle held out to light his path.

I paused for a moment in the chapel; golden-winged angels with faces of unabashed ecstasy fluttered up the white walls. But I dared not delay for long. I hitched up the hem of my gown and made my way carefully down the dark steps behind Pugrue's fluttering flame.

The dungeon was dark and cold, the floor covered with dirt and molded straw. I had explored the granary dungeon before, and was familiar with the pattern of tunnels that connected one room to the next. But I had never been in the chapel dungeon: here were stored the pieces of the count's extensive art collection. The chamber was crowded with crude wooden crates stacked against the walls. As Pugrue lit the sconces upon the walls, I stepped gingerly among the boxes toward a cluster of marble statues mingling in one corner, their heads devoid of noses or ears. I could not help but admire the way my pearl-gray gown seemed to glow, ghostlike, in the dimness.

I jumped at the sound of Pugrue coughing loudly behind me and dutifully followed his candle to a corner of the dungeon, where he set it upon a nearby crate. The candlelight illuminated the corner where we stood: surrounded by stacked boxes, the floor covered with straw.

"Here, I hope, you will not have the chance to be distracted by material things. For the sake of your own soul." He nodded meaningfully and stared at me, his eyes shadowed.

Father had made it clear that Pugrue, of all of the servants, deserved my obedience, for to defy Pugrue would be to defy God. Feeling for a patch of straw upon the floor, I knelt before him in the darkness and offered my confession.

"I have sinned"—my voice trembled with cold—"for I prefer to read poetry instead of the Bible, and I think about things that please me when I should be asking forgiveness for my sins."

"Just as I suspected," Pugrue sniffed, and urged me to continue. "Have you any impure thoughts?"

"Oh, no," I answered solemnly. "I am wary of the desires that plague an unclean woman's mind."

"You are subject to God," Pugrue told me, his palm pressed upon my head, flattening my elaborate hairstyle, "and to your father. Someday, you will be subject to a husband."

My eyes flickered up at Pugrue; though only for a moment, it was enough for him to decipher my reaction.

"Remember this, Erzebet," he said, pressing harder upon my head, his voice rising, "and know your rightful place in this world."

My eyes closed, I held my breath and waited patiently for his ministrations to end.

Pugrue straightened and held the lit candle between us as I stood and brushed the dust from my skirt. In the darkness Pugrue's pale face seemed to float, phantomlike, over his black robe.

"I have some important news for you, Erzebet," he said. "The count has sent word to me that he is planning a journey home this summer, before the harsh weather begins. But first he must accompany Emperor Rudolf to Prague."

"Why Prague? I thought all court took residence in Vienna."

"It seems that the emperor is still unwell," Pugrue said carefully, though I detected a note of disapproval in his voice. "He is moving to Prague to escape the stresses of court."

"Why does my father plan a return to Hungary if the emperor is unwell in Prague?"

"He needs to check upon the progress of his daughter, of course." Pugrue smiled. I folded my hands and waited patiently for his smile to fade; the truth was hiding behind his polite flattery.

"The Turks," he groaned. "They've wreaked havoc over most of this country. It's only a matter of time before they reach Novoe Mesto, which is your father's property no matter where he is. But these are not men of laws, or of God."

I nodded solemnly, familiar with this tirade.

"When the count returns, he will have an army with him to defend his land. He will remain here for only long enough to position them against the Turks, and then he will return to the emperor."

"When the count arrives, will I have my next portrait commissioned?" I asked.

"I feel quite certain that under the circumstances, your portrait will be delayed," Pugrue said, bristling at my mention of it. "And I think perhaps it's for the best. The state of one's soul is far more important than the appearance of one's face."

Pugrue crossed himself, lifted his candle, and moved toward the stairs. I followed the flickering candle up the steps and into the light and fresh air. I stood before the Virgin's pious face when Pugrue turned to me. I felt his eyes, and the eyes of the marble Virgin, observing me closely.

"After your lesson, every day, we will descend to the dungeon for your confession."

I inhaled at the thought of this: descending into that cold dungeon every day, to confess my sins? Pugrue detected my resistance; it made him all the more pleased with his plan.

"The dungeon is a more appropriate place for such tasks, I believe. Lacking as it is in earthly comforts." He cast a critical glance at the angels trumpeting gleefully from the frescoes around us.

Once allowed to leave, I raced into the hallway, where the sun shone from the thin, slanted windows in bright streaks upon the floor.

I stopped briefly in my bedchamber to inspect the silk gown in the mirror—were there any smudges, any snags in the delicate fabric? Assured that the gown was unharmed, I again admired its silken luster against my pale skin. I fastened a string of pearls about my throat and hooked a heavy velvet cape over my shoulders.

This was my favorite time of day, and after submitting to Pugrue's pious whims, I felt eager to enjoy it. Despite Rowena's warning about the weather I was tempted to go outside; it was a spring rain, and the dampness had a fresh smell to it. The sun even managed to shine through its gray veil of clouds. I brushed past the south wing of the castle on my way to pilfer a treat from the granary; the moaning that echoed down that hallway was so familiar, it now made little impression upon me.

The granary was also a dungeon room, this one beneath the kitchen. It didn't have the musty smell of the chapel dungeon, but a more pleasing though pungent aroma of wine and dried fruits. I chewed on the rind of a dried apple while tiptoeing in the cold darkness around casks of wine, barrels of salted fish, and flanks of salted meat.

Upstairs, I was surprised to see that the kitchen was silent, deserted. The door stood open and I could see the kitchen garden beyond it: rows of leafy green plants and herbs straining to grow into their neighbors' boundaries. The green, dewy, spicy scents wafted toward me in the chill breeze: sage, thyme, dill . . . I stepped out into the garden and walked gingerly upon the soft earth, pulling the cloak around my shoulders to protect me from the breeze.

I had taken only a few steps past the garden when I saw the men tying up the deer. I walked closer to watch them, the wind blowing the cloak from my shoulders. A mist had begun to fall, and the sky seemed the same pale color as my dress. One man held her wrapped in his arms while another perched on the branch of an old oak, lashing her back hooves to the strongest bough. The men didn't see me as I stepped closer, watching.

When the man holding her stepped back, I could get a better look at the deer: her fur was a speckled, tawny brown and her belly white as cream. Upside down, her ears hung crookedly from her small, narrow head. She swayed slightly in the breeze, and the men tightened the ropes that held her to the oak tree. I moved closer in order to see what they were doing: moving a large, low basin beneath the deer's head. I moved in even closer, wanting to see the deer's face. Her dark eyes were still open; I could feel her looking right at me. I was standing just behind the men, the wind rippling through my heavy cloak, lifting the gray silk in billows and waves.

Then the tallest man in the group, perhaps the man who had brought the deer in, moved toward her with a large knife. As he pierced the flesh of her white belly, I stepped closer to stand behind him and watch. The man still standing in the cleft of the oak tree grunted in surprise at my approach, but I ignored him, as did the man with the knife. He cut a ragged line down the deer's belly and chest, with a sound like the tearing of raw silk. He paused at times to get a better grip upon his knife and upon the deer, her long body wavering in the breeze. I saw a breath of warm steam emit from the wound, and then the blood.

The stream of blood that flowed from the deer was brilliantly dark red—so red that it made all the rest of the colors around us, the grass, the sky, the oak tree, the dark cloaks of the men, seem dull in contrast. The wind blew as the man finished slicing, and I felt the rain upon my face. But this rain felt different, it felt warm in the chill air. I looked down at my pale hands, my pale dress, and saw that I had been splattered with the deer's blood.

The wind blew again; the deer swayed as I swayed. Her blood drained rapidly into the basin below her. I must have gasped then, for the man with the knife turned and saw me. His eyes grew so wide with fear that I could clearly see the white crescents around the dark centers. He held out his hand to me, as if in solace, but it was covered with blood.

Before he could say anything, I turned and ran back to the kitchen entrance of the castle. The kitchen was still deserted. Hoping to find Rowena, I turned to flee to my bedchamber, but a harsh laugh turned me stiff as stone.

"Don't worry about that, dear," a voice murmured. "It's just a little blood."

I saw a form crouched before the fire. The form turned toward me and I saw it was an old woman, her back curved like a ram's horn. The sight of her made me recoil in disgust. Before I could turn to leave, she moved closer and grasped my hand. Her grip was surprisingly strong.

"Blood is magical. It is holy, don't you know that?" she asked, smiling, inspecting my blood-spattered silk dress with amusement.

"Blood is a sacrament, and sacraments keep us all safe," she told me. I wrenched myself from her grip and ran, her laughter following after me.

I didn't know where to run to. My bedchamber no longer seemed a safe enough place to hide—wasn't there somewhere in this castle where I could be assured of being left alone? The halls were full of servants, and I cowered at the thought of any of them seeing me like this. The laughter of that bent old crone echoed in my head, quickening my steps.

I ran into one of the secret passageways and shut the door behind me; a passageway was my only hope to find safety. Peeking into chambers long unused, I realized that I was in my father's wing of the castle, where all of his apartments were prepared for his eventual visit home.

The ornate bedchambers had already been arranged for his arrival. The air still swirled with dust recently released from the heavy furs draped over the high bed. I looked carefully for the sign of any maids still present as I passed from the bedchamber into a cluttered art gallery. I was adept enough at discovering the secrets of Castle Bizecka that I easily detected another door hidden behind one of the heavy tapestries upon the wall. Here, I hoped, I would be safe.

It was a small room and there was only one window—a narrow slit in the thick stone wall, covered by a thick tapestry to protect those within from the cold outside. The wind swayed and lifted the tapestry, alternately lighting portions of the room, then plunging them back into darkness. After nearly tripping on a variety of boxes that cluttered the floor, I moved the tapestry to allow a weak, pale light to permeate the room.

Once my eyes adjusted to the dimness, I realized that I was in the count's study. A great oak desk by the fireplace was heavily laden with scrolls and charts and piles of parchment. Despite the chill of the room, I sat upon the dusty chair and began to sift through the papers before me.

My eyes scanned a variety of detailed charts and calendars drawn up by astrologers. Special dates were marked during which a body would most benefit from certain herbs, or a bloodletting.

This thought made me gasp, involuntarily, seeing again my blood-spattered hand resting upon the page. I had never been frightened of bloodletting before and had even undergone the procedure myself, many times. It was the best course for remedying an imbalance of humors. Yet somehow it seemed different to me as I looked at the tiny drops of red glinting upon my hand. Blood was powerful—what could taking blood do to you, I wondered, instead of giving?

Now that my breath had slowed and my heart had stopped pounding, I looked down at my dress and sighed angrily. It had been foolish of me to get so close to the deer. I had known, hadn't I, what they were about to do? I had seen the corpses of deer before, already sliced and bled, hanging from the ceiling of the granary. And yet the sight of that red blood had been mesmerizing to me—beautiful, in a way. Perhaps the old woman was right to say that blood was a holy, magical thing.

I sighed and flipped through the pages of a dusty Bible, its Latin text illuminated with florid designs of leaves and fruit, animals and people, nestled in the luscious greenery. In the Bible, I came upon a stray piece of parchment. Despite the spidery handwriting I recognized at once the date as the day of my birth.

The future, the scratchy text read, *is foreseen.* There were many astrological symbols that I did not recognize and mention of a falling star—*a stream of fire cast from heaven,* it said. The next words stood on a line, alone:

The birth of Erzebet Bizecka.

I sat back in the chair, stunned for a moment. My eyes scanned the accompanying pages and found a full paragraph, written in the same labored scrawl:

An image appeared in the scryer's mirror: An angel and a devil stood together in a circle. The scryer could not tell if there was a separate angel and devil, or if they shared the same body. The image lifted its hand and warned us to repent before the end of days. Then the image spoke of a child whose days will end quickly, or whose days will have no end. We are certain the child the angel-demon spoke of is the daughter of Count Bizecka.

I read the paragraph over again, still confused. Despite the clammy cold of the room, my neck felt moist and hot beneath the collar of my dress. I wished I could thrust the paper into the closest fire and forget what I had seen, but I could not. I sat and read the words, over and over again: a child whose days will end quickly, or whose days will have no end. And that child was me.

A gust of wind lifted the tapestry toward me and the cold shook me out of my trance. I stood, suddenly, nearly knocking the chair down behind me. There was a mirror across the room that I had not noticed upon entering, and I was startled by the reflection it offered: my face, neck, arms, and pale silk gown splattered in a fine sheen of blood. The droplets upon my face were the largest, still glinting wet and red. They burned cold into my skin.

This is who I am, I thought. I had known it for so many years but I could not remember when I had learned it; now it came to me, fully realized. This is the truth about me: *I am cursed.*

The wind touched me with ghostly cold hands and a violent shudder ran through my body. With trembling fingers I folded the parchment and secured it in the fold of my sleeve, then scurried from the room like a frightened mouse.

All that night and the next day after finding the prophecy I tried my best to appear as if nothing was amiss. I recited my Bible verses to Rowena, attempted embroidery, ate my dinner, and went gratefully to bed. Once in bed, I did not sleep, despite my weariness, my mind busy imagining all the horrors it could conjure. In the morning I took my usual care in choosing my gown for the day. I began to opt for brighter, bolder colors, in order to balance the grayness of my mood.

Everyone will die someday, I told myself, as consolation. But it is a far different thing to be twelve years old and to realize that it will happen, definitely—not only that, but that it may happen soon. This knowledge seemed to make me already less alive, as if my death would happen slowly and that it had already begun. I even began to imagine how it might happen. A sudden illness? A violent accident? It was amazing the possibilities my imagination could conjure, and these thoughts kept me awake nights. As a drizzly, cold spring shrugged off her misty veil and emerged as a sparkling summer day, I was a pale wraith merely floating through life. I constantly craved something—Rowena's company, a secret sweet treat, the feeling of the sun on my back—in the hopes that this might anchor me more firmly to the world of the living. But once achieved, these desires offered no consolation. Even the distraction of my own face in the mirror was tainted. Though it was still beautiful, something lingered in my eyes that I had never seen before: fear.

Every morning I considered anew who I could ask about the prophecy; I was eager for some comfort, some explanation. I eyed Rowena carefully as she helped me to undress and step into the warm bath. Would she know anything about it? It made me suddenly sick to think that all the servants knew such secrets about me. I gazed at my pale, thin body through the filmy water. It already seemed different, foreign. I listened closely and imagined I could hear it: something deep inside, beyond my control, like the rusted gear of a clock suddenly slipping out of place. Something there since infancy: my death waiting inside of me.

"You're more reflective than usual today, Erzebet," Rowena sighed, nudging me to sit up. She poured warm water over my soapy back. "Are you feeling quite well?"

"I'm fine," I told her, the steam from the bath making me suddenly too warm and woozy.

During my daily lesson I considered asking Father Pugrue, but worried what his reaction might be. Scrying had long been denounced by the Catholic Church as the work of the devil. I was not surprised that the count indulged in the practice, as he was often in the company of an array of astrologers and prophets whenever I saw him. However, I wasn't sure that Father Pugrue would approve of my interest in such matters. Moreover, was all of this to be kept a secret from me forever? I could die young, but no one would warn me?

Then there was the other part of the prophecy: a child whose days will have no end. In the midst of Pugrue's prayer recitation my eyes began to water, and the light-headed feeling returned. I was sweating, the collar of my gown tight against my neck. Pugrue closed his eyes and bent his head in prayer, and I was to do the same. My mouth opened to cry out to him, but something made the words catch in my throat.

Which would you choose? A deep voice asked me. It wasn't Pugrue's voice. I blinked and scanned the chapel, lingering on a fresco depicting the Apocalypse: Christ using a spear to push red-black demons back into a schism in the earth.

Which would you choose? I heard the question again, the voice deep and rich as plush velvet. I watched my fingers tremble lightly against the Bible page before me. The voice seemed to reverberate through my body. It was an easy choice for me: I would choose immortality over an early death. The moment the thought formed in my head, I wished I could take it back. What would God think of such a choice? Never before had I felt God watching me so closely. I winced, waiting for some dreadful judgment to arrive: a lightning bolt to strike down, to shatter the glass window beside me and set the chapel ablaze.

Instead, the voice responded to my panic: *The choice is an easy one for many. You are not alone.*

At the sound of these words my breathing slowed, and the prickly heat on the back of my neck subsided. I swallowed, my dry throat no longer choked with words. I bent my head in prayer, listening to the smooth sound of my breathing, the pounding of my heart sinking deeper into my chest. Perhaps it was God's voice, I wondered; perhaps he had heard me. His words were a panacea: it was a comfort to feel that I was not alone. I bent my head lower in prayer.

Though the voice I had heard was a comfort, at other times my prayers were left unanswered, leaving me feeling only more acutely alone. I needed to ask someone about the prophecy. I needed to know the exact size and shape of this thing that I feared. But it was too embarrassing for me to ask a servant, or even Pugrue; I couldn't bear to let them see this weakness in me, not even Rowena.

In this case, there was only one person left to ask.

It had been four years since I had last visited the countess. I was both doubtful and afraid of what she might offer me, but desperation made me bold. When I was done with my tutoring session I wandered casually to my mother's chambers. Tentative steps brought me closer to her bedchamber than I had been in years—close enough to hear her inside, murmuring to a servant to stoke the fire, complaining of cold. The memories of our last interaction shot through me with surprising force—for so long I had thought of the countess as merely an embarrassment, but the fact was that she frightened me. A fear tinged with sadness for the mother I had lost.

The shameful fact of my own fear urged me forward. What would I do, plod along in my potentially short life, plagued by fears on all sides? I craved action, bold action, to give me some idea of control over my own fate. When a servant emerged from mother's bedchamber, I hid behind a large ceramic vase and waited for her to pass. I slipped quickly into the room in the servant's wake.

The moment I entered her chamber I was consumed with the urge to run. The odor was overpowering; I felt as if it physically pinned me to the wall. By the hearth there stood an urn that burned incense, filling the room with the scent of cloves and sandalwood and emitting a quivering cloud of smoke. Combined with this was a fetid smell of decay. The walls were lined with dark tapestries that blocked out all sunlight. The high bed was draped in heavy red velvet curtains that appeared dusty in the light of the fire in the hearth, which burned so ferociously I feared it might jump out and bite me.

I stood there for a while, as if fixed to the wall, watching a small portion of movement beyond the large curtained bed—the flash of white hands against a full black skirt—accompanied by a low, continuous hiss, that seemed to match the spark and sizzle of the logs in the hearth. It made me realize just how long I had gone without seeing her, living like a motherless child. The smell and the sound and the image of her hands had me so transfixed that I stood there hoping the countess would not see me, considering slipping out as silently as I had entered.

The hissing grew louder. It was the countess, whispering, but I could not see whom she was whispering to. There seemed to be no one else in the room but the two of us.

"You are there," she said suddenly, her voice louder now, but rough and crackling like the fire itself. "I can see you." She sounded triumphant. My breath caught in my throat and my eyes watered from the smoke, but I was surprised when she did not approach me. Indeed, it did not seem that she had moved from her place, and the heated whispering continued.

I couldn't leave now; I didn't want to insult her. I pulled myself from my place on the wall and walked quietly over to the other side of the bed. When I reached the other side, I saw a woman standing before a mirror, talking in a heated whisper to her own reflection. Her face was mere inches from the glass, a stream of whispers pouring from her mouth in a constant hiss. She was standing so close to the mirror that, standing behind her, I could not see the face the glass reflected. I stood by the bed, a few paces behind her. The sight instantly chilled me, in spite of the raging fire.

Was this creature really my mother? She had a desperate energy surging through her that I had never known my languid mother to have. I recognized her hair, instantly, for it was milky blond and reached past the small of her back, but it had grown surprisingly coarse and fragile at the ends, as though from aggressive brushing. She wore a lush black velvet gown, and I noticed how her white hands fluttered around the collar, the bodice, and the corseted waist of the gown, patting herself in a nervous manner. Did I recognize those hands? She fluttered too quickly for me to see. I stepped forward cautiously to get a better look.

When my face appeared behind her in the glass, she jumped in fear.

"I'm sorry to startle you, Countess," I murmured, bowing humbly before her. When I stood to face her I forgot everything I had prepared to say.

Her face was coated in paint, white with a strange tinge of gray. She was dressed as if prepared to attend the royal court. A white standing collar curved in a fan around her neck, the gold lace along the collar's edge reflecting the firelight into her blue eyes. She wore a short gold chain that fit snugly around her neck with a large ruby in the center, nestled in the middle of her collarbone. In addition to this were long strands of pearls that extended to her waist and jewels pinned into her hair. The corset beneath her gown had been tied severely, and her still-small waist was accentuated by the gown's full sleeves, which were gathered together at three different points down the length of the arm and tied with gilt ribbon. This contrast was intentional, I was certain; I was no stranger to the tricks of fashion and vanity. She continued to pat her belly and waist approvingly, almost consolingly, and her breathing seemed harsh and irregular. She smiled at me, and I could see that her teeth had rotted in her mouth.

"It has been a while," she said graciously. "And who are you?"

I remembered this from my last visit with her, but I was not prepared for it. I had imagined that I had grown into more of a person in the intervening years—a young woman instead of a child—and that she would recognize me as her kin. But I shouldn't have been so surprised that she did not.

"Yes, my lady. I'm sorry it has been so long since I have visited you." Her eyes bounced around my face, and I swallowed the lump that rose in my throat. "I am a cousin of the count's," I told her, thinking it best to follow her lead and avoid the truth, for now; I was certainly not eager to admit that I was her dead daughter.

"I see," she said, her eyes narrowing into dark slits. I wondered if I had taken the wrong tack.

"You'd best beware of my husband," she told me coyly, "but I'm sure you already know that. He is at court right now." As she said this she turned back to the mirror, touching her waist again.

"And you are to join him, Countess?"

"Yes, of course," she told me. "As soon as I'm ready." There seemed to be a warning implicit in her voice.

"I wonder if you would mind a brief audience with me, Countess. I have some important questions to ask you, if you don't mind."

"Oh my, you're awfully serious for such a young girl." She smiled at me, but the smile faded quickly and was replaced by a penetrating stare. I felt as if her eyes were devouring me: my face, my hair, my body. I cursed my choice of such a brightly colored yellow gown, for it seemed garish and insulting in the countess's chamber.

"Here," she said, gesturing to a chair by the fire. "Sit here, where I might look at you."

The countess sat stiffly before me and leaned forward as much as her corset would permit. I sat and allowed her to look at me, afraid to ask her any questions before I had been given permission to do so. I could sense that current of energy beneath the surface of the countess, and I knew that her cheerful veneer could be easily shattered into violence. I knew this because we were alike in this way, a realization that made me sweat as much as the fire did.

She hummed meditatively, drinking in every detail of my face. She lifted her hand to touch my cheek and her fingers recoiled as though my flesh burned her. She gazed into my eyes as if they were another type of mirror, one that reminded her of the passage of time. *I am your daughter,* I kept thinking to myself, hoping that she would remember me but afraid of what her reaction would be.

"You are certainly pretty," she pronounced suddenly. She seemed clearly disappointed in this pronouncement. Then I could see what she was doing: the disassembling and comparing of parts, the high art of vanity. It was innate in her as it was in me, for I had been doing it to every woman that I saw, from a young age. Are her eyes more beautiful than mine? Her hair? Her arms? Her neck? Her shoulders? Her waist? Her—

"You're not as pretty as you think you are," she said, her mouth curving into a slow, wide smile. "Nor as pretty as I was at your age. How old are you?"

"I am twelve years, Countess."

"I was very beautiful. Did you know that?"

"You are still very beautiful, Countess," I told her, but I was not sure that it was still true. There was an artificial glaze over her beauty now, as if her face were merely a rendering in paints of a thing that once was—and a poor rendering, at that. She was a tired, rotting creature sealed within the confines of a beautiful velvet gown. The truly beautiful parts of her had been lost in the mire of madness and time.

"Now, my dear," she said, "what is it that you have to ask me?"

"I'm sorry, Countess, but I'm afraid I must ask you about your daughter."

"My daughter? But I don't have a daughter."

"Your daughter who died many years ago. As a baby?"

"Yes, that's right. She died as a baby. You can hardly call her a daughter, really, just a thing that lived inside of me and then died when it came out. Not much of a daughter, anyway." Her hands were suddenly as rushed and furtive as her words, stroking the thick nap of her velvet bodice and skirt.

"Well, my lady, it seems that there was a prophecy about your daughter's birth. Seen by a scryer."

"Scryers!" she said, her voice loud enough to ring off the walls. I worried for the first time what a servant's reaction would be if one entered the room and saw us talking. I fought my urge to glance toward the door.

The countess stood up and spun across the floor, the black velvet gown sweeping in a large circle around her like a roiling thundercloud.

"They were all his doing, the scryers after the falling star. That was all his doing. He hadn't wanted a girl-child at all, and cared even less for one that was cursed."

"Who? The count?"

"Yes, but she was a beauty. He loved her for that. She was very beautiful. A rose in winter, he called her once—*his* rose in winter."

"I thought you said she died as an infant?"

"No!" she cried, spinning back to face me. "You said that, you said that! I didn't say anything about it, nothing." She seemed irritated, as if a child caught in a lie. "I think you've made all of it up on your own."

"But what about the prophecy, Countess? What of it do you remember?"

"It was after the falling star—that was an omen, they said. Cast down in a stream of fire from heaven!" she shouted, and the fire raging beside her seemed to spark in agreement with her words. She laughed at this, and at the look of fear on my face. "Like a falling angel, you see. If an angel falls out of heaven on the day of your birth, that can never be a good sign."

"No, I suppose not."

"So, the men got together with their charts and their mirrors, like fools. They wanted to find out what they could about the baby. Never leave anything to chance, the count never leaves anything to chance. He will have an army of wives when he returns, no doubt." She laughed at this, pleased that such talk made me visibly uncomfortable. I swallowed and tried to look at ease. She sat again and leaned forward, pressing her hand upon my knee.

"He hasn't made any proposals to you, his own cousin, has he, dear?"

"And what happened next? With the scryers?"

Her smile faded. "The scryer saw it, the vision." She paused for a long moment, and her eyes seemed to change in the firelight—watery, but also warm. "They told me while she was sleeping in my arms."

"And then what happened?"

"They told me that she would die, so she did. Words are magic in that way; people obey them without even meaning to. It's simple as that." She shrugged placidly, but her eyes darted in a frantic manner over my face.

"Words can haunt us, too, you know," she informed me, her eyes narrowing, "We make our own ghosts when we're stuck upon this earth. We create them and then they follow us around. In mirrors."

She turned and pointed to the mirror beside her bed. It was the large oval one with the gilt frame that I had watched them hang, years ago, seated upon a stool by this very fire, a dainty child in a womanly satin gown. I remembered.

"Before I was countess, I was Illyana, young and beautiful. She's here in this mirror. Come look." She grabbed my hand and lifted me from the chair with a strange sort of excitement, her eyes wide and wild-looking. We stood side by side before the glass.

"She haunts me here," she said close to my ear, a strange hollow quality to her voice, like the howling of a winter wind. "I see her here every day, mocking me, along with the face of Death."

"A mirror always remembers," I said, my eyes meeting hers in the glass. She stared back at me, defiant, then turned her gaze away.

"And so have you," she said. The words pulled from her so quietly, she seemed unaware that she had even said them. Her eyes settled back upon her own reflection then, and turned harsh and hard as stone. It frightened me to see the way she looked at herself in the mirror. I stepped away quietly, curtsying as I walked.

"Thank you, Countess. I will leave you now." I kissed her hand gently as I would the hand of royalty, but she barely seemed to notice. "Thank you," I whispered again as I left the room. Once in the hallway, I broke into a run and didn't stop until I was outside the confines of the castle's walls.

VII

Nestled among the Carpathian Mountains, Castle Bizecka is surrounded by steep crags, cavernous pits, and a forest alive with the howling of wolves. From the castle entrance you can look down to the crowded, slanted roofs of Novoe Mesto, the village that borders the mountains, and the Vah River. For quiet solitude, I preferred the courtyard of rose hedges behind the castle, the full-blown roses drooping upon their vines.

I ran through garden paths straight to the center of the labyrinth of rose hedges. It was a warm day but gray and damp, and the air I gasped felt thick in my lungs. In the center of the garden I stopped, suddenly panting and dizzy, and slumped onto a damp stone bench. Here I was surrounded by a group of marble men and women posing and dancing, their stone garments fluttering as though lifted by a breeze. Drops of rain dripped from extended stone fingers and arms. I watched it pool in small puddles on the square bases at their feet as I waited for my breath to slow down. I wanted to scream, but the sound that was gurgling in my throat frightened me, sounding desperate and animal. My fingers clenched upon my gown like claws.

I moved over to the sculpture I had named Athenus—a male Athena, for his beauty—and sat upon the base. I leaned against Athenus's leg, my hot forehead pressed to his cold marble knee. The stone cooled my forehead as I choked down my own scream; slowly, the stone turned as warm as my own flesh.

My mother is insane, I repeated in my thoughts, over and over again. *My mother is insane, and it's all my fault.* I wasn't quite sure how I had done it, but it seemed to be perfectly true. If it hadn't been for me, she would still be that same beautiful young woman I had known years ago, humming and singing and pinning jewels into her shining hair.

But I couldn't waste all of my worries on Mother—clearly she had stopped worrying about me. She knew about the prophecy, believed in it, and thought its end had already taken place. My mother did not know that I was alive. I shifted my head and pressed it to another part of Athenus's leg. The roses and vines seemed to stumble and swirl around me; I closed my eyes tightly to block them out. I felt alone in the world, as if I really was dead. Maybe the countess was right, I wondered, and I didn't really exist. The thought seemed capable of pushing me off the edge of the world, into a swirling madness. I squeezed my eyes shut tighter and wrapped both arms around Athenus's leg, imagining he was holding me to the earth. A breeze shifted the hair on my shoulders and cooled my neck. I thought to pray, but had no prayers left in me, none that God wanted to hear.

I was startled from my reverie when I heard rustling. It was an animal raking its claws through the vines, routing its snout into the rose hedge lining my garden, I was sure. The breeze increased and it made my skirt heavier, my clammy fingers tangled in my hair. My eyes scanned the nearby hedge and there it was—the rustling, the frightened trembling of blossoms. Too violent to be a deer; a wild boar, perhaps. A raindrop landed on the tip of my nose as I walked forward. Climbing upon the pedestal of a marble Venus, I peered over to the other side.

I was surprised to see a girl no older than myself. She wore a blue woolen dress, her white apron balled in each fist. This was to protect her hands from the thorns, I presumed as I watched her grasp great handfuls of vines and attempt to vault herself over the hedge.

"What are you doing?" It seemed an appropriate question.

She looked up at me and blinked, panting.

"Do you live here?" she gasped.

"Yes," I told her, "and I've asked you what you're doing."

"I'm sorry," she muttered, curtsying hastily and lowering her head. "I wanted to see inside." I could not help but admire her dark, curly hair and the blush of shame in her cheeks.

"I could have you thrashed for this," I assured her, "or locked up in chains, in my dungeon." I had threatened servants in a similar way, for pulling my hair too hard or lacing my corset too tightly.

"I know," she whispered, and I was impressed by her deference to my authority. I was not even sure if the castle had such chains, or if they had ever been used to restrain an intruder.

"How did you manage to get here?" I asked. "The north towers are always guarded."

"I think they thought me a servant," she said, her eyes flashing at mine for a moment. "I walked stooped over, with my hood up." She pulled her rough woolen hood over her glossy hair. I could see how she could be mistaken for a washerwoman.

"Where are you from?" I asked. Her pink cheeks instantly paled.

"From the village, my lady. My father is a farmer."

"What would you say if I told you that this is a magic garden," I told her, and smoothed my skirt with the palm of my hand.

"I beg your pardon," she said, curtsying awkwardly, "but my mother has taught me not to believe in magic." Her eyes flashed at mine, quickly. "I beg your forgiveness, Countess. It's the most beautiful garden I've ever seen."

"You don't believe in magic?" I asked, though it was an issue I had not long considered—I had grown accustomed to the tonics of healers and the predictions of astrologers; it had never occurred to me to doubt their visions. I had heard other stories, too, of witches gathering at midnight in the forest to meet with demon lovers. Though I had often thrilled at the tales, there was no one nearby to tell me whether or not they were true.

"I know that there are witches," she said cautiously, "and they can curse you with the evil eye, and such, but that's bad magic. I don't think magic like that could make such a pretty garden, is all."

"Do you believe in scryers," I asked, feigning indifference, "those who can divine the future by looking into a mirror and seeing visions?"

"No," she told me, and I was impressed by her conviction. "My mother tells me that they are all charlatans, who tell people things just to scare them."

"What is your name?" I asked her.

"Marianna," she told me, and curtsied again, more prettily this time.

I looked at her quizzically for a moment. How strange it was that I had just met this girl—a girl from the village, no less—and without knowing it, she had told me exactly what I had wanted to hear. I wondered if only she could teach me to reject the notion of a scryer predicting my future. I slid off the pedestal and hurried to the iron gate. Without another word, I lifted the rusted latch, and the gate swung wide.

All that afternoon Marianna taught me how to twist the rose vines into wreaths for our hair. We sat on a low stone bench in the garden, our dresses spread around us, the rose wreaths settled upon our laps. I watched, enthralled by the work of her small, nimble fingers.

"My mother taught me how to do it, when I was small," she told me. Once the wreath was done, she stood and placed it upon my head. "You look like a queen," she said, and curtsied again.

"Sit here and help me with this wreath so that you can be crowned as well." I patted the bench beside me. She sat and smoothed her apron, then pulled the vines from my lap to hers.

"May I ask you a question, Countess?"

"My mother is a countess," I told her. "I am only Erzebet."

"What's it like to live in a castle?" She paused in her work to touch the smooth petals of a rose upon the vine.

"Cold, quiet, and lonely," I told her, but was abashed at the disappointment in her eyes. "There are grand rooms, certainly," I added brightly, "the chapel is beautiful, and the whole castle is filled with beautiful tapestries and paintings."

"A chapel," she murmured, and lifted her eyes to mine. "Does it have colored glass in the windows?"

"Of course," I told her, then stood and smoothed the pleats of my gown. "I'll show you." I held out my hand to help her to her feet.

We exited the rose garden and walked past the kitchen garden—small and dull with its vegetables and herbs. We walked to the chapel tower, though I was careful not to stand in full view of the windows, if by chance Pugrue might be lurking inside.

"Someday I will show you inside the chapel, where you can see the colors more clearly," I assured her. "This tower is always guarded, even though the mountains most likely keep it safe from invasion. A chapel should always be guarded against the Turks."

Marianna crossed herself suddenly at my mention of the Turks. I was so used to talk of war that I was startled by the effect it had upon her.

"Aren't all the towers guarded?" she asked quietly, as if Turkish soldiers might be listening at any moment.

"All except one, which is part of the mountain itself." I shrugged nonchalantly, trying to reassure her and myself. "They would have to scale the mountain at its highest point in order to attack it." The southwest tower—*that's my mother's wing of the castle,* I thought, but dared not say aloud.

As we walked back to the rose garden, I taught her the song I had learned from one of our minstrels, making up the words I couldn't remember as I went along. She laughed and sang the chorus along with me, her sweet voice stumbling over the words.

"I have many songs my mother taught me," she said. "I'll teach you someday if you'd like."

"Of course I would like it!" I exclaimed with rare enthusiasm. "I know another about a fairy living in the forest, but I haven't sung it in a while."

"Oh," she murmured suddenly, and I saw that her cheeks had turned red. She looked to the sky—the sun hovered over the mountains, as though pierced upon the highest peak.

"I'm sorry!" she exclaimed. "I must go! Mother and Father are expecting me home." She lifted her skirts to run and fairly tumbled down the hill. I hurried to catch up to her.

"What's wrong?" I asked. "What did I do?"

"I was to go to the market," she wailed. "My mother is expecting me at home with fish for dinner. I must leave now!"

"Wait!" I grasped her arm. "It's too late for you to go to the market. The sun has nearly set. I can help you—please, just wait here."

I skidded down the slope of grass and through the kitchen garden, then slipped silently through the servants' entrance. Luckily, the cook was shouting at her assistant and did not notice my dash to the larder. I filled an empty satchel with two loaves of bread, then scurried down the spiral steps to the granary and pulled two salted fish from a barrel and dropped them into the sack. Grabbing lastly a fistful of dried fruits, I dashed out again and met Marianna at the edge of the rose garden. I handed her the satchel and filled her hand with the dried fruit. She stared at the fruit with wide eyes and seemed unable to speak.

"I'll fill this with whatever you need the next time you visit."

"It's too kind of you," she murmured, peering into the satchel.

We walked to the gate where I had first given her entrance.

"Meet me tomorrow, by this gate. I'll tell a guard to escort you and I'll meet you here as soon as I've done my lessons."

"Of course, my lady." She lifted her hood and carefully descended the stone path down the hill to Novoe Mesto.

VIII

My day in the garden left me quiet and languid that evening, alternating between dark worries about the prophecy and cautiously giddy anticipation about my meeting with Marianna the next day. Hovering over all of this, of course, was the image of my mother standing in the blazing fire and gray smoke of her chamber. The end result was a feeling of confusion and weariness. In the wake of my horrifying encounter with the countess, my day of twining rose wreaths with Marianna seemed only a misty dream as the hours passed, though pleasant to recall in all its vivid detail. I had never before spoken to a girl my own age—perhaps a servant, but never a girl. I used the memory of the interaction as a kind of talisman against the lingering, ghostly apparition of the countess in her black velvet gown.

After dinner I wandered distractedly until I found Rowena in a sitting room, working on her mending by the fire in the company of other servants. Wordless, I wandered in, inspecting the tapestries on the walls. Their conversation ended abruptly and a familiar barrage of pandering offers took its place (Would you like some tea? Have you completed your lessons?) to which I paid little heed. I couldn't help but see everything in a new way that evening: Would I get to show Marianna this tapestry? Would she like it? The thought made me both excited and anxious. I had never had the opportunity to share these things with someone before, and I only hoped that she would find them—and me—still interesting upon our next meeting.

I turned to the mirror to review my choice of dress. I would wear my blue satin tomorrow, I thought, or would that be too heavy in the sunshine? I wanted her to see the delicate red roses embroidered along the bodice and hem. Perhaps a silk gown? No, somehow I imagined the rich blue would be more to her liking.

"Oh, Erzebet," one of the servants behind me murmured. I could see her reflected behind me in the mirror; she was shaking her head over her mending and smiling, amused.

"Like mother, like daughter," she pronounced.

"What?" I asked, feeling as if the words were a blow to my gut.

"You are just like her, Erzebet," she said, still shaking her head. "You are like her in so many ways."

I approached the woman quietly, until I stood just a pace before her. When she looked up, the smile vanished from her face.

"How dare you say such a thing?" I said, kicking at the woman's legs for emphasis. "How dare you speak of her?"

Rowena stood from her chair and pressed her hand to my shoulder.

"Erzebet, come with me. To your chamber."

"No, no! Not when my own servants dare say such things." I moved forward with a swiftness even Rowena could not have predicted. I grabbed the servant's arm, knocking the threaded needle from her hand, and pulled her to her feet. She was crying as I pulled her up, and it only made me hate her more, the tears running in rivulets down her slack, wrinkled face.

"Forgive me, my lady," she sputtered. "All I meant is—your mother is very beautiful. And you are, too. I meant no ill by it, I assure you."

As her garbled speech collapsed into pleading, I thrust her heavily into her own chair, where she landed with a surprised thud, her cap knocked askew. I turned away and for a brief moment saw my own reflection in the glass as I left the room, my cheeks burning scarlet with rage and shame.

Now one truth was out, after all this time: I knew that my mother was mad. In that moment it became clear to all of them that I was no longer a child, to be lied to and distracted with gifts. My years of ignorance only made my shame burn deeper with the knowledge.

But there was no denying myself this: in the face of my shame it had felt good, satisfying, to lift the woman from her chair, to watch her eyes turn wide with shock and fear. The very thought of it made me smile; a dark type of smile that I saw in the mirror and shared with no one else.

The next day, Marianna and I nestled into the soft grass beside the marble Athenus. Marianna was eager to hear more about the life of a young daughter of a count. I told her about the number of servants employed in Castle Bizecka, the vineyards, the castle grounds, and those dedicated to catering to my every whim.

"They all must do as I say," I told her in what I imagined was a very impressive, austere manner—a good imitation, I thought, of the count's tone. "Or else they must pay the consequences."

"But you are not a cruel mistress," Marianna said, her voice quiet, cautious. I could not tell if it was a statement or a question.

"It is their duty to serve me," I informed her. "It is their lot in life."

She said nothing, and when I turned to meet her gaze, her eyes fluttered away from mine.

"Forgive me. It is not for me to ask," she said, her dark eyelashes casting long shadows upon her smooth cheeks in the sunshine. Suddenly I felt ugly, my clothes and jewels garish in the bright glare.

"You haven't told me anything about your home," I said gently, "or of your parents."

"Your home is simply more interesting, Erzebet," she said, laughing. "We have a garden at home, but it's more like your kitchen garden. I much prefer roses."

"What else?" I asked eagerly.

"It's just Mother and Father and me. There's a brown cow with big eyes and a nervous rump that I milk every morning, and a chicken coop where I gather the eggs. Mother dries herbs from the garden, and Father tills the field. In the evening, Mother and I stitch clothes for me, though nothing quite like yours," she murmured, fingering the smooth satin of my gown. She sighed and remained quiet for a moment, her sigh hanging in the air between us.

"What is the matter, Marianna?" I asked, aware of her averted eyes. "You should tell me; I may be able to help."

"Our problem is the same as everyone's problem." She shrugged, leaning back against her arms and lifting her face to the sun. "The Turks."

This intrigued me more than any of Pugrue's diatribes about the mysterious, heathen Turks. I leaned in close, urging her to say more.

"They've begun to demand taxes from us—I'm sure you know about that."

"But it's only the count's right to collect taxes from you."

"I don't know, Erzebet. We live on the outskirts of the village, near the forest. We may be outside of your father's land, and inside the Turks'."

"But the Turks do not own Hungary!" I said, unable to curb my mounting distress. Marianna, on the other hand, was more accustomed to the subject, though it seemed to make her suddenly weary. She lay on her back, her fingers running distractedly through the grass. Her brow furrowed and her mouth turned down in a way I had never seen before, like a wince of pain marring the sweet freshness of her face.

"Well, they've started to visit us, to collect their share of our produce—*fair* share, that's what they say." She rolled onto her side, a slightly embarrassed smile on her face. "Do you know what my father has started to do?" she asked, but seemed suddenly abashed.

"What? Go on, tell me."

"Are you sure he will not get into trouble if I tell you?"

"I would never get you into trouble, Marianna," I assured her.

She sighed again, but continued. "He's taken to hiding the cow and the goats in the forest when he senses the Turks might visit. Mother and I found a hiding place in the hollow trunk of an old tree, and we've fit jars of honey and jam in there. It's worked so far." She giggled, and it made me giggle, too, though I didn't know what to think about her predicament.

"One day she got stuck." She giggled.

"Your mother?"

"The cow! The Turks had left, but we couldn't get her out; her hooves were stuck under a tree root. I had to climb in and untangle her while my father pulled on her harness, and Mother just stood there with her apron covering her face. She didn't know whether to laugh or cry. I just laughed." Her eyes sparkled at this, and she laughed again. I laughed with her and was amazed at how easy she made it, to find the fun in such things.

"Maybe there is something I can do to help," I offered, in earnest. "My father will be visiting soon. I can ask him." I was eager to help her, though I feared that the count might not approve of my desire to help a peasant. But shouldn't he care if the Turks were stealing goods from his villagers?

"I have a cloak for you, for this winter. It doesn't fit me any longer, but I think it shall fit you just fine."

Marianna sat up, suddenly.

"That's very kind of you—I feel you've been too kind already."

"I don't often have visitors." I paused awkwardly. "If you would like, I can send a letter to your parents, so they know that you're welcome to visit me at any time."

"That would be wonderful—certainly they would ask where I found the new cloak." She smiled. "And what about you? I've heard much about the castle, but little about the count and countess."

"The count is always away," I said easily. "I haven't seen him in years. The countess"—I lingered for a moment, pretending to be distracted by a perfect red rose—"she's not well." I stated this with the same authority with which I had been told all of my life. Marianna smiled a little sadly and asked no more.

A moment passed in silence, then she gazed up at the statue of Athenus and smiled.

"Be honest with me, Erzebet—have you ever wanted to kiss him?" she asked.

"I suppose I have," I admitted. "More so than I've wanted to kiss any other man."

"I feel the same." She sighed.

I shifted uncomfortably; would I have to confess my desire to kiss Athenus to Father Pugrue? It seemed too secret a thing to admit to him.

"Won't your father want you to marry, Erzebet?" She tilted her head to one side, like a curious cat.

"I don't want to marry." I had never spoken these words aloud before, but it felt liberating to do so. I couldn't help but think of my mother, though the thought made my stomach churn. Marriage was certainly partly responsible for her current state, and I suppose my birth was responsible for the rest. As I examined the blades of grass before me, I felt Marianna's eyes upon my face.

"I suppose I just don't want to grow up, at all," I said. I started pulling the blades of grass out by the root, but was careful to keep my voice steady. "It seems that nothing good can come of it."

"You don't have much choice in the matter, Erzebet," Marianna said, laughing. Somehow I couldn't will myself to join her.

"But it's all bad, growing older," I explained. "You get wrinkled and tired and sick. I would much rather stay a child."

"What will you do?" she asked. "Will you not have children? You're nobility—perhaps you could be queen someday."

"I suppose." I turned my face toward Athenus, his long shadow protecting me from the sun. "If I were queen, you could be my closest handmaiden, my lady-in-waiting."

Marianna laughed aloud and stood, damp grass clinging to her skirt.

"At your service, Your Majesty," she said, curtsying with a grand flourish of her brown linen dress.

IX

From the moment Pugrue told me about my father's eventual return to the castle, I had often imagined and reimagined the scene of his arrival while sorting through my gowns and jewels. Would he be impressed with the growth of his young daughter? I studied my face in the glass, trying to gauge what his reaction would be. I had grown quite a bit since his last visit, my limbs growing longer, my waist smaller, the striking contours of my face more defined, my hair and eyes even more lustrous. But there was another change that had taken place, internally, that I hoped he would be unable to detect: my realization of the curse. I inspected my reflection in the mirror for hours on end, trying to discover a defect, marveling that the beauty of the surface was so incongruous with the fears that raged within me. I only hoped that the surface would be enough to hide behind.

Since that early summer day when I'd first met Marianna in the rose garden, my thoughts of the count's imminent visit had changed. I still often looked forward to his return with a certain amount of fretful excitement and anxiety, but now—and for the first time—I had another person to consider in the equation. I doubted the count would approve of my friendship with Marianna. Would I have to conceal from him my whereabouts during her visits? Even with these hesitations in mind, I yearned to invite her into the castle in the days before the count's return. I was eager to share the opulent rooms with her and be able to appreciate their grandness in a way I never had before, being able to see it reflected in her eyes.

Rowena had noticed a change in me, and had begun to ask questions in spite of her usually casual manner.

"You've been spending a lot of time in the garden, I see," she commented one morning, helping me dress.

"I always spend time in the garden in summer," I reminded her.

"I just don't want you to ruin your pretty gown, my dear." She shrugged in her characteristic way. "Besides, it might rain in the garden today. You had best stay indoors after your lessons."

"But I'm not alone in the garden," I blurted out.

Rowena said nothing, only met my eyes in the glass. There was a long pause while she patiently awaited the rest of the story.

"I have a guest," I explained calmly. "She visits me every day. If I don't go outside, she might be waiting for me."

"And that's no way to treat a guest," she said.

Rowena thought it would be best to keep my friendship with a girl from the village a secret; there was no sense in giving the servants something to gossip about, especially considering how the count would react. With Rowena's help, we secreted Marianna into the castle, straight into the parlor where all of my portraits were hung on the walls. The fire was lit and Rowena had set tea out on the table. Before scurrying to shut the door behind her, I saw her cast a quick smile in Marianna's direction. It occurred to me that they might have recognized each other from the village chapel, or the marketplace—there was a whole world outside the castle walls that was completely foreign to me.

Marianna gazed in awe at the lushly appointed room, with fine art upon the walls, a silver tea set, and brocade chairs arranged by a roaring fire. I was glad that we were alone; surrounded as we were by the luxury of the portrait chamber, I couldn't deny the shabbiness of Marianna's sun-bleached blue frock and wrinkled apron.

"They are beautiful, Erzebet. Are you to have another done?"

"No doubt that I will, once the count returns," I told her. Though I tried to conceal it even from myself, this room lacked the sweet dreams it had inspired in me as a child. Those dreams had been obscured by the memory of Mother and Father arguing in this room, so many years ago—the last time I had seen them together—and by my knowledge of the curse. I inspected my face as it appeared in each of the paintings and then compared it critically with what I saw reflected in the large mirror upon the wall.

"Do you know anything about beauty potions, Marianna?" I asked suddenly. The words startled both of us: I had never considered magic before, but here the thought was, fully formed, in my mind. Marianna turned away from the portrait and moved closer, her face reflected beside mine.

"I only know of a few herbs used for healing," she whispered. "There's no magic to it, I assure you."

"But I'm sure there must be such spells. Someone must know them."

"Magic is dangerous, Erzebet—never forget that," she said, squeezing my arm. "Besides, are you not beautiful enough as it is?" She smiled, teasing. Her eyes glittered at my reflection in the glass, but I was too distracted by my own fears to truly enjoy her admiration.

"I just want to stay this way, that's all. I don't want things to change." I stood before the mirror, not looking away from my face.

"You waste your time with such worries." Marianna sighed and turned to sit upon a brocade couch by the fire. "We are meant to simply live each day, and leave our future to God."

"Then you believe that God has decided our future for us already, and there is no way to change it?" I asked, my voice growing louder. "That all the people upon this earth have no free will?"

"It's best to trust God's judgment in these matters, Erzebet," she said placidly, and leaned back upon the couch with her eyes closed.

"I don't see how you can be so at peace with such an arrangement!" Marianna's eyes snapped open at the force of my words. "How can you possibly not wish to have control over your own life?"

She looked at me steadily for a moment after my outburst, the way a mother must look at a petulant child—such as I imagined it, at least.

"That's what faith is, my lady." Her voice was irritatingly calm. "We can do our best to make the right decisions, and use our faith to guide us. Do you truly want for more?"

I lowered my head as the colors in the room began to blur. I clamped my mouth shut, afraid of the words that would come out if given the chance. I wanted to tell Marianna about the prophecy and hear her tell me that it was all foolish, groundless. But to say the words aloud would make them more real. And what if she reacted differently? What if the prophecy were the work of the devil, and made her react in fear? This thought clamped around my heart, making me strain for breath. Marianna stepped closer, aware that something was wrong. She waited for me to speak.

"Don't you fear the future at all?" I asked, not lifting my eyes to hers. She rested a warm hand on my shoulder.

"I never said I didn't fear it," she murmured in my ear, "but I think it's best that we don't know what will happen to us until it happens."

She moved closer and I rested my head upon her shoulder, her thick dark hair tickling my nose and cheeks. She wrapped her arms around me and we stood together for a moment in silence. Deep inside, in the most frightened part of myself, I knew that she was right. It would have been much better not to know.

Along with the new cloak, I sent an elegant letter to Marianna's parents, asking that they allow their daughter to visit me whenever she chose, in exchange for whatever gifts I saw fit to bestow upon her. It took little time for her parents to realize the potential benefits of their beautiful daughter's friendship with the daughter of the wealthy Count Bizecka. After her tour of the portrait chamber, Marianna became more accustomed to entering the castle, particularly on days when the humid weather urged us within the relative coolness of the clammy stone walls.

I also took the matter of Marianna's dress into my own hands, choosing a few of my own gowns to be tailored for her wardrobe. For the task to be done correctly it was necessary to bring Ermengarde, the mistress of the wardrobe, into our confidence.

"I think the pink will suit her complexion far better than mine," I remarked happily as I spread the gown upon my bed. I reveled in the image of Marianna looking like a countess herself in one of my gowns. Ermengarde merely sniffed in response, but I turned to her with narrowed eyes.

"Do you not approve of my use of my own wardrobe?" My eyebrow arched with pointed interest. Ermengarde's eyes darted awkwardly.

"It's not my place to say, my lady," she said through pursed lips, bowing in a cursory manner. "But I doubt your father—" I took a step toward her and she cut her words short.

"You're correct, Ermengarde," I told her. "It's not your place to say anything."

The threatened look in her eyes seemed incongruous with the cheerful pink gown draped over her arm. Despite my irritation, I rolled back on my heels and returned to the gowns, searching for another that would suit Marianna. I saw Ermengarde's shoulders sag with relief.

Later that afternoon Marianna was secreted into my bedchamber for her dress fitting. Though she tried her best to politely refuse my generous offer, there was no concealing the way her eyes danced at the sight of the fine pink lace. I enjoyed the afternoon, watching as Ermengarde dutifully pinned up the hems and sleeves of the gowns, delighting in Marianna's bashful pleasure as she admired her own reflection in my mirror. I walked over to the mirror and stood beside her, our faces reflected side by side.

I can still see that reflected image with startling perfection: she was a bit shorter than me, and a bit fleshier: her shoulders and arms had rounded curves compared to my sharp, winglike angles. Her hair was a dark cloud of ringlets that she was often pushing away from her face or pinning behind her ear. Her face was fair, with a generous pink blush and a soft roundness to her cheeks; my cheekbones were high, and cast a striking shadow over the hollow of my cheek in the low light. I saw her sparkling eyes travel from her reflection to my own.

"Thank you for the dress, Erzebet. It's the most beautiful one I've ever worn."

"It looks far prettier on you than it ever did on me."

She blushed in response and I laughed at her modesty. I had begun to compare us in my mind, the obsessive ticking off of features beyond my control: her face, eyes, lips, cheeks, hair, neck, shoulders, breasts, waist . . . were they more beautiful than mine? Was she more beautiful than me? The sight of her slim waist turning in the firelight made me wince, for a moment, my hands flying to my own waist for reassurance. I turned to look at myself in the mirror.

I was shocked for a moment to see my mother's face in the glass—that ravenous look I had seen in her eyes, as if they were fit to devour me. I didn't breathe for a moment, until long after the vision had faded. The chamber suddenly felt unbearably warm. I turned away from the glass, turning back to Marianna's infectious laughter.

Envy is a dangerous sin. To envy someone you love is to kill a part of yourself.

When the sun dropped lower in the sky it was time for Marianna to leave. After we bid our good-byes at the garden gate, I raced up to an upper balcony to see if I could watch her pick her way down the hill, her pink gown shining in the early evening sunlight.

From the balcony my eyes scanned the scene below, the fresh green hill dotted with darker green trees and crisscrossed with paths traversed by servants on daily treks to the village, vineyards, and fields. The sun, lowering in a cloudless sky, was bright golden upon my face, making me squint in the brightness. I started waving, imagining that though I couldn't see her, perhaps she could see me: I hopped up and down, waving excitedly, laughing at the thought of Marianna doing the same on the ground below.

There was a rhythm to my waving, a beat. With each wave of my arm there seemed to be a corresponding beat: an actual sound. At first I was too distracted to realize it, but then I turned to the sound of the beat, turning to a balcony one story below.

The countess was there, and suddenly I could hear screaming. She was standing on the balcony outside of her bedchamber, her great black gown swirling around her. In one hand she held the wing of a black hen, which attempted to flutter from her grip in a frantic mess of feathers. In the other hand she held a long white cane, cut from the bough of a birch tree.

The countess lowered the flailing hen to the ground, holding it down with her free hand, and began beating it with the white cane. She screamed obscenely as she did this, her words an angry garble. With each strike, the bird shook with greater force, until the balcony was littered with its black feathers. After more strikes than I could count, the hen grew sluggish in its struggle. Eventually the countess was able to let the bird go entirely and strike it with both hands on the cane, unencumbered. The white cane, and her white hands gripping it, were spattered with blood. The setting sun struck the balcony as she did this, casting the countess's black gown and the hen's black feathers in a reddish-golden light.

Beat. Beat. Beat. She dropped the cane. The hen splayed on the balcony, lifeless. The countess pulled a small vial from her belt—I could see it glinting in the sun. She began to run it along her blood-streaked hands.

It was a spell, an old folk remedy. I had heard it spoken of, but never seen it done. The blood of a beaten hen smeared on an enemy's clothing would render them incapable of harming you. It took me only a moment to realize who her enemy was: the countess was preparing for her husband's return.

The earth and the sky began to spin around me as I stood there, watching her. I pitched forward suddenly and caught myself upon the edge of the balcony. As I stood from the railing, I saw blood spattered upon my hands and arms and chest, just as I had seen on the day of the slaughtered deer. The sight of it made me gasp aloud, in horror.

The countess turned suddenly at the sound of my gasp, the sun full and bright upon her face. But it wasn't actually her face I saw: just a blur of white, as though my vision had failed me, my eyes pierced by the golden light of the sun. No, it was a white cotton mask she wore to protect her skin from the sun. She clenched the fabric between her teeth to keep it still during her exertion. There were small slits for her eyes, and the cloth was buttoned closed at the back of her head. Thus hooded, the countess looked more ghost than woman—a grisly ghost at that, for the white cotton mask was splattered with blood. Even though I could not see her eyes, I sensed that she was staring at me with some sort of recognition, the vial of hen's blood clutched in her hands.

I found it difficult to extricate myself from her stare. Once freed, I clambered down the steps, down the hall to my bedchamber. I rushed over to the white pitcher to wash the blood from my hands. Reaching for the pitcher, I gasped again: there was no blood on my hands, or my dress. My fingers, though trembling, were pale and clean. I turned to the mirror in disbelief.

I touched my face with a tremulous fingertip—there was no blood there, but my fear was apparent. That blood would follow me: the memory of the deer's blood on my skin. Closing my eyes, I could see again the red droplets upon my white skin: a symbol of my curse.

That night the angel and the demon came to me, in a dream. From one moment to the next the image seemed to shift, like the flickering of a candle flame. The creature was an angel, holding the mask of a devil before its face, but in the next moment it was a devil, its red limbs flashing from beneath a long white robe.

Repent before the end of days, the angel told me, its voice harsher than I had expected.

Repent before unending days, the devil said, its eyes white and unblinking, its face the color of blood.

I woke suddenly, burning hot and tangled in my bedclothes. Squinting at the weak light from my windows, I determined that it was not yet dawn, the moon still faintly visible in an iron-gray sky. I listened to the rain spattering on the gray stones. The erratic late-summer weather had turned the thick warm air into a steamy rain the night before, but this morning a chill had crept in. I shivered in my thin white nightshift, burrowing deeper under the covers. The images of my dream crept back upon me, even with my eyes opened. I wrapped my arms around myself for comfort.

While I lay blinking in the weak light, Rowena suddenly burst into my room. I sat up in bed at her entrance.

"The count has arrived," she said, her voice steady with false calm. "I'm sorry to startle you, Erzebet. But I must get you ready to greet him." She walked over to my dressing table to begin fussing over which jewels I should wear. The sight of the white kerchief on her head filled me with a feeling of dread; it took me a moment to follow the feeling to its cause, but when I did, the sight of the countess beating the black hen came rushing back to me—her face a mask of white. The hood seemed to replace her face altogether, so I could not recall her features even if I tried. I watched Rowena for a moment, still in bed, and all the while I couldn't stop shivering—the sudden change in temperature had chilled me to the bone.

"Erzebet, are you all right?" Rowena asked. "You look rather pale this morning."

I turned to the mirror to see if this was true. I pinched my cheeks and bit my lips, trying to urge the blood back into them. It was important that I look my best, though I felt far from it.

"I'm fine," I told Rowena, to ease the furrowing of her worried brow. "I'm just cold."

But I wasn't fine. It had been a long while since I had seen my father, and a great deal of change had taken place in his absence. I had learned about the prophecy of my early death—would he be able to see it when he looked at me, this knowledge that had unhinged me from the earth? I wondered if he would visit Mother in her chamber during his visit. I began to wonder if he had visited her at all on his most recent sojourns home. We had both been neglected by him, she and I. This knowledge kindled flames of shame and anger within me.

Rowena hastily dressed me in an elaborate new silk gown. My constant shivering did little to distract her from her work, and I gasped as she laced the new corset with more harshness than usual.

Once my hair was properly braided and pinned, I stood before the mirror. Rowena stepped back in admiration.

"You look beautiful, Erzebet," she told me approvingly.

Meeting my reflection in the mirror, I saw that what she said was true. I was impressed with how the iron-ribbed corset cinched my slim waist. The saffron silk bodice was long, with a point at the waist, the front covered with delicate gold lace that shimmered in the light of the fire. The saffron skirt separated into two petal-shaped panels that revealed the rich yellow silk underskirt beneath. I smoothed the soft, cool silk of the full skirt with an appraising palm.

"You've become a beautiful young woman," Rowena murmured. My eyes turned glassy in the mirror before me, my vision blurred.

"Come, Erzebet," Rowena urged. "Your father is waiting for you in the portrait chamber."

Exiting my chamber, I saw that the castle was already bustling with activity. The count's procession of coaches was being unloaded of art and wares from Vienna and Prague. I wondered distantly of what gift I might receive, perhaps as a symbol of his approval. I lifted my skirt carefully and descended the stone staircase, past the dining hall, to the chamber with tall windows in the front of the castle. The count stood close to a raging fire, the flames licking the top of the enormous fireplace like a hungry beast. He turned from the flames as I entered.

"Erzebet, you've grown into a fine young lady. You look far more elegant than your thirteen years should allow."

"Twelve years," I murmured. I stood still as stone as his eyes brushed across me, as though inspecting a new painting. I didn't dare breathe.

"Recite for me the catechism," he demanded suddenly. The words flew from my mouth in impeccable—if a bit rushed—Latin. After a moment he lifted his hand to cease my recitation and nodded in approval.

"Beautiful." He smiled at me, though the smile did not seem to reach the cold glitter in his eyes. He was dressed sumptuously, in a dark velvet cloak thrown back to reveal the sleeves of his doublet, fashionably torn as though slashed by an artful sword. A stiff ruff encircled his neck, with a thick gold chain protruding from beneath it and extending to his waist. He was tall and lean with a harsh, drawn face, perhaps a bit more haggard than I had remembered him. He stood before the fire as if posing for his own portrait.

"Am I to have my portrait done during your visit, my lord?"

"No," he stated. My heart sank in my chest. I thought back to the face I had just seen reflected in the mirror in my bedchamber: Was I no longer beautiful enough to be worthy of an artist's canvas? Had he expected more from his young daughter?

"Perhaps next time, Erzebet, when I have more time to visit. As it is, I will only be here for a short while, and then I will return to the emperor."

"Will my next portrait be offered as a gift to Emperor Rudolf, my lord?" I inquired.

"Yes, I suppose it may be," he said dismissively. "The emperor has a great interest in beautiful objects, and little else," he remarked bitterly.

I had heard many rumors about Rudolf's ill health and fits of melancholy and rage. From the count's stern expression it seemed clear that all of these rumors were true. Unnerved by his disinterested manner, I urged myself to press forward. I could think of nothing else that I dared ask him.

"Are you planning a betrothal for me, my lord?"

He looked at me in surprise, as if he had not thought of this possibility for some time. I thought I saw the coldness in his eyes melt, if only for a moment.

"Yes, Erzebet, I have been trying to arrange a betrothal. It has become a more complicated issue than I had anticipated. The emperor, as you may have heard, is quite hesitant to commit himself to anyone. And I will admit that there are other matters central to the purpose of this visit."

It is not enough, of course, to visit your daughter or your wife, I thought, surprised by how injured I felt.

"The Turks?" I asked cautiously.

"Yes, indeed." He nodded, settling himself into a large chair by the fire and leaning back languidly, much as I imagined the members of court might sit. He nodded at a nearby chair for me to do the same. I perched awkwardly on the edge of the seat, not wanting to wrinkle my gown.

"This Sultan Selim is nothing like his father. The father they called Magnificent—this one they call the Sot. He's a drunkard, and drinking isn't even allowed in their religion—not a drop. Yet even with a leader such as him, they will conquer all they can. They set their eyes upon Vienna, long ago."

"They have begun to tax the villagers in Novoe Mesto," I told him. His eyes jumped from gazing at the fire to my face. They glittered sharply.

"The Turks have? How do you know this?"

"I've heard it from the servants—the villagers on the outskirts, near the forest. They have begun to tax them, and may move into the village center before long."

A rumbling sound from outside made the count jerk his head toward the window. Another storm was brewing, and distant thunder could already be heard. He stood and peered out the window, as if expecting a siege. The poor weather had likely plagued his entire voyage home, and it clearly unnerved him. A violent storm in the heavens was seen as an omen of war upon the earth.

"Perhaps you should retire to a different residence, young Erzebet, for the remainder of the summer. Far from all of this talk of the Turks."

"Oh, no, my lord. I would much prefer to remain here. If that is agreeable to you." I could not bear to leave Castle Bizecka, and my afternoons with Marianna. I realized that I even felt strangely guilty at the thought of leaving Mother behind, though she had already left me years before.

"You do not seem concerned with the goings-on, though I suppose it is your lot in life. Women are never much impressed by the risks of war—they've never seen what a battlefield is like."

I swallowed the bitter taste of his condescension, along with my pride. I was willing to do anything, even play the role of dutiful daughter, to be permitted to stay at home.

"It's just as well that you remain here, I suppose, and avoid travel in this weather. But you must be warned to stay away from the soldiers, and stop listening to the gossip of those servants."

"Of course, my lord," I said, standing from the chair and bowing graciously.

One of the count's advisers bustled into the room; I noticed the count stiffen against the back of his chair. The adviser took no notice of me, but hurried over to the count and whispered something urgently. I gazed dreamily into the fire, pretending not to listen. The count stood and straightened his doublet.

"I'm afraid I have an important meeting at this time, Erzebet. You are dismissed."

I knew not what to say, so I bowed gracefully. The count had left the room before my curtsy was even complete, his adviser close behind. I stood alone: elaborately dressed and abandoned.

The sunlight shone in pale puddles upon the floor as I left the chamber. None of the other servants paid me any mind, too busy bustling around on the count's orders. Usually I would be relieved to be left alone, but today I felt not simply alone, but forgotten. There was a different current of energy in the air now that the count had returned. I wondered if my mother could feel it, too, while contained in her bedchamber.

I knew that I should make my way to the chapel, to meet Pugrue. It was still early, and time for my lesson. Who, I wondered, would be meeting with the count so early in the morning? It seemed strange to me; the whole castle felt strange to me. I wandered distractedly toward the chapel, but paused in the main hallway. I would just take a walk, that was all—a walk to clear my head. There would be less bustling in the secret passageways, certainly, as the main halls were crowded with servants. After all, I didn't want to get in anyone's way: at least that's what I told myself as I slipped into the passageway and walked quietly toward the count's wing of the castle.

The passageways were narrow, dark. I ran the palm of my hand across the stone wall with each step, careful that my slippers made as little sound as possible upon the echoing stones. When I turned a corner I noticed that a line of wall sconces had been lit up ahead, to aid someone's passage. I walked slowly, listening for the sound of voices. I hadn't been in this wing of the castle since I had found the prophecy, the thought of which made my flesh cold.

When I heard voices, I stopped still in my tracks. I followed the sound to one of the small, windowless chambers in the count's suite of rooms. I slipped behind a tapestry and ran my hands along the wall, searching for the secret door to the chamber. Once I found it, I opened it only a crack. The door was obscured by a tapestry on the other side as well, and this I pushed aside very slightly with my fingertips. The light within the chamber was weak enough—a fire burning in a small hearth—that they could not see me.

It took me a moment to adjust my eyes to the light. Their voices were low, and I could only see a vague outline of shapes. As the count was exchanging pleasantries, he lit a candle with a flame from the fireplace. The candle burned through the darkness and settled upon a low table in the center of the room. In the light of the candle I could see more clearly the form seated across from the count.

I recognized his dress instantly from the tales I had heard from Pugrue and the servants: he was a pasha, a Turkish soldier who collected taxes for the benefit of the sultan. Though I had heard stories and seen drawings of Turkish dress, the overall effect of finally seeing a heathen Turk was rather unexpected: he was magnificent. His robes were made of rich, supple leather, with a scarf of silk tied loosely at his throat. A white turban was wound upon his head—a tight, intricate mass of overlapping widths of silk with a dark purple stone affixed above his forehead. *So this is what the Infidel looks like?* I thought, in awe. Though the pasha's dark-skinned face was lined with wrinkles, he made the count look even older by comparison, rigid in his stiff collar and embroidered doublet. It made me wonder what Turkish women looked like: dark and smoldering, draped in veils.

The pasha smiled at the count across the table, as though amused.

"As you know," the count was saying, "though this meeting must remain secret, I have invited you here as a friend."

With these words, the count pulled a ruby ring from his finger and laid it upon the table before his guest.

"I appreciate your generous offer," the pasha said, nodding. He had a long, elegant nose that I imagined could smell the coins tucked in the pocket of the count's vest. He did not touch the ring. "But it is not necessary. You and I are already on fine terms, I assure you."

But as the count reached out to reclaim the ruby, the pasha's eyes flashed.

"Forgive me if I cannot help but comment on the beauty of your sapphire," he said, glancing at the enormous blue stone glittering on the count's finger. "I'm afraid I have simply never seen its likeness."

"Indeed," the count said, taken aback. He quietly slipped the sapphire from his finger and placed this upon the table before the pasha. At this, the pasha smiled, his eyes sparkling.

"A generous gift indeed," he said, his hand slowly closing over the precious gem. "Now, all gestures aside, how may I assist you?"

"As things have changed as of late, I thought it best that we reestablish our arrangement."

"I agree, things have changed." The pasha nodded. "I assume you are referring to your army?"

"Yes, I'm afraid that is exactly what I wanted to discuss with you. I wanted to make sure that you did not misunderstand my intentions."

"My dear count, we are men of honor, are we not? In my experience, if a man employs an army, he intends to fight a war."

The count shifted uneasily in his chair.

"Or perhaps I want not to fight one," he interjected, "and funding an army is the best way to do so."

The pasha merely smiled in amusement.

"We had an agreement," the count said, in a voice of measured calm. "I would share the taxes of Novoe Mesto with you. In exchange, you would leave the villagers be. I am in power here, and it is important that the villagers see that."

"Yes, you are in power," the pasha said in a flat monotone, shifting in his seat. As he moved, a leather pouch tied to his belt jingled—the sound of silver. He rested a long, elegant hand upon his knee, the count's sapphire ring glinting from the pasha's own finger.

"Yet I hear that you have begun visiting the houses on the outskirts of the town, by the forest."

"Perhaps this was an oversight," the pasha offered, his eyes glittering. "I was unaware that these homes were under your protection. Unfortunately, while your offer was quite generous a year ago, I'm afraid it will no longer suffice. I answer to the sultan, and he, too, has an army assembled."

"I know," the count told him, "and I am willing to make you another offer, in an attempt to keep the peace between us."

The pasha leaned back in his chair, looking at the count calmly, unblinking.

"You may continue to visit the houses by the border, near the forest. I will allow you that. And I will continue to give you a portion of the taxes I exact—but no more can I give. The town center, the marketplace, these areas are beyond the boundaries agreed upon for you and your soldiers."

"And *your* soldiers?"

"They are for the good of the people only. I have no wish to start a war, nor do I want the villagers to feel they are not protected. This will continue to benefit both of us, you see: you will collect more money and goods for your sultan, and I will retain my power over the village. Are you in agreement?"

The pasha smiled, and nodded only vaguely.

"I'm glad that you were able to meet with me on your brief visit home."

The count did not respond to this remark, but spread a map out upon the table. Their voices dropped into a conversation about borders and soldiers' posts as I sank back into the shadows of the hidden hallway.

I could not quite comprehend what I had seen, still swimming with the vision of a Turk in one of the count's inner chambers. I walked forward as though in a trance, lost in the abyss of my own thoughts. Marianna lived by the forest. She had told me that the Turks had come to visit them, and I had offered to help her. I had thought the count would feel threatened by such an intrusion, but I had been wrong. He had invited them, all along: first as a guest in his own castle, and now as an authority in Marianna's home. I knew the count even less than I had realized.

When I awoke from my trance of aimless wandering I eagerly sought the main hallway, wanting to put the close darkness of the passageways behind me. Now the sunlight shone in bright golden spears upon the floor. It was clear that the excitement of the morning had made me late for my lesson. Suddenly I remembered my dream of that morning: *Repent before the end of days*. Lesson or no lesson, confession had become more imperative since I'd learned about the prophecy. The sun patterned my bright gown in streaks of golden light as I ran toward the chapel.

When I arrived, Pugrue was not there. It was late, indeed. The door to the chapel dungeon was open—perhaps he was waiting for me there? I plunged headlong into the blackness, nearly falling down the dark stairs.

"Hello? Father Pugrue?" I heard a rustle in the corner, but no light penetrated the darkness. Bumping into crates that threatened to topple over, I made my way to the corner we used for confession.

"I'm sorry I'm late. Are you there?"

I stopped in my tracks and listened intently. There was the shuffling, again—first in front of me, then behind. I held my breath and listened. My flesh grew moist and clammy.

"I'm sorry," I muttered weakly. "I'm here to confess. I have sinned."

"Indeed, you have," murmured a deep voice startlingly close to my ear. I leaped out of fright, but a strong arm encircled my waist, lifting me from the ground. My back went rigid with fright.

"Tell me about your sins, child."

XI

"Father Pugrue?" I asked meekly, but my question was answered with a dark laugh.

"No," he said, his mouth so close that I could feel his breath upon me. He dipped closer and sniffed my neck and hair like a wolf.

"Who are you?" I gasped.

"You needn't know who I am. Not yet. But I know you, Erzebet, Erzebet, Erzebet . . . " His voice trailed into a string of whispers close to my ear.

"You're nearly a woman," he murmured. "Tell me how you have sinned."

"Who are you?" I begged, panicked. "Did you come with my father, the count?" I grabbed his arm and tried to wriggle from his grasp, but he held me tightly.

"You think so little of your father, do you? That he would have such a friend as me?" He laughed at this, adjusting his arms to better restrain me. I gasped, worried that he might know of the count's secret business dealings.

"Are you a Turk?" I asked. He laughed in response.

"No, my dear. My nationality is of no importance. I have come here of my own volition, only for you. Now tell me how you have sinned."

I kicked with all the force I had, but my full skirt acted as a buffer between us. His arms were like steel bands wrapped around me. Growing weary from the sheer physical exertion of my terror, I felt the tears begin to run down my cheeks. Angry at myself, I did the last thing I could think to do: I bent my head forward and bit him on the arm, hard.

He yelled out in pain, but his yell quickly turned into laughter, like a low growl. He squeezed me tighter and lifted one hand to wrap around my neck.

"Let's start with the sin of wrath," he whispered in my ear.

"I've sinned," I blurted, his hand just slack enough upon my neck to let the words pass, "for I was late for my lesson." I labored to swallow, hoping that his grip would subside.

"And now you are here with me," he said, laughing again. "There is more, and you must tell it." The sound of his breathing filled my head, his arm tight against my ribs. His deep voice seemed strangely familiar to me.

"I've sinned because I've had impure thoughts," I muttered, shocked and ashamed as I spoke the words aloud.

"I'm sure you have," he said, his lips brushing the soft flesh of my ear. "You must tell me, or you will remain unclean." The touch of his lips against my skin felt more impure than all the thoughts I had ever before considered.

"I thought of kissing a man—and of touching." I wailed, tears spilling onto my cheeks, my voice high and whining like a child's.

"Which man is this?"

"Not a real man," I cried, mortified, "just a sculpture of one, in the rose garden. But it was only a dream and nothing more. I know better than that, I promise you."

"There is not a woman in this world who knows better," he hissed into my ear. "It is the weakness of the female sex. Your flesh is weak, and it inspires weakness in others." His fingers tightened around my waist. He released his hand from my neck and began to stroke my hair, his fingers brushing my face. Could he sense some other weakness in me? I tried to kick him again.

"But I inspire something different in you, it seems. I inspire fury—I can feel it raging like a fire in your soul. You'd best beware of that fire, child." He laughed again at this, and seemed merely amused by my struggle.

"I understand," I said, trying to will the tremor from my voice. My eyes roved wildly in the darkness.

"I'm not certain that you do, but I'm here to find out. Do you believe in God, child?"

"Of course I do."

"Don't worry, you can tell me." I could feel his smile against my ear: moist lips and teeth. "God can't hear you, only I can. Now tell me, do you trust God?"

"Yes, of course I do," I said, my voice breaking.

"That's not true. You know the answer," he said. "I only need you to admit it."

"I told you," I gasped, thinking of Marianna's words. If I couldn't trust God, whom could I trust?

"You can trust me," he told me. "You can trust me."

At the sound of these words, I stopped fighting, too shocked to move.

"I've heard your voice before," I told him; I felt certain of this, though I could not explain the strange, intimate familiarity of his voice.

"You're a smart girl," he told me. "That's why I've come so far to be here for you." His arm still rigid against my ribs, the touch of his hand upon my face was surprisingly gentle.

"Let me try another question, one that I know you have the answer to: What if you had to choose, right now, between death or eternal life?"

"I already answered that one—that was you? You've asked me that before." That was where I had heard this voice before: that day in Pugrue's chapel, just after I learned of the prophecy. The deep voice I had heard in my mind that day was the same as the one I heard now. But this was a real person, a living man with his arms wrapped around me, not just a voice in my head.

"This is important; I want you to think about it: early death or eternal life." I tipped my head back against his shoulder, letting his voice fill my head and the darkness around us. "Would you allow God to decide for you?" Suddenly I felt something cold and sharp, piercing—was that the point of a dagger, pressed against my ribs? I tried to wriggle free but he held me fast.

"No!" I screamed in fear and pain. "No! I would choose myself—I choose to live forever!"

"That's right, my dear," he murmured soothingly. "It's often best not to trust God's plan in such things."

"You know about the prophecy, don't you?" I asked him. He only laughed in response. Then it must be real after all, I realized, and not some terrible dream.

"Do not worry so much about the prophecy," he said, this time his voice more gentle. "You have the power over life and death: the decision is yours to make." The pain in my side gone, he put his arms around me again and swayed, side to side. "I know you better than you think. You will never be alone as long as I'm here."

As suddenly as I had been seized, he released me: I slumped to the ground in a heap, my legs giving way beneath me. For a moment I might have fainted, for when I came to I heard nothing—the dungeon was completely deserted, and I was alone. I held my breath until it began to ache in my chest, listening closely for any noises in the dark.

"Hello?" I called, sitting on the dungeon floor. I would have been happy to see Pugrue in that moment. No one appeared. I stumbled forward on weak legs and shuffled to the door.

I could not run from the darkness fast enough. I ran down the hallway, through the kitchen, directly to the rose garden. The rain was coming down heavily now, and the sky was dark. The mud slowed my steps and made my gown heavy. I ran until I was safe within the rose hedge.

"Marianna!" I called, but it was difficult to see through the veil of rain, and I was still gasping for breath. Once I caught my breath, I called her name again, and again. Where was she when I needed her most? Perhaps she wouldn't come today at all because of the rain. I felt eyes all around me, as if I were constantly being watched, from all angles. Reeling in the grayness, I could find nothing to distract me from my fear. I bit the palm of my left hand to let my mind focus on the pain.

"Erzebet! Erzebet!" I heard Marianna's voice call. She stood with her dark hair wet upon her forehead, shaking the iron gate. I fairly tripped over my sodden gown in my effort to reach her. When

I appeared, she smiled, but her smile faded as I drew closer to bid her entrance.

"Erzebet, what's wrong?" she asked.

"Come with me," I said, avoiding her eyes. I grabbed her hand and bent my head low, running through the cold, stinging rain.

"But Erzebet, wait!" she cried, skidding her slippers into the mud to stop me. "The count has returned, hasn't he? What will he say?"

"We'll have to hide. I'll find somewhere."

Moments later we burst into the kitchen, our wet slippers skidding upon the floor. I heard the cook shout "Mercy!" but I dared not slow my steps. I gripped Marianna's slippery hand in mine and pulled her through the kitchen, ignoring the comments of servants along the way. I had to find a place where we could hide, where we could both be safe.

A piercing scream stopped us in our tracks. We slipped on the slick stones and fell to the floor. I looked around, frantically—the count could be anywhere, and I didn't want him to see us. I knew where the screams were coming from: we were near my mother's chambers.

"What is that?" Marianna gasped.

"It's my mother," I told her, then was shocked at the suddenness of my confession. "She's not well," I said, attempting to explain.

Servants scuttled around corners, watching us get up from the floor in our soaked dresses. Mother's screaming continued, and in the midst of it I managed to find a sudden clarity. There was one place where we would be safe from the count. I grasped Marianna's hand and pulled her down my mother's hallway. The hall seemed to grow longer as we ran, Mother's screams magnified with every step. At the end of the hall we reached a staircase that twisted higher and higher, as though stretching into the sky. The stairwell became narrow at the top, no longer lit by torches.

"Where are we, Erzebet?"

"The tower room—the south tower, the one by the cliffs. It should be empty; it's never guarded." Groping along the cold, moist wall, we found the door that took all our might to budge open.

We shivered as we entered the tower: a circular chamber with a high spire in the center and narrow, windowless casements slick with icy rain. Cobwebs clung to the hems of our gowns. The stone walls were burning cold to the touch and the cold seeped beneath our layers of clothes. Marianna hugged herself against the cold, but I relished the feeling, as if it cleansed me of all that had taken place that day: a thin layer of ice slipping against my skin like silk.

"No one ever comes to this tower," I told her, my voice bouncing off the walls.

"A whole room and no one ever uses it, like it's been sleeping this whole time." She smiled thoughtfully and shivered.

"Maybe this room has been waiting for us," I said, excitement making me bold.

"For us?" She blinked at me in awe. "I've never had a room of my own before, not even with just one other person. It sounds so secret and wonderful."

"We can share this room, but it has to stay ours, alone—do you agree?"

"Of course!" she whispered, suddenly breathless. She clasped my cold hand and the wind outside howled; the tower seemed to sway dangerously. "It's our secret." She smiled. My palm stung in her grip, but I pretended the pain did not exist. I took both of her hands in mine.

"Haven't you heard the story of Snow White and Rose Red?"

I asked her, trying to make my voice cheerful and swallow my tears. "They were friends, but they were really like sisters, and there was a song that they sang: *Snow White, Rose Red, would you beat your suitor dead?*" I chanted, and pulled her by the hands into a spiral, our wet shoes kicking up mud from the floor. Marianna nearly tripped over the soggy hem of her gown, but she only laughed and spun faster.

"*Snow White, Rose Red,*" we chanted together, and spun.

This was our very first magic spell. The gray stones, the worn tapestries, the cobwebs in the air, spun around us in a blur. The walls around us and the floor beneath our feet seemed to slip away. The world slipped away. Everything around me spun too quickly to see—everything but Marianna's smiling face.

XII

Day six, tower, night

I'm anxious when the servants leave at night. Only the two guards sit outside the tower chamber, and they've been told not to talk to me. The owls hooting in the distance, the violent caws of ravens, and the occasional bark of a wild dog are all that interrupt the abyss of quiet. I'm never tired enough to sleep. This is how I fill the hours: sitting before this oval mirror, the dressing table before me trembling with candlelight. I spend each night dressing, painting my face, and affixing jewels in my hair.

The bodice of this dress accentuates my elongated waist, the flat front of the bodice embroidered in swirls of sparkling

gold thread. The square neckline exposes my neck and the very tops of my breasts, and the bottom descends into a long, sharp point between my hips. My corsets have grown tighter, my bodices longer, the points sharper as the years have progressed. Each gown transforms me: scintillating, elegant, seductive. I am all of these things and more as I write these words—the mirror tells me so.

I talk out loud sometimes, narrating my transformation in the mirror, in the hopes of filling the terrible quiet and scaring away those old ghosts. I have no minstrels to entertain me, no one to fetch ingredients for a sleeping draft or other potion, and no midnight visits from my girls . . . that would calm me, above all else. I search my dressing table for an abandoned vial of blood, probably long since dried out. But there are none—I think they took them from me, along with the stain for my lips. I drink red wine and pretend that I can taste that familiar metallic tinge, but I know I'm only pretending.

Day seven, night

When the servants arrived this morning, I was resplendent. They paused at the threshold of the door, gazing surreptitiously at my gown and jewels. I'm relieved when they arrive, but even during the day, the tower is eerily quiet. My nights are lonely and my days are likewise, spent in the company of servants who offer little in the way of conversation. Eventually I find my way to the mirror again, to the distraction of my own face.

"I would like to attend Helena's funeral," I inform the servants just before they retire for the evening. They look up from gathering their embroidery hoops and trays of untouched food.

They do not respond to my statement, only stare at me with slackened jaws.

"I intend to write to my cousin Stephan and ask that he grant me permission."

"She was to be married to a Habsburg," one servant ventures. "It will be a funeral for royalty."

"Am I not royalty? I would like to pay my respects to the child."

"Countess, Helena was found dead in your chamber." She explains this slowly, as if I am either a child or mad.

"But I was not the one to wield the blade," I tell them. "Someone must have said that, in all of this. No one saw me kill her."

Their eyes turn back to their tasks of gathering spools of thread and nestling needles in scraps of muslin.

"I'm sorry, Countess," the older servant sighs, but will not look at me. "I am afraid that Stephan will not allow you to attend the funeral." They turn from me and leave the room, closing and bolting the door behind them.

I sit by the fire and imagine Helena's funeral: the corpse dressed discreetly in a long-sleeved, high-necked gown to conceal the wounds still visible on her flesh. Over this, a white veil will stretch from the top of her head to the tips of her toes. She would be carried upon a bier, of course, her face adorned with blooming roses. I imagine that I am there within the crowd, watching the bier pass. The thought of it makes me laugh, and my laughter echoes in the hollowness of the tower. The murder of servant girls isn't the reason why I'm here. It took the death of a noblewoman to attract any attention, and that killing wasn't even mine.

This tower chamber has always been the coldest in the

castle. I turn from this Bible to revive the flames sputtering in the fireplace. I gather old books, the withered pages of a long-dead romance, and feed them to the flames. As the fire grows, the room becomes vivid with light and color. Shadows flicker with streaks of red and gold. There is a gleaming in the mirror, the shine of eyes and teeth. I curse the fire for its brightness, but stand close to it, desperate for warmth. Still, my hands cannot stop shaking. This body is a prison, cold and full of shadows. A log falls in the fire and sprays a shower of sparks in my direction.

Something glints before me: a slice of silver upon the floor. One of the servants left a needle behind. I roll it between my thumb and forefinger, then nestle it securely in the hem of my gown.

In the warm firelight, this tower chamber looks much as it did, so many years ago, when Marianna and I first adorned it with all the comforts we enjoyed. As the sun dimmed and the weather turned cold, we steeled ourselves against the chill with luxurious ermine-lined robes draped over our gowns. We lit candles all around the chamber and covered the narrow slits of windows with heavy tapestries to protect us from the harsh wind. We delighted in arranging the rugs and random pieces of furniture I had procured: a silk divan, velvet-covered chairs, a small wooden desk, and an ornate dressing table with a mirror framed in gold. Over time, the dressing table became a glittering array of small jars of colored glass, filled with scents and oils, herbs, and spices. In the evenings, we often dined in the tower on rich food and sweet wine.

The comforts of the tower room protected us from the wet, cold weather, as well as from the changes that had taken place in the castle since the count's return. The halls were often crowded with servants, soldiers, and the count's band of astrologers, eager to predict the sultan's next move against the Hungarian nobility. They congregated in worried clusters, their conversation falling to hushed whispers whenever I appeared. To avoid all of this, the pattern of our days was simply altered, with Rowena's assistance: after my lessons, Marianna and I were secreted directly to the tower room, through a series of passageways in the south wing of the castle, our progress haunted by my mother's despondent cries.

When Marianna and I had bid our hasty good-byes by the garden gate in the evenings, I was left alone with my fears. I thought about the man in the confessional. When next I entered the chapel dungeon to admit my sins, I trembled at the mere thought of him. I feared that Pugrue knew all about the strange visitation, but was relieved at his apparent obliviousness. He had missed our tutoring session due to a brief illness, for which he apologized.

"We tried to inform you, Erzebet," he told me, "but you were nowhere to be found." The familiar sound of Pugrue's disapproving croak was an odd relief for me.

The memory of that confession was folded and tucked deep within my subconscious, just as the parchment I had taken from the count's study remained hidden in a jewelry chest, concealed by a swatch of linen. His words both confused and haunted me: *You have the power over life and death . . . You will never be alone as long as I am here.* I often thought I heard his voice just as I slipped out of consciousness and into that lost realm of sleep.

Though I didn't dare tell Marianna about my encounter, I did my best to follow the advice I could anticipate she would give: pray to God and ask for guidance. But whenever I did, I was wary of what voice I might hear in answer—could I be sure that it was truly God's?

I saw the count rarely during his time at the castle, and by the beginning of that winter he was already preparing to depart for Prague, to be by the emperor's side. I wondered if perhaps the emperor was dying, and the count did not want to be absent, lest he miss whatever gift of power the emperor might bestow upon him when his departure from this world became imminent. From what I had seen, the count had not once visited his wife in the time he had been at the castle. Though she most likely did not desire such a visit, it made me sorry for the countess. I, too, was acutely familiar with the feeling of neglect.

Though the soldiers stayed behind, the count's departure that winter was a relief. Marianna still preferred the sanctuary of our tower room, but I was thankful to be able to dine with her in my chambers on occasion, or to enjoy a walk in the frost-covered garden without fear of being spotted. Considering how Marianna's presence improved my temperament, the servants knew better than to comment. As the year progressed and the weather turned bitterly cold, we found refuge again in the tower.

That winter I turned thirteen years old: an ominous age that brought with it a mysterious illness. Rowena tended to my complaints with a warm bath and a mug of hot tea, but I kept my fears locked within me, too dangerous to say aloud. To add to my distress, the wind was too harsh to permit Marianna's visit. I sat beside the fire with an aching heaviness in my belly.

I felt certain that I was dying, which led me to desperate thoughts about the prophecy, and the mysterious stranger, whom I had not seen since the summer. In spite of my fear, I could not help but wonder: Could he show me how to choose between life and death, just as he had said? I gritted my teeth through a wave of pain. *I will do whatever he tells me, in order to protect myself.* The moment this thought entered my mind, I spun around my bedchamber, my heart beating wildly. I was alone, but I did not feel alone. I felt certain he was watching me, listening to my thoughts.

I awoke late that night, lying in my bed. I was not sure if I was awake or dreaming. I heard shuffling sounds, the rustling of bedsheets. I blinked in the darkness and noticed, with a distant sense of shock, the feeling of a long form lying in the bed beside me. A body warm and stretched the length of me, curved against my limbs.

"You are a woman now," he whispered in my ear. But it was not merely a voice in my head, it was all of him. My teeth chattered loudly in response; the stranger laid his hand upon my face, brushing his thumb gently across my lips. I braced myself for him to seize me suddenly, violently, but he did not. I was startled, instead, by the warmth of his embrace.

"Do not feel afraid," he assured me. His low, rumbling voice was surprisingly tender. "You have the power over life and death. And I am always here, even when you don't see me."

"I don't see you now," I uttered. He laughed at this and drew himself up upon the bed. A soft ray of moonlight entered the dark chamber and lit one side of his face.

"I am Sinestra," he told me, his face hovering over mine. It was a beautiful face, with strong cheekbones and glistening dark eyes; a face half bathed in pale light, half submerged in shadow. I blinked, certain this was a dream. I lifted a trembling hand to touch his cheek. It was warm and real. He smiled and leaned forward to bury his face in my neck.

"You are a woman now," he whispered again, almost singing the words. "Blood given, blood taken." I wanted to ask him what he meant, but no sound came out of my mouth. My arms were wrapped around him, my fingers tangled in his soft hair.

"It's important for you to act soon, little one. The choice is yours."

When I opened my eyes again, sunshine fell upon the flagstone floor, garishly bright. I rubbed my eyes, still groggy with sleep. Suddenly in need of the chamber pot, I threw back the covers from my bed. That was when I saw the blood—massacre-red upon my silk nightshift and white sheets. For a moment I only stared at the stain, as though it was not a part of me; I hovered above the scene, disconnected. Then I remembered the dream of the stranger.

What did he do to me? The blood was smeared on my nightshift, over my shameful female sex. I opened my mouth and began to scream—a sound of sheer terror tore from my own throat, jolting me back into my own body.

Rowena ran into the chamber at the sound of my voice.

"What's wrong, Erzebet?" Then she saw the blood on my nightgown, and I saw her face turn pale.

"I'm dying, aren't I? It's actually happening, and I'm dying!" My heart pounded as though fit to break free from its cage of bone.

"No, dear, you're not dying. You've become a woman."

You are a woman now, the stranger's voice echoed in my head. Becoming a woman and dying somehow seemed the same thing to me. I nearly fainted with fear. Rowena held me by my shoulders and shook me vigorously.

"Erzebet, listen to me. It happens to all women. We bleed for a few days every month, when the moon tells us to. It means that we may have children of our own someday."

"I don't want children of my own someday."

"That may be, but you can't escape the natural order. It is simply the way that God made us."

"Or the way that God punished us, you mean?" I said, leaning over with another surge of pain. "Are you sure I'm not dying?" I asked, gripping her hand in mine. "You would tell me, wouldn't you—you would tell me if you knew I was dying?"

"Of course, Erzebet," she said, concern mixed with fear in her eyes. "I don't know why you are worried about such a thing."

Rowena did her best to soothe me, bathing me in warm water and then tucking me back into bed. Later that afternoon she returned to my chamber with Marianna. I blinked up at her wearily, uncertain if she was a dream.

"I insisted on visiting you today," Marianna told me, "in spite of the cold. I knew that you would need me—I simply knew it."

She rested her cold hand upon my head. She was real; I sighed with relief.

"Oh, poor Erzebet," she sighed. "How do you feel?"

"I feel sick," I told her. "I'm afraid that I'm dying."

"Erzebet, don't be dramatic. It happens to everyone—every girl, anyway."

"Then you mean you knew about this?" I asked, unable to hide my disgust.

"Yes, of course. I've known for years. I assumed you knew, too."

He didn't hurt me; this happens to all women, I thought, recalling my vivid dream. Was it only a dream, or could it have been a real visitation from the stranger? Or had I dreamed his other visit as well? I considered telling Marianna about it when a glinting across the room caught my eye.

"What's that?" I asked. "On my dressing table? Something silver," I murmured. Marianna stood up to investigate.

"Oh, it's lovely, Erzebet. Is it new?" She walked back to my bed with a silver comb in her hand and held it out to me.

Sinestra—the name came back to me the moment my fingertips touched the comb; I imagined I could see a tiny spark of light at the point of contact. He was real, I remembered it now, and he had told me not to be afraid.

"Would you put it in my hair, Mari?" I asked, wanting to divert her attention from my face. As she slid the teeth of the comb against my scalp, I realized I could never tell her about him. He was my secret, just like the prophecy. I only hoped that he would prove to be my talisman against it coming true.

XIII

It would be years before I again met Sinestra in the flesh. Nonetheless, within that time there were moments when his presence was palpable to me; I often woke with a vague feeling that I had heard his voice upon entering the world of dreaming. The proof I had of his attentions were the gifts he left behind: a pot of paint for my lips, a rouge for my cheeks, and a handheld mirror, the face of a wolf carved into its silver back. I could have explained away these small tokens easily enough if not for the feeling I had when I touched them: I could feel his eyes on me, again, his breath on my neck. Though I still suffered bouts of fear and confusion in regard to Sinestra's intentions, I was also tantalized by the beauty of the objects he left for me. I swore I could hear his laughter rumbling in my head whenever the teeth of the silver comb scraped against my scalp.

The strangest gift was the wolf. Walking out in the garden on a gray afternoon in spring to await Marianna's arrival, I heard men shouting in the distance, close to the kitchen garden. They were dragging a metal trap behind them, but the trap did not contain the rabbit they had hoped to catch. The hind leg of a silvery wolf had been pierced by the metal teeth of the trap. The creature's white ears were flat against his head, his teeth bared, his front legs lashing out in desperation. I thought immediately of the strange wild face carved into the back of my silver mirror, whose features I had traced with the tip of my finger. As one of the hunters reached into his belt for a knife to finish the job, I broke into a sudden run.

"Don't!" I yelled, panting, as I approached them. They turned in surprise, but there was no time for explanation.

"Pull him free!" I did not have to remind them that it was an order. They grasped hold of the trap and released the animal from its rusted jaws. The wolf cantered forward as if to escape, but he slowed to a limp on his wounded leg.

After much cajoling, I convinced a skittish Rowena that the animal was too injured to harm her. The wolf lay on his side in the kitchen garden, his eyes shut and his belly heaving, his tongue hanging from his mouth.

"He's a wild animal, Erzebet. They are not meant to be helped by people." She stood tentatively in the doorway, worrying her apron in her hands.

"But it is our fault that he is hurt," I said, appealing to her sense of responsibility. Truthfully, it was more than that for me. As I helped Rowena bind the poultice over the wolf's wounded leg, I realized that he reminded me of Sinestra—the glint of his dark eyes and bright teeth. This realization made me feel suddenly light-headed; I was wary that the wolf could smell my fear.

"Kyzoni will live in the rose garden," I explained to Marianna, startled when the strange name sprang so easily from my lips; it was his name, I was sure of this. Marianna cast me a suspicious glance, but I dared not reveal my own surprise. "He will protect us."

"You've named him, Erzebet? A wild animal?" Marianna stood at a safe distance, clutching a handful of her skirt in her hands.

"He simply does not seem quite so wild to me," I told her, bending low and offering Kyzoni a sniff of my hand. He growled suspiciously at me; I snatched my hand away and Marianna shrieked in fear. As I caught sight of his glittering eyes, another flash of recognition shot through me, like lightning.

"He won't hurt us, Mari, either of us. We're safe as long as he is here." I told her. I could not tell her why I knew this to be true. If not a literal safeguard against the prophecy, Kyzoni was a symbol of protection, and I was eager to accept all forms of defense I received. I ordered that a leg of deer be brought to the garden, and I watched in silence as the wolf tore the flesh from the bone.

By the first frost that year, Kyzoni would allow me to pet his snowy-white chest, my hands nearly disappearing into the dense fur cuff at his neck. At full height on four healthy legs, his head was level with my waist, his tail huge with his bristly winter coat. I would have even invited him into the tower room if not for Marianna's distrust, though she grew accustomed to his presence on our walks in the rose garden.

The wolf fascinated me, but clearly he could not offer me the protection I required: a way to counteract the prophecy. In the midst of these thoughts, another gift appeared, this time on the dressing table in the tower room: a slender, elegant vial, perfect for containing perfume. I uncorked the top and sniffed, but found the vial empty. I admired it for a while, then hid it in my jewel chest, where the prophecy remained concealed.

A vial, a mirror, a silver comb, stain for lips and cheeks . . . the gifts were a message in themselves. An empty vial—if not for perfume, perhaps for a potion? I turned my interest to spells intended to preserve my youth and beauty. If I never grew any older, I reasoned, I wouldn't have to worry about the prophecy of my early death. I began to ask the cook and various servants about folkloric remedies, magic spells. I made note of all of the details they told me and enlisted their help in gathering the materials necessary. Knowing how Marianna would disapprove, I performed these experiments in secret. They seemed to have no effect upon the condition and quality of my skin.

It's important for you to act soon, little one. The choice is yours. Sinestra's words often kept me awake at night. I still didn't know who he was, and Marianna had warned me against the dangers of dark magic. I yearned to ask her about healing herbs, but my intentions were perhaps not as innocent as she would have liked. However, I had the prophecy to contend with. I was as afraid to ignore Sinestra's words as I was afraid to obey them.

By the time I turned sixteen, my attempt to preserve my youth had grown desperate. Marianna and I were no longer the children we had been the day we first met; the mirror proved this to me whenever I saw our faces reflected in its silver surface. I had grown even taller but remained slender, my young awkwardness transforming into a long-limbed elegance. Marianna had also grown taller, though still a few inches shorter than me. She began to refine her cloud of black hair into a halo of shining ringlets that framed her sweet face. Her figure had become more womanly and curvaceous, and while I glanced warily at how her breasts amply filled out the bodices of my gowns, I knew that she was similarly aware of the slender arch of my neck and the narrowness of my waist.

For all of Marianna's piety and devotion, I knew that she could not resist the temptation to try on all of my gowns and jewels, enchanted by the material luxuries the world of Castle Bizecka had to offer her. It was this same craving that had distracted her from her errands in order to visit my rose garden, years before. Though I would never dare expose this weakness, I did all that I could to indulge it.

We sat in the candlelit tower room one afternoon, a late winter wind whistling beyond the stone wall. Her parents had agreed that she should remain with me if the weather were to turn brutal, and that afternoon it had done exactly that, forcing us into the seclusion of the tower. I was glad to be safe in the tower room with my Mari, safe from the storm raging outside, and safe from the moaning countess.

Unfortunately, Marianna had been exposed on numerous occasions to the countess's mad cries on our way to the tower. I simply chose not to broach the subject, and she knew better than to inquire. Though her family continued to suffer from the greediness of the Turks—sanctioned, as it was, by the count's secret betrayal—I still envied Marianna the tales I had heard of her parents, who had never left her solely to the whims of servants. Still, being so close to Mother's chambers did make me think of her more often. It amazed me that for so many years during my childhood I had thought of her very little, as if she were already dead.

"I don't see how you can enjoy this, Mari," I groaned over a badly embroidered pillow, the needle awkward in my long, clumsy fingers. "It seems such a foolish waste of time."

"Ha! Says the girl who's never had to gather eggs, or dust, or sweep, or bake her own bread," Marianna teased, her dainty fingers tugging efficiently at a loose strand of thread. "You know it's too cold out for walking. What else do you suggest?"

"Do you know anything about medicinal herbs? Just a simple recipe for a good night's sleep, or a beauty trick," I asked, trying not to reveal my excitement.

"You have a fanciful imagination," she said, squinting, rethreading her needle. "I certainly don't know any tricks or magic, as you suggest."

"You know I don't want to do anything bad, Mari, just a little experiment. Besides, I can't bear embroidery"—I shuffled my feet restlessly—"and it may be a long winter yet." The wind punctuated my statement with a vicious gust, howling like Kyzoni against the tower walls.

Marianna sighed heavily. "Talk of tricks and spells, Erzebet . . ." Her eyes flashed at mine only briefly, then lowered again to her embroidery. "It just doesn't feel right."

"You told me your mother taught you some things—isn't that true?" I asked, slumping onto the couch beside her.

"She taught me only a few of the healing properties of certain herbs. Nothing to do with magic."

"What worries you about it, Mari, if the herbs are only used for good?"

"Such things that can name you a healer can just as easily brand you a witch, in the village," she said darkly. I was taken aback by the tone of her voice.

"But we are safe here, Mari. All I want is to learn about healing, you know that." I touched her arm in reassurance. After all, I would not involve Marianna in my quest to defy the prophecy. What I proposed to her might have hidden my deeper motives, but that did not make it entirely untrue.

Marianna struggled with a few stitches in silence.

"The light is too low in here for sewing." She sighed again.

"I can request a small feast to be brought here, to enjoy while we work." The thought of rich delicacies from the castle's kitchen would persuade her above all else. Indeed, she smiled in spite of herself.

"I only know a few things to do with herbs. Nothing more than that."

"We can make it up as we go along. It's only an experiment, after all," I assured her, and stoked the flames in the hearth.

I took careful notes of all of the knowledge Marianna had of healing herbs, and I think she enjoyed the respect I bestowed to her particular brand of wisdom. I tried to convince her to stay with me at Castle Bizecka during winter's cruelest months, but she insisted on returning home, even if it meant we would not see each other until the storms allowed safe passage.

"My parents need me at home, Erzebet," she explained, pulling on her winter cloak. "I'm sure you will find ways to keep yourself busy here, in my absence."

Indeed, I did keep busy, though I constantly looked forward to my friend's return. I rearranged the tower room to suit our newest diversion: I procured a small round wooden table for the center of the room, as well as a variety of wooden bowls, metal spoons, and small jars for our concoctions. I sent select servants on errands to fill jars with rainwater, rose petals, and morning dew, as well as to collect particular herbs from the kitchen garden and the nearby forest. In exchange for secrecy, I asked each servant what ailed her, and assured her that I would create a suitable remedy.

That winter I also began to take more advantage of the count's absence than I had dared to do in the past. I was a tall, austere young woman and the servants were more impressed by my authority now that I had grown. I managed to take over the tasks the countess had once managed: overseeing servants, tending to household affairs, and cultivating trade of our produce with nearby farms. Taking responsibility for these affairs increased my feeling of control over my own life, and assured the servants that I had not inherited my mother's madness.

When Marianna returned to our tower haven I had jars and satchels full of ingredients displayed upon our table, as well as a list of special requests.

"Erzebet! Love potions? Beauty spells? Did you tell these women that we would provide cures for these ailments?"

"I never said that we were experts." I shrugged. "We'll use the knowledge that you have, and make everything else up from there."

The warmth of our tower, the sweetness of the wine, and the delectable treats I had procured for her enjoyment softened Marianna's disposition, and I eventually convinced her to assist me. I wrote the ingredients and purpose of each remedy in a tome I referred to as our book of spells.

In most cases, the results of our spells were as expected: for Rose, the scullery maid, we cinched her corset tightly with a scented purple cord to attract the attention of a certain doorman. A simple success. The poultice we gave the cook's assistant did in fact dissuade her husband from laying his hands on her, for it reeked of garlic and broke her out in a terrible rash. Success, nonetheless, and the results were recorded in our book of spells for further study.

"It isn't really magic, Erzebet," Marianna cautioned, hovering over me as I scribbled. "You don't believe it is, do you?"

"What would it matter if it was magic?" I asked. "If all we are doing is helping people?"

I closed our book and walked over to my dressing table, to check my reflection in the oval mirror. I unpinned my hair and let it tumble over my shoulders, then applied a deep red stain to my lips. The red of the stain accentuated the perfect paleness of my skin. I could feel Marianna's eyes on my reflection in the glass.

"What about beauty spells, Mari?" I asked, my voice low and gentle. I did not take my eyes away from my own reflection. "You have to admit you are at least a bit curious."

"I have heard of women using goat's milk upon their skin," she told me. Her eyes in the mirror seemed glassy, focused on mine.

"Then we shall try it," I said evenly, trying to conceal my eagerness.

From that day on, beauty spells became our chief concern. We tried a variety of different treatments, hoping that we could discover the perfect combination of ingredients to apply to our delicate skin. Even through our enjoyment, I could sense that Marianna was watching me in the same way that I was watching her: we were young women now, with beauty blooming from our bones. Even the closest friendship is fertile ground for envy to plant its wicked seed.

In spite of general enthusiasm for our herbal remedies, it was soon made clear to me that there was one servant who did not approve of our activities.

"It's a matter of propriety," Pugrue explained, extracting a confiscated satchel from his robes.

"After all, the count has high hopes for his young daughter." Pugrue attempted to smile.

"The count's high hopes are his problem alone, not mine. We both know that his stubbornness and greed will come to nothing in the end."

"That is not for you to say, Erzebet," Pugrue informed me, "but the fact is this: the potential betrothed to the Holy Roman Emperor can't be rumored as a witch."

"The count's hopes are high indeed, if he wishes to wed me to the dying emperor." I laughed. Pugrue cleared his throat awkwardly.

"I regret that this has come to pass." I stood from the chapel bench. At full height, I was now taller than Pugrue. "I will need to ask you to leave."

Pugrue's mouth moved for a moment, but no words came out.

"I am here by order of the count." His voice cracked with indignation.

"My father is not here," I reminded him. "We cannot be certain that he will return. In his absence, authority over the servants of this castle lies with me."

"No, Erzebet, I can't do that. I will not. I pledged to serve the count, and serve him I will."

I stared at him for a moment, his watery blue eyes, his sharp chin. His pale skin was red and blotchy with evident irritation. It was true; he would not leave the count. But I could still take action of my own.

"If you are to remain here, you will abide by my rules," I informed him. "I will continue to attend your Sunday Mass, but I think it best that our tutoring sessions come to an end."

"You dare to suggest that you know everything? You are still a child, and a *girl*, you—"

"I do not presume to know everything, Father. But I know that I have learned all that you have to teach me."

Before he could answer, I dipped into a brief bow and exited the chapel. I walked swiftly to calm my rage. I had not seen the count in years, yet still he managed to exercise his authority over my life.

One night late that winter when the snow had begun to thaw, Marianna planned to stay overnight in the castle. A row of small bottles glimmered like amber jewels in the candlelight of our secluded chamber. We giggled over our latest concoction, warm and tipsy on glasses of rich wine.

"I doubt our spells have done much good," I stated, inspecting my face in the mirror. Marianna giggled at my pronouncement, but I could not help but feel discouraged. What else was I to do to keep myself safe? Marianna turned and saw the dark look in my eyes.

"Don't worry, Erzebet. I will never be as beautiful as you. You need not worry about me." She giggled, though awkwardly, and took another sip of her wine.

Then she has felt it, too, I thought, *this envy between us.* I felt ashamed to admit it to myself. I hated that anything could dare to spoil the pureness of our friendship: the one truly good thing in my life.

The weather that night was perfect for a midnight garden walk, a treat we had been planning since the long winter had begun. After an evening spent indulging on wine and a variety of sweetmeats, we donned our cloaks, our cheeks red as roses.

The garden was different late at night, just as we had both hoped: transformed into a bride draped in a powdery dusting of fresh white snow and veiled in a crystalline layer of frost. The rose vines were black and frozen, but in places we could see where the tiny green buds were getting ready to emerge from their winter-long slumber. We huddled close together, arm in arm, walking toward the center of the garden paths. Kyzoni appeared, shaking a dusting of snow from his silvery fur, and followed a few paces behind.

As soon as we reached the marble Athenus, posed on his stage in the middle of our winter theater, I stepped upon his marble platform and helped Marianna up behind me. We brushed the snow from his arms and legs of sinewy stone, taking special care to brush the snow from his face and curled stone hair.

"Now he will be able to watch us dance," Marianna said, jumping down from the stand and stumbling a bit in the snow. Both of us laughed, our voices crackling like sparks in the cold darkness. Breath hovered before our faces in clouds of steam.

"This reminds me of the story of the beautiful lady," I told her, entranced by the sparkling garden around us, bathed in pale moonlight.

"That story scared me when I was little—don't frighten me, Erzebet!"

"No, it's not scary. Because we're one of them, don't you see?" I grabbed her hands in mine and pulled her into a slow circle. "The beautiful ladies lived in the forest. They would gather together in meadows and sing and dance. They would entice their victims this way."

"We are enticing our victims?" She panted, her eyes glittering. Our spinning grew gradually faster.

"Yes! And when they get here, we will dance them to death."

We spun so fast that our cloaks and skirts spread like clouds around us, the cold air reaching up under our garments and biting our flesh. We howled with laughter and a bit of fear: when the circle went too fast our hands broke apart, and we rolled, cold but laughing, upon the still-frozen ground.

"Do they spend every night dancing? Even in the snow?" Marianna asked as we shook the snow from our gowns.

"No. We're the only ones who dance in the snow."

She laughed again, pushing me into a snowbank. I lay on my back for a while, looking up at the stars. The moon was full, and

Kyzoni, nearby, began to howl. Marianna lay beside me and we both began to howl, letting our voices rise from the garden of snow like ghosts, all three of us baying at the full moon. Marianna giggled all through the howling, but I liked the feeling it gave me—the air in my chest pressing out a great burst of sound.

For a moment, if only a brief moment, I could feel completely alive, and pretend that death could not touch me. More than anything else on earth, Marianna had the power to keep my fears of the prophecy temporarily at bay. A night in the garden with Marianna was just that type of night to make me feel normal, and safe. I imagined that perhaps this was how she felt, without a prophecy darkening her every step in life. I envied her this, but also sought to emulate it. Once weary from howling, we lay there side by side for a while, staring up at the stars.

"Perhaps they do dance in winter, Mari. But they build a bonfire. They build a great fire and wait for the devil to come and dance with them."

At this, Marianna sat up. I laughed at the sight of her face; her cheeks had turned even brighter red from the cold air. I was taken aback by how beautiful my friend had grown.

"Erzebet, don't say such things."

"What's wrong, Mari?"

Kyzoni howled again as if in response, but this time Marianna flinched at the sound.

"You know he exists," she said in a sudden whisper, crossing herself. "You tempt him when you say such things."

As Marianna stood and adjusted her cloak, I lay on my back thinking. It had never occurred to me before to reserve a certain fear for the devil. Truly, it was the whim of God and the flames of his judgment that I feared: Was it not God's doing to give me a falling star on the day of my birth, and a prophecy to portend my early death? God was erratic at best, in my opinion, if not thoughtlessly cruel. My fears for how He might choose to alter the course of my life left no room in my heart to fear anything else.

XIV

We walked quietly down the hallway to the tower, keeping our giggling in check. The castle was fast asleep, like an enchanted castle in a fairy tale. We were the only two still awake, and planned to curl upon the chairs in the tower room and sip wine to warm ourselves, and eventually submit to sleep.

The magic of the night still thick upon us, we jumped when a shattering of glass fractured the pristine quiet. Before I could realize where we were or what had happened, the countess emerged from her bedchamber.

I had not seen the countess in years, not since I watched her hooded form beating the black hen to death. For a moment I imagined the hood was still there, as only her outline was visible in the dark hallway, with the firelight of her chamber behind her. The terrible, rhythmic sound of that beating came back to me, an echo of my heartbeat. She stepped forward into the hall and seemed lost for a moment, disoriented. I wondered when she had last been even this far from her chamber. Then her eyes settled upon me.

"You, girl—you need to help me. Come." I recognized this as the brusque tone she used with servants. I could feel how Marianna suddenly stiffened beside me, but I had no choice but to follow, afraid of how the countess might react if I didn't obey her command.

In the light of her chamber, I could see the countess more clearly:

she was wearing a gown of wine-colored velvet with an intricately embroidered bodice. Her hair was sleekly braided in an elaborate style, complete with a jeweled coronet. I could see by the light of the fire, however, that her golden hair had gone stark white. She had also lost her delicate shape and appeared bloated and stuffed into her fine gown, the seams of velvet straining against the bulge at her waist. I tried my best not to notice this, but I swiftly found it was better to focus on these details than to look at her face.

"This broke," she said, pointing accusingly at the shards of a mirror lying on the floor at her feet. Clearly she had smashed it to the ground, not that we would mention this to her. I bent dutifully to begin picking up the pieces, and Marianna moved to kneel beside me.

"Who are you?" the countess spat, nudging Marianna's shoulder. "I recognize the other girl, but not you. Who are you?"

"I am Marianna, my lady," Marianna said, bowing slowly and gracefully. I saw that her eyes were averted. "I am a guest of Erzebet's."

I leaped up at the sound of my name, my hands filled with pieces of glass.

"The spot has been cleared, Countess," I said brightly.

"Yes," she said, with a suspicious glance at Marianna. "Put those pieces over here on the table. I would like to keep them. I've known that mirror for a long time." She cut her eyes viciously at the shards of glass in my hand. "Then he started to say terrible things to me."

"Who did, Countess?" Marianna asked.

"The mirror, of course. Evil things, mirrors. Evil things full of eyes, always watching."

The walls of the countess's chamber were lined with mirrors. Standing in the middle of her room, we could see all three of us reflected upon every wall. Once I placed the shards of glass upon her table, I had no choice but to look at her face: she was bloated, her skin creased with age. Only a few years had passed, but her madness had taken its toll, rotting her mind and now her body. Her sallow skin sagged against the lush velvet of her gown. Her eyes were sharp as needles.

"You have not seen the count, have you?"

"No, my lady," I told her, bowing as well. "I do not know when he is to return."

"It will be soon," she said. "I can sense it." She grasped and kissed what I believed to be an amulet around her neck, but when she released it I saw that it was a small vial, suspended on a silk cord—a vial red with blood. The sight of it sent bile suddenly rising to my throat, and I swallowed hard to push it down.

"The count, my husband—for he is my husband—is trying to have me killed. Did you know this?" She smiled craftily. "I have the servants test my food before I eat it. Every day I do this. Better that one of his young pretties drops dead than I do." She laughed, showing a mouthful of black teeth. She reached for a glass of wine and gulped greedily, staining her lips a lurid red. The chamber was stifling hot; the raging fire in the hearth was also reflected in each mirror, as though the entire chamber were ablaze.

"You two are quite pretty," she told us. It seemed more accusation than compliment.

"Thank you, my lady," I said, curtsying slightly. Marianna did the same.

"Yes, the count enjoys employing pretty girls to care for him and for his wife when he is away. I think they want me dead, too. That's what the mirror tells me."

"I'm sure no one wants to kill you, my lady," Marianna offered; I held my breath as she spoke.

"Ha! You don't know these servants here—they are all peasants from the village. They are the poor, diseased vermin of this earth, no matter how he indulges them."

We stared at her in shock and dismay, but the countess was too busy emptying her wine goblet to notice. The residue from the wine drunk earlier that evening now tasted sour and grotesque in my mouth.

"We had best be going, Countess," I told her. "I hope that you have a restful night."

"Restful? Oh, I don't sleep anymore, dear; it's too dangerous. Time feasts on you in sleep." Her eyes grew wide as she said this, the firelight flickering in their dark centers. "Time scurries around corners like a rat, ready to feed upon you. No, sleep is too close to death. I don't sleep anymore."

"We should leave you be," I said, grasping the edge of Marianna's cloak with my fingertips.

"Yes, of course. You are young things; go to sleep. But I did try to warn you," she said, laughing. The moment her laughter stopped, her smile fell from her face like lead. She moved toward a mirror across the room, studying her reflection—or did she see something else reflected there? I could not dally long enough to imagine. Marianna and I quietly stepped backward over her threshold, then took long strides to the tower room.

We did not speak until the tower door was shut behind us.

"I'm sorry, Mari. I told you that she was unwell."

"Erzebet, don't apologize. It's not your fault." She rested her hand upon my arm. I wanted to tell her the truth in that moment: *it is my fault, I made her this way*. But it sounded too awful, even in my head. I would have to explain the prophecy, and that was something I simply could not do.

I stoked a cheerful fire in the hearth, but a somber cloud had descended upon our night of magic. Wordless and weary, we both retired to our chairs covered in furs and blankets. After we wished each other a good night, I remained awake for many hours, watching the fire slowly die in the hearth. I am quite certain that Marianna did the same.

The next morning when Marianna woke, I was already hard at work grinding rose petals with mortar and pestle, making notes in our book of spells. Marianna yawned and stretched like a cat upon the silk divan.

"You're up early, Erzebet," she remarked. "What's today's task?"

"It's a particularly important spell," I said quietly, not looking up from the table. "A sleeping draft—for the countess."

Marianna sat up suddenly, her dark eyes fixed on my face. I dared not meet her gaze, the heat of embarrassment coloring my neck and cheeks. She pulled up a velvet chair and sat at the table across from me.

"I would like to help, if I can," she said carefully. I pushed a bowl full of rose petals toward her.

"Here, grind these. You said that rosewater aids in sleep, didn't you?"

She nodded in response and began her task in earnest. I carefully measured equal drops of rainwater and oil into an earthenware pot, then added the minced rose petals once they were done. Usually lighthearted over our spells, we performed this task with the sobriety and respect I thought it was due. Once the promising concoction was secured in a small jar, I looked at her and smiled.

"I feel like I should explain," I began awkwardly.

"You needn't explain." She rested her hand on mine. "She's your mother."

"Not that she knows it," I muttered. I knew that Marianna had noticed, but was simply too kind to point it out.

I asked Marianna to wait in the tower as I descended the stairs alone and walked down the hall to my mother's bedchamber. After our encounter of the night before, I knew she would be perfectly agreeable to leaving this task to me. I heard talking inside the chamber, but more quiet than usual. A woman emerged from the doorway carrying a platter—a shallow dish upon it glimmered with blood. I stepped back warily.

"I'm sorry, you can't see her," she told me, securing the door behind her.

"I know." I found myself unable to look away from the blood.

"You don't need to be afraid," she told me. "It's just a little bleeding. The doctor prescribed it—he said it might balance her out."

I nodded, feeling foolish that the sight of the blood should so bother me. Had I not been bled by doctors myself? I glanced at my hands suddenly, remembering the blood of the deer speckling my skin. I was relieved to see only my clean white hand holding the jar. I stepped forward and showed it to the servant.

"This is for the countess," I said, and put it in the pocket of the servant's apron. "It's only a silly potion—to aid her rest."

"Thank you, Erzebet." The servant bowed slightly, careful not to tip the dish in her hands.

I could not help but look again at the dish of blood as the servant passed. *Blood is a sacrament, and sacraments keep us all safe.* The words of the old woman, on the day of the deer's slaughter, came back to me, unbidden.

The countess had been correct in predicting the count's return, for he soon arrived at Castle Bizecka, bringing with him a cool and rainy spring. Though still disgusted by his secret deal with the Turks, I could not help but take extra care in preparing for my audience with him. I had grown into a young woman in the years since his last visit. His appreciation of my beauty was the only form of approval that I could hope to receive.

Once sufficiently painted, perfumed, and jeweled, I swept into the portrait chamber in a dramatic wave of scarlet. I had chosen the color for the particularly vivid contrast against my pale skin. The count was sipping from a goblet of wine as I entered.

"Erzebet," he said, not taking his eyes off my face. I did my best to conceal my pleasure with his reaction. He stepped forward and took my hand.

"I think this new portrait I've commissioned will be the finest one yet, now that you've grown." His eyes passed across my face as though appraising a work of fine art. His own face looked drawn and rather sharp; the count was looking more hawklike as the years passed.

"Have you brought an artist with you?"

"I have procured his services and he will be here shortly, perhaps in the summer, when the weather is best for travel. He is Hungarian born but lives in England. Right now he is in Vienna painting portraits of the members of court. You will be fitted for a new gown for the portrait; I've already procured the fabric and I've spoken to the mistress of your wardrobe." No matter how many gowns I owned, my mind still danced at the thought of a new one—what better way to rediscover and display my beauty?

"I would also like you to wear this." He extended his hand to show me a curve of gold wire with a teardrop-shaped ruby suspended in the center. It was a beautiful piece, and I turned to the mirror over the mantel to watch as he placed it upon my crown of curls. The ruby felt like a cold fingertip pressed upon my forehead.

"Quite nice," he said approvingly, but his expression was cold. I felt as though I were a piece of art, already, to him. I bowed graciously and thanked him.

"There is another important matter I must discuss with you," he said, stepping closer. "I've been told that you've befriended a peasant girl—the daughter of a farmer living in Novoe Mesto. Am I correct?"

I stared dumbly at the count for a moment.

"Is this true?" he asked, shifting his cloak. I could see the scabbard upon his belt glimmer in the firelight; it blinked at me like an eye in the darkness. My voice seemed stuck in my throat. I had never been so intimidated by the count before. In the midst of my panic, a voice entered my head, a low, rich voice that I instantly recognized: *You have more power than you realize.*

"I do have a friend," I said. "She lives by the border, near the forest. They've had trouble with the Turks—"

"Listen to me, child: the daughter of a count does not spend her time with peasants. Unless that peasant is bent over, scrubbing the floor." A sickly smile made his thin lips twitch. "I hope never to see that wench in my castle, or else you will both face the consequences."

"Yes, my lord," I barely uttered, bowing quickly before I was dismissed.

I waited nervously for Marianna's appearance in the garden that afternoon. I would simply cover her in my cloak and bring her up to the tower before the count could see her. I began concocting a plan to keep her secret and rehearsed it over and over in my head as I waited, considering every request I would need to issue to Rowena. So busy was I with planning and pacing that I was surprised when the sun began to set, and Marianna was nowhere to be seen.

I returned to my chamber for my dinner, and after dinner was called to the count to recite for him my lessons. I acted the role of dutiful daughter, but as soon as I was dismissed I donned a black cloak and went to wait by the garden gate.

Surprisingly, I was just in time: Marianna was waiting by the gate for my arrival, but this time she was not alone. A cloaked figure stood beside her.

"Erzebet, this is my father," she told me as soon as I reached the gate. The man lowered his hood and bowed low before me, nearly collapsing to his knees. I noticed that Marianna's cheeks and lips were very pale. Her father's face looked pasty white in the moonlight, in contrast to his wiry black hair.

"Lady Bizecka, I beseech you to help me and my family," he began, his voice breaking as he spoke. I looked to Marianna for a clue as to what was happening, but she averted her gaze from mine. Her dark eyes were raw and red.

"You've been so very kind to my daughter already, I hate to ask you for another favor. But we are desperate, my lady." He wrung his cloak in his hands as he spoke.

"You know that I will help Marianna in any way that I can," I said, placing my hand upon his. "I can promise you that."

"It's the Turks," he said, and crossed himself at mere mention of the word. "They came for their portion of our goods today. We hide part of our produce in order to protect it, you see, but whatever they see, they want to take. We've never had such a problem until tonight. But you see, they've seen my daughter. And they want to take her."

He glanced warily at Marianna as he said this, his hand squeezing her shoulder. The gesture was so tender I felt my heart might burst. It took me a moment to comprehend the meaning of his words.

"The Turks . . . want to take—you?" I asked her, but she could only bite her lip.

"Yes." Her father nodded. "I'm afraid so. Unless we pay them, and I'm afraid that we simply do not have enough."

"I will pay them for you."

"I admit that is exactly what I prayed you would say. But I'm afraid there is more I must ask you. I don't want them to see her again, you see. I want to be certain that she is safe. I cannot keep her safe. Not the way things are now."

"Then she will stay here with me," I told him. I pulled every ring off my fingers and closed them in his palm. I thought to take the ruby circlet off my head, but knew that the count would notice its disappearance.

"Take this now. You can get a good price for these pieces in town. I will send more to you by messenger as soon as I can." As I said this I opened the gate to allow Marianna's entrance.

"I will bring you provisions myself, as soon as it is safe," Marianna told him.

"No, my dear, you are safer here. Now go." He urged her beyond the gate, his eyes squinting as though in pain.

"Do not fear," I told him, shutting the gate. "Your daughter will be safe with me. You'd best hurry home; it's quite late."

Marianna grasped her father's hand once more through the gate. When she released it we ran to the kitchen entrance of the castle. I pulled her black hood low over her face and we scurried down the hallway, close to the wall. I turned for a moment to grasp her hand in mine when I saw her eyes grow wide with fear.

Our path was blocked by a tall man with a black beard, a mop of wild dark hair upon his head. He smelled of beer and sweat and dirt, so strongly that we could have toppled from the pungency alone. Marianna gasped sharply.

"Little countess!" he shouted, and bowed comically low at my feet. Suddenly we were surrounded by soldiers; they reeked of beer and smiled at us with rotted teeth. Their black-haired leader ushered us into the dining hall as if he were welcoming us to his own home. I released Marianna's hand and nudged her, hoping that she would run from the room, but she grasped my arm and remained huddled at my side.

"Little countess, you have come to celebrate with us," he said, withdrawing his sword from its sheath, "our first victory in battle!"

Cheers rang out through the hall. The faces lit by the orange flames of the fire were purple and black with bruises and bloody wounds.

"Victory in battle? Then the fighting has begun?"

"Defending Novoe Mesto from the encroachment of heathens," the soldier explained. "They dared come too close to the center of town for my liking, tonight. And there we were, ready to strike."

The other soldiers laughed in response as the soldier with the sword bent before me. When he looked up, his dark eyes met mine and he smiled. He laid his sword on the floor at my feet—its silver tip was red with dried blood.

"This war is a blood sacrifice to God," he said, his rough palms turned upward. The soldiers crowded around us murmured in response. He reached into his dark vest and pulled free a bloodstained dagger. His smile flashed at me again as he grasped a goblet of wine from the table and swirled the bloody dagger into the cup.

"To drink the blood of the enemy is to consume the enemy's power!" he crowed, lifting the goblet above his head. "With all that we kill, the stronger we become!"

As the cheering around us reached a crescendo, the soldier tilted back his head and gulped the blood and wine. Lowering the goblet, he licked his lips, his eyes burning like flames. He offered the goblet to me.

"Don't take it!" Marianna whispered into my back, her voice muted with fear.

"There is no offering more holy than this!" he told me, urging the goblet of bloody wine into my hand; I gazed into the goblet, hesitant, unwilling to show my fear.

"Does it bother you to look at it?" he asked.

"No," I muttered, though my small voice was swallowed by the noise.

"You must be used to the sight of blood," he roared, and began to laugh. "All women must become used to the sight of blood!"

Their laughter shocked me out of my stupor and forced me into a run. Marianna and I raced down the hallway, the laughter behind us like the mad baying of wolves. We did not speak until we reached the tower and bolted the door shut. Not until we were in the tower room did I realize I still had the goblet gripped in my hand, my fingers sticky and red with wine.

"Brutes!" Marianna cursed, crossing herself. "How dare they frighten us in that way—how dare they frighten you, the daughter of the count! Killing has made them beasts and not men."

She stood facing the wall, fiddling with her cloak, agitated.

"Marianna," I said soothingly, my hand upon her arm. "The Turks are the brutes you speak of, not these soldiers. They are here to protect us."

"They're here to protect you," she snapped, "not me. They may protect a countess, but they do little to protect the peasants in this country. They did nothing when the Turks took our food; they told us there was nothing they could do. And these soldiers steal plenty of the peasants' crops and livestock—just as the Turks do. Soldiers such as these are feared as much as the Turks in the village."

"But it's God's will, this war. It's not their fault that they're willing to fight it, Marianna."

"But they did nothing to help us—they fight for their own glory and little else," she said, wringing her dress in her hands.

And for the count's glory, I thought, but could not say aloud. These soldiers would pay for my father's deception in blood.

"Doesn't this war frighten you?" she asked, a bit accusingly.

"Of course I'm frightened," I told her, for I sought to comfort her, "but these soldiers are merely instruments of God, here to protect Hungary and the Catholic Church. You've told me yourself that we can't change the role God wants us to play."

"I don't want to see them again," she told me. "I've heard what soldiers do to women, especially when they are drunk."

I bent my head solemnly and sat upon the divan beside her.

"Don't worry, Mari," I told her. "Not about the soldiers, or about the war. You're safe here, with me. You shall remain here until we are sure the Turks have moved on."

Though my voice was soothing, she began to cry.

"My parents are not safe," she said, her voice thick with tears. "If the fighting has truly begun they'll be in danger—all of our crops will be in danger as well. I must go back to help them."

"The best thing that you can do for them is to stay here, where they can be sure that you're safe."

"But what about your father?" she asked, her eyes glistening. "What will he do if he finds me here?"

"He won't find you here, as long as you stay in this tower. Only Rowena will know of your presence, and she will tell no one."

She looked around the tower chamber for a moment, her eyes wide. I saw her shoulders tremble and she lowered her head.

"I was so frightened, Erzebet." She began to cry. "When I saw the way they were looking at me. I have never been so frightened before. I don't know what we would have done without you, Erzebet. I feel so—ashamed."

"Don't, my dear. There is no reason for you to feel ashamed."

"We were so helpless. You've saved my life."

They wanted her for their harem. I couldn't stop myself from thinking it. I had learned a great deal about the Turks from Pugrue, as well as from gossiping servants. The pasha the count had met in his chamber no doubt had a host of wives and mistresses waiting to cater to his every need. Had her parents been unable to pay for her safety, Marianna would have gone to live in a harem, in the company of those other wives. These were the type of men my father made deals with, men who would steal a child from her father's own home to make her an unwilling bride. I lifted my hand to smooth her hair, but when I did I saw the red stain upon it again.

All women must become used to the sight of blood! The soldier's vulgar words echoed in my ears. I rested my hand upon the back of the divan so as not to touch Marianna with it.

We were cautious with Marianna's safety all that spring and into summer, which cast dreary, anxious shadows over the days of sunshine. I took occasional walks in the garden, alone, so as not to seem so absorbed in my tower room that it inspired suspicion. Only Rowena knew that Marianna lived in the tower, and she supplied us with the necessary garments and food to keep her comfortable. The other servants were so distracted by the demands of brutish soldiers that they didn't notice anything amiss.

I began to allow Kyzoni to stay in my bedchamber for companionship. I tried to bring him to the tower as a much-needed diversion, but Marianna refused.

"He is a wild animal," she reminded me. "It's bad enough that I can't leave this room; I refuse to share it with that beast."

From then on, I made sure to order Kyzoni to my bedchamber whenever I walked the spiral steps to the tower.

"I think that wolf has replaced me as your companion," Marianna told me one day, a tinge of sourness in her voice, "now that I'm encaged in this tower."

I shivered at her words. We did not usually spend the warm months cooped up inside, and the tower chamber seemed to retain its wintry chill in spite of the balmy summer outside its walls. I tended to the fire and to Marianna's every earthly need, but I seemed unable to relieve the chamber of its inherent iciness.

Two months into her captivity, Marianna had lost interest in our book of spells, and the tower was littered with abandoned embroidery samples. I made a habit of reading the Bible to her on a daily basis, as she could not attend church, and she insisted that we both kneel upon the flagstone floor to pray.

Despite my efforts to distract her, Marianna often spoke of returning home to find if her parents were still well and to see if there were any provisions that could be offered to help them. Each time she mentioned such a visit I reminded her of the risk involved. From servants' gossip I learned of the dangers the peasants of Novoe Mesto faced, threatened by the Turks and by marauding Hungarian soldiers willing to take advantage of those they had sworn to protect. I never broached the subject with Marianna, hoping that staying with me in Castle Bizecka would offer her a new life and she could leave the old one behind.

Late at night, I dreamed about the tall, dark-haired soldier. He greeted me in the dining hall and took my hand, the sheath of his sword visible behind the folds of his great black cape. He led me to a table heavily laden with platters of roasted goose and boar and deer, great pots simmering with stew. He smiled at me from across the table and lifted his glass to drink. I reached forward to lift the silver lid off the nearest platter, only to reveal Marianna: white as a corpse, lying on the table before me.

From this dream I would wake in a frenzy, biting the palm of my hand to suppress my screams.

Marianna and I were treated to a much-needed diversion at the arrival of the artist, that summer. I began to exert even more than the usual efforts in preparation for the portrait sessions: milk baths for my face, neck, and arms, scented oils applied to my skin, and special herb pouches soaked in water and placed upon my eyes.

Though Marianna was my closest friend, I still felt sheepish about the spells and potions I had begun to employ. Perhaps she thought me merely vain, but I knew it was imperative to preserve the youthful beauty of my face. If I could only keep the aging process at bay, then perhaps death could be kept at bay as well. I sat at the dressing table in the tower room, inspecting my reflection and taking notes on my latest treatments in the book of spells. Marianna eyed me quizzically in the mirror.

"What charms are you considering imposing upon your guest this evening?" she asked, stretching from the divan like a sleepy cat. She stood and approached the dressing table where I sat, her face reflected beside mine in the mirror.

"I don't quite understand your fixation, Erzebet." I could not help but wince at this remark—how could she understand? She had no prophecy hanging like a noose around her neck.

"What do you mean, fixation? I simply want to look my best. It's been years since I've had my portrait done. It would be a shame for this one to pale in comparison."

"Indeed, it will not," she assured me, "but there is something else." She began pacing the small room restlessly. She reminded me of Kyzoni, but I knew better than to mention the resemblance.

"Are you worried about witchcraft, my dear?" I teased.

"No," she told me, her cheeks coloring. "It's just that you seem to think about your appearance all the time, always looking at your face in the mirror, always worrying. Why is that?"

"I just don't want things to change," I told her; this was as close to the truth as I dared admit, but it only made her more puzzled.

"Mari, you seem uneasy. I'll not be long tonight, I promise you." I turned from the glass to look at her. "Once the count returns to court you'll have more opportunity to wander the grounds. Please be patient."

"I know." She slumped into a chair close to me. "I just can't stop thinking about my parents. This could be my last chance to see them, after all."

"I'll not hear you talk about leaving. It's too dangerous."

"But can you blame me for worrying, Erzebet?"

"There is nothing you can do to help them now." My voice was a touch too loud. "I'm sorry, but I refuse to take any risks," I told her, softening. "Castle Bizecka is your new home, it's where you belong."

"How can it be my home if I'm locked in this tower all day?" She stood, backing away from me. "Can't you remember? This isn't really me. This is your gown, your jewels. The village is my home. It's the land of my birth, no matter where I may sleep."

"So, too, it shall be your grave," I hissed, but thought better of the words as soon as I said them. Her eyes flashed at me reproachfully.

"I'm sorry." I grasped her hands in mine. "You're a sister to me, Marianna. I would be alone in this world without you."

Perhaps it was the rare tears that glistened in my eyes, but her face softened upon me. Without a word, she touched the curls by my ear with a delicate finger, then pulled me close in an embrace. I breathed in the scent of lavender from her thick black cloud of hair.

That night I met briefly with the artist as he lounged with the count before a raging fire in the portrait chamber. I swept into the room in a gown of dark purple velvet, the rich color an excellent contrast to my smooth ivory skin. I could feel them both appraising my beauty as the eyes of my previous portraits exacted their own judgment upon my new, womanly form. I felt both exultant and afraid.

The count introduced me to Konrad, the artist. I was taken aback by how young he was, for I was used to posing for haggard old men. I had seen Konrad's paintings and knew his talent to be stunning, but his appearance was less so. His hair was long but unkempt, and his long arms protruded awkwardly from his rumpled jacket.

"Good evening, Erzebet," he said, his dark eyes darting from my face to the count, betraying his nervousness. "You are even more beautiful than the count described. I'm honored to paint the portrait of so elegant a lady." As he took my hand I noticed that his were rough and weathered, not the soft hands of aristocrats to which I was accustomed.

"A gift from your father," the count pronounced, handing me a small wooden box. I gritted my teeth in anger, but only smiled and curtsied in response to his offer.

Inside the box was a magnificent scarf of saffron silk. My fingers trembled as I rubbed the smooth fabric between my thumb and forefinger.

"It's Turkish," the count murmured, and chuckled devilishly. "Their fabrics are very fine. I thought that you would appreciate this piece."

"It is beautiful," I uttered; I would not attempt to deny this, but the feel of the silk in my hands and the smug smile on the count's face made me boil with rage. *This is the sin of wrath*, I thought, remembering Sinestra's words. The thought of him reminded me of my own power, helped me to contain my rage.

"Konrad has brought a new painting for us to admire, Erzebet. I have told him of your love of art—though it seems most keen when you are the subject." The count laughed. I ignored him and took Konrad's arm, and he pulled me closer to a large, framed portrait propped against two high-backed chairs.

The portrait was of a young woman with skin pale and soft as flour and glossy, golden hair. She wore a simple cotton blouse, but the rest of her dress was undefined. It was her face that Konrad had focused upon, delicately bringing her to life with his paints. The sight of the young woman's face filled me with conflicting emotions—is she more beautiful than I am?—but it was the familiar gaze of her wide blue eyes that rendered me speechless.

"She looks like your mother, doesn't she?" the count said, suddenly close to my shoulder.

"The girl was a peasant in a small town in Italy," Konrad explained. "I bought her a meal so that she would allow me to paint her portrait."

"A meal well worth it," the count stated, bemused. "What do you think, Erzebet?"

"It does look like her," I said, and faltered. "Strange, isn't it, that someone else could have that face?"

"You must forgive my emotional daughter," the count explained.

"Her mother has been ill these many years." The count laid a heavy hand upon my shoulder; my flesh prickled at his touch.

"I can assure you, this was the face I saw," Konrad offered. "My paintings are truthful, if nothing else. I have had some very unhappy customers because of it."

"Many people don't want to see themselves truthfully," I murmured. "I have long wondered myself why my father has never commissioned his own portrait."

The count shifted uneasily, lifting his hand from my shoulder.

"It's no small feat to reveal yourself to an artist's scrutiny," Konrad stammered, "but I see that you have already done so with beautiful results." He gestured toward the paintings on the walls around us.

"Perhaps a touch of fantasy is necessary in art, at times." The count sneered. "After all, to catch the eye of an emperor, the one thing that is required is perfection."

Konrad opened his mouth to respond, but by the gleam in my father's eyes he realized that a response was not required. He bowed his head obediently. My eyes blurred for a moment as the count's words pierced me, like a needle sliding between my ribs. I could not bear to meet his gaze.

Perhaps this is how the countess felt, I thought. *Never good enough.*

XVII

Late that night, my return to the tower was labored, the saffron scarf clutched in my hand, the purple gown weighing me down. Despite my weariness, I paused near the doorway to my mother's chamber, listening intently to the low voices beyond the half-opened door. I wondered if they were still bleeding her, and what effect the bleeding could have had. Despite my curiosity, I could not will my stiff limbs to cross the threshold of that door. I continued down the hallway and dragged my velvet train up the spiral stairway.

The one thing that is required is perfection. My father's words echoed in my head. Entering the tower, I fought the desire to rush to the mirror in search of what imperfections the count might have detected in my face. I owed Marianna my attention now, more than ever. I could take up my treatments again, the next day.

"Are you asleep, Mari?" I asked the darkened chamber. The fire had burned to its last embers, and the chill nipped at my neck and arms.

"Dearest, are you all right?" I said in my sweetest tone. I moved to the silk divan and pulled back the fur cover—Marianna was gone.

"Your friend is not here," a low voice rumbled in the darkness—I jumped with recognition, and a hand reached out and grabbed my own.

"What happened? What did you do to her?"

"Nothing," the stranger assured me. "She is not my concern. You are my only concern." His hand still clutching mine, he moved over to the hearth and lit a candle from the dying flames, placing it on the table in the middle of the room. I gasped in shock: he was real, he was real . . . this was the face I had seen, so long ago. I had often wondered if it was all a dream.

He smiled and lifted my hand, prying the silk scarf from my clenched fist.

"How lovely," he murmured, moving closer and drawing it around my neck, letting the silk brush slowly against my skin. The chamber was cold; he stood close enough that I could feel the warmth of his body on my flesh. He was taller than I was, with broad shoulders that

I could have just rested my chin upon, in an embrace. In spite of my trepidation, I had to resist the urge to place my hand upon his chest.

"I must leave," I murmured. "I have to find her. I have to know that she's safe."

"She was gone when I arrived here," he said, and pulled me closer. "Besides, I was only looking for you. And now I've found you." His grasp was gentle—persistent, but not unpleasant. He wrapped me easily in his arms.

"Who sent you here?" I asked. "Shouldn't I at least be able to know that?"

"Of course, my dear," he said, smiling against my neck, "God sent me here."

"God sent you here?"

"Yes, of course. And He sent you here as well. And He made you beautiful. Then He gave you a falling star, and a prophecy."

"What do you know about the prophecy?" I breathed, my limbs suddenly rigid in his embrace.

"I know as much as you do." He lifted his head and looked straight into my eyes. "God sent me to you. God does all things. Isn't that what you've been taught?"

He brushed his hand against my cheek gently. For a moment my eyes fluttered, my vision blurred. I forgot about searching for Marianna; thoughts of her drowned in the low rumble of his voice.

"I've received your gifts," I told him.

"Yes, and have you enjoyed them? Have they made you think of me?"

"Yes, they have," I said, though the admission made my cheeks warm.

"Have you thought about the choice you've made? Between eternal life or an early death?"

"I didn't realize it was my choice to make," I said.

"And yet you've read the prophecy." He sighed mockingly, with an affectionate squeeze. "I expected more from you, truly."

"What? What did you expect?" I demanded, suddenly frustrated. I was tired of what people expected of me.

"It's just like a mortal human to read and remember only what is feared and to leave grand possibilities undiscovered." He leaned forward and pressed his forehead to mine, his eyes shut, long dark lashes curling against his cheeks.

"Now tell me, Erzebet, what did your prophecy say?"

"It talked about an angel and a demon, and the angel and the demon predicted a child whose days will end quickly, or whose days will have no end. And that child is me."

"The words are written upon your heart, and yet you've never really thought about what they mean, have you?"

"How dare you!" I hissed, pushing his arms away. "I've thought about it every day since the moment I found it. Of course I've been afraid. It's made me feel like less of a person—less alive."

"But why? After all, the prediction is both good and bad: a child who will die young, or a child who will never die. And you've already made your decision, there."

"Yes, though I don't see why it matters. There is no such thing as living forever."

He looked at me again, steadily, his eyes inky black and glittering in the low light. He held my hand in his.

"I find that when someone is faced with a future they fear, they can either give up and blindly follow the path laid out before them, or find the strength to divert it. I've already told you that you have the power to decide. You are stronger than you realize."

"But it doesn't matter how strong I am." I sighed.

"Of course it does." He clasped me to him again and smiled. It was a beautiful smile; I basked in its warmth.

"I spent some time reading your spell book." He laughed. I pushed against his chest, trying to release myself, but his embrace only tightened.

"I thought that was what you wanted me to do—spells and magic. Isn't that what all of your gifts were telling me?" I asked, petulant. "Perhaps you should make your messages more clear."

"No, you have done well. But there is another book you should consider. Now listen." He bent low to speak into my ear. *"For the life of the flesh is in the blood: and I have given it to you upon the altar to make an atonement for your souls: for it is the blood that maketh an atonement for the soul."*

"Leviticus?" I whispered.

"You know your Bible well. Now think of this: the life of the flesh is in the blood." As he repeated the words I felt mesmerized, as if his voice were inside my head.

"You already know the power of blood," he said, stepping back and brushing his fingertips against the bodice of my gown. My belly ached in response; I knew that my blood was coming again, just as it did every month. The thought of it filled me with dread.

"Erzebet." He sighed, and cradled my face in his hands. "It hurts me to see you in pain."

"I feel like I am dying, slowly drained of life."

"Don't worry," he whispered, his lips close to my ear. "Think of what I've told you. We'll meet again soon." He released me, sinking back into the darkness without a sound.

As soon as I returned to my senses I tore from the chamber and hurried down the stairs, down the hall, lifting the purple gown from the floor, hoping that no one would notice the haste of my stride. I came upon Rowena in my bedchamber, spreading a fresh silk night-shift upon my bed.

"Rowena!" I cried, gripping her arms. "Marianna is missing—she's gone. Have you seen her?"

Rowena blanched, her skin the color of yellow cream.

"I thought you knew, child. I saw her getting ready to see her parents one last time. I tried to convince her not to go, but she was determined. I saw there was no stopping her, so I at least gave her food to bring to them, so that they might not starve. Please understand, Erzebet, they are her parents. She said she would be back tonight, as quickly as she could."

"How could she?" I gasped, shocked by her betrayal. "I was trying to keep her safe—everything I did was for her protection!"

"Erzebet, please sit—you look very pale. She didn't do this to upset you. I'm sure she'll be back."

"But how can she invite such risk?" My hands were shaking, and Rowena urged me to sit beside her upon the bed. "How can anyone take such a risk? There are so many things out there," I murmured. "There are so many things ready and able to harm us. I don't know how she can live without thinking about them all the time."

"Oh, Erzebet, do you really think that way?" she said, and rubbed my arms vigorously. "That's no way to live at all. Please, Erzebet, I will help you into bed. Marianna will likely run right to the tower when she returns."

"The tower," I breathed, holding a clammy hand to my forehead. "I will wait there for her."

I climbed the stairs back to the tower, the candle in my hand casting a shaky dance of light upon the stone walls. When I opened the door, I thrust the candle in first.

"Is anybody there?" I asked, but no one answered. The room the candle illuminated was empty; I was relieved that Sinestra would not be there to intrude upon Marianna's return. I lit a fire hastily before pulling a fur blanket over my gown and sitting in a chair to wait. I thought to pray for Marianna's safety, but could think of no words that sounded sincere. Only anger welled inside of me—for her uncertain fate and for mine.

"How could you be so cruel?" I asked God. There came no answer. I shut my eyes and imagined I saw stars falling, one by one, in streams of gold across a dark night sky.

I was torn from these visions by a rough bang at the door. I sat up, disoriented in the darkness. The flames in the hearth had died; the only light in the room was a pale silver glow from the full moon. The dark-haired soldier entered the room and stood over me, his face half lit with jagged shadows in the moonlight. I was so shocked at the sight of him that I felt sure I was dreaming.

"I found something on the road that may be of importance to you, young countess," he said, his rough voice waking me from my half-dream. He was no vision, after all. He let loose what appeared to be a large, lumpy sack from beneath his arm; it rolled to the floor with a thud. The blue cloak revealed Marianna, lying on the floor, her face covered in her hands.

I prepared to speak, but the soldier lifted his hand to silence me.

"She came to no harm, I assure you, though she nearly did through no fault but her own."

Marianna gasped and began to cry, a high, keening wail. She rolled over on the floor at the soldier's feet and hid her face beneath her hair.

"See to it that she doesn't leave here under any circumstances—I will not be responsible for her again."

With these words he turned and left the room without looking again at the girl writhing upon the floor. I knelt at her side, pulling her hair from her tear-streaked face.

"I couldn't get to the house," she wailed. "I tried to but the Turks are heading straight for the center of town. The soldiers were there to ward them off, but there was so much fighting—I saw it." She winced, her eyes shut tightly, then moved her hands to cover her ears. "I cannot tell you what their screaming sounded like."

"We're lucky that you got out alive, we must all be relieved with that." I drew her close in a tight embrace; she shook against me with the force of her sobs.

You tried to leave me, I thought, but did not say aloud. *After all that I have done for you, you tried to leave.*

"Did you hear him, Marianna? He said that you're not to go back there—do you understand? There is nothing left there for you."

"I had to see them once more, and now I never will."

"I will take care of you here, Mari. Here you will be safe. Wait here a moment." I propped her against a pillow and scurried to the door to find Rowena—she would surely know how to help calm her. But when I opened the door I jumped back, startled. Konrad stood before me in the dark hallway—he, too, jumped at the sight of me.

"I apologize, my lady. I didn't mean to frighten you," he muttered, bowing awkwardly. "I saw the soldier enter with the young lady and I came to see that she is unharmed, and to offer my assistance if needed." I saw him wince at the sound of Marianna's crying.

"If I am not needed, I will leave you, my lady. I am sorry to have startled you."

"Konrad, wait," I whispered harshly. "Did my father see her? Did anybody else see her?"

"No, the count has already retired for the evening."

"You will tell no one." My voice struggled to be heard over Marianna's cries. "You will tell no one that you saw her—tell no one that she is here. Especially the count."

"Of course, my lady," he said, his head bowed. "If I can be of any service, you need simply to ask." When he had turned down the hallway, I shut the door firmly.

I held Marianna close to me, tightly, until her cries weakened and she finally slept.

XVIII

The next morning, soft sunlight filtered into the narrow windows of the tower room, a soft slant of light falling across Marianna's sleeping face. It was the type of fresh morning she always gloried in, her hazel eyes sparkling in the golden glow. I let her sleep in the patch of sunlight, only to be roused once Rowena brought breakfast to the tower.

"How are you feeling?" I asked her when she sat up. She rubbed her face for a moment and sighed before answering.

"Still tired," she murmured, glancing only briefly at the tray of food. I filled her teacup and placed it on a saucer before her. Despite the sunshine, the air around us still seemed to echo with her cries of the night before.

"You should eat something." It seemed the kind of thing Rowena would suggest. "It may make you feel better."

She nestled down under the covers, her lids still heavy with sleep. She blinked, but did not look up at me.

"Thank you, Erzebet," she uttered quietly.

"My first portrait session is tomorrow," I told her, trying to keep my voice bright. "I thought you might help me prepare."

"You've been preparing your gown and jewels for weeks now. I doubt that you need my help," she said, yawning. "Besides, I'm stuck in this tower."

"But I would like your help, Marianna."

"I'm sorry, Erzebet." She held her hand out and I grasped it, warmly. "You know how tired I am. Please understand."

"Of course I understand," I told her. "I'm sorry that things have not worked out well for you—it's unfair."

"What is fair, Erzebet? There is no such thing as fair in this world."

"But you should be protected," I told her. "You above all others. Your faith should have protected you, and your parents."

"I suppose you must think me rather foolish," she murmured, her voice still rough with sleep, "to have preached to you about trusting God's plan for us all. His plan for me hasn't turned out as I had hoped."

"I've never thought you foolish, Marianna," I said carefully. I noticed the shadows beneath her eyes, like smudges of ink. Her cheeks and lips were pale in the sunlight.

"Perhaps I feel a bit foolish myself." She laughed lightly.

Now she understands, I thought, *now she understands: God does not deserve our trust.* As much as I had always wished she could understand my fears of an unknowable future, hearing her speak in such a way filled me with a strange despair. I felt the words of the prophecy rise in my throat, but I swallowed them like a lump of hard bread.

"But I am protected, Erzebet. God still protects me—especially now," she said, managing to smile over the words. I sensed she was saying this aloud more for herself than for me. She reached for the teacup and I caught her gaze; her eyes were red and raw at the edges.

"I wish I could help you, Mari," I uttered, reaching for her hand again.

"You *have* helped me, Erzebet," she said, smiling. "You already know that you've saved my life. There is no way I can repay you for that."

I waited for her to tell me what she needed, but she said nothing. After sipping her tea, she managed to return to sleep.

As I turned to leave the tower, something on the dressing table caught my eye. A small, leather-bound book was nestled among my array of jars and jewels. I paused for a moment before approaching it, but my eyes and the mirror's reflection assured me that it was real. When I lifted it in my hands I realized that it was a Bible, the leather cover carved with intricate patterns. I flipped the book open to reveal the page that was marked with a satin ribbon.

Leviticus. My encounter with Sinestra the night before came flooding back to me. As my eyes passed over the same words he had recited, his voice echoed each word in my head. What could Sinestra have meant by this? What could God have meant by this?

"What does God mean by this?" I asked Pugrue during my lesson that morning, hoping for guidance. The count had insisted that I resume my lessons, so I sought at least to use them to my advantage in spite of my bitter loss of authority. I wrinkled my brow like a curious scholar to conceal the significance of my question.

"Blood is a holy sacrament," he explained. "It is the liquid of life, you see." I listened to Pugrue's explanation, searching for a clue. Memory of the soldier back from battle shot through me like lightning: *To drink the blood of the enemy is to consume the enemy's power . . .*

With all that we kill, the stronger we become! Could blood work like this, transferring the traits of one to another, through the blood?

I stared at the small goblet of sacramental wine upon Pugrue's altar: before my eyes the color seemed to change, turning from the clear jewel-red of wine to the thick, dark red of blood. The sight of it made me dizzy, and I saw the deer's blood upon my hands again. Just as I had been years ago, I was enthralled by the contrast of the red blood upon my white hands.

"Beautiful," I breathed.

"Erzebet?" Pugrue called; his voice at first sounded very far away, but slowly it broke through—the blood on my hands disappeared.

"Are you all right, Erzebet? You suddenly look quite pale."

I looked to the goblet on the altar—it was wine again. I took a deep breath.

"Yes, Father, I feel fine."

But truly, I didn't feel fine. There was a heaviness in my belly all day, as though I had swallowed lead: I was suffering merely one of many afflictions of the female sex. That afternoon I took a walk with Marianna in the garden, for she was looking wan and pale and desperate for release from the tower room. The count was busy tending to business outside of the castle, and we were confident that the rose hedges would conceal us from intruders. I welcomed the kiss of cool air upon my face and neck.

"It is nice to take a walk outside." Marianna sighed, breathing the fresh air in greedy gulps. "I was afraid I would have to remain in the tower indefinitely."

"It is the safest place for you to be, Mari. But I don't think a walk on a day like today can hurt. Look, the buds are really blooming now."

We walked arm in arm, inspecting the progress of the tight rose-buds upon their curled black vines. Though my cloak was pulled back over my shoulders, Marianna was huddled in hers, shivering. I stopped suddenly at the sound of leaves crunching. I lifted my hand for Marianna to be quiet, but it was too late. A moment later, Konrad stood in the path before us. Marianna bent her head, her dark hair covering her face.

"I apologize, my lady." He bowed to me, but his eyes flashed quickly to Marianna. "Your gardens are quite beautiful. I wanted to take a closer look. I hope I'm not intruding."

"Don't worry, Mari," I murmured. "He saw you last night. He promised not to tell."

Marianna lifted her head, her cheeks flushed and rosy.

"Marianna, this is Konrad, who is to paint my portrait tomorrow. Marianna is a special guest of mine."

"Pleased to make your acquaintance." Konrad bowed formally before her.

"Your portrait is to begin tomorrow, is that true?" Marianna asked as we continued our walk.

"Yes, I already have a chamber arranged in the guest quarters," Konrad stated.

"Are you excited, Erzebet? I would certainly be excited if my portrait were to be painted."

I was surprised by Marianna's sudden enthusiasm. I mused that the fresh air had improved her mood.

"I suppose I am," I said, wary of revealing my apprehension. "It's been many years since my last portrait was painted."

"I'm sure this will be the most beautiful one yet, without a doubt," Marianna pronounced admiringly.

"Beauty is a very powerful force—and a dangerous one, at that," Konrad mused.

"You are an artist, of course you will believe that beauty is powerful," I teased.

"Oh, but a portrait of a beautiful woman is the greatest power an artist can invoke. There was a great painter in London, Hans Holbein, whose portrait of Anne of Cleves charmed the late King Henry into proposing to her, although they had never met."

"And the portrait had been very flattering, was it not?"

"Indeed, it was a very effective portrayal, but not a very accurate one. The marriage did not last long."

Marianna giggled; it was good to hear her spirits rising from the despair of the previous night. In spite of her giggling, I could see her visibly shivering beneath her cloak.

"I'm afraid it is getting too cold for a walk," I remarked. "We'd best get inside. Konrad, perhaps you could dine with us some evening, perhaps once the count returns to court? We would be most grateful for your company."

"I would be delighted, my lady," he said.

When we turned to enter the castle, Marianna gave my arm a little squeeze.

"You must be more excited about your portrait than you let on," she said.

I felt many things about my portrait, indeed, but I could not answer her. With each step my belly felt heavier. I had begun to grit my teeth to distract myself from the pain.

XIX

I spent the next morning in bed, resting, with soaked bags of herbs placed upon my eyelids. The count had released me from my lessons for the day so I could spend all of my time preparing for the portrait. Rowena enlisted the help of a meek young lady to assist in my wardrobe, and she even aided in Marianna's safe journey to my bedchamber, to soothe my spirits with her company.

Rowena secured an iron-ribbed corset, and I urged her to employ the necessary force to tie the stays tightly against my ribs, regardless of my pains. Despite the warm summer weather, the gown was heavy, elaborate court dress: lush red velvet with detailed embroidery in gold thread lining the long, pointed bodice and the edges of the full skirt. The opened front of the skirt and the slashed sleeves revealed a layer of fine gold gauze, and the stiff collar of gold lace that rose behind my head reminded me of a peacock's fan of feathers.

After a night of feeling my life slowly drained from me, the gown made me feel vividly alive. The gold thread sparkled against the red velvet like fire, and my red lips glistened like the ruby that dipped low upon my forehead. This was my power, I realized: my beauty was my power. Even the count would not dare to deny me my beauty if he were to see me now. Even the prophecy, still a thorn in my side, seemed to curl a bit at the edges in the livid, powerful flames of my perfection.

"You look unimaginably beautiful, Erzebet, you truly do," Rowena assured me. I knew that this was true. Since childhood, my angles had grown more elegant. I inspected my face in the mirror and approved of my milk-white skin, ink-black eyes, and intricately pinned cascade of shining dark auburn curls. After the bustle of getting ready, the women gathered around me and I felt each set of eyes settle upon my reflection in the mirror. I was transformed.

"You look like a painting already," Marianna said, and I reveled in the admiration in her voice. "You've become severely beautiful, but tonight you are even more so. You look, somehow, unreal. Somehow—"

"Not human." I said, and smiled slightly, a curve of a full red mouth. Marianna shuddered at the thought, but I rolled the words deliciously over my tongue.

"Your hair, my lady," a servant began timidly. Her fair face was reflected for a moment beside mine in the mirror. She was pretty, with rosy cheeks and full breasts, but I tried my best not to notice, not to compare her looks to my own. I saw her tilt her head, looking at me, and I turned back to my own reflection. *My hair is like fire, like sunlight, like—*

"Your hair is crooked on this one side. You need another pin," the servant said.

She moved toward me slowly, as though walking through water. I held my breath and watched her, my eyes fixed on her movements. *How dare she? How dare she undermine my power?*

"Here, my lady, I will fix it for you."

One swift motion of my arm sliced the air like a scythe. Voices spiraled into silence. The girl bent on her knees at my feet, hands shaking on either side of her face. As I straightened, I felt suddenly taller, watching the servant cower before me as though from a great distance. It had been a while since I had allowed myself the luxury of lashing out at a servant, and now I could not help but revel in the release of my rage. I was so full of fear and rage all the time, it felt good to let it out. The servant remained crouched in shock, then a moment later scurried from the room.

When I turned back to the mirror I saw that my ring had cut the girl's face as I slapped her—there was a spot of blood on my hand, and another on my cheek and chin. The echo came to me—that day in the count's chamber, after first reading the prophecy, then looking into the mirror to see my face splattered with deer's blood—as if that moment and this were somehow connected, existing together in my reflection in the glass. But this moment was wholly different. Far from realizing I was cursed, I felt powerful. Sinestra had told me I had more strength than I realized. The servant's blood on my face reminded me that this was true.

I took a moment to admire the contrast of the red blood upon my white skin before I began to carefully wipe the blood from my face. As I did so, I noticed immediately how clear my skin was, how smooth and white it appeared, once the drop of blood had been wiped away. *Blood is a sacrament, and sacraments keep us all safe . . . the life of the flesh is in the blood.* I was not cursed, I realized, looking into my reflection as if I were staring into Sinestra's eyes: I was blessed. I had been chosen.

Marianna's face hovered beside me, her brows furrowed. I did not meet her gaze, her frown already tarnishing my moment of satisfaction.

"Erzebet, how could you?" she asked me. "She was only trying to help. Sometimes I don't understand you at all."

"I have never expected you to understand," I told her. She turned and stared insolently into the fire. Still captivated by my own reflection, I tarried before the glass. When I bid Marianna good day, she did not respond.

Before I met with Konrad for the portrait, I turned up the stairwell and entered the tower room. I lifted the book of spells from the table and looked again at my face in the oval mirror. A wave of pain surged through me, and I held my breath until it had passed. Suddenly things made sense in a way they never had before. I was no longer a child, as evidenced by the blood that seeped into a cotton rag between my legs. I looked again at my face, inspecting my skin in the mirror. Sinestra's words echoed clearly in my head: *the life of the flesh is in the blood . . .* Blood lost, blood gained. This is what he had meant all along. Perhaps he understood me better than I could have imagined—perhaps even better than Marianna ever would. I pushed this thought aside swiftly, feeling in it some sort of betrayal. I looked back to the mirror to focus on my face. This was about me: my prophecy, my life. Blood is powerful—it had taken me this long to realize this, to learn how I could use this power for my own protection.

Eternal Beauty, I wrote on a blank page, in flowing script.

Believe me, Marianna, when I tell you now that it was the alchemist in me, the scientist and not the murderess, who wrote on that page about the refreshing effects of warm blood upon the flesh.

Day ten, night

I can still create that face, just as it appears in a portrait more than ten years old.

"Won't Stephan be surprised to see how young I look," I remark to my face in the glass. "Won't they all be surprised, when I see the peasants at the trial?"

The meek servant lingers for a moment, her eyes snagged on my reflection in the glass. When I look at her, she looks down and begins to fiddle with her apron.

"The prince has already arrived, Countess," she tells me. "I thought that you knew. The trial has already begun, in the village."

"How am I to know anything if you don't tell me?" My face is flushed with anger. "Why did he not visit me? Why am I not at trial, to defend myself?"

The girl's eyes shift from side to side, then back to me.

"Who has been called to testify?"

"There have been a few witnesses, Countess, who have testified."

"There were no witnesses, you fool," I snapped. "Who is there? Rowena? Pugrue?"

"Yes, Countess. And a few of your servants."

Mary, Elizabeth, Althea, and Sarah . . . my girls—or at least they used to be.

"Konrad is not there?"

The servant blinked dumbly.

"I'm afraid that name isn't familiar to me, Countess."

I was not surprised at this. Likely he had disappeared the night of Helena's death—vanished in time to hide her killer.

"Why have I not been called to trial?" I demanded.

"I don't know that you will be called to trial, Countess. The prince thought you would be safer here." The round-cheeked girl says her words carefully. She pretends to be calm, but I think she is afraid. I smile at her.

"Will I be asked to confess?"

"We don't know that, Countess. You will have to wait for the prince to call upon you."

"It's just as well. I don't know why I should have to confess." I sigh, moving to the mirror again, watching their expressions reflected in the glass. "After all, I don't see that I did much of anything wrong."

At night, the ghosts come to the tower to disagree with this notion.

We didn't want you to be alone. *They laugh.*

I try to recall the moments of peace and power I experienced in their death in order to keep my calm.

"I've won, you see," I remind them. "I'm here and you are gone. You are nothing but shadows."

Still, my hand trembles as I grip the quill to write.

I stood before the artist in a chamber draped with black velvet curtains and lit golden by a roaring fire. The moment I stepped into the room, I could see my beauty reflected in the dark pools of his eyes. The gown shimmered in the firelight. Konrad fumbled with pleasantries and took my hand, showing me where to stand before the black velvet, which kept out the light of the sun.

"Firelight creates a special warmth, for a portrait," he explained. "And that dress—the red and gold are the color of the flames."

Despite the persistent ache in my belly, I could not help but think about the blood of the servant upon my hand. I meditated not merely upon the satisfying sound of my palm colliding with the face of the young maid, but on the warmth and vivid redness of the blood itself, and how it felt against my skin. *He will be so proud of me,* I thought, and I realized I was thinking about Sinestra. I reveled in the feeling of his pride. Then Marianna's visage rose before me: reproachful, injured. The memory of her gaze wiped these thoughts away.

"Is the light quite right for you, Konrad?" I asked coyly.

"Of course, Erzebet. It's perfect. You look perfect," he stammered.

Ignoring the heavy ache in my back and belly, I enjoyed how his eyes flickered nervously as he perfected my pose, tilting my chin in the light. I smiled as I watched the way he tugged at the loose collar of his shirt and patted a dry cloth to his forehead. Meanwhile, I stood still, austere, like a sculpture in the garden, the firelight glowing golden upon my skin. He arranged the pots of paint before the canvas with awkward, clumsy fingers. He tipped over one jar and scattered a handful of slim paintbrushes upon the floor.

"You're not nervous, are you?" I teased. "You have painted a live model before?"

"None quite so impressive, my lady, forgive me," he said, with a hasty bow.

In the years I had spent awaiting this portrait, I had long fantasized that the gaze of an artist was much like the gaze of a lover, drinking in each detail of his inspiration from my face, my limbs, my slim waist. As the hour progressed, Konrad grew quiet and focused on his work, and something in his face changed.

"It's been many years since my last portrait was painted," I prattled, continuing my flirtation. "I'm certain I've changed a great deal."

"I need the right expression," he murmured, more to his canvas than to me. He ruffled his hand through his hair for a moment, thinking. When he turned to me I saw a smudge of red paint on his face. He might have said something to me, but I didn't hear it; I was distracted by the red paint, like a smear of blood across his face. I remembered again the sound of my hand against the servant's face, the feel of her blood on my skin. I felt that I had been granted a secret in this, a secret that not all humans are privy to. It made me feel more than human somehow. I could not help but smile.

"Don't move," he told me. The clumsiness of a first lover disappeared and only the penetrating gaze of the artist was left behind.

My romantic notions about art were untrue. I learned that the soul of art is not love or lust, but creation. The artist's passion is not for the subject arrayed before him—a young woman laced into the constrictions of her finest gown—but for the creation of the art itself.

By the time I reached my bedchamber that evening, I felt drained.

"Erzebet, are you well?" Rowena walked toward me as soon as I entered. I saw that a white silk nightshift was already spread upon the bed and I sighed with relief.

"Let me help you undress. You need your rest."

I stood still and allowed her to release me from the confines of the opulent gown. When I stood in my underclothes, I was careful to close my eyes when the bloodied bandage was removed from between my legs. It was as though I was wounded, I thought, suddenly dizzy at the smell of blood.

"You looked beautiful today," Rowena murmured, urging me into bed.

I thought distantly of the face I had seen in the mirror only hours before: harsh, beautiful angles reflected in the glass. I did not feel like that girl anymore. It was not just the blood that drained me of life, but the eyes of the artist as well. I felt as though a living part of me had been removed, to be rendered in oils upon the canvas and made immortal.

"Where is Marianna?" I asked, my voice weak.

"She's in the tower, asleep. Don't worry," Rowena said, piling a heavy fur upon the bed. "You're chilled to the bone, Erzebet. I hope you're not unwell."

"I'm not unwell," I told her, but it was not merely the cold that had made me shiver. *Time scurries about at night like a rat, feasts on you in sleep . . .* My mother's voice echoed in my head, magnified, as if part of a hideous dream.

XXI

I woke early the next morning, hours before Rowena's visit. It was surprisingly chilly, a portent of the cold winter already on its way. I pulled a dressing gown tightly around my shoulders and poked at the embers in the fireplace, urging the flames to warm my skin. In the steel-gray light of dawn I lit a candle and sat before the mirror to contemplate my reflection. Despite the cold I slipped the cloak from my shoulders, then pulled down my nightshift to inspect all of my curves and angles in the glass. While part of me thrilled at the glow and softness of my young skin in the candlelight, a dark cloud hovered over my enjoyment. I was a woman now, and according to the prophecy, death could come to me at any time, without hesitation, despite the soft white curves of my new breasts or the unblemished skin of my face and throat.

I thought, of course, about the blood. The gold-and-emerald ring that had sliced the flesh of the servant's face the night before now glinted darkly in the candlelight. I rifled through the sundry items on the table before me—pearl necklaces, ribbons, rings—and found a sapphire brooch and unfastened the crooked clasp. Delicately, I pierced the flesh of my thumb with the pin and watched as a bead of blood rose to the surface.

This was so different from my monthly blood, pulled from me by unseen forces, beyond my control. This blood seemed clean and pure, like a sacrament. I patted the spot dry with a wad of muslin until the bleeding ceased. I looked at the stains the blood had left behind upon the swatch of cotton: red roses blooming on a field of white.

It was clear that I needed blood for my next experiment. Piercing my own flesh would not produce nearly enough, and I was loath to risk scarring my own flawless skin. Clearly I needed the help of a servant, much as I had required their help in the past to offer me the necessary leaves and herbs for my potions. Blood was simply a new ingredient that I required.

I could make this argument quite convincingly to my own reflection in the glass. As soon as I remembered the look upon Marianna's face the night before—reproachful, a bit frightened—my own courage faltered. I swallowed my misgivings, resigned to keep the experiment a secret.

After dressing in a blue satin gown, I went to visit Marianna in the tower, carrying a tray of tea, bread, and jam: a peace offering. I set the tray upon a low table and rallied the fire in the hearth as she sat up upon the divan, wiping the sleep from her eyes.

"Good morning, Mari," I said, as sweetly as I could. Marianna smiled, her eyes brightening when she saw the thick white bread slathered with jam.

"Such dutiful service," she said. "It's lovely, Erzebet. Thank you."

"It's my pleasure. I thought I would visit with you briefly, before my lesson. I know that you're restless when I'm away."

She made ready to bite into a piece of bread when she paused, gazing at it for a long moment.

"There is something I feel I should talk to you about, Erzebet, but I feel sorry to say anything, as you've always been so kind to me."

"You can talk to me about anything, Mari." I smiled to hide my apprehension.

"It's about last night, when you were readying for your portrait. I know it's not my place to say, but you had no right to treat that young woman as you did."

"I wasn't feeling well—you know that," I uttered vainly, to suppress my guilt. "I don't think it was as terrible as you make it out to be."

Her eyes flashed at me reproachfully, her lips parted to speak.

"You must understand, there are nobles who treat their servants far more harshly than I do. That's how they deal with their servants, to make sure they know their place."

"Their place?" she cried. "Do you realize that it could very well have been me? That girl is probably from the same village in which I was born."

"Your parents never sent you into service, Marianna."

"But don't you think they would have, if it hadn't been for you?" Her eyes blurred with tears and she sighed angrily, averting her gaze from mine.

"Some people don't have much choice in the matter," she murmured. "Where you are born is where you are born; God gives you a life and you must make do." She looked up at me warily. "That life may not be easy for many people."

"Life is not easy for anyone," I told her, putting my hand upon hers. "Not for you, or for me. I'm sorry, Mari," I sighed, softening. "I'm sorry that you saw it at all."

Later that morning, after Pugrue's endless lecture about sin and salvation, I learned the whereabouts of the count.

"He has been in the village of late, with his soldiers. He will make a voyage to court before long, before the weather turns," Pugrue explained. "He plans to take your portrait, when it is done, and make a gift of it to Emperor Rudolf."

"Am I to be betrothed, Father?" I asked, most innocently. Pugrue responded well to innocence.

"That seems to be his plan, of course. He has long been set upon a match between you and Rudolf, though I confess I think it unlikely."

"Why is that?"

"The emperor is not well, has never been well from what I've heard, and seems to have no intention of marrying anybody. He was engaged to his cousin Isabel for years before she finally got tired of waiting and married his younger brother. Now that the count—your father . . ." He paused for a moment, feeling abashed at having revealed so much. He scratched his balding head, making the white strands of hair stand up like reeds.

"Your honesty is much appreciated, Father," I reassured him. "I'm afraid I hear very little honesty, least of all from the count."

"Over the past few years, the scourge of Protestantism has infected the nobility," he grunted, disgusted. "Your father will wed you only to a Catholic, of course, but those options are dwindling, I'm afraid."

"I'm not afraid, Father," I told him, and bowed most regally. "Please do not fear for my sake."

I was glad to hear that the count would soon be back at court and unable to meddle in my affairs. I had spent so many years of my childhood concerned with how I would impress him upon his return, and now the thought of him only filled me with anger and disgust. He was a coward who made deals with the enemy just to retain the illusion of his power. I sought real power, and his weakness sickened me. But in spite of my bitterness, I still remembered the pain caused by his neglect: no one should be made to feel so insignificant. These thoughts pulled me gradually to my mother's bedchamber.

The countess was lavishly dressed, lying upon her bed.

"You again," she announced upon my entrance. The servants turned and looked at me with wide eyes; one nearly dropped a pitcher of wine. I lifted my hand to silence their concerns.

"Good morning, Countess," I said, bowing. "I thought I would pay you a visit; I hope you don't mind."

I waved a hand to the servants, and they retreated to the hearth, the wardrobe, giving us some semblance of privacy. I lifted the wine pitcher from a table and filled a glass for the countess. When I held it out to her, she shook her head.

"Try it first," she insisted. "You try it first."

I sipped the wine, and when she saw that it was safe, she took the goblet from me and drank.

"I remember you," she croaked, her voice thick. "You were here asking about my daughter, about the prophecy."

"You're right, I did. In fact, I've been thinking about that prophecy."

"Here, sit," she said, patting the side of her bed. As she lay back, the skin of her face and neck fell slack; her eyes were glassy. She smelled of wine.

"Do you really think the prophecy was true?" I asked.

"What do you mean, do I think it was true? She died, didn't she?"

"Did she?" I asked, but the countess only shook her head. I decided not to press the matter; perhaps she would not be so willing to let me visit her if she knew I was her daughter. She seemed more comfortable believing that I had died.

"The prophecy was unclear," I explained. "It said she would either die young or that she would never die."

At this she laughed loudly, the sound of it making me jump from her in fear. Her eyes gleamed as though bright with fever.

"What if there was a way to stay young forever?" I suggested.

"I would bless you if you could find it," she said, snorting, "though God may think differently. Mark me"—she leaned forward and whispered close to my face, her sour breath reeking of wine—"He is a vindictive God, who does not look kindly upon the perfection of his poor, pitiful creatures upon this earth. I know."

"Careful, my lady, it's blasphemy to say such things." I shifted my eyes, wary the servants might be able to overhear.

"It's too late for me anyhow." She waved me off the edge of the bed and pulled herself up from it, suddenly seeming agitated, wringing the fabric of her gown. She stood and smoothed the silk with the palms of her hands, but I could see that her fingers were trembling.

"Why would I want to live forever like this? No"—she frowned and shook her head—"eternal beauty comes with eternal life. No one would choose one without the other, because the first makes life worth living." The countess laughed, a harsh, barking sound that degenerated into a fit of coughing. She waved her arms frantically as I tried, in vain, to calm her. A young servant girl shuffled forward, but the countess stood and backed into her dressing table to avoid the girl's touch.

"Who are you?" she croaked viciously.

"What's wrong?" I asked, but the countess could only point at the girl before her. The servant was a bit younger than I was, and even slighter and paler in complexion. Her hair was braided into a golden rope that hung down her back.

"I'm sorry, Countess," the girl, curtsying, said miserably. "I am Anastasia."

"Is she a ghost?" the countess asked me. "Are you a ghost?" she shouted, lunging at the girl and pinching her harshly on the breast.

The girl shrieked in pain and fear. The other servants ran forward and snatched her away.

"You must lie down, Countess," they said to her. "You're not well, you must rest."

"None of you are well!" she shrieked. "Not a single one of you!" Then she turned her glassy eyes to me. "You saw her, didn't you?"

A servant urged a goblet of wine into her hand; the countess gulped, dutifully.

"You saw her," she repeated to me, her voice thick. "It was Illyana—the girl I used to be. She's climbed out of the mirror to mock me. That mirror is playing tricks on me," she hissed. "You watch her, will you? You must watch her for me."

"Of course I will." I stepped back, horrified at the sight of the bloated countess muttering under her breath. I turned and walked out of the room with my head down, aware of the servants' eyes upon me. Once in the hallway and free from their gazes, I broke into a run. When I was halfway down the hall, with the staircase to the tower in view, a cold hand grasped my arm and pulled me into a dark room. Before I realized what had happened, I heard the door slam shut behind me.

"I've missed you, Erzebet," said a familiar voice.

XXII

We were in one of the countess's chambers, the walls lined with her collection of mirrors. Sunlight streamed in through the puckered windows. For a moment I was dizzied by the sight of everything multiplied: his rich velvet cloak, his hands, his face, all stretching into eternity around me. And there I was in the room with him.

It occurred to me that I had never seen him so clearly, either in my dreams or the dimly lit tower. He was not much older than I, with high, sharp cheekbones, a long narrow nose (to rival my marble Athenus), fashionably long and curling brown hair, a square chin, and dark brows arched over glittering black eyes. The cloak was fastened at his throat by a golden clasp. Though my heart raced, I realized that I didn't feel surprised to see him. I had been expecting that he would find me again soon, especially after I slapped the servant in the face. I knew that he would know about that, as if he had been there to watch it happen.

"You're an awfully sweet child"—he smiled, grasping my hand and pressing it to his lips—"to visit a mother who will not claim you as her own."

I pulled back at his insolence. "I don't want to talk about her," I told him, surprised by my desire to defend her. "She may be mad, but at least she's not completely made of lies."

"Falling from your father's grace so soon?" he murmured, amused. "I suppose we all do; it's just a matter of time. Though some of us fall farther than others." He laughed and pulled me close to him, the bodice of my gown brushing against his rich satin doublet.

"My father's grace affords me little honor. Yet there is little I can do. I have no power here," I blurted in frustration.

"Do not worry, young one. When your chance comes to seize the power, you will know it."

I considered his words while gazing at his face; I strove to act composed, though my head was full of nagging questions.

"Who is *your* father?" I asked.

"My father," he mused, "is much like yours in some ways: domineering, never satisfied. But I'm not here to talk about him. I wanted to tell you how impressed I am with you."

He knew about the slap, of course. My mind raced: there was so much I wanted to ask him, so much I needed to know.

"What else do you know about the prophecy?" I asked.

"I know as much as you do. There is little to know and much to interpret. You certainly believe in it."

"I don't know what else to believe. Is it true?"

"What does it matter whether it's true or not? What you believe is more important than what is real. What seems real can change, can alter—like light, or like time."

He took my hand and spun me around to face a mirror. He stood behind me, his arms wrapped around my waist. The sight of our faces side by side made me light-headed. His eyes were dark and glittering; I loved knowing that he was looking at me.

"You have changed—you can see it in your face. You have grown into a young woman. You will continue to grow older, unless you can stop it. And I've already told you: you have the power to choose."

"And I made my choice, for eternity," I told him. I knew it was what he wanted to hear.

"That's right," he whispered, and bent his head low. The touch of his lips against my neck made my flesh tingle.

"I come here to offer you guidance, Erzebet. Your next experiment may benefit from some caution at first."

"What experiment?" I asked warily.

"The blood, of course," he said, lifting his head to meet mine in the mirror. Of course he knew; he always seemed to know everything. I felt a strange thrill that someone knew my darkest secrets and did not judge me for them.

"I will be careful," I answered, and sighed for a moment in the warmth of his embrace. "What about Marianna?"

"What about her?" he asked. "She matters only if you let her matter. I suggest you not let your companion's moral standards interfere with such an important task. Remember that your life may very well be at stake."

"Why do you care so much about me?" I asked. He squeezed me again, affectionately.

"Because you have power, Erzebet," he whispered, his voice tunneling deep into my head again, "and I'm drawn to it. You're still unaware of what you're capable of."

A moment later, he spun me around again, my vision blurring in the sunlit, mirrored room. When my vision cleared, he was gone. I left the room and walked quietly to the tower, feeling watched at every step.

That night I was kept awake by beauty: all of the traits of beauty I did not possess, haunting me like a ghostly pageant. All of the women I had ever seen in my life paraded through my mind, showing off the very attributes I did not have. The sight of beauty so unlike mine robbed me of my greatest power. Envy burrowed deep into my heart, and the pain made me squeeze my eyes in agony.

I rose from the bed and sat before the mirror, the book of spells open on the table before me, and studied my face periodically as I wrote. I had begun to keep the book of spells in my bedchamber, safe from Marianna's eyes. On its pages I made notes on the physical characteristics of all the young women in servitude in the castle. By each name I had a list of those attributes that inspired jealousy within me—jealousy was powerful, indeed—making me wish for the soft curves of their supple arms and full breasts instead of my angular frame; their straight, silken hair in place of my wild auburn waves. Since I was a child I had begun to automatically crave any trait that I saw as beautiful that I did not yet possess. Now my cravings kept me awake at night.

Just as the stranger had warned, my next experiment required the utmost care and planning. But it was all connected; my envy served to show me that, as did the blood of the pretty servant upon my face. Her pretty blood. Somehow that beauty could be transferred to me, through her blood, to preserve my own youth and beauty. If I could stop aging then I need never fear death again. I stared at my face in the mirror, imagining it being this way forever, as if carved from glittering marble.

Once the book was put away, I wondered if Marianna was also having trouble sleeping. I pulled on a velvet dressing gown and went to visit her in the tower. As I turned down the hallway toward the tower, the sound of a light, familiar voice made me stop in my tracks. I followed the sound to a nearby sitting room, lit golden with dim firelight. Peering inside, I saw Marianna seated before the fire, her face buried in her hands. Konrad sat in a chair beside her.

She lifted her face to him and spoke, waving her hands in agitation. I saw that her cheeks were wet with tears, but her face was vivid, expressive—not the same listless girl I had seen of late. Konrad leaned forward, nodding, his brow creased with concern. This visage was far different from the critical gaze of the artist to which I was subjected every night. He spoke for a moment and I strained to listen, but his voice was not above a whisper. Little could be heard over the crackling of the fire.

Had she been looking for me? I wondered. Had she ventured from the tower to find me but come upon Konrad instead? I watched as he handed her a crumpled linen handkerchief; she used it to dab at her eyes and nose. I wanted to move forward from the shadows, to wrap my arms around her. But somehow I could not move into the warm glow of the room before me. I was not a part of this tableau.

He reached out his hand and gently rested it upon hers. She sat quietly for a moment, looking at his hand. She turned her face up to smile at him, her eyes still brimming with tears.

I had never seen such a smile upon her face before. The sight of it ran through me like a spear.

XXIII

As the count was still away tending to his war, I invited Konrad to dine with Marianna and me after my portrait session the following day. With Rowena's assistance, a table was prepared in a private room adjacent to my bedchamber. I wore a lavender gown with silver lace, as a contrast to the dramatic red velvet that I donned every day for the portrait. Marianna wore her favorite pink lace gown, and I noticed the extra care she took in pinning her shining ringlets away from her face.

Konrad shared with us tales of London, his home. I leaned forward to hear more about Queen Elizabeth, for I had heard great reports of her beauty and power.

"She never intends to marry, no matter what all her eager courtiers think." He leaned forward in a conspiratorial manner. "The day she took the crown, she wed England."

"I think it sounds rather lonely," Marianna commented, her cheeks flushed from the wine.

"I don't see why she would need a husband; she's done a fine job without one trying to take control away from her," I remarked. I watched Konrad carefully as his eyes brushed over Marianna's face.

"It's not a question of needing one, but of wanting one, you know," Konrad said. At these words, Marianna blushed even more deeply.

"I doubt she ever intended to take a husband," I suggested, "seeing what little luck her father had with all of his wives."

"I will have to agree with you there." Konrad smiled, his own eyes sparkling.

"I think it's much wiser for her to rule alone, without a husband to influence her decisions with his own selfish desires."

"I think you and the good queen are cut from the very same cloth."

"But won't England need an heir to the throne?" Marianna asked.

"I'm sure there will be no shortage of takers," Konrad said darkly, swirling the wine in his glass.

The evening passed in delightful conversation. Though I often contributed to the talk, I did so from behind an invisible barrier. My mind was elsewhere, and I already felt strangely separated from the two people seated at the table with me. I kept a careful watch on Marianna's face to gauge her reaction to Konrad's company, trying to detect what secrets she might be hiding.

That night after dinner, I followed Marianna up the steps to the tower, regardless of how the book of spells called to me.

"Konrad is a very nice young man, and very talented," I said carefully. "Have you had a chance to spend any time with him before tonight?"

"Well, yes, I have," she admitted, though warily. "You are not angry with me?"

"Why would I be angry with you?" I asked, trying to hide how neglected I felt. "Why didn't you tell me?"

"I didn't know that you would approve. But he knew that I was all alone up here while you were at your lessons. He says it's a welcome break from his work."

"That is kind of him, though I didn't suspect he would be such interesting company," I said, adjusting my hair in the mirror but keeping a keen eye on Marianna's reflection.

"I thought he was quite entertaining tonight—and so did you, don't deny it."

"He's just rather dry during our sessions together. I had expected more passion in an artist."

"He's hard at work when you're with him," she explained. "He's focusing on the painting."

"You're quick to defend him, aren't you? Is there something you're not telling me?"

"Erzebet, please," she began, but the color in her cheeks betrayed the false calm of her voice. "You have a wild imagination."

"When were you going to tell me about your engagement?"

"But there is no engagement!" she whispered fiercely, though no one could possibly overhear us in the tower. She sighed and began again, more calmly. "He was very kind to me when he heard I could not return home."

"You know that you're better off here—you told me so yourself." I turned from the mirror.

"Erzebet, you know I don't wish to offend you, but I'll never see my parents again." She bent her head over her folded hands. "I wish that you could understand."

"I'm sorry. I didn't mean it in that way, I just wasn't thinking." Perhaps Konrad could do a better job of understanding what she was going through, which made me feel unnecessary. I rarely saw the count and countess, but I considered for a moment how I would feel if I were never to see them again. For the count I felt only relief. But the thought of never seeing the countess again made me pause; it bothered me more than I had expected. I slumped onto the couch beside Marianna, my head resting upon a satin cushion.

"I'm sorry I was harsh, Mari. I'm a bit tired. Posing for the portrait seems to have drained me in some way."

"He is a talented artist—" She blushed again. "I can only imagine what he has created."

"I will show you tonight, when everyone is asleep. But you must promise not to tell him that we peeked. He hasn't agreed to reveal it yet."

Her lips curved into a slow smile.

"You know that I keep all of your secrets," she whispered breathlessly.

Late that night, certain that Konrad had retired to the guest chamber, we slipped quietly down the hallway to the artist's study.

The canvas was draped with a sheet, looking ghostly in the darkness. For a moment I was afraid to look, afraid to find out what this man saw when he looked at me so deeply. Marianna lit a candle and carried it over to the easel. The glass jars of oil paints glimmered slickly in the flickering light.

"Oh, how exciting!" she breathed. "Are you ready to look? Do you think it's nearly done?"

Without a word I pulled the sheet aside. It billowed in the air for a moment and sank to the ground. As though looking into a mirror, I saw a face I recognized well, for I had rehearsed it to great effect: elegant hands folded against the red velvet gown, a defiant posture. There was a hint of the sinister in the arch of the brow and the curve of full red lips. There was also that coldness, that inhuman quality that I had relished the night of the portrait: the power I had felt after slapping that young woman's face. I was a woman etched from ice.

"Oh, it's truly you, Erzebet," Marianna murmured in awe. "It's so perfect; I saw that smile on your face that night." Her voice seemed to falter a bit over the memory.

I broke my gaze from the eyes of the painting and walked away, feigning interest in the scattered sketches littering the nearby table. I could feel the eyes of the painting follow my every move.

Among the sketches on Konrad's table I saw a different face, clearly not mine, rendered softly in gentle strokes of charcoal against vellum. A simple, lovely face crowned with black ringlets, each line added with not only precision but also warmth, an intimacy I found haunting. Marianna burst forth from the paper in my hands in a way that I thought only I had been able to see.

I thrust the drawing under a pile of sketches before she could see it. Without looking, I covered the canvas with the sheet and took her hand.

"We must be going," I said. "We don't want to be seen."

XXIV

Mother's chamber was calm on the morning of my next visit. The countess was confined to her bed, though fully dressed in a gown of black satin and lace. She had a small mirror that she had especially requested, which she held before her face in the dimness, whispering harshly to her reflection for hours on end. I tarried in her chamber for a time as she engaged in this ritual, then sat upon the edge of her bed to interrupt her reverie. She sat up, somehow amused at my intrusion.

"Poor girl, you look heartsick," she said in a mocking-sweet tone. At least she remembered me, I thought, even if she didn't know who I was.

"It's this frost, I suppose," I sighed, unconvincingly. "The summer was bright but brief, and now the cold days have returned."

"Don't bother me with prattle about weather, child," she barked, then smiled again, knowingly. "Tell me what you have on your mind. A young girl's heartache mends the wounds of my old soul." Her murmured laughter was not unkind; I shifted closer to her on the bed.

"I think I feel a bit left behind," I started cautiously. "My friend has found a lover," I went on, my voice low.

"It isn't the count, is it?" she asked.

"No," I whispered, wary of the ears of the servants. "A young man in his employ."

"Oh, I see." She seemed both disappointed and relieved that the count was not implicated in the affair.

"Why so upset?" she asked, a bit teasingly. "You're a pretty young woman. Have you no lover of your own?"

"No, of course not," I said quickly, my cheeks hot with the memory of Sinestra's embrace. "It's just that I never wanted her to marry. I never wanted things to change."

"Was childhood so kind to you that you never desired to become a woman?" she inquired mockingly.

"Why would I want to become a woman, knowing that my age pulls death so much closer to me?" I whispered fervently. I was not sure how she would react to this, but she only laughed.

"Ah, now you understand. Every day pulls death closer to us. We're dying every day of our lives. People find different ways to escape death, or at least they think they do." Her eyes wandered for a moment over to her mirrors. She seemed to be greeting someone there in the glass, but I could only see her own reflection staring back at her.

"Who is this friend of yours, dear?" the countess asked, her eyes narrowed suspiciously.

"She is from Novoe Mesto," I told her. "She is a farmer's daughter."

"Well, then, what did you expect?" She slapped my hand as she spoke. "Why do you think she spends her days here, if not to catch a husband—her thick arms and peasant's breasts stuffed into one of your costly gowns?"

"She is different! We've grown up together."

"Ah, *she* is different," she groaned. "I don't see how you could be so foolish. They're all the same, child. No matter how finely you dress them and parade them about."

"You told me you were from a village. You were not born a countess."

"I was a wealthy merchant's daughter, my dear, not a mere farmer's daughter. That's more than you can say, I'm quite certain."

"I'm your daughter," I blurted, surprised at the tears that sprang to my eyes. A servant nearby gasped, nearly toppled a goblet of wine to the floor.

"Don't tell horrid lies," the countess scolded, giving me a harsh shove. "Lies have the devil in them. Get on with you now." A group of servants began to gather in the doorway, but I held up my hand to prevent their intrusion.

"Can't you listen to what I'm trying to tell you? I'm your daughter. I didn't die. At least, not yet. I know the prophecy, but it hasn't happened yet." I shrugged, desperate for her to believe me. "I'm sixteen years old, and I fear it every day. Isn't there anything more you can tell me, to help me?"

"Why should you be given a warning, whoever you are?" she

spat. "Why should you be warned of death, when the rest of us must muddle through our lives?"

"But I'm your daughter. And I'm not dead."

"I think you're a ghost," Mother told me, her eyes glassy, distant. "I think you're a lying ghost. The mirror thinks so, too."

But the fact was this: she was looking at me differently than she had before, as if she could see me more clearly. Love is immune to madness. I've learned this time and again.

I sat in a fog for the rest of the day. When Rowena entered my chamber that evening to say that the count had returned, I felt a dangerous anger boiling within me. It was his fault: the prophecy, Mother's madness, Marianna banished from her parents' home only to meet the artist—the count was my enemy as much as he was the countess's enemy.

I met him that night in the portrait chamber, surrounded by the different incarnations of my face. He lounged before the fire in an ivory doublet, lavishly embroidered.

"I've heard you've still had little luck in procuring a betrothal for your daughter?" I said, striding into the room and standing before the fire.

"Indeed," he said, surprised by the question, "but it shouldn't be long now. Rudolf is being pressured to take a wife—he must produce an heir as soon as possible, else the throne will fall to his brother, Matthias."

"What is wrong with Matthias?" I asked.

"Too sympathetic to the Protestant cause," he said, wrinkling his nose as though from a foul odor.

"It's interesting that you are still so hopeful that I will be wed, as I have no intention of ever taking a husband."

He turned to me, and his eyes narrowed.

"Do you dare to defy me?" he asked.

"I don't see it as a terribly difficult defiance." I stood before him, silhouetted by the flames behind me. "I'm sure you know I would not hesitate to embarrass you at court—there have already been rumors of witchcraft. It would take little to encourage them to flourish: a pentagram, a dead hen. Rudolf already seems a troubled sort; I think it might be simply too much for him to take."

"You would risk persecution, just to deny my wishes?" He rose slowly from his chair, his eyes not wavering from my face. "You would not dare."

"There is little risk in it for me, I assure you. There are many in our family in higher ranks of power than you, and all would be eager to cover up your humiliation. I think our glorious name will keep me safer than you think."

"I've never heard such rubbish from the throat of a girl-child," he blurted angrily. "Are you some sort of demon?"

"I am as God made me—isn't that what you believe? In fact, I am your seed." I laughed. "I am as you made me."

He leapt forward and struck me across the face with his open palm. I fell back against the mantel, close enough to the fire to feel its heat upon my skin. The slap stung and brought tears to my eyes, but I winced through the pain—even delighted in it, relishing the fear I had managed to conjure in the count. I tossed a wave of my hair over my shoulder and looked up at him.

"You will do as I say, Erzebet," he told me. "Whether you want to or not is not my concern."

"No, I won't," I said. I brought my hand up to my mouth where he had slapped me; my fingers came away from my mouth red with blood. I laughed at the sight of it. "You and I are enemies," I informed him, "and only a coward makes deals with an enemy."

I lunged forward and smeared the blood on my hand onto the

count's satin doublet. I stepped back for just a moment to relish the scene: the count's ivory doublet grotesquely smeared with blood, his face blanched and his eyes frantic.

"You are mad, just like your mother," he spat. "Both of you are mad."

I smiled at him, enjoying his fear. Mother would have been proud of me had she seen the look on the count's pale face. With this pleasant thought in mind, I turned on my heel and stalked from the room.

XXV

In spite of the chill of early autumn, Marianna and I took to the garden for a late-night walk. It was her idea to do so, and she hooked my arm in hers as we had done as children.

"It's a beautiful night," she mused, staring up at the sky. "We always pick the perfect nights to be out here."

"The moon shines just for us, didn't you know?" I squeezed her arm. I was glad to be with her, but dreaded what was to come. Kyzoni appeared from behind a rose hedge, and though he kept his distance, I was comforted by his presence. There was something different about Marianna that night, something wholly jubilant in a way I hadn't seen in a long time.

"I have something important to tell you, Erzebet," she told me. "About Konrad. I want you to be the first to know."

That was all that I needed to hear. I grasped her hand suddenly, desperate to stop her from saying any more. I pulled her faster toward the center of the garden.

"Do you hear that?" I asked her.

"Hear what?"

"The beautiful ladies—they are singing our names."

"Erzebet, I was trying to talk to you." But her words were cut short—I clasped my hands over her wrists and started to spin.

"Hold on tight," I told her.

"Hold on tight," she repeated, her dark mouth forming shadows into words. We spun in a fast circle, spinning ourselves like a magic spell: like the very first spell we cast, together, on our first day in the tower room. Everything spun—roses, sky, moonlight—until the earth was only a blur. Marianna's face was as bright as the moon. I felt as if life was suspended and wished we could somehow exist there, inside that vortex of spinning, untouched by time.

"I can't breathe, Erzebet!" she howled, laughing. "Please, let's stop!"

My fingers clenched upon her arms. I felt the skin break beneath the pressure of my fingernails. Her arms broke from mine suddenly, and we rolled upon the grass. The darkness had never been so silent. We sat on the ground panting, breath hovering in clouds before our faces. She lifted her arm to see what I had done: a line upon her white flesh, blurred with blood.

"I'm sorry, Marianna. I didn't mean to hurt you, I didn't." I moved closer and watched the blood glisten in the moonlight, like a ruby. Unable to stop myself, I reached out to touch the bead of blood. Marianna scowled and turned away.

"You hurt sometimes, Erzebet." She stood and brushed the grass from her gown. "You don't mean to but you do." I lay on the ground at her feet for a moment, feeling too small and weak to move.

"You hurt sometimes, too, Marianna. You're leaving me behind."

"Oh, please don't think of it that way!" She reached out a hand

and pulled me to my feet. "I was hoping you could be happy for me, Erzebet. I want you to approve of my choice. You are family to me."

"I suppose I can't stop you, though I find it a foolish choice."

"Erzebet, I promise that someday you will understand how I feel, when you—"

"I don't suppose I will ever feel as you do." I released my hand from her grip. "I know better than that."

"But Konrad is a kind man, and I feel I know him quite well."

"You know nothing!" I spat. "As soon as your beauty starts to fade, he'll abandon you and find another for his bed."

The fear in her wide eyes quickly sharpened into anger.

"Not all men are like your father," she snapped. We stared at each other for a moment. I waited for her apology, but she said nothing.

"We are different, Erzebet," she began, cautiously, again taking up my hand. "We have always been different. Please understand. All I have ever wanted is a husband, a family of my own, just as my mother had. I know that you want other things. I hope that we may both be happy."

"Have I not made you happy enough?" I said sadly, knowing I had been defeated. She lifted my face with her hand. I could see that she was crying, but there was a smile upon her face.

"Of course you made me happy, and it is true that I owe you my life," she said, "but please do not expect me to offer it to you in gratitude. It is still mine to live. Some things must change, Erzebet." She lifted her shoulders and sighed. "It's the way time works."

I swallowed harshly, but only squeezed her hand in my own. Time was passing, beyond my control. I had to stop it while I still had the chance.

Once Marianna had retired to the tower room, I walked slowly back to my bedchamber, preferring to be alone. A sight at the end of the hallway made me slow my pace. It was night, and moonlight fell in awkward shapes upon the floor, as though twisted through the windows of wrought iron and glass. A young girl stood, half in shadow, but in the moonlight her hair shone the color of new cream. For a moment my breath stilled—she seemed ghostly, otherworldly, this girl. I could see only her pale hair and the graceful movements of her arms in the moonlight, but my memory of her fair face was clear as glass: this was the servant who had inspired my mother's jealous rage.

She was speaking to someone, quietly, someone hidden by shadows. A moment later two hands emerged from the darkness of the hall and clasped a necklace around her neck; the stone suspended from the end looked black against her pale skin. She touched the gem timidly with her fingertips. One hand gently touched her hair, her face. Less gently, a greedy finger traveled slowly down her neck, down the bodice of her gown. In the darkness I dared not move, or breathe.

I recognized that hand, that ruffle of lace at the wrist, the velvet coat from which it protruded. I knew well the ruby ring, like a dark drop of blood upon the count's finger, the finger he used to caress the fair skin of the young peasant girl.

"Anastasia," I whispered to myself, savoring the taste of her name in my mouth. Surely there were other places a young woman could spend her time at such an hour, and the plan became clear to me—like a key turning in a lock I had long sought to open. The child could be claimed as a victim by only one of us: the count or myself.

Then the feeling came to me again: another set of eyes in the darkness, watching me as I watched them. I turned and stared into the dark hallway, expecting to see Sinestra. I even took a step forward, my hand outstretched, searching for him. I found nothing in the darkness, but still felt his eyes upon me as I went to my bedchamber. I reveled in the feeling of being watched, for it meant that I wasn't alone.

I found Anastasia in my bedchamber the next afternoon. In the sunlight her hair had a golden luster, not the silvery shine of the night before. She looked more girl than ghost in that light, humming a wispy tune as she scrubbed the hearth with a dirt-caked brush.

"Anastasia," I startled her with my voice. "This mirror has spots upon it. Have you polished it yet?"

"No, my lady, I haven't yet." She pushed a lock of fine hair behind her ear with a filthy hand. "I'll be sure to do it as soon as I've finished the hearth."

Are they really all the same, I wondered, *these peasant women?* From the corner of my eye I observed her white neck in the sunlight, the bare expanse of flawless flesh. I thought again of the blood of that young servant upon my face, the night of my first portrait session. The memory of how clear and white my skin had appeared came to me again as I stood before the mirror and touched my chin and cheek.

"You're a pretty girl, Anastasia. Do you hope to be married when you leave this castle?"

"If my work pleases you, my lady," she said awkwardly, "yes, that is what I hope."

"What your father hopes as well, I'm sure."

"Yes," she said, smiling thoughtfully as she turned back to her scrubbing. "Miss Marianna's father must be quite pleased with her match."

"What was that?" Turned to the hearth, she did not detect the coldness of my voice.

"The daughter of a farmer marrying a successful artist, who has traveled the world. That's a good marriage for Marianna," she explained. "She would never have made such a match in the village."

I grasped the child by her hair and nearly lifted her from the floor. Her dirty slippers struck out against my satin gown as she turned her watery eyes to mine in fear.

"Do not talk of her in such a way, do you hear me?" As the girl struggled, I realized the absurdity of my anger and let her go. She was only a peasant, a foolish one at that. She sniffed and wiped her nose on her arm, pathetic. Another surge of anger welled within me, but I pressed it down with a calm voice.

"I'm sorry to startle you," I told her, "but I don't enjoy foolish prattle, even from young girls." I looked carefully at her face. She was maybe fourteen, two years younger than I. Young enough, perhaps, that her monthly blood had yet to begin.

"But there is something you can do for me."

"Yes, my lady, anything, of course," she said, sniffing.

"I need your assistance in the tower room tonight, at midnight." Since Marianna's engagement to Konrad had been made public, she had been freed from her tower imprisonment. Finally I was glad of this, for now I could claim the tower as my own sanctuary.

"Here is the key." I handed her the slender silver key, which she took dutifully. "I generally allow no servants of any kind in the tower, do you understand? I need a diligent young girl to tidy, and I think you will do nicely. But tell no one—you can do your work in secret, at midnight tonight."

"Midnight." Her pale eyes roamed around the room nervously. Was there a secret tryst already planned? I could only hope to thwart my father's passion in order to indulge my own.

"I will be there," she said resolutely. Of course, she had no other choice.

Every night at midnight for the following month, Anastasia came to tidy the tower room, and every night I was there waiting for her. She became accustomed to her work in the tower, sweeping the flagstone floor, beating the dust from the tapestries, and dusting and arranging the many bottles of perfume and cosmetics upon my dressing table. I often noted how she examined each bottle before setting it down. She also enjoyed the sight of her own reflection in the glass, and I never saw her without the sapphire necklace the count had bestowed on her. From the corner of my eye I saw her admiring the look of the dark stone against her pale neck, then nestling it carefully into the bodice of her gown.

I was pleased that she had become comfortable in my presence, but was abashed that I was not quite as comfortable in hers. I decided to delay any blood experiment until we had achieved a relaxed, trusting relationship. As the days and weeks progressed, Anastasia thrived in her work, even hummed cheerfully in my presence. The count left on another of his journeys, so I knew that my usurping of the girl's time would be challenged by no one. Every day I practiced the steps involved in the bleeding, then hid the necessary supplies beneath my dressing table. And every night, as Anastasia bustled about, dusting and sweeping, I sat at that dressing table staring at my own reflection, losing my resolve.

This would have been an opportune moment for the stranger to arrive and encourage me in my mission, but he did not. I read the passage about blood in Leviticus on a daily basis, and though my desire to protect myself from aging and death did not diminish, I struggled to find the strength to actually do it—to take the blood of another person for my own devices.

Marianna's ties to Konrad kept her safer from the count's judgment than my friendship ever could, and she was installed in guest quarters in the same wing as his. I insisted that they marry in the small chapel in Castle Bizecka. In preparation for the wedding ceremony, I had Ermengarde create a wedding gown especially for the bride. Marianna chose to use white lace for the gown, which she loved for its pure, angelic properties. The final fitting took place in my bedchamber.

"I thank you so much for this, Erzebet," Marianna sighed, and gazed into the mirror as Ermengarde bustled around her with pins.

"Well, let me see it—turn to me."

"Wait just a moment! It has to be perfect first. You know I had never expected you to buy me a dress. I had planned on wearing my pink one."

"The bride deserves a new dress for her wedding day. Now turn and let me see."

She did turn, and I held my breath at the sight of her. She really did look like an angel, standing upon a footstool, the hem of the gown still lined with pins. Her curls were glossy in the firelight and cascaded past her shoulders. The gown itself was pure white and simply sparkling, fitting snugly to all of her curves. Marianna and I had always harbored a secret rivalry between us; I dared to guess that the jealousy was not solely my own. But never before had I been consumed with such jealousy for my friend. She appeared as never before, as perfectly beautiful and perfectly happy. It was more than just the dress, I realized, it was the glow of a young woman in love looking forward to what life had to offer her, not hindered by fear. I wondered, distractedly, if such a glow of happiness could be bled from a girl.

Could happiness be bled from a girl? The moment the thought rushed to my head I became light-headed and too warm, perspiration collecting on my upper lip.

"You look beautiful, Marianna. Absolutely perfect," I told her, and smiled. I needed to escape; I didn't want her to see me like this. I feared my desperate thoughts were visible on my face, and it made me feel panicked and weak.

Late that night, I sat before the dressing-table mirror in the tower chamber, Leviticus open in front of me. I stared at my reflection: if the mysterious stranger would not come to me, I would evoke his presence here myself.

You are more powerful than you think, I told my reflection. *The choice is yours.*

I watched Anastasia moving in the background of my reflection. And so it would happen, I decided: the night before Marianna's wedding would be the night of the first bleeding. I challenged myself to this in the mirror, committing myself to the act.

In the eyes reflected back to me, I saw a familiar power. I saw the red mouth curving into a smile.

XXVI

The night before Marianna's wedding was bitterly cold; winter sank deep into the frozen earth. A light snow had fallen upon the town, like a sheer cloud. The trees were crystalline with frost, the river sheer black with a layer of ice. And something burned cold inside of me: fear had crystallized into an icy flame. I had made my decision, and did not intend to fail.

I had studied the art of bleeding in countless medical texts and felt confident that I could execute the task with as little mess as possible. I even practiced once, on my own arm, and took notes regarding the size and depth of the wound, the amount of pressure required when wielding the blade, and how long to let the bleeding continue. Things were slipping away from me, and quickly: I was soon to be seventeen years old, in the height of the youthful bloom of womanhood, but I was certain that bloom would not remain for long. I looked into the mirror and touched my face—my fingers recoiled, as though my skin burned them.

I watched Anastasia carefully that night as I sat quietly before the fire, trying to calm my breath. It was important that she not notice any difference—there had been many nights that she came here to clean for me, and this night was no different from any other. I saw her hover over my dressing table and touch a gold comb encrusted with pearls with delicate, wary fingertips.

"Pretty, isn't it?" I asked her. She pulled her hand away, startled.

"Do not be afraid." I smiled. "Sit down."

She sat stiffly before the dressing table, and I swept up her golden locks and secured the teeth of the comb close to her scalp. Her eyes moistened, but she did not flinch. This girl already understood the marriage of beauty and pain.

"You look like a princess," I murmured in her ear, glancing only briefly at the sapphire glinting from its hiding place in the bodice of her gown. She devoured her own reflection, the metallic comb reflecting the warm candlelight onto her glowing face. I smiled at her reflection in the glass, and she basked in the warmth of my praise. I held her left hand in my own—my own hands were clammy, trembling slightly. I watched her face to make sure she didn't notice, too distracted by her own reflection to sense my fear.

"I feel that I can trust you, Anastasia," I told her. I pulled a chair close to hers at the dressing table. Without slackening my grip upon her hand or breaking our gaze in the glass, I reached down and grasped the wooden bowl I had hidden beneath the table. I rested the bowl upon my lap. "I feel that we are more alike than you realize," I said, gently brushing my finger across the delicate skin of her wrist, the web of pale blue veins.

"Really?" she asked me, and her eyes fluttered bashfully. "You've been so kind to me, my lady."

"I like being kind to you," I told her. "You've helped me feel a bit less lonely these last few weeks."

"Why do you feel lonely?" she asked. "Is it because your friend is getting married?"

"You're right—see, you do know me." I smiled at her reflection in the glass. I reached beneath the layers of my skirt for the cold, hard handle of the blade.

"I'm always happy to help you, my lady. You've been a kind mistress to me."

"I'm happy to hear you say that," I told her.

She smiled at my reflection in the mirror, then looked back at her own. She was concentrating too hard on her own reflection to see me lift the knife.

I had little time to think, only to act: one delicate slash across the thin skin of her wrist would do, I knew. But concealment was vital. I pulled up the sleeve of her gown and pressed the point of the blade just below the wrist, then sliced quickly across her flesh. It was more difficult than I had expected, for my hands were shaking, and the line I cut was crooked. For a moment it seemed that nothing would happen, that perhaps I hadn't cut deep enough. Then the blood welled up all along the slice. The blood looked red-black in the candlelight, startlingly vivid against the whiteness of her flesh.

We both gasped at the intoxicating sight of it, and for a moment we just watched her arm bleed, the dark red tracks of it running off the sides. I gasped with delight at how easy this was, the precious blood welling out of the wound and running into the bowl below. I wondered if Anastasia was also taken aback at the beautiful sight of the blood. I had never felt so much power at my fingertips. It made me feel light and warm at the same time, my fingers tingling as I held her arm steady over the bowl.

She gasped and tried to stand, but my grasp upon her arm was firm. I turned her arm upside down so that the sliced area was facing the bowl below.

"I'm sorry, my dear, I didn't mean to startle you," I said, nearly laughing, still a bit nervous. "I thought this was the easiest way. I didn't want you to be frightened."

"What are you doing?" she asked, breathless. I smiled at her reflection again, measuring my expression carefully—I had rehearsed every moment, alone, before the glass.

"Just a little bleeding," I explained lightly. "Haven't you ever been bled by a doctor before?"

"I suppose," she murmured, watching her blood form a small, glistening pool in the shallow center of the bowl.

"You told me I had given you so much; I was hoping that I could take just a little bit more from you in return."

"But why my blood? What will you do with it?" Tears began to well in the corners of her eyes.

"Hush, dear. There's nothing for you to worry about," I told her, smiling gently at her reflection. I lifted my other hand and placed it on her shoulder. She flinched from my touch.

"Just breathe," I told her. "This is a great gift that you are giving me. I hope that I can give a gift to you in return. Bleeding rids the body of bad humors, did you know that?"

"Yes, I have heard that," she said, sniffing, her eyes trained on mine in the glass.

"I'm letting you in on a great secret, my dear. How do you think all those noble ladies stay so fashionably thin and pale?"

"Bleedings?" She was suddenly motionless.

"Of course." I nodded. "I won't take very much, but you will feel light as air when I'm done. You will feel—new." I smiled at her reflection, and she smiled back. Vanity was a powerful weapon; I already knew this to be true.

I looked down at her arm, still suspended over the bowl in my lap. The bowl had filled considerably. It was imperative that I move quickly: I wrapped a length of gauze around her arm and tied it taut. I put the bowl on a nearby table out of her eyesight and turned from the glass to look directly at her.

"This is our secret, Anastasia. I'm asking you to hold this secret of mine inside of you—can you do that for me?"

"Of course I will, my lady." I could see myself reflected in the flat pools of her eyes.

"You will be my personal handmaiden, and you may keep the comb as a gift, from me to you. That, too, will be our secret." I folded her arm close to her body and helped her up from her chair.

"It looks very pretty on you, Anastasia," I said admiringly. "And don't worry, I think we may find a proper match for you."

She lifted her other arm and touched the comb with her fingertips.

"Thank you," she breathed, then turned and left the chamber.

XXVII

Day twelve, night

The ghosts in this chamber play tricks on me. First emerging from the dimness of the mirror, one by one they climb out of the glass and crawl along the walls. Anastasia is the most mischievous; she smiles at me, white teeth gleaming in the dark like fangs. She steals my gloves when I'm not looking: my ruby ring, my string of pearls. I seem to be always in search of some lost treasure, and that is when I hear her voice, from inside the mirror again. Her laughter shivers like icy water down my spine.

It's certainly too cold here to undress. I pull a velvet robe over my shoulders for warmth, slip my hands into the once-missing gloves. Other eyes glimmer in the darkness.

"Sinestra?" I ask, my voice desperate. The glimmering vanishes and I'm surrounded only by flickering candles. Where is he when I need him most? The mirror turns from dark to golden and I can't resist the face reflected there.

Marianna's face is cast in vivid, warm colors over my vague outline. The sight of her face makes my heart feel like cracking open; I have to hold my hands to my chest and remind myself to breathe. Her cheeks flush red at the sight of me, her brows furrow over wide, glittering eyes.

How could you do such a thing? *Marianna asks me again. She looks too angry to cry.*

I told you, Mari, that I must start at the beginning to confess.

This is where it all began. I assure you it was not as hideous as you might think.

As soon as I had dismissed Anastasia I sat at this wooden table where we so often concocted our magical potions. The candles glimmered darkly in the shallow pool of blood in the bowl before me. I knew there was no chance for hesitation, lest the liquid cool and congeal, drying black at the edges of the bowl.

I leaned my face forward, suspended over the bowl, and tentatively dipped my fingers into the blood. Thankfully it was still warm. I began to bring it up to my face with my fingertips, as though covering my face with paint, or a new cosmetic. At first the odor made me pause, but I urged myself forward. The blood felt warm and soothing on my skin. Of all the poisons and paints that women use to coat their faces, what could be more natural than the source of human life, the most basic element of our human selves? I slowly grew accustomed to the musty, metallic scent; women have grown accustomed to strange things in the quest for beauty. But this felt pure to me, like entering the womb again.

You shrink from this, Mari, but remember that blood has always been the first sacrifice: the blood of a goat, the blood of a virgin, the blood of a son. The Bible I write these words in now admits that this is true. On the day of your wedding, as you knelt in your white lace gown in the stained-glass sunlight of the chapel, Father Pugrue handed you a goblet of wine with which to sanctify your marriage vow. Each time you sipped that wine, you drank the blood of Christ. When the wafer was placed over your tongue, you consumed the flesh of Christ.

This was my own sacrifice: the pure blood of a beautiful virgin, given, if hesitantly, still willingly. We all have our own religion, Marianna. All I wanted was to be beautiful, and deathless. Beauty is, after all, a physical manifestation of the divine. I would be somehow more than human, living on earth but knowing the secrets of the angels. In this chamber I found my sanctuary: bathing my face in the sacred blood of life.

I had a basin of warm water nearby, to rinse my face as soon as the blood had lost its natural warmth. The water was a fresh contrast to the blood upon my skin. I washed carefully with a soft wet cloth, making sure to clean my hairline and down my neck. Once clean, I wiped my face with a dry cloth. When I stood and looked in the mirror, I looked renewed. Reborn.

I stood the next day in the castle chapel, my beautiful chapel nearly garish in its effusion of ecstatic angels. I watched you commit to your wedding vows. I stood as still and as beautiful as the sculpture of the goddess Athena, upon whose perfection only priests are allowed to gaze. I watched as you closed your eyes and savored the taste of the sacrament, heavy upon your tongue, and I smiled. Sacraments keep us all safe, Marianna: God's sacrifice of blood will protect you. A sacrifice of blood will protect me as well.

You were not as innocent as you thought.

XXVIII

Because of the toll that war with the Turks had taken upon the ravaged countryside, I insisted that Marianna and Konrad be installed safely in a guest wing of the castle until the danger had diminished. Though they offered polite protestations, they were relieved to have a safe place in which to wait out the war. Not long after their wedding day, Konrad visited me in my sitting room.

"I hope I'm not bothering you," he said, with his characteristic awkwardness.

"Not at all," I told him. "I trust that you and your new bride are feeling well?" I smiled over the words, though the smile made my cheeks ache.

"We are well," he said, bowing his head. "I wanted to thank you again for offering us rooms here in the castle. It's true that life in the countryside is still uncertain."

"Is not life in the countryside always uncertain?" I asked him, still a petulant child.

"I suppose you're right, accustomed as you are to life in this castle," Konrad answered, "but there is much about the village and the riverside that Marianna and I miss dearly. I was born in a village much like this one, after all."

I did not acknowledge his musings, but gazed calmly into the fire. I did not want to hear about my Marianna desiring to leave, much less to live in some poor peasant village by the filthy Vah River.

"There is something else for which I feel I must thank you," Konrad began again, cautiously. "It seems that I have taken from you something which you highly treasure," he said, the color rising in his cheeks. I turned from the fire and looked at him directly. His eyes seemed liquid black and warm as the fire that crackled beside me.

"I assure you that I will treat her well," he said, "always."

"Thank you, Konrad," I uttered, again smiling and extending my hand, which he kissed, though quickly. "I know that she shall do the same for you."

Despite my yearnings to visit Marianna after her wedding day, I was wary. I could only imagine how the vows of marriage and, even more, the wedding night could have altered my young friend. But there was more than simply the wedding that had taken place. While Marianna had undergone her transformation from young woman to bride to wife, I had undergone a change of my own.

Each night, Anastasia and I spent time in the tower chamber, alone. Each secret bathing in her blood temporarily rejuvenated me, and my reflection in this oval mirror on those nights seemed to offer evidence that my experiments were taking effect. My skin did appear more clear and even-toned; my cheeks even seemed softer and firmer beneath the gentle press of my fingertip.

The entire ritual was a heady experience for me: wielding the blade, watching the blood pool, then wrapping the wound in cotton once I had taken just enough, infused me with a new power. Not only could I expect a young woman to care for me, serve me, and cater to my every whim, but I also proved that I had the authority to take the essential ingredient of life itself. Blood is sacred, and I treated these rituals with the quiet respect they deserved. As I began to crave the feeling of the blood upon my skin, the bleedings became more frequent. Anastasia was increasingly obedient and compliant to all of my demands in the tower, certain that if her blood was extracted a handsome reward would be paid in return.

I worried, at first, of any relationship she might have engaged in with the count. It was the blood of a virgin I desired, just as I had learned from the Bible—a virgin girl-child is the most valuable sacrifice, her blood the most pure. I had to make sure Anastasia would be unavailable if the count were to return, so I made her my most devoted servant. Her presence was required every evening in the tower, and often during the day as well. Anastasia was simple and greedy enough to be more than willing to enter into this arrangement.

One evening I pulled a string of delicate pearls from a carved wooden box. I held them over a candle for a moment, enjoying the way the golden light reflected off each pearl. Anastasia was vigorously polishing the flagstone floor and did not see the gift.

"This will surely draw attention to the delicacy of your neck," I told her, for I knew she loved to hear such things. Slowly standing, she abandoned her rag upon the floor and stood before me, lifted her hair so that I might fasten the strand around her neck. She spun and stood before the mirror.

The bleedings had transformed Anastasia: her high color had paled and her cheeks and limbs turned thin, a style quite popular among aristocratic ladies who viewed eating as crude, unladylike behavior. Her eyes were pale and glassy, like twin mirrors I could see myself reflected in.

"They are lovely," she uttered, swallowing; the harsh movement of her throat made the pearls jump. I was certain I was assimilating her former youthful, vigorous beauty by bathing my face in her blood, sometimes adding a drop of blood to my wine to savor the salty taste. Though I found myself shuddering at the sight of her now-drawn face, Anastasia only smiled, clearly pleased with her reflection.

We sat across from each other at the table, her right arm poised over the bowl. I had already marked her left arm with cobwebs of thin scars, always careful to choose areas easily hidden by a sleeve. The slice of my blade had become deft with practice.

"These marks will disappear completely before your wedding night, I assure you," I told her, tracing my fingertips over the abandoned paths of the blade. She giggled, almost soundlessly, then gasped as the knife cut into new flesh.

"Do you not think of such things?" I asked, holding her arm steady over the bowl; this cut was in the soft, unscarred flesh just above her elbow. "Of course you do. You're a young woman—it's natural to think of such things."

Her pale cheeks blushed suddenly, her eyes turned down.

"I'm afraid there is something I must ask you, my lady," she asked, eyes focused on her bent white arm. "I will not be able to help you tomorrow night. The cook has asked me to assist her in the kitchen, very late. She needs my help, and I was hoping you would understand."

"I see," I murmured.

"It's not that I don't like working for you, in your secret chamber. I'm very grateful for all you have given me. But when I am needed elsewhere, it's difficult to keep it secret."

"Certainly you can keep my secrets," I assured her. "It is your duty as my servant to do so, don't you agree?"

"Well, yes, of course," she uttered. "I understand if you need me here."

"I will tell you another secret of mine. About the blood." We watched it slowly pool in the bowl between us. "It's pure blood that I need—the blood from a pure young girl, a virgin. Do you understand?" I asked her, but she said nothing.

"If you are spoiled, I will have to find someone else," I told her. Her gaze was still vacant. I seized her bleeding arm with sudden force.

"Would you tell me?" I asked her. "Would you confess your sins to me? Or would you lie, for the sake of a string of pearls and a silver comb?"

"No, I wouldn't lie to you, I wouldn't!" Her glassy eyes turned up to mine in fear. She shivered so drastically I had to renew my grip upon her arm. I watched as the fresh blood stained my fingertips.

"Would you lie to me and take my gifts, like a dirty whore?"

"No, I wouldn't! I wouldn't!"

I released her suddenly and she sat crouched before me, pitiful, her body racked by deep, wrenching sobs. Her blue eyes looked like melting ice. I thought of my mother for a moment and wished that she could see this girl whose beauty had once enraged her with jealousy. I wished she could see her for the pitiful, greedy creature she was. I watched for a moment, relishing the disgust I felt for her.

"You may leave," I told her, and stood from the table.

XXIX

I did visit Marianna finally, though wary not only of how she might have changed but worried that she might detect some difference in me as well: the warning fingerprint of God upon my flesh, for all to see. I strained my eyes before the mirror, willing myself to perceive such a difference. I could see nothing beyond the smoothness of my clear, young skin.

She greeted me in the doorway with a familiar warmth and excitement, but something in the way she gazed into my eyes made me flinch. She greeted me as a vision, I was sure, a part of a life she had left behind. She was a wife now, and her new relationship with her husband was paramount to her friendship with me.

In spite of these changes, we took up our familiar pastimes: chatting by the fire over steaming cups of tea in her quarters and taking long walks in the rose garden in spite of the weather. She had no interest in visiting the tower room, as she had spent more than enough time there during her concealment. I was glad of this; since the bleedings had begun, the tower had become a private, sacred place for me.

Marianna and I were most natural with each other when Konrad was sequestered in his study, busy with a new painting. Though I was curious to ask Marianna about the physical and emotional life of a wife, I suppressed all of my questions. I did not feel ready to admit my curiosity, so devoted was I to the notion of my own unending childhood and the importance of my physical purity. I was not willing to be spoiled by any man—through marriage or otherwise. I had read tales of ancient Greek goddesses whose suppressed sexuality imbued them with magical powers. Virginity was one ingredient of eternal youth—one I was not yet willing to part with, despite my curiosity.

Marianna, Konrad, and I dined every night in the parlor I had arranged beside my bedchamber. We celebrated the new year together with full glasses of sweet wine.

"We had better toast," I cautioned them. "We do not know how many years we will have left."

"That's awfully dreary talk for such an occasion, Erzebet," Marianna scolded.

"Oh, but it's true." Konrad smiled. "They've predicted that the world will end, just as the year turns 1600."

"What a perfect excuse for revelry that will be," I suggested, pouring more wine into each of our glasses.

"You are quite right. We should enjoy our more sedate celebration while we still can." Konrad smiled again, his eyes twinkling at Marianna in the candlelight.

"You're quite terrible, both of you," she said. "All this talk of the world ending."

As she lifted her glass, I saw her unconsciously rest the palm of her hand against the bodice of her gown in a strange, protective gesture. The realization hit me with undeniable force: Marianna was with child.

The room began spinning suddenly, my skin too warm beneath my ornate velvet gown. I stood abruptly from the table and walked over to the fire with my wine.

"Marianna is quite right, Konrad," I said, trying to keep my voice steady between gulps of wine. "This is no way to talk on such a night as this."

I stood and stared into the fire for a moment, the flames licking hungrily at the stones of the hearth. I kept imagining that I could see Sinestra's face there, trying to urge him into being with my mind. But the longer I looked into the fire, the more my eyes stung and watered. Marianna and Konrad were sitting close to each other at the table, and he was whispering something in her ear.

Why must he feel so far away from me, I wondered, *just when I need him most?*

As that winter transformed into spring, the change that had taken place in my Mari was undeniable. The sight of her filled me with regret and fear.

"Forgive me for not rising to greet you, Erzebet," she sighed as I entered her chambers. "I'm afraid I'm simply too tired."

"Apologies are not necessary, my dear." I kissed her hand warmly and smiled, but the change that was now clear separated me even more completely from my closest companion. Her once-graceful curves were utterly misshapen beneath the formless dress she was wearing. This newfound girth was not only unsightly to me, but also awkward and tiring for her to carry. Though the rest of her seemed full and fat, her face appeared drawn and pale, with bruise-colored circles beneath her sleepless eyes. The baby within was taking over Marianna's body, like a disease, draining her of beauty and of life. Her face reminded me, in fact, of Anastasia's, but I did not think long on it.

"You look simply striking, Erzebet. You make me feel like a regular country dumpling. That is, even more so than usual."

"You're looking very well, dear. Don't say such things about yourself."

"I know, Konrad says the same."

A shadow must have passed briefly over my eyes, for she did not mention him again.

"I assure you that I don't feel as terrible as I look," she exclaimed, squeezing my hand. "Just weary and more than a bit anxious. But I've been told it's perfectly natural to feel this way." She patted her round belly thoughtfully.

Even while I saw her in her ruined state, the memory of Marianna in her wedding dress burned like a flame in my memory, along with the envy it had ignited. I wondered: Had I ever managed to inspire such envy in her?

"Here." I offered her a gleaming amber vial. "This may help you rest. Nothing more than a few herbs, of course."

"I see that you're still hard at work in the tower, mixing your concoctions. Has Pugrue ever given you any trouble?"

"Pugrue is far too comfortable in his quarters to give me much trouble. I don't worry about him." I did not feel like talking about Pugrue's old reprimand. I eased into a high-backed chair as Marianna meditated on the smooth vial in her hand.

"You will be careful with your spells, won't you? I know you think me foolish, but it could be dangerous. There are those eager to blame someone else for their own suffering. And because of the Turks, there will be much suffering yet."

"What did we ever do that could have caused any danger?" I asked, trying not to think of the bloodstained bowl in the tower room—only in Marianna's presence did an uncomfortable guilt surge within me. "Besides, this one is just a gift, for you," I assured her.

"I know, dear, I just . . . I've heard things," she murmured, color rising to her cheeks. "Some people are very afraid of such things, they think it evil work—no matter how innocently you mean it."

"Oh, dear!" I crowed playfully. "Are you talking about witchcraft? Magic? You've been listening to the tales of too many foolish servants."

Her eyes fell to her hands, folded in her lap.

"Would you care for some tea, Erzebet?" she asked, without looking up.

"Of course, but you stay seated, I'll get it for you." I touched her tenderly on the shoulder and she lifted her eyes to mine.

"You're too kind to me. You always have been." She sighed and smiled. I turned and hurried into the hallway to request the help of a servant.

"I will be glad when this is all over," she told me as we sipped our tea in privacy. "It's not just that I feel I can tell you, but I think that you know it already. From the way you look at me in this state, I doubt that you will ever choose my path in life."

"The count is entertaining notions of a new betrothal, last I've heard, though he has yet to inform me of any decisions on my behalf." I sighed dreamily. "I simply don't think I was meant for it, though. I think if I do have a husband, he shall have a very terrible time with me."

Marianna laughed, her eyes sparkling.

"I've simply always wanted a child of my own. I suppose you think me silly, but it's true." She settled the teacup carefully upon the table and peered into my eyes. "I thank you for all you've done for me, Erzebet," but her smile weakened over the words. "I'm sorry if I've disappointed you."

"No, don't say such things," I told her. I sat beside her on the couch and smoothed my hand over her soft hair. "No matter what happens, we are deeply connected, you and I. We are like sisters."

"Of course," she told me, and rested her head upon my shoulder, as if we were children again, napping side by side before the fire. "We have always been sisters," she murmured.

Everyone and everything is changing," I told my mother, who was still confined to her bed, "just as you told me it would." I assumed that she had either forgotten or ignored our last interaction, when I had tried to convince her that I was her daughter. She probably assumed that I was crazy.

"I am a harbinger of ill tidings, my dear," she murmured with a low laugh.

Her eyes gleamed at me with an unnatural shine, and she did not blink. They shone like moonlight through the thick fog of incense filling the room.

"There is something different about you, child," she told me, and I felt at once admired and accused. "It makes me tired to look at you. You've been listening to too many mirrors. Am I right? What do they tell you?"

"They tell me nothing, Countess."

"Hmm, you lie. You are getting very good at lying. But I can always tell." She shut her eyes and sighed. I sat beside her and held her hand in mine, the thin flesh of her hand purple-white in its paleness. The countess, it seemed, was dying. Indeed, she had been dying for years.

I wanted to lie back upon that bed beside her and whisper to her what I had discovered about beauty and blood. Had she noticed the change in me, the new freshness of my face, the new power gleaming from my eyes? I rested my head upon her shoulder and spoke close to her ear.

"What price would you pay," I asked her, "for eternal youth and beauty?"

Her eyes opened suddenly, pale and unfocused. "They are the same," she announced. "Who would choose eternal life without beauty?"

"What would you pay," I continued quietly, "to God or the devil, for immortality?"

"Only the devil would make such an offer," she said harshly. "God would never be so generous."

I sat up suddenly, my skin prickling at the sound of her words.

"I am in league with no devil," I blurted out, then lowered my voice, wary of who might overhear.

"You are in league with whoever makes such an offer," she said, gripping my arm. Suddenly her eyes turned wide, her breath coming in short gasps. Her grip upon my arm tightened. I imagined that she was looking into death, as if it were a mirror, and she was somehow enraptured with what she saw.

"Tell me!" I urged, before the servants could hear. "What do you see?"

"I see—you—" she uttered, then was overcome by hysterical laughter. Her eyes, still unblinking, flowed with tears.

I sat numb with shock as the servants tended to her with wine and damp cloths. In time, her breathing became more regular and her eyes shut as she rested. Though her grip did not lessen from my arm, she did not speak to me again that night. I pursed my lips and held her hand in silence.

XXX

That night I walked the rose garden paths alone, to visit in solitude the marble Athenus, the object of my childhood longings. I still fantasized about him in my early womanhood, it's true—the dreams of a child are the most indelible of dreams. Despite my distrust of men and marriage, I was still curious about men and their passion. Here was the one man I could trust: dear Athenus, with his long narrow nose and full lips, the cluster of curls upon his head cool in the warm summer air.

Standing upon the pedestal beside him, I rested my cheek upon his cold shoulder, as if we were perfect dancing partners. My fingers trailed along his sinewy arm until I reached his outstretched hand. I noticed one finger on his hand was missing and the marble exposed by the missing digit was as clean as new snow. This is where his soul broke free, I mused. Perhaps Athenus had been a real man once, then turned to stone. I dreamed for a while that he would turn real again, and his arms would wrap around me in a safe embrace.

In the midst of dreaming, my eyes snapped opened. Had I heard something rustling in the rose hedge? My ears strained in the silence, but heard nothing. Still the feeling was unmistakable, for I had felt it many times: in the hallways, in the chapel, in my bed at night. Always, constantly, I felt that I was watched. Generally I enjoyed Sinestra's attentions, but this time I bristled from the seeming intrusion; I had called for him when I felt most alone, and he had not answered me. It seemed I had no choice but to be patient with his whims. I jumped down from the pedestal and landed heavily on the thick, dewy grass.

"Am I interrupting you," he teased, appearing from a rose hedge, "alone with your first love?" I could see only a slice of his face in the moonlight, his teeth gleaming in the dark.

"Kyzoni," he called suddenly, and the wolf rushed to his side. I looked on in awe as the wolf permitted him to scratch his snowy-white chest, the thick fur at his neck—even his soft white ears and the top of his head, which he still growled at me for attempting to touch. Though I suppose I shouldn't have been surprised; Kyzoni was his gift to me, after all.

"You've done well," he told me, still lavishing attention on the wolf. finally he looked up to meet my eyes. "I can tell just by looking at you. The treatments have taken effect."

"Do you think that it will work?" I asked eagerly.

"Do you believe that it will?"

I sighed, frustrated with his response. I wanted a straight answer: Would the blood preserve my youth and beauty and save me from an early death?

"I've been thinking more about that prophecy." He stood and moved closer, Kyzoni following at his heels. "What about it do you fear, exactly?"

"Why shouldn't I fear it?" I asked, pulling my cloak about me. "Wouldn't you?"

"But what, specifically?" he said, grasping my cold hand in his. "Tell me how you felt when you first read it."

"I felt like . . . my life was done." The words surprised me as I said them aloud. "God had decided my path in life, and it would be a short one. There was nothing I could do to change it."

"Feeling that you're not in control of your life," he said meditatively. "You know that there are ways to break free." He squeezed my hand for emphasis.

"How do I do it?" I asked, my voice louder than I expected.

"Choose your own path, don't let fate decide for you," he said simply, as if it were an obvious answer.

"Choose my path—how?"

Clouds rolled in across the bright white moon, blotted the stars from view. I moved closer instinctively.

"God has made all things in this world," he mused. "But do you think we never surprise Him? Do you think we never act in a way He hadn't intended? Free will is your power, remember that."

A cool, moist wind lifted his cloak and fluttered it around both of us, like the flapping of wings.

"The blood of one is not enough," he said, his eyes dark and serious. "You'll need another soon."

He released my hand, and with a snap of his cloak seemed to disappear into the night. Kyzoni whimpered, pawing the ground impatiently. I suddenly felt how dark and silent the garden had become, as though it was only moments before a sudden storm. The rose vines trailed on the ground like twisted hands. I pulled my cloak closed and ran.

Walking the castle halls late that night, I was wary of shadows, and anxious about what I might find in them. There were voices in the darkness, a low cooing sound that seemed to echo in the vast quiet. I walked past the dining hall, into a sitting room where the servants sat and spun wool into thread by a roaring fire. The door to this chamber was open. For a moment I watched the scene within from a distance.

Rowena was there, seated upon the couch beside Anastasia, who was bent listlessly over a cup of tea. Rowena rubbed the girl's narrow shoulders, nearly upsetting the teacup. She urged her to eat a piece of bread, but the girl refused. The thin arms that protruded from her dress were no more than skin and bone.

"Is something wrong?" I asked, entering the room and removing my light cloak. The fire made the room exceedingly warm, but I could easily detect a shiver in Anastasia's narrow limbs.

"I've been trying to get her to eat something," Rowena told me. "Can you see? She's worn through."

Anastasia sipped her tea and did not look at me. I felt a strange twinge of envy at watching her be coddled by Rowena.

"Child," I asked her, "are you quite well?"

"Of course, my lady," she uttered.

"I think we can all see that's not true." Rowena tutted, unfolding a fur blanket and draping it over the girl's shoulders. As Anastasia set her teacup upon the table before her, the slack sleeve of her blouse pulled up to reveal her pale, thin arm. Rowena grabbed the arm before it could disappear beneath the blanket.

"What's this?" she asked, holding the bone-thin arm close to her face in the light of the fire. "Erzebet, do you see this?"

The weaving woman looked up from her loom, her brows furrowed. Ermengarde sighed heavily and set down her mending to look. Thin, pale scars were visible, like a white spiderweb printed against her pale flesh. Anastasia's eyes flashed at mine for a moment, her gaze reeling helplessly.

"What happened to you, child? What did this to you?" Rowena asked, breathless.

"No, nothing. I don't know what it is," she stammered.

"What's the meaning of this?" Rowena demanded, her face red with indignation.

"I think we should all stay calm here, for Anastasia's sake." I moved closer and rested my hand upon her shoulder. "Don't you agree?"

"Thank you, my lady," Anastasia muttered. Lightly I rested my hand upon her shining hair.

"See that she sleeps well tonight, Rowena. And be sure that she eats tomorrow morning." I smiled at Rowena reassuringly.

I turned from the room and made my way to the tower, my fists clenched. Now that they had seen her scars, could I keep my bleedings secret? Pacing the tower chamber in anger, I realized what had become of me: I had begun to crave the blood, like a monster in the folklore of peasants.

I looked in the mirror at my face, my smooth, unblemished skin. This was not the face of a monster, to be sure. I could not stop now—it would be dangerous to stop. I had to keep going. I needed the blood in order to survive.

XXXI

Day thirteen, night

This far into my confession my quill just splintered; ink dribbled darkly onto the page. The dark ink glistened in the candlelight, and I couldn't look away.* It's only ink, *I reminded myself, my voice a harsh whisper, my mouth dry. I touched the glistening pool carefully with the tip of my finger, my breath caught

in my throat. It was only ink. I stood from the table weakly, wary of the faces crowded in the mirror. The mirror is the eye of madness.

I watch the dawn fill the small windows with a bleak gray light. I haven't slept, couldn't sleep—the ghosts keep me awake at night. The only thing that seems to quiet them is the writing. My words scurry across these pages like the legs of a spider. I watch as the blots of ink dry.

This morning the timid servant arrives first. I detect her shudder as she enters the room to find me alone in it. I close the cover of the Bible over my scurrying words.

"Good morning, Countess," she says, curtsying. I watch as she pokes at the weak flames in the hearth, then settles into a chair with her sewing.

"If you had to choose between immortality and dying young, which would you choose?" I ask. I know I only have a few moments alone with her.

"I would choose to live a long and healthy life, of course." Her eyes are wide, vaguely panicked, her voice small but steady.

"No, you fool, that's not an option I offered to you. There are only two: eternal youth or an early death."

"How early?" she asks, considering.

"Soon," I tell her. Her shoulders turn rigid.

"That's a terrible choice to have to make," she says.

"Not so terrible as you might imagine."

For the next few days I abstained from blood, knowing that Anastasia needed time to regain her strength. I considered Sinestra's warning—*the blood of one is not enough*—but since Rowena's revelation of Anastasia's scarred arm, my confidence had begun to waver. What if Marianna had seen those wounds? In spite of my need for blood, I could not deal with the possibility of choosing another servant to bleed. I was already plagued with anxiety that Anastasia might divulge my secret.

Meanwhile, I spent my time visiting Marianna, now in the final days of her pregnancy and confined to bed. The sight of my once young and beautiful friend turned weary and bloated frightened me. She was becoming a specter of death, much like my mother, I thought for a moment, but pushed the thought as far from my mind as I could manage. The sight of her only magnified the cravings within me.

During our next midnight session, Anastasia was more listless than usual, her arm limp over the edge of the bowl.

"I have a new corset for you," I told her, hoping the thought of a gift would brighten her spirits. I held the pink brocade corset before her, showing off the fine lining and the smooth satin ribbons in the back. She inspected the workmanship for a moment while my eyes alighted upon the bowl of blood.

The bleeding seemed to take longer than I had expected, and I implored Anastasia for patience as I paced the floor, agitated. Anastasia did not seem at all impatient, sitting drowsily hunched over the bowl. According to the medical texts I had read, humans were equipped with pound upon pound of blood—surely there was still enough inside of her that could be spared. I glanced again at the measly pool and sighed, frustrated.

"We may have to try again," I told her, inspecting the cut upon her arm. "Perhaps a cut upon your leg—that might yield more." When I turned to look at the girl in the chair, I jumped back at the sight. Her head had fallen forward onto the table.

I pulled her up by her shoulders and shook her vigorously, then slapped her cheeks repeatedly. Her eyelids only fluttered. When I stopped shaking she slumped backward, her neck limp and her mouth slack.

"Wake up, Ana!" I cried, the sound of my own frightened voice only heightening my panic. "Please, child, wake up!"

I lifted her from the chair and listened closely. Heartbeat? Breath? I could hear nothing. Though she weighed little, her long limbs made her cumbersome in my narrow arms. She slipped silently from my grasp and landed in a heap upon the floor.

I looked again at the bowl, gleaming in the candlelight. The wind howled and the tower itself seemed to sway with the blows. I felt suddenly that I was on an enormous ship in rocky waters, the floor undulating beneath me. But when I looked down, Anastasia's pale, thin body did not move. Her skin was the color of marble and cold to the touch.

There was only one thing to do. No one could know what had happened. I had to get rid of her as quickly as possible. What about the blood? Should I complete my skin treatment now, while it was still warm? The walls of the tower room seemed to spin around me. No, I couldn't wait that long. I lifted a tapestry to inspect the window—her body would never be found once thrown down the cliff below. But the window was too narrow; I could fit no more than my hand through the narrow slit in the stone wall.

I threw a black cloak around my shoulders and then reached down to lift the girl into my arms, concealed beneath the cloak. Thankfully, the hour was late. I labored down the tower stairwell with my grim cargo. I could carry her outside, drop her body in the gulf between the mountains, if I could manage to carry her that far without being seen, or without tempting the nearby wolves with my own scent. It would be best to get rid of the body completely.

Would I have to give her final rites? I wondered. But the thought was short-lived—there were voices at the end of the hall. I wouldn't make it outside without being seen. Another stairwell led from the tower down to the dungeon below. Once the door was shut behind me, I dropped the girl on the floor.

The dungeon was dark. I groped for a moment through the darkness for a candle, which I lit from a flame in the hallway, then nestled the candle in a sconce upon the dungeon wall. I was surrounded by crates packed with sculptures and paintings: the overflow of the count's affinity for objects of beauty.

I looked down at Anastasia again: she could have been sleeping peacefully, if not for the awkward, jagged line of her arm against the cold dirt floor, or the way her eyes remained half open. I reached down and lowered the lids for her. Was this a part of her destiny, I wondered, to die young? I rolled her toward the wall of the dungeon.

I found an empty crate in the corner with a splintered lid. I stuffed her inside, hastily. Though her limbs were difficult to manage, once she was folded into the crate, I was amazed at how small she seemed, like a sleeping child. I pushed the crate against the wall, obscured by barrels of wine. I would choose a different night to finish the job.

By the time I returned to the tower, Ana's blood had turned too cold to bathe in. I was loath to waste the blood, not knowing when I would find another supplier. I busied my trembling hands with the task of siphoning the meager amount of blood into a few empty vials I had on my dressing table. Once done, I sat before the fire, stewing, wondering what to do next.

One thought did stick in my mind about young Anastasia: when she was a baby, if a scryer had predicted her future, is this what he would have determined? I wondered if God had seen what I had done, if it had been part of His plan for both of us, or if my actions had surprised Him. Would it be possible, I wondered, to act against God's will, as the stranger had suggested, to stray from the predetermined path He had chosen for me to live?

I stared at my hands in the firelight. They were young hands, still, but perhaps something had changed about them. In the silence I could feel the eyes of God upon me, burning me like a brand. There was a mark upon my heart, a scar no mirror could detect.

I didn't mean to do it, I thought, but these words made me shiver, sounding so much like an admission of guilt. It had been an accident, nothing more than that.

A knock at the chamber door broke into these thoughts.

"Erzebet! It's Marianna, she's calling for you," Rowena blurted out as I opened the door. Her brow was moist, and her hair was streaming from its tight knot.

"The baby is on its way, Erzebet. The midwife is already with her."

I raced with Rowena down the hallway. Though my arms were now unburdened, something in my chest felt heavy as lead. The cut-glass windows in the hall sliced the moonlight into icy spears upon the floor. The closer I came to Marianna's chambers, the heavier the lump in my chest became.

When I arrived in her chambers, I was greeted by the harsh screaming of a wounded animal. I saw Konrad's shapeless form hunched in the shadows.

"Erzebet," he called to me, but I walked past him toward the light burning in the bedchamber.

The infant was the first thing I saw upon entering the room. The creature was naked and pale blue, kicking and clawing at the air in a fury. The midwife's apprentice noticed my grimace of disgust.

"The child is healthy, my lady. She is healthy and strong," she announced.

I walked to the midwife, who knelt beside the bed, pressing a cloth to Marianna's face. The sheets were drenched with more blood than I had ever seen, or imagined. I stepped back at the sight of it, and was surprised by my sudden desire to run. The midwife looked to me and stood, gesturing me to sit.

"She murmured your name," she told me. "I thought you might want to calm her. She has lost a lot of blood." She looked back to Marianna, breathing shallowly upon the bed, and shook her head. "The infant is healthy, but for her there is much danger."

"Leave," I told her, finding the strength with which to speak. "Right now. Please remove the child."

"My lady, please be careful—"

"Leave us." I commanded. I shut the door behind them.

Marianna's eyes fluttered as I knelt beside her.

"Mari, can you hear me?" I asked.

She looked at me beneath drooping lids.

"Don't talk, you need your strength." I rifled through the midwife's satchel for a knife. A goblet of wine stood on a table beside the bed. I held my forearm over the mouth of the cup. The slice of the blade through my own flesh was quick and clean. I watched the careful drops by the light of a candle and clenched my fist to urge my veins to drain. Then I lifted the cup to her face.

"Marianna, please drink this." I slid my hand behind her neck in order to support her drooping head—so much like the limp Anastasia, but I banished the thought from my mind.

She struggled to take a sip, but wrinkled her nose at the taste.

"Trust me, Mari. This will improve your strength. You must trust me." Her dark eyes focused on mine for a moment, her breathing still shallow. I held her head steadily in my hand as she took another sip of the wine. It stained her lips red. Her head fell slack against the pillow and I could not lift it again. I felt that I was still stuck in a dream. All of the colors in the room were too vivid: Marianna's red lips, her pale white skin, her dark curls loose and wild upon the pillow. The wound on my arm still bled, fresh drops blooming upon the white sheets like red roses. The sheets were crimson with my blood and hers: the stain around her was so huge and red I could not help but look at it. It was Mari's life, spilled out upon the bed before me.

"It's a girl, did you see her? Is she all right?"

"Of course, the baby is fine," I told her, touching her face gently. "Please rest—you need your strength."

"I will name her Ilsa," she murmured, dismissing my pleas, "after my mother. She's so white, from head to toe—I think that we should call her Snow."

"Whatever you would like, dear," I said, and kissed her upon the forehead. "Please sleep soon. You need your rest."

"You must promise me that you will make sure they're all right—Snow and Konrad. I know that you will do that for me. You've always done everything that I couldn't do for myself."

I nodded, numb. She sighed again, and squeezed my hand.

I watched in horror as her eyelids began to droop. When I shook her vigorously, her eyelids flickered for a moment, but did not open. She did not wake again.

I stood so quickly my skirt toppled the chair behind me. I could not look at her body once her soul had left it—her body was only an empty shell. When I left the room, I saw servants huddled around the baby in the adjacent chamber, saw them lift their heads and follow me out into the hall. I turned to look at them—their mouths were moving but no sound came out. I walked down the hall and then outside, where the late-summer night was drenched in a cold rain. I could not feel the cold against my skin. The wind howled through me, empty as a reed.

Dawn glowed upon the horizon with a cold white light. I closed my eyes, desperate for the void of darkness. But when I closed my eyes I could not find peace, for brilliant images filled my mind: full-blown red roses drooping in the rain, a rope of black hair gleaming between my fingers, hazel eyes flecked with gold, wet brown leaves stuck to Marianna's face.

Part Three

DUNGEON

I am the Lord and there is none else.
I form the light, and create darkness;
I make peace, and create evil:
I the Lord do all these things.

ISAIAH 45: 6–7

XXXII

I did not sleep that night. I walked in the garden, the rain plastering my hair to my neck and shoulders, my steps tracing over the same muddy tracks down the garden paths, then back again. Time moved in a blur of stars, moon, and sun. At dawn I found Rowena asleep in a chair in my bedchamber, no doubt waiting for my arrival. She woke the moment I stepped into the room and blanched at the sight of my face.

"Erzebet! I looked for you—when I found you in the garden I thought you might want to be alone."

I lifted a hand, as if to protect myself from her words of consolation. I could not look up into her eyes; I could detect their shine in the dimness.

"You will have to help me—someone must care for the infant. A wet nurse, perhaps. The infant needs caring for."

"Of course," she said, grasping my hand. She said nothing more. I crumpled on the floor before her chair, resting my head on the fur upon her lap. My wet hair smelled musty and my dress was like a cold, damp shell. Raindrops still poured down my face, but I did not weep. I shut my eyes tightly. Rowena stroked my hair until I slept.

Rowena enlisted the help of an experienced young mother in the village to act as wet nurse to the infant. Konrad and the child were quickly bundled up to leave the castle, and I prepared purses heavy with coins to give to the wet nurse and to Konrad before his departure. Marianna's body was to be buried in a small village cemetery near the church she had visited as a child.

"I'm sorry to make you go," I said to Konrad when our paths accidentally crossed in the hallway the next day.

"I understand completely, Erzebet. You needn't explain," Konrad told me. I dared not look at his wretched appearance, preferring to feel only anger toward him. I had only enough sorrow to feel for myself.

"I think the countryside will be the best place for you. I've asked a few of the castle guards to accompany you, to make sure you reach your destination safely." I concentrated on the folds of my gown as I spoke, my fingers fluttering nervously. It seemed as if I would never stop shaking. "You will have two of the finest horses from my stables, as well as a covered wagon for your journey."

And a coffin, I remembered, but did not say the words aloud.

"Thank you for your kindness, Erzebet," Konrad said, bowing. I gave yet another purse of coins to Rowena for the infant's provisions. Merchants arrived with soft blankets and small linen dresses of the finest quality. I heard the servants cooing over the dainty items as I turned down the hallway toward my bedchamber. In those days after Marianna's death I spent long hours pacing the floor of my bedchamber like a caged beast. I dared not return to the tower room, though I longed for such privacy. The cries of the motherless infant seemed to follow me wherever I went.

My eyes had been fractured in half by memory, and shards of the past kept piercing my vision; even closing my eyes did nothing to help. When I walked down the hallway, a memory of Marianna in her wedding gown flashed through me so vividly and brutally that I had to stop, my arm outstretched to find a wall to lean against. Was this her destiny, or some terrible mistake? She wouldn't have wanted to know the future, regardless, and if she had known I doubted she would have lived her life differently. I was angry at the infant, and angry at God most of all. Not for what He had done to me, but what He had done to her, His truly faithful servant. He had forsaken her and allowed her to die.

Without thinking of what I was doing, I swung out into the hallway and rushed down my mother's wing, toward the tower room. I lifted my gown and hurried up the stairs on quiet feet, to slip unseen and unheard into those familiar shadows.

My progress toward the tower was stopped short by voices.

"Erzebet, please—the countess has been hoping to see you," a servant said, gripping my hand with cautious urgency. "She's been most worried about you—we all have been."

She guided me reluctantly into the room and I stood beside my mother's bed, though the heavy clove scent of the burning incense made me feel light-headed.

"I heard about your friend. I thought that you would never visit me again." She smiled warily as I entered the room. "Here, sit beside me, dear." She patted the edge of her bed. She lay upon the bed dressed in a black velvet gown, a string of pearls hugging her slack neck. I sat dutifully.

"How are you, Countess?" I asked.

"I am as well as I ever am. And how are you, child?"

I did not want to answer; I merely took her hand in mine. I studied the strange, frantic map of veins that showed through her translucent skin.

"I see," she murmured. "I'll not chide you about it, for this once. After all, I suppose this is your first real loss."

"You're wrong," I stated. "You were my first loss."

She looked at me for a moment, her eyes odd and unfocused.

"Don't you feel fortunate to have me here now?" She laughed cautiously. "Don't worry, dear. I think life is not as wondrous as it seems—particularly marriage and babies. Perhaps your young friend is better off where she is now."

I leaped from the edge of her bed.

"I don't want to hear it!" I shrieked, kicking her oak end table with my foot. "I don't want to hear anything about her, from anyone!"

The servants moved swiftly toward me. I knocked a glass of wine from one's grasp and sent it shattering to the floor. As they began to back away, I noticed something familiar gleaming from their eyes—recognition. They looked upon me as the same violent, wrathful child they had had the misfortune to care for, years ago. After years of respite, she had returned.

"No one is to speak of her, do you hear me?" I turned the full force of my rage upon my mother, who cowered among her silk pillows. "No one is to speak of her at all!"

"I'm sorry, child," she croaked quietly. I realized in shock that her eyes were wet, as though they were melting in her face. "I'm sorry."

"What are you sorry for?" I asked, not willing to let go of my rage.

"When I'm gone, you'll be alone," she told me. "Alone with your mirrors." Her voice was at once pitiable and cruel. I trod upon broken shards of glass as I left the room.

When I opened the door of the tower, the room was uncannily bright with sunlight: thin rays of it penetrated the narrow windows and fell in spears of light upon the floor. Immediately my stomach began to churn in the uneasy quiet. I crept inside, wary of what shadows might be lurking in corners, ready to pounce: for a moment I thought I saw Anastasia's face on the opposite side of the room, and I jumped in fear. But it was only the mirror showing me my own pale reflection in the glass.

I ran to the dressing table and groped wildly through the jars of powders and paints until I found the slim glass vial still glimmering with a drop of Anastasia's blood.

What was I? Was I a monster? The image of Anastasia folded, childlike, into the crude wooden crate flashed across my mind. I clamped my eyes shut and held my head in my hands, hoping to hide from the vision, but it was stuck deep inside of me. I would never be free of it, just as I would never be free of the memory of Marianna's eyes, staring blankly up at me, her face as white as snow.

I caught another sight of my own face in the mirror. Was there a change already stamped upon my face? Just as God had branded Cain for killing his own brother, leaving it clear for all to see the nature of his sin.

I tore down the stairs to my bedchamber, the vial in my hand. When I rushed into the room, I saw that the servants had descended upon it in my absence: inspecting my gowns, sweeping the floor, dusting my dressing table. Their eyes gleamed at me strangely when I entered. I clenched my fist over the small vial of blood.

"Erzebet, why don't you sit? You need your rest." Rowena came forward and urged me into a chair close to the fire, then gently pushed a goblet of wine into my hand. I looked up at her questioningly.

"It's all done, Erzebet. You needn't worry—I've made all the arrangements. Now you must rest, please."

I nodded sleepily and she turned away. The vial was hot in my grasp. When the servants had turned back to their work I carefully removed the cork and peered inside to see the blood glimmering like a jewel. I tipped the contents of the jar into the goblet of wine, too tired and weary to think of what I was doing. I only needed comfort, for a moment, and somehow the thought of the blood comforted me: blood was life, and life was what I craved in the face of so much death. The drops of blood did not alter the flavor of the wine at all, though I imagined a salty aftertaste. I drank and drank and focused on the wine and tried to forget all that I had seen. I sank into the warmth of the chair and slept.

She was supposed to put the kettle to boil this morning, but she never arrived. Has no one seen her?"

"I checked her bed and it's empty."

I opened my eyes slowly but did not rustle from my spot. The fire before me had grown brighter; the room was dark, nighttime. I sighed, relieved that I had slept the day away.

"She's been more listless than usual lately. Do you think something happened to her?" a servant asked.

"I don't know what to believe," one woman said quietly; I strained my ears to hear. "I heard about the scars on her arms."

"Was that true?"

"I didn't see them myself, but Rowena was worried."

"I would only believe it if I saw it with my own two eyes. The child must be lurking round here somewhere. She's got enough sense to know not to leave."

"We're all lucky to be living here." A servant sighed. An uneasy silence followed. When a moment had passed, I rustled in my chair. A young woman rushed forward to tend to me.

"Are you quite all right, Erzebet?" she asked. "I hope we did not wake you. We have dinner ready for you, whenever you would like it." Though she looked at me with a sweet smile, a heavy crease was visible between her brows. The only sound in the room was the crackling of the fire. All the servants waited nervously for my response.

"No, thank you." I stood and smoothed my wrinkled skirt.

"The count mentioned that he would like to see you," another servant said, cautiously.

"He will have to wait," I stated, the thought of visiting the count making my stomach lurch. "I would like to be alone for a while."

"I'm sure he will understand," the servant told me, though she didn't sound at all convinced. "We are only concerned with your well-being, my lady."

Her kindness comforted me, but at the same time I was repelled by their pandering smiles.

"I should like to be left alone," I said, and left the room.

XXXIII

Thankful for the darkness nighttime offered me, I hurried through the shadows to the dungeon below the tower, trying not to think of the errand that lay ahead.

I brought only one candle for my descent, barely enough to light my path around the crates of wares and barrels of wine. I wandered for a bit, as if to pretend that I was merely investigating, carefully picking out a path through the crates and barrels stored there. I was surprised to find old, rusted chains attached to the walls in one corner. I wondered how long it had been since people had been chained here, imprisoned in this cold, clammy cave.

It was simple enough to find Anastasia, crumpled like a limp doll in a half-opened crate in the corner, her rest undisturbed. Had it been one day, two days, since I left her here? I could not remember; Marianna's death had unhinged me from the normal order of time. The corpse still looked like little more than a sleeping child. When

I moved the crate from the wall she rolled out onto my feet; she had grown stiff while tucked inside, and her arms and neck retained the same crumpled posture. The candle trembled; dim golden shadows flickered over her face. I set the candle on a nearby crate, preferring darkness for my task. In a corner of the dungeon I started to gouge at the dirt floor with a pitchfork.

The work was difficult, but I was glad of it; the vigorous digging allowed me to seal off all other thought. I had never done such physical labor before and I was grateful for the way it allowed my mind to go blank. I was nothing but motion, bending, fighting against the earth at my feet. The stays of my corset snapped with the strain of my labor, and my neck and arms grew damp. My fingers cramped around the handle of the fork like claws. I did not cease digging until I heard a sound—a low, rumbling laugh in the darkness.

"Who's there?" I asked, whirling around.

"I'm here, Erzebet." It was Sinestra, and his voice resonated within me. I gripped the pitchfork tightly and shifted over to the corpse, covering her with my full skirt. I stood still in the darkness, searching. His footsteps drew closer. He lifted the lit candle and used it to light the sconce upon the wall. For a moment the candle seemed to float of its own accord, a stream of fire through the darkness like a falling star. Then the wall sconce sizzled and burned brightly. He turned toward me, the candle still in hand.

"Why now?" I demanded. I held the pitchfork in front of me, defensively.

"Because you need me now, most of all. Don't you?"

"I needed you before, I've needed you . . . " I felt the tears burning behind my eyes, and it made the rage rise like bile in my throat. "I don't need anyone now!" I yelled, my foot bumping the corpse still hidden by my gown. My legs trembled convulsively.

He moved closer and placed an elegant hand on my leg. Slowly, he lifted my full skirt just enough to reveal the face of the corpse.

"A shame when such things happen," he murmured, but did not sound surprised.

"Are you a spy?" I croaked anxiously, struggling to my feet. His laughter crackled like fire.

"Why are you suddenly so mistrustful of me, Erzebet?"

"You've given me no reason to trust you," I growled through gritted teeth.

"I think your anger is rather misdirected," he informed me. "It's God you're angry at, not me. Or perhaps you are angry at your friend, for making herself so accessible to death."

I lifted a hand from the pitchfork to strike him in the face, but he grabbed me before I could make contact. My legs buckled and I fell, toppling over Anastasia's corpse and into the shallow grave behind me.

"I wish we wouldn't fight, Erzebet," he said, standing over me at the edge of the grave, his dark form outlined by the flickering candlelight. He turned to gaze around the dungeon for a moment. "This is much like where we first met," he remarked, then extended his hand.

"Confession," I answered, the word pulled from me. It seemed to hang, visible, in the air. The thought of confessing had taken on a more sinister quality now that I had a substantial sin to confess.

"You're not here to confess tonight, are you?" he asked.

"That's no business of yours," I hissed. I took his hand and he lifted me out of the grave easily. I was standing very close to him, the pitchfork still gripped in one hand.

"I suppose you're right. We've already discussed the power of faith. I couldn't expect you to let go of it so quickly."

"Let go," I breathed, though it was not a question. I realized that what he had said was true: though my trust was tarnished, my belief in God still existed, woven into the threads of my soul.

"What do you hope for, Erzebet?"

"I don't know," I said, my voice breaking. "Forgiveness?"

I lowered my head and saw Ana's limp body at my feet. My eyes blurred, and her features seemed to melt and transform: Marianna's corpse on the ground before me. Sinestra clasped his hand upon my shoulder. His touch was tender, but not gentle. It felt familiar to me, strangely comforting.

"Don't worry about it," he told me. "finish your task." He lifted my chin to meet his gaze, his eyes glittering darkly. "You need never ask any forgiveness from me."

Caressing the side of my face, he moved closer, paying no mind to the pitchfork in my hands or to the dirt that covered my dress.

"You have been strong, Erzebet," he whispered in my ear, "and I'm drawn to your power. Besides, no one should be alone in this world."

With these words he leaned forward and kissed me, tenderly, on the lips. The kiss filled me with an undeniably sensual warmth, something I had never experienced before, outside of a dream. My eyes still closed, I reached out a hand to pull him closer, but I faltered instead. He had already sunk back into the shadows, and I was alone.

I felt my grip upon the pitchfork loosen. The hole before me was large enough. I rolled Anastasia into it and she fell to the bottom with a dull thud. In the weak candlelight, something glimmered from the bottom of the hole, like a wide-open eye in the darkness. I moved closer and realized it was the sapphire necklace the count had given her. I stepped into the hole beside her and leaned forward, pulling the chain from her neck. At first the chain wouldn't give and simply pulled her slack neck forward. I placed my foot on her chest to brace the corpse, and the chain broke with a snap.

Securing the necklace in the bodice of my own gown, I climbed out of the hole and covered her up with renewed fervor. Once finished, I marveled at how smooth the earth again appeared. I set forth rearranging the wooden crates in order to cover the patch of broken soil. When I was done it was as if nothing had happened at all. Perhaps I could pretend as if nothing really had. But Sinestra was right, I knew that now: there are those things that even God does not foresee.

I blew out the lit sconce and departed the dungeon with only one candle to guide me up the stairs, directly to the tower. I felt uneasy in this chamber, as though it had been tainted by the accident of Anastasia's death. The mirror had seen everything, and a mirror remembers everything it sees. Still, here at least I could be assured of my privacy.

I found the basin of water that I had left there the night of Ana's last bleeding. Though it was cold, I set to work washing the dirt from my hands and face. In doing so, I accidentally looked up and caught my own reflection in the mirror: my face and gown were covered in dirt. But there was something more than that, really, something that made me choke on my own breath: I saw that lonely girl that I had been, years before Marianna's arrival in my rose garden. That child who felt alone on this earth, alone with her fear—she had been waiting inside of me, all along.

Was this my punishment for the accidental killing of a foolish serving girl: the loss of my dearest friend? Then God was just as bitter and vengeful as the humans He had created to roam this desolate earth. Why should I be so harshly punished for taking a life, when God would do so on a random whim?

You are no better than I am, killing one of Your most devoted servants, I thought.

Grief and sadness swirled within me, along with rage. The grief was a living, breathing thing, devouring me from the inside out. The rage was familiar, safe. The rage had power that I could feed on, while the grief merely sapped my strength. I could see this choice transform my face; the eyes that welled with tears gradually dried, turning hard as stone, glittering darkly. I looked to my dressing table before the mirror and saw the Bible there, opened to the passage in Leviticus. It was a message from Sinestra, to remind me that I was not alone. Unlike Marianna, he had seen the horrors of my heart, but did not shrink away.

XXXIV

I was impressed with the further transformation a fresh gown offered me. Once my hair was braided and my mouth painted, I stepped down the tower stairs and made my way to the count's wing of the castle, knowing that he would soon call upon me.

"Erzebet, I'm glad to see you looking so well," he said, a bit surprised, as I strode into his sitting room and stood before the fire. I looked at him but said nothing.

"I'm sorry to hear of your loss," he said lightly. "I heard about your friend Marianna."

"You're sorry about nothing," I spat.

"I suppose you would think that, but I am sorry for you, and for Konrad." He averted his eyes from mine and gazed into the fire. "But perhaps now that your friend is gone you will better understand your place in this world."

"And what place is that?" I asked, a mockery of innocence.

"As the daughter of a count!" he yelled, slamming his fist against the arm of his chair. "As my daughter—a child of one of the most ancient noble families in this country, whose role it is to marry and bear children to keep her royal blood alive."

"I can't imagine you will procure a betrothal for your daughter." I laughed. "After all, who would want a bride born under a bad omen?"

He stared at me in shock, not sure what to say.

"That's correct. I've read your prophecy." I sighed. "I feel it gives me a sort of freedom."

He stood from his chair and approached me. "And why is that?"

"Because I have so little to lose, of course. Which reminds me." I stepped toward the count and rested my hand upon his arm. "I'm sorry to hear of your loss."

In answer to his confused expression, I reached into the bodice of my gown and pulled out the sapphire necklace. I dangled it for a moment before the count's face and smiled.

"Where did you find that?" he hissed, but his thought was disturbed by an adviser who entered the room, bowing hastily.

"I'm sorry to intrude, Count, but your visitor has arrived."

"Indeed," the count said. He turned to me with furrowed brows, already taking a step back. He seemed ready to grasp at the sapphire, but I had already tucked it back into the bodice of my gown.

"You are dismissed, Erzebet. I must go."

"Thank you, Father," I said, curtsying. I stood in his chamber and watched him turn to leave.

There was only one type of guest I could imagine would have pulled the count away at that moment: the type of guest who sneaked into the castle via secret passageways. Indeed, the count's deal with the enemy hadn't ended, even after the injury and death of his soldiers at the hands of the Turks.

I walked down the hallway to the main dining hall. The dark-haired soldier was there, the one who had saved Marianna that night when the fighting had just begun.

When your chance comes to seize the power, you will know it. I remembered Sinestra's words. Once I caught the soldier's eye I paused for a long moment before turning down the hallway. I walked slowly, certain that he followed, and opened the door to the room adjacent to my bedchamber, bidding him entrance.

"My lady," he said, bowing, "is there some way in which I might assist you?"

"There may be a way in which I can assist you," I told him quietly. "There is information that may prove important to you, and your fellow soldiers."

"And you will be good enough to share it with me, my lady?"

"I cannot tell you myself, but I can show you where to find it." I described to him the secret passageway and told him where to go. The soldier's dark eyes flashed at me warily.

"One moment," I said, and stepped into my bedchamber. When I returned I held a scarf of saffron silk in my hand.

"I intend to keep this conversation secret. Take this as a token of my honor."

His eyes grew wide at the sight of the scarf, which he stuffed hastily into his black doublet.

"It will remain a secret with me," he assured me. "Thank you for this guidance, my lady." He bowed solemnly.

"Make haste," I told him, pressing my hand upon his shoulder, "and be careful. It is best if you are not seen or heard."

He bowed again, and followed my instructions.

Darkness pressed against the windows in the hallway. Though wary of what ghosts might seize upon me in sleep, I was weary and could think of nothing else to do. I struggled from my gown and corset and slipped into bed in my underclothes.

After waking late from a fitful sleep, I remained stony-faced as Rowena offered me breakfast and a warm bath. I noticed that she had not cared for me so diligently since I was a child—years ago, before Marianna and I had ever met. Perhaps nothing had changed, after all.

I almost fooled myself into believing this until I glanced down at my own body beneath the film of soapy water. Though small, my breasts were decidedly womanly, and my hips and thighs had become more rounded with age. I tried to listen again, as I had before, to the sounds of my body, as though listening to a machine to detect where a defect might lie.

"Erzebet! Sit up, child—are you all right?" The steam had made me light-headed and faint. Rowena urged me to sit up from the warm water and began to dry my head and shoulders briskly with a scratchy cloth. In spite of Rowena's comforts, I refused the breakfast and returned to bed.

I spent all of my time in a dim haze of restless sleep. I rarely rose from bed and the smell of food sickened me. After a time, the aid of astrologers was requested. Some prescribed bleedings, baths in scented oils, or vile purgatives. I submitted to all of this listlessly, often closing my eyes and separating mind from body, hovering over my thin white form in bed. The sight of a dish of blood made me soar with excitement until I realized the blood was my own.

There were brief moments in which I considered death, in the way someone considers a ride through the countryside—perhaps I should simply submit to it, and give up this fight, after all? I could not bear the thought of waking and dealing with the grim, lonely reality that lay before me. But then I would remember Anastasia, and fear the retribution that awaited me on the other side. Where I was going, I would certainly not be reunited with Marianna. These thoughts shocked me back into my own body, wrapped in blankets and sweating out an illness that bled my spirit dry.

It was an accident, I thought. *Death was never my intention.*

Life is your intention, a voice told me. It was Sinestra's voice. It was nighttime, and he was in the room, kneeling upon the floor beside my bed. *Choose your fate; the choice is still yours.* I fell into a deep, restful sleep at the sound of his voice.

Through a rippling haze I saw Pugrue seated beside my bed, his head lowered solemnly. I wondered if he had come to offer me my last rites, and the thought revived me a bit. I rustled beneath my heavy covers and he started at the sound.

"Erzebet, can you hear me?" he asked, his face close to mine, his eyes blinking rapidly. "I'm afraid I have some terrible news to share with you." He pulled his chair closer to the side of my bed. I could see Pugrue's scalp through his wiry nest of hair; it reminded me of the stone-smooth head of a skeleton.

"Erzebet, your father is dead."

"Dead?" I asked, my voice louder than I thought possible. "How?"

Pugrue's eyes shifted nervously about the room; he lifted his hand to the servants, requesting privacy. He turned back to me once the door had been shut behind them.

"It appears as though he was killed by the Turks, four days ago. He was found in his bedchamber, strangled with a silk scarf. We would have told you immediately, but your illness forbade us from doing so."

A saffron silk scarf, I thought. For a moment I worried I had said the words aloud. But Pugrue suspected nothing; strangulation was a popular method of murder among the Turks.

"Unfortunately, word of his murder has already spread through the village, and the people are afraid. It's important, in such dangerous times, that they feel protected."

"By me," I said.

"Yes, Erzebet. You are their protection now."

"I will visit them," I told Pugrue. "I will visit the village myself."

"We will discuss the details when you are well," Pugrue said, resting his old, spotted hand upon mine.

Though still weak, I rose from bed that day for the first time since my illness had begun. I called for Rowena to bathe and dress me.

"Oh, you've grown so thin, Erzebet," she moaned, adjusting the stays of my smallest corset. "You must promise me to eat something today."

"I promise I will, don't worry," I told her. I did appear bonier than usual, but there was a vibrant energy that seemed to sparkle around my reflection in the mirror. My eyes shone brilliantly and my skin was pale as flour.

Now that the count was dead, I felt liberated. I moved into his chamber and rifled through the papers on his desk to learn about the administration of the castle, the local farms, and payment of the servants in his employ. What interested me most were the documents regarding the collection of tithes, which had grown steadily over the past few years. In order to gain the trust of the villagers, I would need to formulate a way to help them with their financial burden. Ideally there would be a solution that would benefit me as well.

Though I did not return to my blood treatments at this time, I was very aware of my appearance. I had a simple gown of pink silk fitted to my fragile frame—the silk was pretty but void of ornate embellishment. It was imperative that I appear not only lovely, but also warmhearted and caring to the people of Novoe Mesto. Within the week of rising from my bed, I was already discussing with Pugrue our visit to the village. We would travel on a Sunday and speak to the crowd just before the Mass. Then we would join them in their devotions.

"Do you know what you are going to say to them, Erzebet?" Pugrue asked, his voice strained with nerves.

"Yes, Father," I assured him. "Do not worry about me. I am in control now."

The glassiness of his eyes showed me that he was realizing this was true. Perhaps he feared that I would follow through on my earlier threats of banishment, but now that the count was gone, Pugrue posed no threat to me. I laid my fingers upon his hand in consolation.

"Your guidance has been invaluable, Father. I will not forget it."

The servants watched with cautious eyes as they readied me for the carriage ride to Novoe Mesto.

"Are you sure that you are well enough to go?" they asked.

Looking at my reflection and stiff walk, I could see their cause for concern. But they could not see the energy—like a bolt of lightning—that surged through me.

Stepping beyond the castle walls, I was shocked by the cold: winter was on its way again, and the chill seeped into my bones. Pugrue, though frail himself, did his best to assist me into the carriage. We rumbled uncomfortably over rough roads for a while, and I cautiously peered through the black curtains to survey the hillsides as we passed them. Finally we arrived in the center of the town, where we entered the church—a simple white steeple—where the whole of the village stood at attention.

A hush fell over the murmuring crowd as I walked, regal though weak, to the altar, accompanied by Pugrue and the village priest.

"It's good of you to meet with us," the priest offered, his bloated fingers trembling nervously. "I'm afraid that our village has been seized by fear."

"If Count Bizecka is not safe, how is anyone safe?" a voice shouted out from the crowd. A murmuring followed, and the priest tried to shush the uprising.

"What about our crops, our livestock? How will we have money and food for our families if we are all at the mercy of the Turks?"

"How can we afford your taxes if the Turks threaten to tax us as well?"

"The Turks have no right to tax you," I answered. The murmurs ceased. "That is why the soldiers will remain, to protect you."

"The battles hurt us, too, and we've barely recovered."

"But many of you have recovered, and I sense that you are all stronger for it," I told them, and smiled proudly. "You were not conquered and you will not be conquered. More soldiers will be stationed at the borders and within the town, and the Turks will dare not penetrate our borders again—if they do, we will be prepared for them. You have my word on that. I'm here to help you."

The truth was that the Turks had already begun to move north. They took little interest in the crops grown in the village, and were more interested in siphoning wealth from other, richer towns than spending more time with meager Novoe Mesto. Still, I did not intend to remove the soldiers in my employ from their stations, if only to remind the people of potential danger.

"What will you do?" numerous voices asked me. My eyes scanned the crowd, and like an expert, I was able to pick out a series of faces: young women, young girls, with smooth skin and shining hair. My legs shivered, still weak. But I would not remain weak for long.

"I offer you an opportunity," I told them. "Give to me your daughters—they may work in my castle for five years. For those five years I will see to their daily needs. When their service is done, I will grant them each a handsome dowry, allowing them to marry and begin households of their own. Each of you will be paid, in advance, a small portion of the dowry, to replenish your own crops and livestock. And you will be relieved of the burden of daughters to feed. When they return, they will have husbands to feed them."

There was some laughter in the audience; their whispers sounded like the shushing of waves.

"This is how I will help you, and you will help me," I repeated, my voice growing stronger. "Give me your daughters," I told them.

And they did.

Day sixteen, night

I've been sitting here alone in the dark, but I don't think I've been sleeping. A soft thud startles me and suddenly I'm alert, eyes scanning the darkness. A thin slice of moonlight outlines the frame of the oval mirror on the wall.

"Who's there?" I ask quietly, hoping the guards will not hear me. "Are you there?"

"Don't worry." The low rumble of his voice instantly soothes

me. "The guards are asleep. I put a special something in their wine."

"Sinestra!" I leap up into his arms, his cape folding over my shoulders. I stand in his embrace for a long time, without speaking.

"You must be careful. It would be very dangerous for them to find you here. They could put you on trial," I warn him, my face buried in his shoulder.

"Don't worry about me; you know that I'm perfectly safe." I can see his teeth gleaming in the darkness.

"Have you heard any of the trial?"

"Bits and pieces." He sits upon the couch and I sit close beside him, our legs touching. "Rowena and Pugrue offered their testimony, as well as a few serving girls."

"My girls—they did testify? Have they told them everything?"

"Everything they could dare to imagine," Sinestra moans. "There were no direct witnesses to Helena's murder, but they've all told vivid tales."

"And what about the rest of it—the box of dead girls? The girls showed them, I'm sure of it."

"Calm yourself, Erzebet." He squeezes my arm. "What your girls have confessed is their own problem now. They were your accomplices—none of them have been able to escape that fact."

I sit quietly for a moment, considering the import of his words.

"They will be put to death," I murmur. "They will be put to death for assisting me."

I squeeze Sinestra's hand; I can't deny the loneliness that casts a shadow over my heart. My girls were with me, here in this very chamber, not so long ago.

"They betrayed you," Sinestra reminds me. "They do not deserve your pity." The moonlight slants against his sharp cheekbones, as if they were cut from stone. I press my palm to his face; he moves it to his mouth and gently kisses the base of my thumb.

"They've all lied about Helena?" I whisper, though I already know the answer.

"Of course they have. There's only one other who knows the truth, and she has simply vanished." He sighs, the sound like blowing out the flame of a candle.

"Where do you think she is?" I murmur.

"With her father, I suppose. Unless she's taken to the woods again." He wraps his warm fingers over my shoulder. "Do I detect a touch of concern in your voice?"

"I'm not sure," I tell him, "but I feel better now that you're here. Please stay with me. It might help me to sleep." I lean forward and nestle into the crook of his arm.

"Of course," he says, pressing his lips to my forehead. "Don't worry. I'll always be with you."

When the women began to arrive that winter, I watched them from a safe distance—safe for them, and for me. Their presence both inspired and disturbed me: at night I was forced to watch Anastasia crawl up from her dirt grave in the dungeon floor to haunt my dreams. My sleeplessness often led me to the portrait chamber, where I compared my most recent portrait to my reflection in a warped and puckered mirror. I tried to move to get my reflection to come out right, past the defects in the glass. I could not tell what was real and what distortion.

The count's death rejuvenated the countess. We began to take dinner together in the dining hall, and even enjoyed an occasional walk in the rose garden if the weather permitted, when she was feeling well enough. The only place I did not take her was the tower room.

When Mother was asleep I would walk around the castle until late at night, wandering aimlessly through sitting rooms and chambers I rarely visited to watch the new host of servants diligently at work. I even wandered into the kitchen, surprising the cook and her assistant over a bubbling pot of stew. I was always looking for something—perhaps Sinestra, or Rowena. Deep inside I knew what I was looking for; I wasn't yet willing to admit to myself what it was.

Every night, I sat before the mirror in the tower room, at the dressing table alight with candles, and inspected the lines of my face and the tones of my skin. I undressed in the cold of the tower chamber to better inspect my slender neck, my young breasts, belly, hips, and thighs, wary of any sign of change. I spent long hours appraising my own beauty. The flesh of my inner thigh was my favorite, for it seemed still fresh and soft and new, though the nest of hair between my legs filled me with shame. Though often I delighted in the golden image reflected in the mirror, there were other nights when the lines upon my face seemed deeper, the skin more sallow, my young breasts drooping. I left the tower and wandered the halls late into the night, watching the snow fall beyond the windows, blanketing the world in white.

Winter had already begun its slow, groaning thaw the night I stumbled upon a scullery maid, polishing a silver platter in the dining hall. She admired the platter as she polished its smooth surface, or admired her own reflection. I stood behind her for a moment in silence, transfixed by the strange, graceful movements of her narrow limbs, her shoulder blades moving like the wings of a bird. I stared at the smooth skin of her neck, her tawny hair falling across it in feathery wisps. The sight of her made me shrink inside; my heart clenched like a fist. Then she lifted the platter and saw me reflected there, standing behind her.

She dropped the platter; it fell to the floor with a loud crack.

"I'm sorry. I didn't mean to startle you," I told her, bending to lift the platter from the ground. Her eyes were wide, her lips plump and bow-shaped. I looked away from her face, feeling suddenly angular and ugly. My fingers gripped the platter in my hand.

"I'm sorry, my lady," she said, and bowed briefly. I wondered if perhaps every woman feels this way at some time, cowering before the beauty of another woman, a younger woman. I had just turned eighteen years old, but I had long been wary of the signs of age, of change. This girl was no more than fourteen, her beauty maddeningly new and fresh, as if still discovering itself. But this wasn't only jealousy, I reminded myself: the words of the prophecy were seared upon my brain.

I asked the girl to follow me to the tower room. When we arrived, I asked her to light the fire. As the flames grew in the hearth, the room came vividly to life, just as I remembered it. My hand trembled as I poured a goblet of wine and offered it to the girl.

She smiled and took the wine gratefully. I sipped eagerly from my own goblet, still nervous.

"You have pretty hair," I told her, tugging at a lock that fell loose upon her shoulder. "Sit here and let me fix it for you."

"You needn't trouble yourself, my lady," she said, and bowed hastily.

"It's no trouble. I would like to do it. Please sit. What's your name?"

"Therese," she told me.

She sat at the dressing table and I untied her kerchief, letting long wisps of golden-brown hair fall loose upon her shoulders. I moved my hands quickly over the locks so that she could not see them trembling.

It could be so simple, I realized, though it was not at all simple. I let the servant's hair slip through my fingers like silk. Then I stepped back and placed the small wooden bowl and the silver blade on the table in the center of the room; my hand remembered the feel and weight of the blade in my palm. The servant looked at them for a moment, then stood suddenly from her chair. She looked up at me, confused.

"Don't leave," I told her. "I have only one request, and it's not as difficult as you think. All I need is a bit of your blood. Are you willing to give me that?"

"What are you going to do with it?" she asked, her lips twitching slightly in disgust.

"That's for me to decide. But you will be rewarded handsomely for your offering." I merely nodded toward the dressing table. When she turned, the mirror betrayed her wide-eyed awe at the array of glistening jewels. She sat slowly, obediently, in a chair, her eyes lowered away from the wooden bowl before her. She was a very brave girl. I held her arm flat against the table.

"Are you going to drink it?" she asked me.

"No—I'm not a vampire. I don't even believe that they exist."

"I think they do, sometimes." Her eyes flashed at mine, warily, then she shut them tight as I lifted the blade.

"You enter into a secret in this offering—look at me." I shook her gently to open her eyes. "Do you understand? Keeping the secret will keep you safe."

"I am safer here than I am at home, with the threat of the Turks," she told me. Her chin still tilted toward her chest, she cast her eyes up to mine; her eyes were large, with dark blue lines around the soft gray centers.

"You are right." I smiled at her. "You are a smart girl. I will be sure that you are paid well for your sacrifice."

I lifted the blade again, but this time she did not look away. She watched the sharp edge slice her flesh and shuddered at the feel of it, tears springing to her eyes. Taking her hand in mine, I turned her arm so that it might drain directly into the bowl. I lifted my hand and wiped the tear from her cheek.

Sitting across from each other at the table, we became connected. I was a little more of her, and she a little more of me. She watched as I wrapped her wound tenderly in cotton. When I gave her a ruby ring from my dressing table, her eyes sparkled. She thanked me.

They always thanked me for their gifts.

After my success with Therese, I took to the castle halls over the following month to carefully choose other young girls to induct into the blood ritual. Sinestra had been right: the blood of one was not enough. Anastasia's death had taught me that lesson. To avoid the messy consequences of an accidental death I would need a small army of girls willing to be bled.

The choice was inspired by my own primal feelings of jealousy; I had raised the sin of envy to a fine, if maddening, art. I walked from room to room, where clusters of servants were dusting vases and scrubbing the flagstone floors, stirring pots of stew, and plucking fresh fowl for dinner. I pretended to be inspecting their work, but really I was looking at their faces, their bodies, their movements, searching for that certain trait that caused a strong physical reaction in me.

Mary was petite and delicately boned; I found her scrubbing the surface of a mirror. She saw my face reflected behind her before I laid my fingertips upon her shoulder.

Althea had enormous dark eyes and great waves of dark hair, set against alabaster skin. Her long eyelashes fluttered up at me like butterflies when I approached.

Elizabeth had a slim waist and full breasts. I found her sweeping the floor in one of the parlors; she paused and set her broom aside and stretched backward, graceful and sinuous, catlike. She straightened quickly when I walked into the room.

All of them I told the same story I had used years ago with Anastasia: I needed help tidying my tower chamber. And it was a secret. They were to arrive at midnight and the door would be unlocked for their entry. I would be awaiting their arrival.

And Therese—sweet Therese, who looked at me with knowing eyes when I approached her across the kitchen garden, her hair honey-golden in the afternoon light. She, too, was invited, and smiled warily at me. She had hidden her cotton bandage craftily beneath a full-sleeved gown, and she wore the ruby ring I had given her with the stone turned inward so no one could see it. She would be a good leader for the rest.

All that day I prepared for their arrival. The tower room changed, in some ways reverting back to the atmosphere of revelry that Marianna and I had shared years before. I procured trays of sweet dried fruits and decadent pastries the girls would not have otherwise been offered. I had a crystal wine goblet for each of them set upon the wooden table in the center of the room, beside a full pitcher of dark, rich wine.

Near midnight, I heard footsteps on the stairs. The fire was roaring in the hearth, and more than a dozen candles were lit around the room. They entered the room in a hesitant cluster, and as soon as they entered they were enchanted with the circular chamber, the fanciful tapestries, the Turkish rugs, the velvet and silk cushions on the sofas and chairs.

"Mary and Althea, would you polish my mirror? You can see that it's a bit smudged." I pointed to the mirror over the dressing table, in its gilt frame.

"Elizabeth and Therese, would you clean and rearrange my dressing table—the tiny perfume bottles capture a great deal of dust."

They set eagerly to their tasks, and I watched from a corner of the room. Once these tasks were completed, I allowed them to pore over the jewelry displayed upon my dressing table, under the guise that they must polish it. At this point I filled their wine goblets: red wine is always the first sacrament. It eases confession, makes the truth easier to tell.

While they polished the jewels, the conversation became more animated. They even tried the jewels on, wiggling their fingers to see how the gems glistened in the candlelight. I stood back and watched the scene, relishing their enjoyment, watching their innocent eyes grow wide with greed—and perhaps a bit less innocence. Only Therese held back from the lively scene. She watched the girls quietly from the divan, twirling the ruby ring around her finger.

Eventually their attentions turned to the trays of treats, and the jewels were put aside. They each chose a sofa on which to lounge. Ever the dutiful maids, they made sure to refill one another's wine goblet as well as my own. I imagined that the tower room appeared as a Turkish harem might have: women in fine gowns lounging on silk pillows, drinking and eating by a warm fire. But the luxuries of the tower room were not spoiled by the threat of men. The girls giggled freely in my presence, their cheeks rosy with wine and their eyes bright in the candlelight.

When the time was right, I called them all over to the table in the center of the room. Therese and I exchanged a brief, knowing look; I think she even smiled, slightly.

"I'm glad that you're all here tonight. It's for a very important reason that I've invited you here."

I held their hands as I spoke, and I nodded for all of them to do the same. Once all hands were held in a ring around the table, I released myself from their grip. I reached under the table and pulled the wooden bowl and the blade from their hiding place. I placed them on the table for all to see. Their eyes gleamed upon the blade; its sharp surface reflected in all of their eyes.

"I will explain, and it is important that you listen. You understand that you are all safe here, do you agree?"

"Safer here than we are in the village," Therese offered, "with a war going on."

"Thank you, Therese," I told her, and smiled approvingly. She blushed deeply and squeezed Elizabeth's hand.

"So you agree that I am keeping you all safe. I want you to know that you can all trust me, and we will keep one another's secrets. But first I must be sure that I can trust you. Althea, Mary, Elizabeth, Therese: What sins do you have to confess to me?" The candlelight glimmered in the tower room, a sacred, golden glow upon all faces circling the table.

"Sins?" Althea inquired. "Like confession?"

"Exactly, Althea. It's important to be cleansed of your sins." I smiled at her encouragingly. Her gaze bounced frantically around the table to the eyes of the other girls. Therese nodded slightly in encouragement.

"One of the stable boys went to kiss me, but I wouldn't let him," Althea hiccuped nervously, her dark eyelashes fluttering.

"Is that entirely true, Althea?"

"I did let him kiss me—but only quickly. How did you know?" She blinked, awestruck.

"I know a young girl's heart"—I laughed—"for I have one myself."

I think you've had a few young girls' hearts, Sinestra once told me. The thought of him made me smile.

We went around the room, and they confessed their sins. Elizabeth was hesitant and shy, which accentuated her sultry appearance. Mary was sweet and eager to please, chirping like a delicate bird. Therese was elegant, and made her confession with the somber attitude that the act deserved. All of the girls learned from her pious example.

"Very good, girls," I praised, joining hands with them again. "Now tell me your dreams," I said.

"I dream that I might have a husband someday."

"I dream that I might fall in love."

"I dream of having a daughter of my own."

"That's the most foolish dream of them all," I told her, and Elizabeth blushed, biting her full red lip.

"I had a dream that I kissed one of the soldiers," Therese said, her solemn tone mesmerizing us all. "I kissed him in the dream, and let him touch me. Please forgive me for my weakness." She lifted her gray eyes to mine in supplication as she said this.

"Of course. I will forgive all of you your sins. But first you must give something to me, in return for keeping you safe, and for offering my forgiveness."

"You need our blood," Therese said. The girls looked at her in shock.

"It is a small price to pay, my dears. You must understand that I make the final decision: whether you leave here or stay. Whether you live or die. By giving me your blood, you pledge that you understand."

I taught them the line to recite, and they repeated in unison, as though in prayer:

"We offer you our lives, through our blood."

"Then you understand my power here," I stated. I lifted the blade in my hand and positioned the bowl.

"Yes, my lady, I understand," the voices answered, overlapped.

"I understand and I am thankful," Therese said. She offered me her arm and all the others watched. One by one, they followed suit.

Isn't God like this, after all? At times embracing all who love Him; other times offering no protection to His greatest believers. God gives us life only to later wield the crushing final blow—we are all but waiting for the end to come.

"I offer you my forgiveness," I told them, lingering on each of the faces before me. "Your sacrifice is a generous one."

Each girl left soon after the bleeding with a bandaged arm, a glittering trinket, and a secret to keep sacred in her heart. The secret bound each of us together—bound us as one. When the door shut behind them I sat at the table with my back to the fire, before the wooden bowl. I stripped off the bodice of my gown, then leaned forward and swiftly, quietly, bathed my face, neck, hands, and arms in their blood. I did not look at myself in the mirror as I did this; I was not a monster. Blood is holy, and this was the holiest of sacraments I could attain. As soon as the blood became cold, I washed my face clean with warm water and combed and braided my hair. I lay in bed and dreamed another girl's dreams.

XXXVI

Over the course of that spring I gradually began a regular schedule of bleeding these select servants. The four girls I had chosen proved loyal and trustworthy, and remained my bleeders for years. Together they attended each midnight blood ritual, though I often bled only one or two of them at a time, giving the others a rest between bleedings. It was best, I thought, to be as discreet about my cravings as possible. These girls were devoted to me, and I attended to their well-being. There was an occasional alternate bleeder inducted into the group, who was dismissed once her beauty began to fade or her purity came into question. But Mary, Althea, Elizabeth, and Therese were my core group, and I did not fear that they would transgress against me.

Only bleeders, past or present, were allowed to know the secret, and it was kept as sacred within the group. Each girl respected this rule, eager to please me with her sacrifice and receive my approval. If a girl's health began to fail, she was released from her duties for a time and her loyalty was rewarded. Over time I became skilled at noticing when a girl might teeter close to the brink of unconsciousness, or death—I wondered at the fact that doctors seemed still unable to notice death's approach.

I kept the servants privy to the nightly ritual closest to me. These servants learned that the blood not only did wonders for my skin, but for my temperament—it quenched a sudden rage just as surely as cold water abates a flame. I did not begrudge them my protection if it made them more willing to offer their sacrifice to me. Servants not selected for the ritual were never invited to the tower room, and my girls were as protective of the tower's secrets as I was. While I coveted their blood, they coveted the attention and approval I bestowed upon each of them.

I understood their desire for approval.

Entering the tower room late one night with Kyzoni at my heels, I was startled by the smell of fragrant smoke. A smoldering flame across the room caught my eye: it was Sinestra, lounging upon a cushioned chair and smoking a hookah.

"Are you quite comfortable?" I teased, trying to conceal my delight at his visit. I still often saw him in my dreams, but that did not compare to a meeting in the flesh. I could feel my heart beating through my embroidered bodice.

"It is rather lovely in here," he said, smoke pouring out of his mouth. He set the pipe aside and stood before me. Again, I was taken aback by his beauty, transfixed by his fair, angular face and dark eyes. Distractedly, I could not resist extending a hand to touch his doublet: fine black silk embroidered with red roses. As my fingertips met the fine fabric, I blushed deeply at my boldness. He only laughed, and grasped my hand in his.

"You've done well, Erzebet," he murmured, his voice very low. "I wanted to visit you here, in your sanctuary."

"It is a sanctuary," I mused, smiling. "My own private heaven: replete with deadly sins."

"And without any men," he teased, pulling me closer.

"You know that you cannot stay for the ritual," I cautioned him.

"I understand," he said. "I wouldn't want to interrupt you with your pretty playthings."

"It's not that. You are a powerful presence, Sinestra," I explained.

"You've always thought so, at least." He smoothed his hand admiringly over my hair; it tumbled in dark auburn waves over my shoulders.

"To be fair, you were a bit intimidating at first," I stammered.

"You mean I don't intimidate you anymore?" He leaned in close as if to kiss me, but I pulled back with a nervous laugh.

"There must be many other women who are pulled closer by your charms," I stated.

"You should know by now that isn't true." He was reassuring though mildly scolding. "I am not one for court—or courtship, for that matter. I am only here for you."

"And what does your father have to say about such an arrangement?"

"My father is of as little concern to me as yours is to you." At this he smiled knowingly. "His arrogance makes him blind to his own lack of power. He is no father to me." He stroked the front of his doublet, the gold buttons twinkling in the firelight. I felt the heat rise to my cheeks again and looked away from his face. I turned to stoke the flames in the hearth.

"You do have heaven here," he murmured approvingly, caressing one of the many velvet cushions piled upon the chairs, "but what does it all mean, really?"

I stared at him pensively. Had I not done exactly as he had advised? He only laughed at my expression.

"What do the delights of heaven really mean without the torments of hell as the alternative?"

"I think you've been listening to too many tales of the Apocalypse," I accused.

"They've predicted it, you know. I have to admit I'm surprised that you're not a bit more concerned."

"I've already faced the prediction of my own death. I face it every day when I look in the mirror. I have little fear left over for much else."

"But you wouldn't fear hell at all, once you've witnessed its glory for yourself."

"What do you mean by that?" I laughed, though warily.

"You will see, in time," he remarked. "No God can keep control with merely heaven to use as a tool. Don't you remember from your lessons? The agony of hell is what truly convinces people to repent."

"You told me that the blood of one would not be enough," I reminded him. "Now I have the blood of many, just as you suggested. Isn't that enough to protect me?"

"Yes, indeed, and I'm very proud of you." He smiled, a bit consolingly, as if I were a child. "But there is more that you can do, to be truly safe. To completely divert your path from God's plan."

My eyes fluttered away from his, my vision blurred with fear. I didn't want to show any weakness to Sinestra, but he knew me too well for me to try to hide it: Anastasia's pale hands tearing through the crumbling earth below me, her glassy eyes searching for me. Ever since her death I had made sure that the ritual performed in the tower room was completely within my control. How much more did he expect me to do?

"Your girls will be here soon," he said, running a finger along the side of my face. "I will leave you to your ritual; but we will talk about this again." He bent forward and pressed his lips to my neck, and whispered, "When you're ready."

All aspects of the blood ritual fascinated me: the act of taking it and the blood itself. Over the years that followed I perfected both my method for extraction and my manipulation of the blood as a key ingredient to my immortality.

The bathing of my face was still integral to preserving my youth and beauty, but during that first summer of bleedings I began to put aside separate vials of blood for different purposes. I mixed a few drops of blood into a bowl of rainwater and crushed rose petals to create a heady perfume. I put a few drops of blood in my wine, for I had begun to savor the flavor of the substance as well. My most successful experiment involved using blood as a key ingredient in cosmetics. I ground flakes of dried blood into a powder and brushed this onto my cheeks as rouge. I also added a full vial of blood to a small pot of melted candle wax and animal fat; mixed while warm, then let alone to congeal. When solidified, the substance created an impressive stain with which to paint my mouth a glistening red.

These perfumes and cosmetics became popular aspects of some of the midnight rituals, at which the girls beseeched me to brush their cheeks and paint their mouths with my special paints. I often wondered, watching them smile at their red-lipped reflections in the mirror, if they realized these concoctions contained their own blood. But insecurity drives many of us to desperate acts; I certainly did not fault them for their indiscretions.

Envy is, after all, the most exhausting of all the deadly sins.

Rowena remained a comfort to me, at times, but no longer the confidante she once was. I knew her well enough to be able to predict her reaction to the blood ritual. She was never allowed admittance to the tower room, though I still saw her most mornings in my bedchamber, or sat with her during my meals. It's important to know whom you can trust in this world; I had Sinestra, and my girls. I knew that Rowena would not understand the particular fears that had plagued me all my life—nor would she condone my methods for easing those fears.

On a cold day marking winter's return, she entered my bedchamber, her hands fretting with her apron. She looked at me worriedly and closed the door. I sank back upon the bed and sighed, knowing what was to come.

"There's an important matter at hand, Erzebet," she blurted swiftly, mumbling over her words. "Something I've noticed about the servants—Mary and Althea."

"What is that, Rowena?"

"They have scars—I've seen them before upon other girls, but none of them will tell me why. They seem afraid when I ask them." Rowena studied my face as she spoke. My eyes did not falter from her gaze.

"I know the scars; I've seen them myself," I told her.

"You have?"

"Don't act the fool with me, Rowena." I sighed and stood from the bed. "I'm sure you've known the truth for some time, though I doubt you would admit it—to yourself or to your God."

"What are you doing to them, Erzebet?" she asked, falling heavily into a chair.

"Haven't you ever wondered why I've never changed, Rowena, in all these years?" I turned to look at my face in the glass: the same face I had seen reflected since the night that my last portrait was begun. In fact, my skin had become even clearer, ever since the bleedings had begun with Anastasia. I saw Rowena's face reflected behind me, but her expression was inscrutable. She did not respond.

"Nightly bleedings," I said lightly, and smiled in enjoyment of my own confidence. "It's part of my beauty regimen. Don't worry, the girls are all willing participants, and they are treated well."

"Are you a murderess?" she asked, her eyes suddenly blank with terror.

"Why would you say that?" I looked away from her accusatory gaze, inspecting the emerald ring on my finger.

"Because I remember her. I think I'm the only one left here who would remember her." Her face crumpled with tears, and her voice became thick. "That girl so many years ago—Anastasia."

My eyes flashed to her in the mirror at the mention of that name. Didn't she know better than to call out the name of a ghost?

"I saw those same scars on her," she continued, "and then she vanished. What became of her, Erzebet?" she asked, a challenge trembling in her voice.

"Her death was not intentional, Rowena." I turned to face her, unable to keep the anger from my voice. She shrank before me, fear gleaming in her eyes.

"Erzebet, don't you fear God's judgment?"

"Why should I, if His acts are even more arbitrary and cruel than my own?"

"But God's will is divine—you don't compare yourself—"

"I don't adhere to the will of God, Rowena. My will is my own and I do with it as I wish."

"Then I worry for your soul," she cried.

"Perhaps you'd do better to worry about your own." At this suggestion her face turned a shade paler, her eyes wide with dread.

"You've called me a murderess," I said calmly, "and yet you live in my castle, you sit with me at dinner, you dress me in the mornings and ready me for bed each night. Why would you do all this for a murderess? What would God think of your actions?"

"I want to protect you, Erzebet! I've wanted to protect you ever since you were a child."

"You are protecting yourself, Rowena. Just because you won't admit it doesn't make it any less true."

I turned away from her and walked to the window, tired of the conversation. The delicate branches of the trees below were crystalline with an early frost.

"I never expected you to understand, which is why I never told you," I said, my voice gentle. "All I require is your silence."

"Who could understand such a thing?" she snapped. I looked at my own vague outline in the window and smiled. It's important not to be alone in this world.

"You won't undermine me, Rowena. You would be doing more harm than good if you dared such a thing."

"I don't deny your kindness to me, Erzebet, but how could this be good for these girls?"

"They are good, sweet girls, looking for someone to protect them. They need me. Don't you see, Rowena?" I turned to her and smiled. "I am their religion."

XXXVII

Five years after my ritual bleedings had begun, I felt stronger in the face of death than ever before. But that did not stop death from touching my life in other ways; near the end of a long winter I sat with my mother on her deathbed.

"Have you found your key to immortality?" she asked me, in a sudden, surprising moment of lucidity.

"I'm still alive, aren't I?" I mumbled, uncertain if she would understand.

"If you've found it, keep it and protect it for as long as you can," she told me, in the moment before her death. "For as long as you possibly can . . ."

As the ravaged body of my mother was laid to rest in the tomb, I recalled suddenly the scent of rose oil from her skin when I was a child, the feel of her silken hair tangled in my tiny fingers. The memory made me quake with sorrow and fear.

I sat and stared at my face in the mirror for the rest of the day. I painted my face and even put on different dresses, finally settling on the black silk gown embroidered with red roses—a gift from Sinestra. The bodice was lined with whalebone and came to a sharp point in the center of my waist, where the black skirt divided, revealing an underskirt of dark red silk. I thought to call my girls in for an early bleeding, but the thought of this made the earth rumble: the sounds of dirt and stones moving, just as I had heard them in my dreams. Anastasia's white hands breaking through the earth below me. I squeezed my eyes shut to escape the thought.

"Erzebet," a voice whispered, and a hand pressed upon my shoulder. I fell heavily into Sinestra's arms, too glad to find him near me to play my usual coquettish role.

"How did you get here?" I moved behind him and closed the door of my bedchamber as I spoke.

"Your door was opened. I assume you don't mind the intrusion. I could tell that you needed me." He pulled me back into his embrace, then turned with me to face the mirror again.

"You look no different than you did in your portrait, Erzebet. I assure you."

"Are you certain? Do you really think it worked?" My eyes flickered from his reflection to my own.

"Can't you see it?" His eyes sparkled like jewels in the candlelight. "It's been more than five years since your portrait was painted. Not a day of change has been marked upon your face."

"Sometimes I think that's true and other times I'm not sure. I'm twenty-three years old; the prophecy could still—"

"There is always more that you can do, to be sure." He wrapped his white hands around my slim waist. "To alter your own fate, irrevocably."

"Are you going to talk to me about heaven and hell again? I assure you I've already learned plenty about them from my childhood lessons."

"No, I want to talk to you about killing," he stated. I stared into his dark eyes in the mirror; they were black and glistening, a mirror of my own eyes.

"I'm not a murderer, if that's what you're telling me," I whispered to his reflection in the glass.

"But that's where you're wrong. There was a young girl—what was her name, Anastasia?—who would say differently. Would that she could speak."

"That was an accident," I hissed, my throat suddenly dry. "I'll never do it again." I moved to release myself from his grip, but he held me fast.

"Don't pretend that you are remorseful about Anastasia, because you are not. That was not remorse, it was fear for yourself and for your own safety."

"And what of my punishment, then?" I said, pulling myself angrily from his embrace, shocked by the tears that burned my eyes. "God certainly had his vengeance upon me. I'll not put myself at risk of such reprimand again."

"It was love that put you at risk for such pain, Erzebet," he stated simply. "Marianna's death had nothing to do with your supposed crime. Anastasia was your servant. Her life was yours to use as you wished."

I stood by the fire and stared into the raging flames, suddenly frozen to the core. Sinestra came up behind me and pressed his warm palms to my arms to calm my shivering.

"What are you afraid of?" he whispered in my ear. "You have free will, and this would release you completely. Freedom from the hands of God."

"That's what I need to do?" I asked hesitantly, turning to face him. "I need to kill, to be sure I will live forever?"

"We are all God's children"—Sinestra smiled wryly—"but what better way to break free from a father's control?"

"And that would give me my own life? My eternal life?"

"That's how it worked for me," he told me, his eyes bright as flames. "I am only a man, Erzebet, but I am not a mortal man. I made my break from God many years ago. Many years."

My breath caught in my chest at these words. I looked closely at Sinestra in the firelight. His face was perfectly constructed, like a handsome marble sculpture—I could not imagine a face more beautiful. In fact, I often thought I had imagined him, assembled him from a variety of childhood dreams. I touched his cheek and lips with tentative fingers.

"Then you are—old?"

"Yes, I am very old. I saw in you the power that I saw in myself, knowing that I could break free. I am here because I have chosen you to receive this gift of eternity. I hope you don't refuse it."

"We would both live forever," I said, the words taking on a new gravity I hadn't fully realized before.

"And I will always be with you, of course." He wrapped his arms around my waist and pulled me close to him.

"What happens if I'm killed?"

He laughed harshly in response; it sounded wolfish, like barking.

"Why would you think of such a thing?" he asked.

"Why wouldn't I think of such a thing?"

He sighed and stared into my eyes, as if he were traveling deep inside them, searching.

"If we were killed, we would rise again. Then all would see our glory."

He smiled; his eyes glimmered in the dimness like the sharpest of knives.

I couldn't sleep that night, too wary of the ghosts crowding my bedchamber: not only Anastasia, but young Illyana, my mother's ghost. Now that my mother was dead, Illyana had come to haunt me; when I looked into a mirror out of the corner of my eye, I could see her there, sparkling and sylphlike, admiring her own reflection. When I looked toward the mirror she was gone.

I wandered down hallways, distracted, watching the moonlight cast slanting shadows across my pale skin and black gown. Eventually I was drawn to the warm firelight emanating from the kitchen. Upon arrival, I paused, standing in the passageway between kitchen and dining room.

A girl was seated at a table in the kitchen, covering pots of golden honey with layers of cheesecloth. She had a pleased smile on her face and a blush in her cheeks. I was perplexed by this until I saw a young man emerge from the shadows of the kitchen.

"You're here expecting a taste, aren't you?" the girl asked. She was plump and pretty with a sweet round face; not the usual type to inspire envy in me, but I found her flirtatious tone captivating. And I was not the only one.

"Sweet Pola," he said, smiling, sitting in a chair beside her. "You are the queen honeybee."

"Don't tease me," she warned, "or I won't give you a taste."

She dipped her fingertip into a jar of honey; it glimmered like liquid gold in the candlelight. She offered the fingertip to the young man, and he took it slowly into his mouth. Pola's cheeks turned pink; she stifled a giggle as she pulled her finger free.

"That's all you get," she said. "I'll not have you eating all of the honey."

"It's delicious."

"I know," she said. "Everyone loves honey."

As she turned back to her jars, he leaned in and kissed her on the mouth. His rough hand touched her smooth face, then traveled into her dark hair. The kiss seemed to go on for a long time, and I watched from the shadows. When she pushed him away, her eyes were glistening: she was far prettier than I had realized.

This one would offer something special, I thought. I realized I wasn't considering just a bleeding. I remembered what Sinestra had told me, how he had encouraged me not to hold back my power. There was a spark about this girl that I craved, and I wondered if he was right: though the blood was helping, perhaps it wasn't enough to make me truly deathless, truly free. To kill a girl, to drain her blood entirely, to bathe in her blood . . . that would be the ultimate transference of one life to another. I could take them in, take them all in, and be infused with their beauty.

I thought back to the night of Anastasia's death. I had felt out of control that night, and the memory still made me quake with fear. But time had proved that I was, in fact, quite in control: I had killed her, buried her, and little fuss had been made over her disappearance. She was the unclaimed dead, likely to have been killed by illness or childbirth eventually. They were disposable, these extra humans stumbling blindly around God's earth. No wonder she was such an angry ghost—haunting was the only device left to her, and she was far more effective as a ghost than she had been as a living girl.

Perhaps Sinestra was right: I had more power than I realized.

XXXVIII

A few weeks later, I watched from the dark hallway as three young scullery maids were herded into the kitchen by the cook and her assistant.

"You're to have dinner with the countess tonight," the cook explained.

"Why us?" one girl asked. She had clearly been cleaning a fireplace—her hands and face were smeared with soot.

"Because the countess wishes it," the cook told her. This explanation seemed to suffice, and the girls hurried quietly, one of them tripping over the hem of her own gown in an effort to keep up with the cook's brisk strides.

I had chosen them all myself, carefully, if a bit hastily. Once I had made the decision to act, Sinestra urged me to waste little time. These were not my midnight blood girls, who would be kept safe in gratitude for their sacrifices. After all, I would only have to choose other girls to replace them, and I wanted these killings to be a secret, even from them. So I chose three new girls: Pola, whom I had seen kissing the young man in the kitchen, and two others who impressed me with their youth and innocence. They looked so young that it was possible the monthly blood had not had time to start. There was something mystically powerful about the virulence of their youth.

I kept to the shadows as I watched a few of the older servants follow my instructions: in the kitchen, the girls were stripped of their worn clothes before the fire and each took a turn in the warm bath. Once they had bathed, their skin was perfumed with oils and lavender. Each girl was given a fine gown to wear, and I watched their eyes turn wide at the opulence of crimson velvet, blue and gold satin, green silk embroidered with a garland of wild flowers. One girl held the gown up to her bare chest, no longer ashamed, or even aware, of her naked body.

The cook's assistant moved patiently from one girl to the next, securing each corset with unmasked severity. Their hair was brushed and swept up from their necks. I rushed back up the stairs to conceal myself from my guests. From the top of the staircase I saw them crowd in the hallway around the enormous mirror, straining to catch a glimpse of their newfound loveliness, twisting to show off their minuscule waists.

Assembled in the dining hall, they awaited my arrival, seated at the polished wood table and warmed by a roaring fire. I overheard their chatter from a shadowy corner, before my entrance.

"Oh, I'm hungry." Pola sighed. "I wonder what we'll eat."

"Pipe down, fool," another snapped. She sat straight as a rod in her chair, her sandy-blond hair piled high atop her head. "At least pretend that you're a lady, even though you're only dressed as one."

"Listen to you," Pola whined. "You've worn that velvet gown for two minutes and already think yourself a queen."

"Please stop bickering," said another cautiously, her face thin and pale. "No good can come of such indulgences—why do you think the countess chose us?"

"I don't know why"—hungry Pola sighed—"but can't we simply enjoy it without worry?"

"I've never spoken to the countess before," the quiet girl whispered. She looked down and stroked the green silk of her gown with frightened reverence.

"I haven't spoken to her either, and I've been here months longer than you."

"Will you both be quiet, please?" the blond queen said, and rustled in her chair.

Their conversation crashed to a halt upon my entrance. I swept into the dining hall and sat at the head of the table as the girls stood and curtsied awkwardly. I reveled in the way their eyes burned upon me, like live coals upon my flesh.

"Good evening, ladies." I smiled.

"Good evening," they croaked.

"Thank you for joining me. It gets lonely sometimes, dining alone." I waved my hand toward the side door, which connected the kitchen to the dining hall. "I hope you enjoy your dinner."

Bowls of soup, platters of meat, bread and cheese were brought to the table, along with copious glasses of wine. Minstrels played and sang to each girl about her immeasurable beauty. Pola enjoyed the soup so much she slurped it. Sarah, quiet and sweet as a flower in her green silk gown, seemed the only one wary of the sudden luxury in which she found herself. The blonde was Ursula, who had been scrubbing the floor mere hours before but turned cold and proud as her beauty was lauded in song.

When dinner was over, I lead them all to the tower room.

"What is that for?" Ursula, the blond girl, asked. She walked over to the tub that stood in the middle of the room and peered inside, scowling. "It's empty," she remarked, "and there's a grate at the bottom. Why is that?"

"I could fetch you more water if you need it," pale Sarah interjected. Ursula's cheek twitched in annoyance.

"No need," I told her, stirring the pot of water bubbling over the flames in the hearth.

"But I've already had a bath tonight," Pola remarked.

"It's not simply a bath," I explained. "It's a beauty treatment. You lie on top of the grate and I will pour the water into the tub beneath it. The steam is an excellent treatment for your skin."

"Have you done this treatment, for your skin?"

"I have, many times," I told them. They seemed satisfied with this.

Make them disrobe, Sinestra's instructions echoed in my head. *They are animals. You are not.*

"You must remove your gowns before you can take part."

Carefully, they disrobed. Ursula was the most deliberate in her undressing, admiring herself in the mirror as she did so. She made it easy for me, or so I told myself, watching her twist proudly before the glass. Once her flesh was exposed, she was so charmed by the way it appeared in the golden firelight that she did not see the blade in my hand. I stepped forward and grasped her arm firmly, leading her to the tub.

"You can go first." I smiled at her. She pursed her lips in a prim smile at my kind offer, stepping daintily onto the grate that lay atop the tub. The feel of the grate beneath the sole of her foot made her stumble a moment, but I steadied her against my arm. I helped her lie down against the grate, the black wire mesh a stark contrast to her moon-white skin.

"Is the grate too cold?"

"No, not too cold," she insisted, in spite of her slight shivering.

"Relax," I told her. "Close your eyes. You will feel the warm steam soon."

I marveled at how calm the moment before chaos could be. Sarah fiddled with Pola's corset stays in the corner by the mirror, the two of them chattering as they slipped from their rich gowns, admiring the corset and the silk underclothes beneath. Ursula lay before me in the tub, her eyes shut, a smile still playing at the corners of her mouth. The blade gleamed in my hand, winking cold and silver in the light of the fire, though no one saw it but me. The handle of the blade seemed suddenly like an iron brand in my hand, the searing heat of it traveling up my arm, up my neck, filling my head with poisonous fire.

I am not a murderess, I thought desperately, though Sinestra had told me not to shrink from my own power. But was this power, or weakness? Perhaps this chaos could be contained inside of me, and we could all ride out the storm. They could each take turns lying in the steam. I would watch them and curse their youth, but do nothing more than help to dry their skin in scented cloths and send them off to bed.

God decides who lives or dies. Sinestra's voice roared in my ears. *To these women you are life and death, you are all-powerful. To these women you are God.*

"I wield the crushing, final blow," I murmured beneath my breath. I looked at Ursula lying in the tub. A series of images blinded me: a devil and an angel in the same body, just as I had seen in so many dreams; Marianna lying upon her deathbed, the sheets vivid with blood; the portrait in the parlor of my own haughty, smiling face. My hand upon the blade began to shake. When my vision cleared I saw Ursula again, her pale young body lying before me, a virgin sacrifice.

No one saw me lift the blade. It sliced through the voices in the room just as it sliced through Ursula's flesh. first her belly, then her arms and legs. She started up, surprised, and gasped at the sight of her own blood. She struggled to stand, the grate making a horrifying scraping sound against the side of the tub. Her legs quickly buckled beneath her, and she fell backward. Prone again, her eyes wide, she did not stop me from cutting her arms and legs—more cuts than I had ever given one girl before, at one time. There was no sound at all when I did this: the eye of the storm is silent. The blade seemed to work as an extension of my own hand; even Ursula, on the other side of the blade, seemed to be an extension of me. I felt, as I killed her, that I had become a part of her, and that she was a part of me. I could see myself, my power, my glory, through her eyes.

As soon as I stopped, the floor seemed to move beneath my feet. I lurched forward, catching myself against the side of the tub. Peering beneath the grate, I could see a dark pool of blood spreading over the bottom of the tub, but blood had also splattered over the side of the tub, and onto the floor, and onto the walls. The only noise in the room was the crackle of the fire and the sobbing of the two remaining girls, huddled in the opposite corner, cowering before me. They would watch and wait their turn.

The blade slipped from my hand and clattered to the floor. My hands were red and slippery with Ursula's blood. The front of my gown was wet and vivid red.

"Can't have that," I muttered, bending down to lift the knife. "I'll need this again, soon enough." I suddenly felt extremely tired, a bit dizzy. I tried my best to walk a straight line to the dressing table so as not to expose my weakness to the other girls. The colors in the room seemed very bright all of a sudden, and looking at them made my eyes water. I sat before the mirror at the dressing table, setting the bloody knife on my lap as I did so. I removed a silver pin from my hair and took a deep breath, letting the auburn curls cascade upon my shoulders. The tub behind me was reflected in the glass. Only a limp hand was visible over the edge of the tub, and waves of golden hair spilled over the side like flax. Ursula did not make a sound. Though my hands were sticky with blood, I fiddled with my hair for a moment, finding that it calmed me. I pinned it at the base of my neck, then pinned it higher. My face was smudged with blood as well.

I made sure to grip the knife again before returning to the tub to inspect the delicate bend of Ursula's knee, the blood a swirling pattern of red-black against her pale skin. Her breathing was shallow.

"The body is a prison," I murmured, looking down at her. She opened her eyes at the sound of my voice but could no longer focus; her eyelids drooped heavily.

"Tell me what you see," I whispered to her, for her death was mine, just as her life was. "Tell me."

I was startled from my reverie by the sound of the door swinging wide. The second victim—greedy Pola—had escaped. I paused in the doorway to see her gown swish down the stairs. I followed, watching Pola run while clutching her unfastened dress to her body. Desperation made her faster than I had expected, and it wasn't until we were outside of the castle that I managed to reach out and grasp the skirt of her gown.

She shrieked, horrified, and suddenly the vastness of the sky above made me release my hand. I was no longer within the safe confines of my tower room, but standing upon the earth, in full view of the sky and whatever might reside there. It was not the eyes of God I feared, but the sudden flash of Marianna's face that I saw, as if looking down at me from among the stars.

"I am as you made me!" I shouted in vain, but I couldn't tell who I was speaking to. I ran back to the castle, up the stairs to the tower, to the crying girl and the corpse.

"It's over," I told her. I slammed the door behind me. The girl only shuddered in response, huddled against the wall.

"I'm not a murderess," I told her, "not usually. This is different for me." I walked over and put my hand upon Ursula's—her skin had already turned cold, as had her blood. I turned from the corpse and lifted Sarah's green dress from the floor.

"Here," I told her, holding the garment out to her in my bloody hand. "You may dress and go to bed. I will take care of her." I imagined the mirror watched me do this.

Sarah gripped the dress around her shoulders and fled from the room. Innocence was still tender to me. I was not completely without kindness.

"I am not a murderess," I repeated to the corpse when we were alone.

XXXIX

Thankful for the nearby stairs, I carried Ursula down to the dungeon below the tower for burial.

"Somehow I knew that I would find you here," I remarked when Sinestra appeared, "to scold me for my failure."

"I see no failure," he murmured, glancing down at the corpse wrapped in a blood-soaked sheet. "I thought you were wonderful."

"Is that so?" I said, pushing angrily at the dirt before me. "I had to dispose of the blood. It was too cold for me to use. How is that wonderful, for anyone?"

"But you felt that power I told you about—didn't you? You can't deny it." He moved close and enfolded me in his arms, not shrinking from my gown and hair stained with blood and dirt. He pressed his hands against my rib cage and squeezed.

"I felt out of control," I told him. I accidentally glanced at the corpse and felt suddenly light-headed.

"No, no," he murmured, his face in my hair, his mouth on my neck, "you were completely in control. It will only take some time."

"One girl got away," I reminded him.

"I know, a sad loss. But your release of the third girl was masterful. You show more fairness and kindness than God, from what I've seen."

I pushed him away angrily. I often thought of sinking into his embrace, but I was unnerved that he would approach me during such a grim task.

"I don't know what you're talking about," I told him, returning to my digging.

"But you do, you're just not ready, not strong enough to admit it. It will take time. You'll remember, and you'll crave the feeling again."

He put his hand on my arm and immediately a lightning bolt shot through me. I did remember, and the memory made me quake with fear and awe: that one moment, hovering over Ursula, realizing that her life and her death were mine. I had never felt so powerful before. I felt that I was floating above the world and all its pain, untouchable.

When he released my hand I was gasping for air. The dungeon was dark and I was alone.

The task of cleaning the tower chamber fell to Sarah, the quiet servant, the one I had released after Ursula's death. I called her to the tower the next morning to give her this task; she was visibly relieved that my request was merely cleaning. Though to be frank, it was a grim and frightening assignment—the walls and floor were so grotesquely spattered with blood that even I felt uncomfortable spending time in the tower until it had been cleaned. In need of reassurance, I brought Kyzoni with me to the tower; Sarah's eyes turned wide as she watched me pet his coarse, silvery fur.

Sarah was instructed to tell no one of what she had seen. She was eager to comply, as if she had been an accomplice in what had taken place the night before. Perhaps cleaning away the evidence made the entire episode—and her witnessing of it—seem less real, scrubbing it from the wall and from her mind. I did detect gratitude from her, for sparing her on the night of Ursula's death. I had saved her life, after all. She became my dutiful servant from that time forward, though I refrained for a time before bleeding her. The night I did welcome her to the tower room, her back was rigid with fright. We held a special secret between us, Sarah and I. The other girls detected this without remark, though I sensed their jealousy. I had the tub and grate removed from the tower and taken to the dungeon, where it would remain.

Over the next few years, Sinestra often broached the subject of an intentional kill, but I managed to dissuade him. He told me that I would change my mind, in time. I preferred not to think about the prospect, assuring him that I was satisfied bathing my face in the blood of my girls, every night after our midnight ritual.

But Sinestra knew me better than anyone else: I was not completely satisfied. Fear was holding me back from fully appreciating that act of ultimate power, my final break from God. I just needed something to inspire me to action.

One evening I sat with Sarah before the mirror in my bedchamber. I stood behind her and pinned back her coffee-brown curls in a cluster atop her head.

"What have you been learning in Sunday Mass with Father Pugrue, child?" I had stopped attending his services after my father's death, having assured Pugrue that I kept my devotions in private, which was true. Still, it was important for the sermons to continue for the sake of the servants, to further protect my secrets with a veneer of God-fearing normalcy.

"About the Apocalypse," she told me, "and the Second Coming."

"It's depicted on the chapel walls—did you notice it?" I surprised myself with the sudden memory.

"I've seen that painting!" she exclaimed, unable to hide her enthusiasm. "I couldn't stop looking at it—Father Pugrue accused me of not paying attention, but I think I was paying the most attention."

"Do you really believe it will happen—the Day of Judgment?"

"To believe anything else is heresy," she said, but blushed deeply. The minds of the innocent are easily plied.

"What about me?" I asked her. "What do you think will become of my soul?"

"I can't say," she muttered, "but there may be someone else you could ask."

"I tired of Pugrue's sermons long ago, if that's what you mean," I assured her, shaking my head.

"No, I meant—someone who deals in prophecy."

"Prophecy?" My voice broke over the knife-edged word. "I'm surprised that you condone such practices."

"People are driven to strange things out of fear." She shrugged. "Many people hope for visions to reveal to them when they will die, or what may be in store for them in the afterlife."

"I'm sure that few are truly blessed with such abilities," I murmured. "The rest are spouting their own delusions." Sarah again shrugged at this notion.

"For a glimpse of the future, the people in the village visit the scryer."

"What scryer?"

"She lives in the forest—they say she made her house there so people would leave her alone, but people are desperate. And they say she can see things no one else can."

"Can she see the future?"

"They say she's seen the afterlife—both heaven and hell. But I've never visited her myself," Sarah told me. "They say she has been blessed by God."

XL

The next morning, at dawn, the gold rings clinked against the dressing table as I removed each one from my fingers. In my wardrobe I found a forgotten wool cloak—gray and moth-eaten. It was voluminous enough to conceal my rich velvet gown, the dark hood covering my shining hair. Looking into the mirror, I wiped the red paint from my lips and tied the cloak close to my chin.

I filled my gold silk pouch with coins, then tied it tightly to my wrist. I hurried to the stables, walking a bit hunched to avoid any distraction from my errand. Preferring to be alone for this uncertain journey, I chose a simple gray mare with a smudged white nose that took me swiftly to the bank of the Vah River, the outskirts of the marketplace.

The sun had fully risen by the time I reached the marketplace, and villagers were bustling about tables setting up their wares. Once tied to a thick tree, the mare stamped the dry earth as I wended my way between the tables of cloth and wrinkled potatoes. The sun had begun to rise, streaking the blue sky with smears of pink and gold. I walked to a table where an old woman sat hunched, embroidering a piece of linen. When I fingered a piece of cloth upon her table, she croaked out the price of each.

"I have a need for more than your embroidery," I told her. "I have a request. Tell me where I can find the scryer."

The old woman clucked knowingly and did not lift her eyes from her work.

"You'd best not do that," she warned. "It's an evil thing, knowing what no one should know. They say the child is blessed, but I say she's cursed."

"I agree with you," I said, pulling the purse of coins from my wrist, "but I would still like to meet her. Tell me where she is."

Her pale eyes darted from the fat pouch to my face. She blinked her wrinkled lids and lowered her eyes back to her embroidery.

"Follow the river," she said. "She lives in a rude hut in the forest, near the river. I hear that her visitors have cut a path through the brambles to her door."

"That was kind of them."

"Kind? They are cruel. The girl would rather be left in peace."

"A girl?" I asked, surprised. "How old is she?"

"Some say a child, but others say older. It's difficult to tell, and not for us to know. I think it would be better if you left her alone."

"Thank you for your assistance." I reached out and discreetly nestled a handful of heavy coins into her palm. She snatched my hand before I could take it away.

"I haven't seen your kind around here—your hands are soft as a baby's skin."

I struggled to release my hand from her grasp. She laughed at the fear that flickered across my face.

"Go to your scryer," she told me, thrusting my hand aside. "I've already seen enough of you here."

As we followed the river, the mare and I, the sun rose to its highest point in the sky. Winter was waning and soon it would be spring, but even the sight of new leaves upon shivering, naked branches seemed tinged with sadness this year. When we reached the forest the horse bucked in fear, but I urged her forward. We were plunged into a misty twilight, the sun blotted out by the expanse of trees above us.

All the while my ears were peeled for the threatening sound of voices, or the howling of wolves that were sure to prowl these grounds.

By the time I saw the house—a misshapen hut nestled in a cluster of rocks and trees—we were nearly upon it. I heard the sound of rushing water, the nearby hiss of a tiny stream. I tied the horse to a tree and let her drink, walking closer to the house on foot.

I peered into a gap in the rough slats of wood, but could see nothing. It was so dark inside that I doubted anyone lived there at all. But as my eyes began to adjust, I detected the flickering of candles within, though I could see no fire to ward off the cold. I shivered in the late winter chill, pulling my cloak more securely around my shoulders. I found a roughly fashioned door and knocked upon it.

"Is anyone there?" I called when there was no answer. When I moved closer to listen, the door opened slightly, hitting me in the face. I stood and watched it sway in the wind for a moment, unsure if I should enter. I cautiously rubbed the sore spot on my cheekbone.

"It's cold," a voice croaked quietly. "Shut the door."

I stepped hastily over the threshold and shut the door behind me. Once my eyes became accustomed to the dim light, I looked around. It was a small, one-room hut, with fat, bulging candles lit in every corner. The walls were covered with layer upon layer of overlapping scraps of parchment, each one scrawled with a frantic drawing or strange symbol. In the center of the room there was a table, its surface painted with a large pentagram, a candle lit at each point. The table was crowded with bowls of water and oil and a variety of herbs that made my eyes water. But where was she? When I began to wonder if I was alone in the hut, I heard a shuffling from the other side of the table and a low voice mumbling an incantation I could not understand.

"Pardon me?" I ventured deeper into the dim room. There was a mirror lying on the table—I gasped at the sight of white fingers dancing over its surface.

"Be careful," she croaked again, then continued her incantation. I could see nothing else of her but her hands, which dipped into a bowl of oil and then touched the mirror again. I stepped closer and saw that she was shrouded in a thick black veil that stretched to the floor; I felt I was standing before a ghost made of shadow and smoke.

"Who are you?" I asked, not knowing what else to say.

"You know me, or why else would you be here?" she answered.

"What are you looking for?" I said, peering into the glass before her. She paused for a moment, her fingers trembling slightly over the slick surface.

"Your future," she stated.

"Don't you need to know who I am?"

"I know enough." She shuffled over to the corner and grasped a wooden cane from against the wall. She dragged it on the ground around her, drawing a circle on the dirt floor.

"What are you doing?"

"The circle is protection. What are you doing?"

"I came to ask you about scrying. What you see and how you see it."

"Don't you want to see your future?"

"Yes." But suddenly I was uncertain. "I wanted to ask you," I started again, "is it possible to change your future, once it's been seen, or scried?"

"Prophecies are often misunderstood," she said, not looking away from her mirror. Did she get this question often? I wondered. How many people on this world could be living under prophecies they wished to escape?

"What was your prophecy?" she asked.

"That I would die young, or that I would live forever." The words rushed out of me with surprising ease; I couldn't believe that it was my own voice saying them. The girl only shuffled back to her mirror and murmured in response. The seemingly disembodied white hands came forward again, swirling over the glass.

"Is this what you scry in?"

"This mirror, bowls of water, oil, a dish of milk. Anything."

"When did you have your first vision?" I asked, stepping closer as she bent over the mirror, wanting to peer into it myself.

"I was a child. An angel came to me in a dream and told me I would see the dead reflected in every surface. The dead who were not finished living."

"How awful," I breathed. "Are you sure it was an angel?"

She looked up suddenly from her mirror. I could not see her face beneath the veil, but I could feel her eyes upon me in the dimness.

"No, I'm not sure," she stated, then crossed herself quickly beneath her veil. "Everyone told me it was an angel. Everyone was sure but me," she murmured.

The glass had seemed ordinary to me, when I managed to look into it—my own face foggy and distorted on its surface. She turned back to her mirror and lifted her veil, letting it fall like a tent over herself and the glass. She was small, perhaps a bent old woman best concealed beneath a black veil; but her hands were the smooth hands of a child. The low incantations began again, and I stepped back, wary of the magic circle drawn around her in the dirt. Her voice was eerie to me—the voice of a hoarse child or a weary old woman, I could not tell. I began to inspect the drawings on the walls.

The dead certainly had a lot to say to this woman. The sketches were hurried depictions of angels or demons holding a sword, a bloody chicken, a string of pearls. In some drawings the angel was missing a mouth, or eyes. The only thing that was clear in these descriptions was the girl's terror at whatever lived in her own mind. The evidence of her fear filled me with awe and recognition.

"The mirror is fogged," she murmured, "a dark cloud. I can't scry for you today. You can return tomorrow." She paused and shifted her feet. "How will you pay me?"

"What payment do you require? I have many fine jewels that I'm sure you will like," I told her, but she only sniffed. "Perhaps a well-tailored gown of fine silk? Embroidered handkerchiefs?"

"I don't look into a mirror to see my own reflection—only the reflections of the dead."

"I see," I murmured. "I could offer you a fine meal."

"No!" she fairly shouted, clearly agitated. "Don't talk to me about food. The visions require that I remain pure, and abstain from human pleasures."

"Even eating? How do you remain alive?"

"God sustains me."

My eyes wandered around her crude hut at this sobering thought. I scanned the furtive drawings, and finally my eyes landed upon a Bible, its pages frayed. I moved closer to it and rested my hand upon it.

"Do you attend Mass?"

"No," she told me, much softer now. "I prefer not to be seen."

"You read the Scripture on your own?" I asked carefully.

Her shuffling stopped; she did not respond.

"I could read the Bible aloud to you each time I visit, if you would like."

"Yes," she said, and seemed to instantly regret her own eagerness. "That sounds like a suitable price, at least."

"Then I will return tomorrow," I told her, moving toward the door.

"I think I see a face," she murmured, her voice suddenly more monotonous than before. Her face was bent low over the mirror.

"Is it my face?" I asked, suddenly intrigued.

"A woman's face," she said, almost chanting. "Black hair, in curls. Fair skin. She is lying on a bed. You are kneeling beside her—"

"No—that's enough, I don't want any more." My voice trembled nervously.

"You're holding her hand. The bed is white and red."

"Stop!" I spun on her and grasped her arm. "Stop! I don't want to hear any more."

The girl yelped and jumped backward, flailing from my grasp.

"I didn't come here to be reminded of my past," I told her.

"I'm sorry. There is no way for me to know what the mirror will show me."

For a moment there was silence. I wrapped my cloak around my shoulders, preparing to leave.

"I will visit you another time, when you may have other visions."

She moved toward me, closer to the candlelight. Her fingers gently brushed my arm.

"I've seen that woman before," she told me. I could see her pale, gaunt face dimly through the sheer veil. The shadows upon her cheekbones were jagged as mountain rocks, as though her face were crudely cut from stone.

"Who is she?" She moved forward, but I leaped away from her touch.

"I will visit you another day," I told her.

"If God wills it," she said, turning back to the glass.

XLI

Pacing the hallways until late that night, I felt old ghosts shiver through my fragile bones. My nightmares had grown fangs, over the years, and could come to me even in my waking hours. Unable to sleep, I rose from bed and began searching for Sinestra. I wandered down hallways, attempting to distract myself with the paintings my father had collected over the years. I hadn't noticed before how many depictions there were of the Day of Judgment upon the castle walls: human bodies ascending to heaven on the wings of angels, or plummeting through clouds of smoke to the livid fires of hell. Looking at these paintings I could feel Sinestra gazing over my shoulder, but his physical presence eluded me.

Finally I went to the tower, where I knew Kyzoni would still be sleeping. In the tower chamber I turned to look at my reflection and saw Anastasia in the mirror instead, her arms and face patterned with thin cuts. When she smiled, the sliced skin puckered red. She has always been a mischievous ghost.

Then the image changed, softened. Marianna stood there, staring at me from the glass. For years I had been haunted by the death mask her face had become in the last moment I looked at her; but this vision was Marianna at her most beautiful and alive.

How could you do it? she asked me. Her voice was like a spear through my chest.

"What do you mean?" I asked her, but I knew what she was talking about—the ghosts were flitting around in the mirror behind her reflection.

"You left me here," I told her. "What could I do?"

Her mouth crumpled in pain. When she opened it again, the scream of an infant tore from her throat.

Suddenly I was looking at an image of Ursula, lying on the metal grate, covered in her own blood. Her pale eyes clicked open and she stared at me. She lifted her head from the edge of the tub and slowly stood, her naked body a glistening red sheath.

"A perfect face," a voice murmured, and rested a heavy hand upon my shoulder. I shrieked and turned from the mirror, only to see Sinestra looking at me, puzzled and concerned. He wrapped his arms around me warmly.

"I was looking for you," I said wretchedly. "Where have you been?"

"You haven't needed me. Or so I thought." He pulled me closer to his warmth.

"How do you know that I haven't needed you?" I grumbled, pulling free from his embrace.

"I admit, I thought you might have little need for my company now that you've sought the guidance of the village witch."

I sighed angrily and started a fire in the hearth, urging the flames to rise.

"How is it that you always know?" I asked, but he only smiled at me, and made no attempt to answer.

"And you asked her about your prophecy, I'm sure. Did she tell you what you wanted to hear?"

"Indeed, she did not." I paused, unsure of how much I wanted to reveal. "What kind of scryer tells you about your past?"

"She doesn't deal in prophecy," he scoffed, settling into a sofa near the fire, "just in ghosts and visions. The vision she saw is one that you carry around with you at all times." He smiled knowingly at me in the dimness.

"She told me she had seen her—the vision—before," I said uneasily, sitting beside him. Kyzoni stretched from his corner to rest his head upon my lap.

"Maybe she knows others who harbor the same loss," he said carefully, and reached out to smooth my hair. "You will visit her again."

"Will I?"

"Of course you will. You're drawn to innocence. From what I hear, that child has been made a victim of her own innocence."

"I doubted there was such a thing, anymore," I murmured, slowly warmed by the touch of his hand and the fire in the hearth.

"Only one who is particularly pure of heart may read the future, so they say."

"What else do they say?" I asked, leaning against him.

"Well, the scryers I've heard of abstain from all earthly delights: food, drink, affection, intimacy." He trailed his fingertips lightly along my arm.

"It seems a great deal to give up, for a chance to be haunted all your life," I murmured.

"And what would you know about being haunted?"

I moved away from him, suddenly embarrassed.

"That prophecy still has a hold over you, doesn't it? Even after all these years."

"Even after all I've done to escape it."

"There is more that you can do, my dear, to make sure that you are safe, and in control of your own destiny."

"I've had my intentional kill," I reminded him. "I just prefer to remain fully in command of the situation."

"And that prophecy will stay with you, until you learn the full extent of your power." He rested his hand heavily upon my shoulder as he said this, and I felt an old thrill of memory run through me: Ursula's murder. I shivered deliciously at the thought, but would not admit it to him. Kyzoni snorted, then returned to his rest.

"I've heard she's seen the afterlife, this scryer." I sighed, trying to change the subject. "Both heaven and hell."

"But haven't we all?" he murmured thoughtfully.

At these words I moved to turn away, but he grasped me by the shoulders and kissed me on the mouth. The kiss was warm and suffocating, like thick, red wine. At first I thought to pull away, but then I allowed it to wash over me. When I glanced across the room to the mirror, there were only the two of us in the room; no ghosts peered from its silver surface.

I stood to fiddle with the fire, unnerved by how brightly the flames lit the room.

"Do you want us both to freeze to death?" Sinestra asked. I laughed and moved away from his hands. I lit incense and breathed in the thick smoke, willing it to soothe me. I poured a glass of wine for each of us and began to drink. Then I turned and allowed him to kiss me.

I returned to my favorite dream as a child, that Athenus would suddenly shake his head and break free from his stone prison in order to be my love. Sinestra's hands were warm, his touch tender, just as I had dreamed. When he began to unlace my corset, I broke free from the kiss.

"Close your eyes, please," I blurted desperately. He laughed in response.

"You take such pains to be beautiful," he said, smiling, "yet you don't want me to look at you?"

"You already think I'm beautiful. I don't want reality to spoil the dream."

As we kissed again, I fell deeply into the dream of Athenus. As he was transforming, perhaps I was, too. I was turning into a different type of girl, one not so haunted, or cursed. I thought back to young Pola, whose easy flirtations I had observed from the shadows. As I lay back on the sofa, among the silk cushions, I imagined myself like her: sweet, giggling, beguiling. It was, after all, very tiring to be me.

Sinestra hovered over me for a moment, his eyes glistening in the darkness. Then he lay on top of me, and I could feel his heart beating, beating against mine. I knew what was happening; I was not so naive about men that I did not know. I pushed my reservations aside and let him kiss me. I let it all happen: his warm hands against my bare skin made me feel real and beautiful and definitely alive. I was weary of always needing to be in control. Let Sinestra be in control while I lay there with him and let him kiss me, and felt his breath on my neck, his whispers in my ear. I lay there and drank in his love for me like sweet, red wine.

I awoke at dawn from a deep, dreamless sleep. I was still in the tower room, nestled into the cushions on the sofa, my gown lying on the floor in a pool of cold sunlight. I was alone in the room but for Kyzoni, curled up asleep in his corner. The fire in the hearth was dead and I shivered at the sight of my own nakedness. I grasped my gown and covered myself with it. My eyes scanned the room eagerly, adjusting to the bleak light. My dressing table, the mantel over the hearth—all was just as it had been the night before. There was no gift, no message left behind.

I leaned back against the pillows, wondering about the nature of innocence.

Day eighteen, night

The sound of a long, low howl broke through the thin veil of my dream. It was a very familiar howl coming from the rose garden—Kyzoni. It was just the sort of sign that Sinestra would

leave for me when planning a visit to my prison. The howl came again—I was to meet him in the garden, I was sure. I tiptoed over to the door and grasped the cold handle with both hands. But the door was locked. Suddenly, my hand still resting on the handle, the door swung wide. A tall man stood in the doorway, silhouetted by the sconces lit in the hall behind him. I was ready to jump into Sinestra's arms when I realized it was one of the guards.

"I wasn't trying to escape," I attempted to explain. "I know better than that."

"I'm not sure that you do, my lady. We're assigned to sit here, and we're to sound an alert if you try to leave."

"You needn't bother," I told them. "I'm going to sleep. I won't try to leave again, I promise."

Now the guards watch me, suspiciously, as I sit upon the couch and cover myself with a blanket. Sinestra knows I'm restless here, sleepless. The one time I slept was curled up in his arms upon this couch. Tonight he must not have drugged the guards properly.

"I promise you, I'm going to bed," I tell them, and they shut the door again, shutting me into my prison. It makes me realize how Marianna must have felt, so many years ago, when she was stuck here and unable to leave.

I know I won't fall asleep tonight. I light a candle and return to my confession.

I visited the scryer again that morning. In daylight I could see more of the hut, and I realized how small the room was—only large enough for the table in the center, and a pile of dirty blankets in the corner where, presumably, the girl slept. The four walls covered in her drawings seemed to encroach upon us. From inside it looked like a house made of paper, ready to be downed by the slightest breeze.

"Why do you live here?" I asked her.

"I thought here I would be left alone." She shuffled forward like an old woman, lifting the dirty hem of her veil from the floor.

"I can leave if you would like."

"No, I was hoping you would come back. I wanted to ask you again about the vision."

"Why do you wear that veil?" I asked.

"I told you," she said self-consciously. "I prefer not to be seen."

"I see." I turned back to the notes on her wall. "You look into your mirror for the people in the village?"

"They come to me wanting to hear from those who have died, or to ask about their own futures."

"Do you tell them what they want to hear?"

"I tell them only what I see or hear in dreams, or in visions. I tell them only the truth."

"You are confident that you know the truth?"

She only shrugged beneath the black veil.

"How did you know that black-haired woman? Will you tell me that?" she asked abruptly.

"Wouldn't your mirror tell you?" I answered, sitting upon a low stool in the corner and lifting the Bible to my lap. As she seemed to have no intention of answering, I began reading aloud. I thought little about the words as I read them, but I could tell that the girl listened in rapt attention. She barely made a sound during the readings, but sat crouched on a stool across the table, melting into a corner of shadow. If not for the occasional sniff or sigh, I could have easily imagined I was alone in the room.

When I grew tired of reading I stood from the stool and placed my candle on one point of the painted pentagram. Patiently I waited as she mumbled her incantations over the glass, pressing her veiled face close to its shadowy surface.

Unfortunately, what designs fate had in store for me the mirror would not yield. I began to wonder if this was God's trickery, not wanting to reveal a fate He knew full well I would only attempt to circumvent with my own actions.

"I see a wedding—you are wearing a beautiful white satin gown," she told me.

"Rubbish!" I exclaimed.

"You are smiling happily," she told me the next day, a bit warily, "with a beautiful baby in your arms."

"Blasphemy!" I shouted. "Where do you get these ridiculous ideas? I could do better myself, gazing into the cook's ladle."

"I'm sorry," she said, and wavered for a moment, as if faint. "The mirror won't show me anything aside from what I've already told you: the woman with black hair." She sighed heavily, her shoulders hunched forward beneath her veil. "You did not want to hear the truth; I thought I would try to guess what you wanted to hear."

She took a step closer, her veiled face hovering over the candlelit table like a dark ghost.

"Won't you tell me about her, please?"

"I'm beginning to doubt your power," I told her angrily. "That angel who blessed you was nothing but a foolish child's dream." I clasped my cloak at my neck, preparing to leave.

"But I've seen her, the woman with the curling black hair. And I've seen you with her. That much is true, you can't deny it."

I paused for a moment, suddenly embarrassed. I turned away from her and faced the wall.

"She was a friend of mine, long ago," I told her. "A very dear friend."

"And then she died," she said.

"Did you see that in your mirror?" I asked.

"I can hear it in your voice," she said. "What else can you tell me about her?"

I opened my mouth to speak but instead caught a flicker of recognition, like a tiny lightning bolt striking in my head. Right before my face hung a particular piece of parchment on her wall. It was a drawing that I knew well, though I had not seen its likeness for years: a young woman's face rendered by the gentle strokes of an artist's pencil.

"What do you know about her?" the child asked again, petulant. Her voice had never sounded so young before.

"Perhaps I should ask you the same thing," I said, moving closer to the door. "You've seen her in your mirror before?"

"Many times," she told me, "and in dreams."

"Who asked you about her—did someone ask you to find her?"

"No, no one asked me. I've seen her all along." She lowered her head over the mirror but did not crouch over it to scry. "She was my first vision. I saw her on that white bed, and I saw the sheets turn red with blood. Not until now did I see you sitting beside her."

"Why are you telling me this?" I muttered angrily. "I was there, I don't need to know."

"I need to know," she stated, and stepped forward. "I need you to tell me—please."

"Perhaps your angel will reveal it for you," I told her. I slipped out the door and fled into the night.

But I did go back to visit her, though at the time I wouldn't admit to myself the reason why.

"How old are you?" I asked her, the Bible unopened upon my lap. "Does anyone know that you are here?"

"My father, he is traveling," she explained. "He knows where I am."

"And your mother?" I ventured.

"My mother is dead." She sighed, and the words made me shiver. "I think that is why I am this way. I think you're right, that I was cursed."

I could understand that, the feeling of something being wrong with you, living under an ill omen.

"Why do you think you were you cursed?"

"Because my mother is dead, and I think it was my fault," she told me.

It is your fault! The thoughts began screaming in my head, so loud that I could not ignore them. I squeezed my eyes shut, but all I found in that blackness was memory: the white bed covered in blood, the sound of an infant's strangled cries. Opening my eyes to see the child before me, I had the urge to lash out at her violently. For a moment I sat perched on my chair, unable to move, my fists clenched and my teeth gritted.

This is the sin of wrath, I thought, remembering Sinestra's words. *Embrace its power; don't reject it.* It tore through me with frightening force, the opening of an old wound.

Finally, I stood from my chair and turned to leave.

"You'll be back to read more tomorrow?" she asked me.

"Of course I will," I uttered, my throat too tight for speech.

But I didn't go back, and attempted to avoid any thought of the scryer. When I saw her again, the village would be seized by flames, and hysteria, and fear.

XLII

Seeing the scryer changed me. The ghosts of Anastasia and Ursula still paced the tower room while I tried to sleep at night, but I responded with rage instead of fear. I threw things at them—a string of pearls, a book, a wine goblet—until they scurried back into their hiding places. Though bathing my face in the blood of virgins each night continued to offer me some form of peace, the rituals themselves were lacking in something I desperately craved. I felt that my power, my rage, was being constricted inside of me, waiting to break free.

One night the girls—Mary, Althea, Elizabeth, Therese, and Sarah—lounged in the tower room just before our ritual. Therese lay with her head resting upon a velvet pillow beside me, and I petted her silken hair distractedly as she closed her eyes.

"Therese had better rest while she still can." Althea giggled, her eyes glassy with wine. "She may not have much of a chance, before long."

Therese's eyes opened, her neck stiffened against the velvet pillow.

"What was that, Althea?" I asked, but the conversation on the other side of the room had abruptly shifted to the comparing of jewelry; I had given Sarah a pearl pin that was the envy of all. Therese lifted her head slowly from the pillow and stood to take a sip of her wine.

"What was Althea talking about, Therese?" I asked her. Her

eyes shifted away from me nervously. I had never known Therese to act so skittish around me before. She had long been the leader, the bravest and most accepting of all my girls.

"Countess, I've been your servant for five years now," she informed me.

"Yes, I know that, Therese."

"You promised that we would be released after five years."

"Of course, dear. I had no idea that you wanted to leave, if that is your decision."

"The decision has been made." She shrugged and smiled slightly. "I am getting married this summer. I hope that you approve, Countess."

"I simply don't see why you would want such a thing for yourself, Therese."

"My father has made arrangements with the village butcher. He seems like a kind man, and my father approves of the match," she explained, ever pragmatic.

"And that is enough for you to leave me?" I asked, my voice suddenly loud. All other talk in the room ceased; though only Sarah had been witness to my killing, all of the girls were familiar with my periodic rages.

"I saved your life here. And you will leave to be the servant of a man who will give you nothing but work, and children? You will be his slave, with none of this luxury," I told her, referring to the candlelit chamber, the wine goblets glistening red in the firelight. "What I ask of you is comparatively little."

"I know, Countess, and I am sorry. But I'm afraid I must do this, for my family. It's what my father has long planned for me, once my years in your service were complete. I hope you can understand."

She was a dutiful daughter, I realized. I shouldn't have been surprised, for she had been a loyal servant to me. She would make this butcher a good, honest wife—would that he deserved her.

"Of course, dear, I understand," I told her, and smiled. She rested her head back upon the cushion and shut her eyes, her dark eyelashes curving against her cheeks. I nestled my hand in her golden curls to hide its trembling.

The desire came to you last night." Sinestra's voice rumbled in my ear, waking me from a deep sleep. "I saw it, as you looked at Therese. I could feel how it surged through you."

It was barely dawn and he was lying beside me in bed, my bedchamber lit with candles.

"What do you know of my desire?" I asked, but I could not conceal the hurt in my voice. He pulled me close to him and kissed me, deeply.

"Don't deny that you've thought of killing her—your favorite, no less." His voice lilted with admiration. I could not help but revel in it.

"Perhaps"—I sighed, realizing the futility of denial—"but it was only a thought."

"It doesn't need to be. It could be so much more than that. I know you, and I know what you are capable of."

"How is it that you know me so well?"

He placed his hands on either side of my face and forced me to look directly at him, his eyes reflecting the candlelight.

"Because you and I are the same," he told me. "We are the same mind, the same heart."

"If am your heart, then why don't you come to me when I need you—at night, when I can't sleep for thoughts of old ghosts."

"You give the dead too much power over you, Erzebet," he

scolded, gripping my arms. "Your measly kills, your mother—and that friend of yours."

My eyes flew open at this, my back suddenly rigid.

"You never talk about her, but I can see her death still clinging to you, like a silk shroud."

"How dare you!" I shrieked, pushing him away from me. The ghosts were not the only thing that haunted me, I realized in shame—my days and nights were plagued by my desires for him. And here he was in the flesh, spurring me to anger. He gripped my arms in his, but I lashed out only more viciously, scratching him across the chest. As I grew tired of the fight, he pulled me close to him again.

"Let go of it, Erzebet," he murmured, his voice surprisingly compassionate. "Let go of her. She certainly let go of you, long ago, even before her death."

He knew all of it, then, all of my feelings of betrayal when Marianna had married, when she became swollen with child.

"She was not chosen," he reminded me, "but you are."

I felt the tears rise within me—stale tears, unshed over years of stifled grief. I pushed them down again, feeling them harden within my chest. Sinestra kissed me again, the heat of his kiss warming the coldness inside of me.

"Am I not enough for you?" he asked. "I will always be here for you, and I offer you everything—I offer you eternity."

"Of course you are enough for me." I responded in kind with a kiss.

I was not prepared to put myself at risk. This lesson had been hard learned after Marianna's death; I had only needed Sinestra to remind me. To love was an indiscretion that I dared not commit again.

I began a habit of calling Therese to the tower at odd hours for bleedings. I reasoned that I wanted to have my fill of her blood while she was still a virgin, and still mine. But both of us knew there was more to it than that.

By the time the spring buds had opened their hearts to the sun, Therese was merely a shadow of the girl she had been. Her skin was glaringly pale in the sunlight, her limbs skeletal and lacking the reliable, resourceful energy she generally exuded. Ever the brave acolyte, Therese told no one about the additional bleedings that I had been demanding, and hid her weakness with stunning efficiency. I continued to present her with gifts after each of these secret bleeding sessions, which she accepted with a solemn nod of gratitude.

"You could wear this on your wedding day," I told her after a bleeding, ushering her over to the mirror so I could clasp the circlet of pearls in her hair.

Her eyes appeared flat and glassy in the mirror, her face drawn. It was not unlike the transformation Anastasia had undergone before her death, but there was something more precious, more sacred about how it took its toll upon Therese. She was not naive about my intentions, and seemed to realize that I still held sway over her life, and that I might do with it as I pleased. She submitted to her death gracefully, with the full knowledge that she was still under my control. As the day of her wedding drew nearer, Therese's life waned to a close.

It was a day in early summer when we both knew the end was near. She gazed at me over the wooden bowl, her gray eyes glassy and solemn.

"Why are you doing this to me?" she asked, but she seemed to know the answer already.

"Because you have faltered in your devotion," I told her, tightening my grip upon her hand. She sighed knowingly. Weary, she rested her head upon the table. She did not lift it again.

Once certain that her heart had ceased beating, I mused that I had saved her from a worse fate at the hands of a brutal husband. Still, the fact that she had rejected the life I offered her left a sour taste within my mouth, even as I inspected the motionless beauty of her bent white body, her honey-golden hair spilled over the wooden bowl. No one was safe, anymore, from my whims. No one was safe but me.

I called Mary, Althea, Elizabeth, and Sarah to the room, where we stood for a moment in silence over Therese's frozen form.

"There has been an accident," I explained, but they knew the truth. I left the task of Therese's burial to them, as a lesson to them all.

I feared I was losing what grip of power I held over these girls. It made me think back to another night in my past, and the far greater power that I had possessed, if only for a moment—the night of Ursula's murder. The memory awoke a craving within me that had been dormant for years.

That night I waited for Sinestra in the garden; Kyzoni paced around my legs as though circling prey. When Sinestra appeared, I fell into his embrace. The night was warm and he spun me around in a slow, sinuous dance.

"Tell me about the glory of hell," I whispered in his ear.

He took my hand and pulled me to the tower, breaking into a run in the middle of the dark hallway. By the time we reached the chamber we were both panting and laughing with excitement.

"Why are we here?" I asked him as he lit a fire in the hearth; it sprang to life with startling ease. He turned to me, his body outlined by the flames.

"Because this is where you will begin," he said, grasping my hand in his. "This is where you have created heaven, for you and for your victims."

"Victims—not my girls?" I asked. I filled a glass of red wine and took a sip, then passed it to him.

"That choice is entirely yours." He smiled. "Though you might need the assistance your girls could offer you. Those that you choose for killing should be girls easily disposed of."

"There are plenty of them here," I thought aloud, imagining the kitchen assistants and scullery maids sleeping side by side in the servants' quarters, beneath the shadow of this tower.

"You will choose them," Sinestra said, pulling me into a twirling dance around the tower room, "and you will invite them here to your haven—your heaven. Here they will taste the delights of music, and food, and laughter, and wine. Delicacies such as they have never tasted before." He grasped me by the waist and lifted me from the ground; I laughed, breathless. "You will dress them in fine clothes that will make their vanity bloom within them; you will cover them in your sparkling jewels, like goddesses."

"Like angels," I corrected him, my head spinning with the dance.

"What is heaven," he asked, staring into my eyes, "but freedom, and beauty, and comfort?"

"And salvation," I added.

"Yes, of course"—he smiled—"but what is heaven alone? It is a dream for these pitiful creatures blundering through their common lives, eager to see what lies in the world beyond in the hopes that it may be better than what they have here."

"That is greed," I told him, "and pride. The sins are a part of us all. I sometimes think that humans were made entirely of sin. No wonder they are so consumed with a fear of damnation."

"This idea of heaven is meant to show people the right path to walk, in order to end up sleeping in the arms of angels," he mused, lowering a candle over the flames of the fire; I heard the wax sizzle as it sparked a flame. "Heaven is a gift from God—or is it a gift from the Church?"

"That's blasphemy!" I laughed nervously. "And what of your fascination with hell? If heaven is not real, then most likely hell is a construct of imagination as well, to terrify people into behaving themselves."

"What have I taught you, Erzebet?" he asked, enclosing my hand in his. "It does not matter what is real, but what people believe is real. You must make them believe."

He pulled my hand swiftly toward the chamber door; we raced down the stairs, then down more stairs into the dungeon. He released my hand and for a moment I stood motionless in the darkness. Then I saw him toss the lit candle into the hearth, where the fire sprang to raging life.

Though I had been to this chamber before for burials—first Anastasia, then Ursula—I had never taken the time to explore it. Still littered with crates storing the rest of the count's art collection, this dungeon was smaller than the granary or the dungeon below the chapel where I had taken my confession, years before. It branched off into other, smaller chambers, but the main portion of the dungeon was encroached upon by the side of the mountain. Near the jagged face of the mountain I spotted the chains I had seen on my first visit here, protruding from the stone wall.

"Do you see how the stone is curved here"—Sinestra pointed,

resting his hands upon the base of the mountain—"as if carved at over years of waiting."

I looked again and saw, for the first time, the disintegrating bones—barely distinguishable—littering the dungeon floor. It made me suddenly, frightfully aware of the dead lying in the earth beneath my feet.

"There were prisoners here?" I wondered aloud.

"Castle Bizecka has secrets that she has not told even you, her favored only child."

I stood beside Sinestra and pressed my hand to the place where the ancient mountain and the castle fused together as one. It was a castle already livid with its own ghosts, its own evil; I could feel it pulsing beneath my hand like a living, breathing being. It was as if the castle had grown here from the mountainside, sprouting like a dark plant from an evil seed.

"I belong here," I murmured, pressing my cheek to the rough wall to hear the ghosts clamoring from within. I felt that the castle had given birth to me, and had done more to make me the woman that I was than the count and countess ever had.

"I knew I would find you here," Sinestra said, leaning against the wall for support. "My kin, my love, born in such a place, and of such a family, with an ancient name. And under such an omen."

I thought of the shooting star on the day of my birth with a familiar fear.

"Do you think it really was an angel, falling from the sky?" I asked.

"Perhaps it was that angel's time to fall," he suggested, smiling at me. "It was a good omen, remember? An omen foretelling your birthright; if you are only brave enough to claim it."

"The child whose days will have no end." I murmured the words of the prophecy with a strength and happiness they had never conjured in me before.

"That's right," Sinestra agreed. "Eternal life. All that you need to do is commit your ultimate break from God."

"Will it happen here? The scene of my crime?"

"Of course it will happen here." He smiled, caressing my cheek. "You have created heaven, Erzebet, and you have made your girls worship you like a god. But if you are truly a god, you must show them the full breadth of your power. Creating heaven and sharing a sacrament is not enough. This castle is your world, Erzebet, your own creation. You've created Eden—now banish them from it."

"Banish them," I murmured, intoxicated by the images the words conjured in my mind, "and bring them here."

"Show them the power of one more than merely human," he said, and the fire seemed to jump higher at his words.

"What is the one thing that never dies?" he asked.

"God never dies," I answered.

"God? No—God dies in the hearts of men every day. God's power relies solely on the belief and devotion of His subjects: without belief, God is dead."

I swallowed, my throat strangely dry; my vision blurred in the red-and-orange light.

"It is blasphemy only if you believe in such things," he reminded me, "as you have been taught to believe. All else in this life is a mystery, and what lies beyond life a greater mystery still. There is only one thing that we can be sure of: the one thing that never dies."

I stared into his eyes, awaiting his answer.

"Death," he said.

"I will create heaven and hell," I told him. "I will be like a god to them. I will be their death, exacting their final judgment. What then? Will I be safe forever?"

"Yes," he said, kneeling before me and wrapping his large hands around my small waist. "Nothing will be able to touch you then, not even a prophecy made about a little girl—you are not that little girl anymore; you've already transformed. But soon the transformation will be complete. You will be beyond all judgment but your own—all-powerful. In this castle, you are God."

I leaned back and spread my arms out as if I were flying, feeling the flames rise, letting the voices of old ghosts wash over me in waves. Sinestra held me by my waist; I knew he would not let me fall. I was bending, exultant, beneath the power of Castle Bizecka; her power and my power fused into one.

I threw a special celebration that summer. I secretly referred to it as a blood party: a more genteel form of slaughter, as the prey is well fed and entertained long before the night's true entertainment begins. There was much preparation required for the event. My blood girls were responsible for clearing the boxes from the main chamber of the dungeon below the tower, moving them all into one of the small adjacent chambers that we would not need. Once it was cleared, I could detect the inconsistencies in the earth left behind by our burials—including the most recent burial of Therese.

"Put that empty box in a separate chamber, over there," I ordered, enjoying how my voice echoed confidently in the cleared space. The girls dragged the large empty crate over the dirt floor, over the grave of their former companion; they were eager to meet all of my demands. I can understand now why God inspires fear in His subjects: there is a certain security of the self, a certain power in being feared.

Three girls were chosen as my companions for the night of the sacrifice, and we took our meal in the dining hall. Dinner was accompanied by minstrels, laughter, delicious food, and copious glasses of red wine. Dessert was enjoyed in the tower room—an enchanting heaven, indeed—where yet more wine was imbibed. All the while in the tower I would check my face in the mirror, smiling at myself knowingly.

I waited until the moon was high in the night sky, and then I penetrated the laughter and the singing with my own voice:

"To the dungeon! Follow me!"

Like willing sheep, they followed me: giggling and tripping over themselves all the way. I held a torch to light my steps, and threw the torch into the hearth as soon as I emerged in the dungeon, making the fire leap to life. I stood by the fire and watched the girls pitch forward from the dark stairwell into the eerie red light.

First I taught them how to dance: I grasped one girl's wrists and started to spin her in a circle, faster and faster, until she tripped over her own feet with dizziness. All the girls paired up in twos or in threes, spinning in circles—dancing over the graves of other, similar girls who had been there before them. I watched them for a while, their howls and laughter filling the chamber, echoing tenfold against the stone walls.

A tub was set up by the roaring fire, a tub with a wire grate inside.

"A beauty treatment," I told them, and that was enough to get them to drunkenly pull off their garments and toss them aside. From all the wine and all the dancing, their garments were already loose and dangling, and they were glad to be free of them, to dance naked like witches at midnight.

This is when my assistants emerged from the adjacent rooms: Mary, Althea, Elizabeth, and Sarah. They waited patiently in the shadows for my signal. They would be rewarded handsomely for their assistance with only this: their lives. I would choose to allow them to live. For this they were grateful.

I grabbed one dancing girl and stabbed her, but only enough to injure her, to slow her down, not enough to kill her. Not yet. Her friends were too busy delighting in the way the firelight lit their bodies golden to distinguish their companion's cries of pain. I dragged her over to the grated tub and stabbed her again—not to death, but to the brink of death. The act filled me with awe at my own power: I had been born to do this, I was sure, blessed with an innate skill for hunting and killing prey. By the time the others realized what was happening, my assistants had rounded them up and chained them to the walls.

One by one the girls were slaughtered on the grate and bled into the tub below. The rest would watch and wait. I stood over each girl to watch her die, and said her name aloud over her body, singing it like a lullaby to a child, savoring the sound of it, as if it were a word I had just created myself. No one else would say her name. These girls were swallowed whole by time.

The blood harvested from three girls was enough to allow me to indulge in a full bath, once all were dead. My assistants dragged the bodies to the adjoining chamber, where the large crate was ready for the disposal of dead girls. Meanwhile, I was enjoying their blood by the light of a raging fire, the flames casting gold-and-crimson shadows upon the walls, the girls' shrieks still echoing in my ears. I felt my own fear and anger melt inside of me, extending to my toes and my fingertips like liquid fire. The sin of wrath is powerful, and I had finally claimed this power as my own.

In the days following the sacrifice I asked my faithful assistants to act as spies in my defense: listening to conversations, asking questions, all to gauge the reactions of the other servants to what had been going on beneath the castle's main floor. According to their reports, the late-night cries of the dying were overheard as the howling of the wind, or the sighing of old ghosts. Even Rowena and Pugrue had nothing to say on the matter, and reported having slept well enough.

I can only speculate on the lies people tell themselves for the sake of self-protection. There is no such thing as innocence in times like these.

XLIII

The full bath in blood left me feeling strong and triumphant. I was already planning another as the leaves began to crisp and curl in the autumn wind. Though at times I was eager for another full bath, the preparation for such an event took careful consideration. It was not enough to choose three girls to kill—they had to be the right girls, whose appearance lit that spark of envy within me until it burned bright within my heart. I would walk the halls of the castle to watch them from the shadows, letting the flames of envy grow brighter, fiercer, fit to consume me. But another flame was fed there, too. I held the knowledge of their death close to my heart, waiting for the right moment to claim my power.

Late that autumn, I visited the village for All Hallows' Eve to watch the villagers perform their annual Hell Parade at midnight. I took my white-nosed mare down the steep incline to the village, then settled with her on a lower slope in order to watch the festivities from a distance. Torches were lit in the darkness, and a great bonfire was already smoking in the village square.

A group of villagers had begun snaking through the town in the red robes of devils, or the white shrouds of the dead. They held torches and bottles of wine and shouted the lyrics to bawdy songs. I laughed at them, the brisk wind nipping at the back of my neck through my cloak; I shivered deliciously. The behavior of the peasants fascinated me. They paraded down the streets, making a mockery of the damnation they so feared while kneeling in church, in the daylight. I was certain that a pious few were still indoors, disapproving of such debauchery and apparent disdain for all things holy. But for this one night the people of the town felt safe from the devil's touch by taking on the aspect of the devil themselves.

As the crowd snaked closer, the voices grew louder, escalating to screams. There was one particular devil in the front of the crowd who was creating most of the stir: he was dressed in a red cape with a white turban tied upon his head. This was a devil that everyone reviled: the sultan. The crowd grew wild, throwing bottles at the turbaned head before them, running in a mad rush to the town square. I could not help but laugh at their antics: were they now too drunk to realize that it was one of their neighbors they chased, and not the sultan himself? I nudged the gray mare with my heel and we descended our hill, moving closer to the town square.

Another devil was in the center of the square, and his voice boomed over the cries of the crowd. He was a large man wearing a robe that would have suited a devil or a bishop, his face smeared with red paint—blood? I wondered. He held a torch in his hand that he waved while he spoke, the sparks and embers streaking through the air.

"There is evil in our midst!" he cried. "Evil in our midst! We, as a people, have been deceived!"

This pronouncement grasped the full attention of the crowd. They all gathered around the large man, who held his torch high. I hung back near a large oak tree to watch the scene from a distance. The smell of the smoke made my eyes sting.

"Evil has lived side by side with us for years. The time has come to remove it!"

The peasants around him shouted in approval; I wondered if any of them knew what the man was talking about.

"She was to protect us," he cried. "She was to warn us of what the future might hold. But she has failed us all—everyone here, she has betrayed! She protects no one, aside from the devil whose bidding she does."

"The witch!" the people started chanting; the mare began to buck anxiously, the smoke becoming thicker by the moment.

"Tonight—a sacrifice!" the man yelled. "To rid our town of evil! Burn the witch!"

"Burn the witch! Burn the witch!" the crowd shouted in response. They touched their torches to the bonfire in the town square until they each blazed forth into crackling life. Then the crowd turned in one mass, toward the forest. It became all too clear to me the witch they meant. I gripped the mare's reins in panic. Suddenly I thought I saw Sinestra's face in the crowd of villagers before me.

"What do I do?" I called out to him, my voice barely audible over the screaming. "Tell me—what do I do?" But his face disappeared before the words left my mouth, melted into the smoke and fire.

You must promise me . . . Marianna's voice echoed in my head, magnified above the shouting of the crowd. *You must promise me*—I covered my ears with my hands in the hope of blotting out the words, but they were there inside of me, and I could not escape them.

You give the dead too much power over you, Erzebet. Sinestra was right. After all that had changed, why should Marianna's words haunt me now? But this didn't just involve the dead: it was a promise about the living. A promise still burned like a brand upon my soul.

I'm a killer now, that's who I am, I tried to explain, but the dead do not accept an explanation. A promise is a promise; I wasn't ready to reject Marianna's wishes.

Still not certain of what I would do, I spurred the horse forward, toward the river. That would be the quickest way to get to the scryer before the crowd, which would be slowed down by the overgrown forest.

The mare pounded the earth at a gallop, all the way down the river, the echoes of the screaming crowd following us all the way. Finally we reached the stream that trickled a path through the trees to the scryer's house. I pulled the horse to a sudden stop and she reared up in fear. The forest was full of men and women shouting, "Burn the witch! Burn the witch!"

We dove into the trees, rushing into the crowd in the hope of reaching the hut first. Villagers lunged from the path of the horse's pounding hooves. When we reached the hut, I swung from the saddle and leaped toward the door.

"Are you here?" I ran into the house, pushing the table aside. A mirror fell and crashed to the floor. I heard a shriek in the darkness.

"You must come with me—I can save you from this."

"Why would you save me?" she asked, leaping away from my touch. "Where will you take me?"

I grabbed her roughly by the arm and pulled her toward the door. Her knees buckled at the sight of the horse.

"I made a promise long ago," I muttered.

"A promise to whom?" the child whined.

I grasped her hand and lifted her clumsily onto the saddle, then swung onto the horse behind her. Just as we made ready to ride, the horse reared up again, shrieking with fear.

"Burn the witch! Burn the witch!"

A man had grabbed hold of the horse's tail and pulled it violently. The horse stamped the earth, her eyes livid. There were men standing in the path before us now, surrounding the house. Women were behind us, throwing clumps of dirt and stones.

Then, in one moment, it happened. Kyzoni appeared, his fur silvery white in the darkness. He must have followed me from the castle, from a safe distance. Now he lunged forward and seized a man's leg between his jaws. The shriek of the man made the villagers jump back in fear. The other voices around us diminished, and the horse reared up again, whinnying shrilly. Kyzoni's ear twitched at the sound of the horse, but he did not release his grip upon the man's leg.

With a swift pull and a bracing kick, I turned the horse away from the forest, back toward the river. The two of us crouched low, gripping her mane tightly.

"You'll be safe now," I told her.

She bent her head low upon the horse's back. She did not lift it until we had climbed the mountain, leaving the raging fire and voices behind us.

XLIV

When we arrived at the castle it was not yet dawn, but I knew the kitchen would soon be bustling. We dashed through the door and into the hallway.

"I don't want to be seen," the scryer croaked urgently.

I was eager to conceal her for my own reasons, anxious to hide what I had done. I knew of only one place completely secluded, but the thought of taking her to the tower made my stomach groan. Panicked, I regretted having brought her to the castle at all. I began to pull her down the hallway toward my bedchamber, but there was a rustling at the end of the hall; she stood stock-still in fright. I sighed in despair as I urged her up the spiral staircase, my arms nearly lifting her weak body over the threshold.

"No corners to hide in," she uttered upon entering the tower, awed and afraid. As I rushed to light a fire she stood still as a statue in the middle of the room, the black veil swaying softly around her.

"It's cold in here," she whimpered.

"It's always cold in here," I told her, "but once the fire is roaring, you'll be warm."

I moved forward and tugged at the veil, but she resisted; the fabric was scratchy to the touch. Lifting pillows and a fur blanket, I made a bed for her upon the small couch.

"You can sleep here. I'll move it closer to the fire," I told her. She sighed audibly and I saw her shoulders droop; in defeat or relief, I could not discern which. I tugged at the veil again and this time she relented, slipping free of the sheer shroud and crawling into the bed. She was a child, indeed, and nearly wasted to the bone. I detected something animal-like about her as I watched her burrow into the heap of blankets by the fire, her face obscured by a mass of knotted black hair. I listened closely as her breathing began to slow.

"Where did you get those drawings of the woman with the dark curly hair?" The words pulled from my throat like a ghost.

Her eyelids fluttered. "My father gave them to me," she said, as if speaking from the edge of a dream.

I sat in the room the whole day and watched her sleep. Near sunset she began to rustle, burrowing deeper beneath her nest of blankets. I poured a cup of tea and set it on the table beside her, along with a plate of bread and cheese. She peered warily over the edge of the blanket, her face still hidden by her hair.

"I have food for you," I told her, but she only shook her head, vehemently.

"You have to eat. I can have the cook prepare whatever you would like."

"If I eat I won't have visions," she said. "That's what the villagers told me."

"That's because they wanted the food for themselves. You have to eat something, Snow."

Snow: the name slipped out of me, like pearls from a broken strand; I could only stand and watch them scatter. It had been the last thing Marianna had said to me before she died, but I had never spoken the name aloud. Now there was no denying to myself who I thought this child was. Her eyes flickered over my face.

"That's not my name," she said warily. "It's only what my father called me. How did you know?"

"Where is your father?" I asked, shifting uneasily in my chair.

"I told you, he's been traveling for years now. He missed my mother too much to stay with me; it was like a needle stuck inside of him all the time." She studied my face for a moment. "I am the needle," she said.

"Please eat something, Snow," I urged gently. "You don't need to have any more visions. Wouldn't you like them to leave you alone, for a time?"

"I would like the villagers to leave me alone," she remarked bitterly. "They are foolish people. The devil and his minions are nothing to make a mockery of—they are something to be feared." She crossed herself hastily at these words.

"Then the whims of God should be feared as well," I suggested, "for He created the devil, did He not? God created both heaven and hell."

"I suppose He did," she tentatively agreed. "But I do not deny his blessings." She gazed for a moment at the bread on the plate before her. "Perhaps this is a blessing. None of the villagers will visit me now," she said darkly. She grasped the bread and ate hungrily, like a desperate animal, chewing too quickly to speak. When she finished her meal she fell back asleep.

As Snow slept, I noticed that all of the artifacts of Marianna that had remained in the tower over the years suddenly seemed to shine brilliantly in the firelight, demanding attention: a pink silk handkerchief, a bracelet of pale beads, a dried rose on a curling vine. I considered rushing to conceal these objects, but thought better of it: I had other work to do. I hung a kettle of water over the fire and had the clean tub I used for my morning baths carried from my bedchamber into the tower room. At first glance I saw a white body streaked with blood stretched within the tub. I looked to Snow—thankfully, she was asleep. When I looked back, the vision was gone. Even in the daylight, ghosts winked at me from the silver brightness of the mirror.

When she woke again she seemed startled to see me.

"You're used to being alone, aren't you?" I said as I transferred hot water into the tub. "So am I."

"Who is the woman in the vision?" she asked bluntly. I poured the hot water into the tub, the steam rising in a cloud around me.

"How did she die?" she asked, and my eyes flashed at hers for a moment. I sensed that she knew more than she dared admit.

"It's time for your bath. We'll talk about that later."

"No," she said, burrowing deeper in the covers, "I don't want a bath."

I stood and stepped toward her, taken aback by my own lack of authority. During other episodes in this tower room I had felt powerful—all-powerful. But standing in front of that stubborn child, I didn't know what to do.

"Please, Snow. It won't take long," I told her. But would it? I wondered. I had never even bathed myself, let alone another person.

"I won't do it."

"You must."

"I won't!"

I stomped my foot on the ground like a frustrated child. Furrowed and brooding, I left the tower room and closed the door behind me. I walked down the hallway toward my chambers, peeking into rooms to see what servants were available. But all of the girls I saw were too young, none of them motherly enough to care for Snow. Finally, I found Rowena. I hesitated for a moment, unsure I wanted to involve Rowena in this situation, but I didn't know what else to do. She curtsied stiffly at my approach and did not meet my eyes.

"Rowena, I have an important request. I need you in the tower."

I detected a bright flash of fear in her eyes. Her thin lips lost their color.

"It's not that, Rowena," I reassured her awkwardly. "There is someone else who needs your help."

Rowena followed me cautiously, unsure of what she would find. Her presence hadn't been requested in the tower room since the days of Marianna's confinement. When she stepped in, her eyes scanned the room anxiously. Finally they settled upon Snow, shriveled and dirty, curled upon the couch. Rowena warmed to her instantly, as if to a wounded animal. As she coaxed Snow out of her dark layers and into the tub, I stepped aside, feeling suddenly out of place. This was a fragile, intimate moment that I could not get too close to, as if it might shatter like glass at my touch.

"Oh, what have you done to yourself, child?" I heard Rowena moan.

"I haven't done anything," Snow retorted.

"I can see that," she murmured. "Clearly you've had no one to help you."

Snow was nearly completely submerged in the tub, her white body folded neatly under the water, her chin resting upon the already dingy surface. Rowena had begun to attack Snow's nest of black hair, pulling free clumps of dirt, leaves, and hair as she did so. Still obscured by dirt, Snow's face was a mask of pain.

Even in the sanctuary of my tower, the child's presence made me feel awkward, even powerless. I did the only thing I knew how to do in Snow's company, just as I had in her hut in the forest: I lit a few candles, sat in a chair, and began to read the Bible aloud. Rowena's eyes flickered at me suspiciously.

It was near midnight when Rowena was done. She poured water from a pitcher over Snow's newly sleek head, the water running into her eyes. Then she set to work with a washcloth on the child's face. I watched, afraid of what the gray lump of soap would reveal. I could not have prepared myself for the results: her skin was pure white and smooth as glass, though her cheeks still retained the hollowness of starvation. Her black eyes gleamed as though with fever, her lips a natural berry red. She stood from the bath and let Rowena dry her bone-china skin. I felt something clench deep inside, making my spine bend and my knees buckle.

"Now you've been set to rights, and so prettily," Rowena gushed over the girl, her face glowing with perspiration and praise. "How old are you, child?"

Snow did not answer, only shrugged and wiped her nose on the drying cloth.

"Ten years old, I would guess, or even younger. We need to get some padding on those bones." She helped her into the white dressing gown I had laid out for her. The white silk made her even more ethereal, as though made of air.

"So nice," Rowena murmured approvingly. "Wouldn't you like to look?" she asked, leading her over to a mirror.

Snow's legs became rigid and she shook her head vehemently.

"I don't look in mirrors," she said.

"That's not true," I blurted out. "You look in mirrors all the time."

"That's different," she told me, with a sideways glance at Rowena. "I'm not looking for myself—I've never even seen myself. Mirrors are vain, a sin."

Just then I heard voices on the stairs. I stood to walk to the door, but I didn't make it in time. Mary, Althea, Elizabeth, and Sarah entered the chamber—it was midnight, after all. They stopped short at the scene displayed before them: Rowena and I standing in the candlelight, and the white-gowned child standing between us. I saw their eyes widen at the sight of Snow, glowing like an angel in her nightgown. Snow gasped under the shock of their sudden stares.

"I'm sorry, girls," I said, trying to divert their attention. I noticed that they were hesitant to look at me, unable to look away from the girl. "The chamber doesn't need cleaning tonight. Perhaps later this week; I will find you if I need your assistance."

As they turned to leave, Rowena shot a wary glance in my direction.

"I'll get you something to eat," she murmured to Snow, and left the room.

Snow did not want to leave the tower room. Seated upon the divan, she feasted upon the dinner of roasted meat, hard bread, smoked fish and cheese, and the goblet of goat's milk that Rowena provided. When she was done, she leaned back and let her eyes wander over the room meditatively. Then she settled her gaze upon me.

I moved over to the jewelry chest and emptied out the bottom drawer of its trinkets. *Why am I doing this?* The thoughts screamed in my head, but I felt compelled to pull the worn scraps of paper from the bottom of the drawer. Perhaps if I shared Marianna with her—only a little bit—then she would share her visions with me. I was still curious, though afraid, of what the child had foreseen. Careful not to look at them, I handed her the drawings.

"They are like the ones on my wall—where did you get these?" she asked, nearly breathless.

"I took them from Konrad, many years ago."

"She's the woman in the vision," she murmured. I could not tell if she meant to say the words aloud. "How did she die?" she asked warily.

"Didn't your vision reveal it to you?"

"Please don't tease me," she muttered. "Just tell me, how did she die?"

"In childbirth," I told her. "That was the end of your vision. I was there when she died—I held her hand."

"And the baby?"

"The baby lived, Snow." She kept her head lowered, staring at the drawings in her hands. Now dry, her black hair fell before her face like a veil of silk. "You knew that I would say that, didn't you?"

She paused for a moment, thoughtful, not daring to meet my eyes.

"The baby lived," she murmured, as if trying to decipher the meaning of the words. "Konrad is my father," she told me, lifting her eyes to mine, only briefly. "He never spoke about my mother at all. I think I knew what happened, but I pretended that I didn't know—I did very well at pretending."

"You didn't even know her," I said, unable to hide my bitterness.

"I know," she murmured, "but I was worried—afraid, even—of what it would mean about me."

"What do you mean?" I asked.

She was quiet for a moment, then lifted her head.

"I was born with death," she told me. "What could that mean about me?"

"I've wondered the same thing," I said, and closed my eyes.

Over the days and nights that followed, Snow indulged in the luxurious quiet of the tower chamber during the day and lurked the halls at night like a ghost. Those servants who caught a brief glimpse of her told tales of the phantom they had seen, creeping quietly around corners at night. Her skulking reminded me much of myself, in the days before Marianna. She reminded me more of myself at her age than of her own mother, who had always been friendly, and not given to hiding in shadow. The same tower imprisonment that Marianna had despised offered the security Snow preferred.

While Snow rested, my mind raced with what I should do. Winter was on its way, and I knew that Snow would have to stay with me, at least until the warm weather returned. I didn't trust the child, but I was wary to think such things around her, afraid that she might be able to see the thoughts forming in my mind. I tried, at times, to ask her about her visions of the future, but she demurred, unwilling to talk about it. Snow's presence made me feel closer to my own prophecy than I had in years. I hated the child and blamed her for Marianna's death—but these thoughts waged a constant battle with the promise I had made to her mother, to keep the child safe.

One day while we were dining together in the tower, Snow leaned back in her chair and studied me with her dark eyes. I felt awkwardly exposed, as though she were using me as one of her scrying mirrors.

"Do you have trouble sleeping here?" she asked me.

"Sometimes," I admitted. "It does get very cold here at night. Perhaps you would be more comfortable in a bedchamber on the main floor. I could have one prepared for you."

"No, I'm used to this room," she told me. I was eager to move her from the tower chamber: my regular schedule of monthly bleedings had been interrupted by her presence in the tower, and the sight of her flawless face made me yearn for them all the more.

"It seems like there are other people who have trouble sleeping in this castle. I find them when I take walks here late at night."

"Indeed? Perhaps they are servants, still attending to their tasks."

"Hmm, perhaps," she said thoughtfully. "They are very nice girls." She blinked sleepily; when she looked up at me, I noticed an uncanny glitter in her eyes.

"Anastasia," she pronounced suddenly.

"Who is that?" I asked, hiding my expression behind a goblet of wine.

"One of the girls I met, wandering around at night. And Ursula, and Therese. And a few others—I'll have to ask their names."

"I think you should try to stay in your own quarters late at night, Snow. You'll never get to sleep wandering about the halls of this castle."

"They all want to come here," she told me, her voice an eerie monotone. "This room is their favorite."

"There are many more things you could do if you were awake during the day with me," I said quickly, standing from my chair. I walked over to the dressing table; once my back was to Snow, I took a few deep breaths, trying to calm myself.

"Like what?" She sighed sleepily at this notion. It was still early evening, and I could tell she would doze after our meal was complete.

"I thought we could invite a minstrel to play some music for us, if you would like, or perhaps a recitation of poetry."

"I don't know anything about poetry." Again she sighed.

I scanned my eyes across the dressing table, peeking into drawers, searching. Finally I found it: a copy of *Tristan and Yseulte* that Marianna had asked me to read to her again and again. This would be exactly the type of gift that might distract Snow from her midnight walks, but still I hesitated to share it with her. Did I really want to share my Mari with this child? I looked into the mirror to see Snow's reflection in the glass. I was startled: she was looking right at me in the mirror, her eyes dark pools. The girl had power, I realized, a dangerous power, for I wondered in fear what the dead might tell her.

I returned to the table and placed the book in Snow's hands.

"But I don't know how to read," she informed me.

"I know, I'll read it aloud to you—just like I did for your mother."

Her eyes flashed up at mine and then back to the book. She began to scan the pages greedily, as if the symbols upon them would suddenly yield the answers to all of her questions.

"Did your father really never tell you about her at all?"

"No," she said. "He was too sad. For a long time I thought I had been born from magic, and not from a mother at all." She tried to laugh at this, but it came out awkward and sad.

"Your vision told you differently," I remarked.

"Yes, but I can never know if I can trust my visions—but please don't tell anyone I've said that." I was taken aback by her insistence; she even gripped my arm in fear.

"It is sinful to doubt one of God's gifts," she explained.

"Then I will doubt it for you, for I'm not afraid," I said, returning to my seat.

"You don't think I've been blessed?" she asked.

"No, Snow. I don't think being followed by the dead is much of a blessing."

I knew this to be true. Late that night I made my own walk down the castle halls, willing the ghosts to come out of their hiding places and face me. They did, one by one, but they would not let me see their faces. I heard light whispering, a few giggles, their footsteps following mine in a procession: Anastasia, Ursula, Therese, Katarina, Josephine, Susannah . . . I repeated their names to myself, like a prayer. I had recorded all of their names in the book of spells, to mark the day they gave their lives and deaths to me. They were a part of me; I knew their names by heart.

It's me you want, I reminded them. *It's me you're angry at. This has nothing to do with the girl.*

I chanted their names in a low tone until it became a kind of song, their footsteps like drumbeats. I hoped to find Sinestra, but knew that I would not—this night I would bear the burden, alone.

You will be untouchable. Remembering Sinestra's words gave me some solace, but this thought made the girls behind me laugh, their voices echoing sharply off the stone walls. I was not untouchable, and they knew this: the dead knew my secrets as well as I knew them myself. If I was God to them, then they were my fallen angels.

They followed me down every hallway. They followed me into bed, beneath the covers. They followed me to sleep, running and screaming through the chambers of my dreams.

That winter, despite the comfort of regular meals, and a warm bed to sleep in, Snow returned to her old habits.

"The people from the village would bang on the door of my hut, day and night, anxious to have their future foretold," she told me one day over a mouthful of bread. "I still wake from sleep, thinking that I hear them."

"What do the visions feel like, Snow?" I asked. She was surprised by this question, and mulled it over slowly while chewing a mouthful of cheese. Finally she swallowed, and spoke.

"It feels real. It feels as real as you sitting across from me right now," she told me. Her eyes seemed to glow in the candlelight.

"And what about the Apocalypse?" I laughed casually. "There

are those who seem certain our world is soon to end. What have you seen?"

"The world is ending slowly," she told me, "but it is ending. The end will always feel very near." As she said this, the tapestry covering the narrow window shuddered, the bitter wind pushing more snow onto the floor of the tower.

In the midst of the storm, she begged from me a roll of parchment, a quill and inkhorn. Seated at the round table in the tower room where I had performed my midnight bleedings, she began drawing her disconnected dreams and visions with a fervor I found fascinating. If she hung them on the wall, I mused, the tower would soon look like her hut in the forest. I watched her from a safe distance.

"What have you seen, Snow?" It was late at night and she had set the quill aside. She stared at the parchment before her quizzically, a deep crease nestled between her eyebrows. She scratched her face and left a smudge of ink by her nose.

"These visions want to be seen, but I don't quite know what they're telling me." She lifted her head to meet my gaze. "Your castle is quite haunted. Did you know that?"

I leaned over her shoulder and looked at the pieces of parchment laid before her. At first they looked like a frantic mess of scribbles and shapes, but slowly the forms began to emerge with startling clarity: a naked girl lying in a tub, crisscrossed with lines to show the wounds, the blood; a pile of dead bodies lying in a wooden crate, their eyes still opened. The sight of the crude drawings transformed into startlingly clear memory in my head: the dead bodies, the blood, their eyes open and looking at me. I blinked my eyes, trying to clear my vision: the ink upon the pages looked like blood.

Why are you so weak? I shouted in my head. *What has happened to you?* The sight of the drawings made my hands tremble. I was afraid of this child, afraid of what she would see in me. I was angry that she, of all people, would inspire my fear.

"They were murdered, and they are angry. That much is clear," Snow stated, crossing herself. I nodded, anxious to hide my reaction.

"Don't you ever attend Mass?" she asked suddenly.

"No, I don't—and neither do you," I said.

"But I would like to," she confided bashfully.

"Are you sure you're ready to be seen? I've already disposed of that black veil you wore—it was so filthy it stunk up any room it was in."

For a moment this thought made her cheeks red. She looked down at her simple blue gown, as if realizing that she was exposed.

"I think I am," she said bravely. "I need to go to Mass."

I enlisted the help of two servants, who woke, readied, and escorted Snow to Mass every morning. Even Pugrue praised her pious devotion. As winter transformed into spring, Snow became even more beautiful, and I watched everyone become intoxicated with the child's ethereal innocence.

One morning while Snow was busy with her devotions, I went to the tower room to find Sinestra waiting for me. He was bent over Snow's drawings and sipping lazily from a goblet of wine.

"Erzebet," he said as I entered the chamber, "I wanted to encourage you to take advantage of this day, when your young friend returns." I saw that he was placing my knife and bowl on the table, over the drawings.

"No," I uttered weakly, "I can't do that." I hid my trembling hands in the folds of my gown.

"You've been wanting to bleed her since the moment you saw

her," he told me, walking around the table toward me. "More than that, you've been wanting to make her one of your victims in your dungeon-hell. Then the girl can live among your precious ghosts; I can see that they have already embraced her."

"I can't do it," I uttered; he leaped forward and grasped me roughly by the arms.

"Why? Why can't you do it? I've given you so much power—don't deny it now, when you need it most."

"I can't kill her. I made a promise to keep her safe."

"Don't kill her, then, but don't let this child take your power from you. Don't be ashamed of what you are."

"What am I?" I asked, stunned at the words as they came out of my mouth.

"Don't you remember?" He pulled me into his insistent embrace. "You can do anything you want to do here; this castle is your world."

"She has made me weak, and afraid of her—the things that she sees." I could not explain to him the girl's connection to Marianna, and how I felt it had brought her back to me again, after all of these years: Mari sweet and loving, but also judging and fearful of what I had become.

"The things that she sees are true; why must you be afraid of them now? They are your glory. Give the girl something to fear—you know fear so intimately, I am certain that you can inspire it in her."

"I know fear and fear knows me," I murmured, feeling suddenly faint.

"You can't let her have the power, Erzebet. This weakness puts you at risk."

The thought of being at risk made my head spin: *time scurries around corners like a rat, feasts on you in sleep.* I felt myself spinning on the edge of a very familiar madness.

"It has been too long," I blurted out, touching my hand to my face. "I need the blood—it's been too long."

"That's right," he said, and lifted my chin to look directly into his eyes. "Don't fear the girl; she is not a threat to you unless you allow her to be. Besides, you two are very much alike."

"We are alike?" I murmured. "How?"

"Two girls born under ill omens," Sinestra pronounced, his eyes glistening. "It's as if you are sisters."

I waited in the tower for Snow's return after Mass. A warm fire was lit and I had a feast already prepared, knowing that she would be hungry. The knife and bowl were tucked away, again, but the drawings were still spread upon the table. I took greedy gulps of red wine as I studied the frantic scribblings, this time keeping Sinestra's words firmly planted in my head.

"I've prepared a bedchamber for you on the first floor of the castle," I told her over dinner. I was eager to reclaim the tower for my own purposes—it had been too long since my last blood treatment, and I dared not take any more risks.

"Not in the north wing," she uttered, suddenly panicked. "I don't like it in that wing."

Of course she wouldn't like it there: I hadn't visited those rooms myself since Marianna's death, on the day of Snow's birth.

"Do not be afraid," I assured her. "Your chamber will be right beside mine; you will be quite comfortable there. And you will still be welcome to visit this chamber during the day. I think perhaps you will sleep better in a proper bedchamber, not so plagued by visions."

"I suppose you are right," she said meditatively, gazing at the pile of parchment. I saw her look away, as if it pained her to recall her visions. They must frighten her, if they felt so real.

"What if God has not chosen me, after all?" she asked me suddenly.

"Would that be so terrible to be rid of your visions?"

"I fear I will never be rid of them, but I don't know what the dead want from me. I don't know what God wants from me."

Her gift from God was clear enough for me to see: her face was so smooth, as though sculpted from snow-white marble. Over the months since her arrival her body had become sturdier, a radiance glowing from her skin. Her innocence was like an impenetrable shell, keeping me at a distance. Her beauty made me feel shriveled and old and wrinkled and ugly, my breasts sagging sorrowfully and my chin beginning to droop. The effect was so strong that I wondered if she was some sort of witch, emanating a spell that would destroy me.

"I think you were chosen, Snow, but not by God," I told her, my voice placid, hiding the venom within. "Have you ever thought of that?"

She stared at me with wide eyes. I was impressed by the magnitude of her fear; I felt a surge of my power return. I sipped from my goblet of wine to hide my smile.

"Yes, I suppose I have," she admitted, in a low whisper.

In the bedchamber next to mine Snow prayed, paced the floor, and scribbled on her parchment all hours of the night.

Once Snow was safely installed in her bedchamber, the blood rituals resumed in the tower chamber at midnight. Mary, Sarah, Elizabeth, and Althea were perhaps a bit wary as they climbed the spiral staircase, but they were devoted to me and eager to please: their laughter crackled warmly in the tower, just as it had so many months before the long, cold winter had begun.

The blood ritual had changed since the previous summer. The girls had seen what I was capable of: not only the blood party, but Therese's death had made an appropriate impression. Confessions were observed with an impressively somber air of which Therese would have approved. They were harsh on themselves and their transgressions in the hope of receiving my forgiveness. This, along with their assistance the previous summer in the dungeon, had proved that their fear and devotion were real.

I'm sure they all wondered if the sudden cessation of our nightly sessions that winter had been due to the arrival of the strange young girl to Castle Bizecka, whom all of them had now seen wandering the hallways or praying in the chapel during Mass.

"Are there any preparations you will need us to attend to, in the dungeon?" Sarah asked carefully once her arm had been bled. She looked at me with large, round eyes. There had been plans for another blood party in the fall, but it had never occurred. In spite of my loss of confidence upon Snow's arrival, the desire to kill had not dissipated within me. The girls looked at me anxiously, eager to help and assure their place on the safe side of my rage.

"Thank you for the offer, Sarah. I suppose we will begin planning again, very soon."

But even as I said this, I was filled with a frightening doubt. Snow was Marianna's child. Would I be able to kill with her living here, under the same roof? I could not help but think of Snow as a part of Mari, and an extension of her judgment upon me.

Why can't you kill? my thoughts screamed. *It's what you are. It's what you do. You give the dead too much power.*

I patted Sarah's hand and thanked the girls for their offering. When they left, I indulged in the feeling of the blood upon my face. It soothed me, restoring my old strength. It reminded me of my very first bath in blood, on the night before Marianna's wedding, and the thought of that first rush of power made me smile.

Once my face was rinsed with water, I walked quietly to my bedchamber for sleep. In the light of the dying fire, I lay wide-awake upon the silk cushions of my bed. My hunger had not been entirely sated. After experiencing the thrill of killing, I could not find the same satisfaction in the blood alone. It was the killing that infused me with real power—the greatest that any human can hope to achieve.

As the shadows of a gray, rainy spring were replaced by sunlight streaming through the high, arched windows, Snow became more apt to wander the halls in daylight, letting the warm light shine upon her dark hair. She also grew more comfortable in the company of the servants, sitting with them until I emerged from my bedchamber. I preferred to sleep late the morning after a blood ritual, and the thought of having to face Snow made it all the more important that I feel refreshed and strengthened. I indulged in at least an hour of staring at the mirror and perfecting my hair and face before looking for her.

One afternoon I came upon Snow and Rowena in the sitting room near her bedchamber. Rowena looked over Snow's shoulder as she worked a trembling rose vine onto a swatch of linen. Snow glanced up when she saw me but quickly turned back to her stitching.

"Rowena has taught me embroidery," she told me. "She thought it would take my mind off other things."

Snow's fingers were stained with ink the same color as the shadows beneath her eyes.

"You've come quite far already, I see," I remarked.

"I couldn't sleep last night." She sighed. "Today, Pugrue offered to teach me how to read Scripture," she blurted excitedly.

"That was kind of him, wasn't it? To want to teach a young peasant girl how to read." Snow lifted her head from her embroidery, her brows furrowed.

"Did my mother ever learn to read?" she asked suddenly.

I caught the frantic flash of Rowena's eyes, but I dared not meet her gaze.

"Your mother?" she asked Snow, taken aback. "Did your mother live in Novoe Mesto?"

"Yes," Snow said. I listened, panic-stricken, unable to quiet her. "The countess and my mother were great friends. Isn't that right?" She turned her gaze back to me.

"That's quite right, Snow," I murmured. *Why hadn't I told her not to talk about her mother?* I wondered frantically, but it was too late. Rowena was already looking at me, her face pale with both shock and suspicion. I would have to deal with her soon enough.

"I didn't realize she was your mother, Snow," Rowena murmured.

"Did you know her?"

"Yes." Rowena smiled, her eyes suddenly glassy. "I knew her quite well. She was a very sweet young lady."

It made me angry to hear them talking about her; she was my Marianna, not theirs. Her death had burned me more indelibly than it had either of them, I was certain.

"Rowena, could you bring us some tea? And perhaps something to eat. Aren't you hungry, Snow?" I asked, knowing that food was one of Snow's favorite distractions.

Rowena nodded, patting Snow gently on the back before departing.

"Will you tell me more about my mother?" Snow pleaded. There was one thing aside from food that Snow hungered for.

"I thought I had told you quite a bit already." She was greedy, this girl, eager to take my memories from me.

"You said she was your dearest friend."

"Yes, that's true. She was like a sister to me," I said. At this, Snow's eyes fluttered away from mine. I smiled, glad that I could make her jealous of our connection.

"You look a bit like her, you know."

At this she lifted her head.

"Really?" she breathed. "In what way?"

"Well, your hair is your father's hair, and you have his dark eyes. But your skin, and the shape of your face. Maybe your smile, but I've never seen you smile. Your mother always had a smile on her face."

She lowered her eyes a bit, embarrassed. She seemed to consider trying to smile, but decided against it.

"Don't you want to look and see?" I pointed to the mirror on the wall behind her, but she shook her head and turned back to stitching.

"I don't want to look," she said. "I'm afraid of what I'll see."

"You're very beautiful, Snow," I told her, though the truth made me wince in pain. "You have nothing to be afraid of."

"I have everything to be afraid of," she said, her dark eyes burning with anger. "There are too many ghosts here," she informed me. "They will find me if I look in the mirror."

"I think you've been spending too much time around the dead," I informed her, "and I'm sure that your mother would say the same."

I sat beside her on the couch and put my hand on her hair. I was here to protect her, I reminded myself. In spite of the killer that I had become, that promise had remained intact inside of me, and I found I was incapable of ignoring it. Aside from my anger and jealousy toward Snow, there was something else pulling me close to her. I could understand her, and I think that she could understand me—better than Marianna ever could. We had something in common: we had both been born wrong.

"Here, for when you're ready to look at yourself," I told her, and handed her a golden circlet for her hair. I couldn't dare give her a gift once owned by one of the dead girls—it would only tempt them to try to reclaim it.

"It's beautiful," she murmured, "but I don't know how to put it on."

"Here, I'll do it for you," I said, and set to work smoothing my fingers through her black silken hair.

I suppose I was the closest thing to a mother that she had ever had.

XLVI

By that spring, with the bleedings at their usual frequency, I chose another servant—Dariah—to take Therese's seat at the table. I knew that I would need to alternate between the girls, allowing them respite from bleeding in order to preserve their strength. Instinctively, the other girls kept their distance from Dariah, not knowing what my full intentions were in her regard. Wisely, Dariah was never informed about the murderous night of the summer before.

"Dariah, I chose you to join us because of your dove-white skin and your long black hair."

I told each girl why I had chosen her, just as Sinestra had suggested. I considered each girl carefully before I spoke.

"Mary, I chose you for your delicate bones, like a bird. Althea, I chose you for your lustrous hair and eyes. Elizabeth, I chose you for your sinuous grace. Sarah, I chose you for your pretty mouth."

Each girl smiled strangely at the pronouncement laid upon them: their smiles mixed with wonder and fear.

"You will all be a part of me," I explained. "I will take your beauty into me, assimilate your beauty through your blood." The blade glinted in my hand. I had seen fit to reveal more of my intentions to them, as a reward for their loyalty. "First you will offer me your confession, and then you will be rewarded for your sacrifice."

"I've nothing to confess since the last time. I avoid those stable boys, just as you told me. They could only lead to trouble," Dariah said convincingly, "and I think purity is best."

"Purity has its own power," I murmured, watching the way the light flickered over the edge of the blade. She sat across from me and dutifully offered her arm.

"I strive to be as pure as your young friend Snow," she said cautiously. I sliced through the words, through her flesh: the sight of her blood calmed me. She had been part of enough blood rituals to have become accustomed to the bleeding, but not to the sacred silence that accompanied the act. Therese would have cautioned her, but the other girls were too quiet, wary.

"When she prays her face looks like the marble Virgin," she said. "I think I've never seen someone so pure."

"Indeed." I stared at the blood as it dripped into the bowl.

"Will you bleed her as well?" she asked, her voice edged with concern and fear.

We all lifted our eyes to Dariah. I gave Dariah a moment to

consider the silence in the room, to feel my eyes burn into her flesh. Then I grasped her bleeding arm and lifted her from the table, slamming her against the stone wall.

"It is not your place to make judgments!" I hissed, twisting a rope of her hair around my hand. I pushed her against the wall again, her head colliding against the stones, and she cried out in pain. The sound of her cry had much the same effect as the blood had had on me in the very beginning—a surge of power. It had been nearly a year since my last killing, and I craved that feeling of ultimate power.

Holding the girl against the wall by her hair, I realized how like Snow she was, the paleness of her face against the dark contrast of her hair. Her dark eyes welled with tears. She stared at me in shock and fear, her eyes wide as a deer's in a hunter's snare.

The deer, I thought, considering this image. It was both a brutal and beautiful memory for me: the day I saw the slaughtering of the deer, seeing my own pearl-gray gown splattered with the animal's glistening blood. And later that day, I had found the prophecy, and saw my reflection in the mirror . . . it all rushed through me in a blinding moment while I held Dariah against the wall. The other girls sat at the table, patiently awaiting their turn to be bled.

"I am not a monster," I whispered in her ear, and wrenched at her shoulder as though pulling at the joint of a fowl. I pulled her down the stairs with my hand clamped over her mouth. I brought her to the dungeon below the tower. The girls followed in silence.

In the chill of the cavern her cries subsided to whimpering. I saw the way her pale skin seemed to glow in the dim chamber. I pulled her over to where the rusted chains protruded from the walls.

"Take off your clothes," I barked, remembering my instructions. She wept as she disrobed, and I watched her. She was like an animal, just as Sinestra had said: pale, awkward, weak.

"Are you strong enough for this?" he whispered behind me. "For all of this?" His voice was always so close to me—inside my head, in my dreams—that I no longer felt surprised to hear it.

I grabbed the creature before me by the wrists. I secured each wrist in the chains, the cuffs screeching as they clamped over her flesh.

"What are your intentions with the girl—the one you would truly love to bleed? Do you know what you will do with her?" he asked.

"I never said I would do anything to her!" I screamed, still staring at Dariah's panic-stricken face. "I made a promise and I intend to keep it. I'm not a monster."

"You made a promise to keep her safe, and you could do it." Sinestra sidled up to me and put his hand on my arm. I saw the other four girls lingering in the shadows of the dungeon, awaiting their cue. But I hung on to Sinestra's words: "You could teach her," he told me.

I paused for a moment. Dariah's weeping was only a vague echo behind the rumble of Sinestra's voice.

"This could be your greatest act against God," he told me, his eyes burning like fire. "To corrupt the most innocent of his followers. Then your promise would be fulfilled: you and the girl would both be safe, forever."

I did not answer him, my mind suddenly filled with too many voices, my vision blurred by the red and golden flames in his eyes.

"Are you strong enough?" he asked again, a challenge hidden in his voice.

I nodded toward the girl chained to the wall.

"She will wait for her death," I announced, and returned to the tower room, the four girls following behind me.

What are your intentions with the girl? Sinestra's voice followed me to my bedchamber that night, where the ghosts kept me awake with their screaming. The noise grew so loud that I pressed my cold palms to my head, for fear my skull might split open from the force of their cries. Though I implored Sinestra to save me, he did not come when bidden. Only his question, not fully answered, remained:

What are your intentions with the girl?

I looked to the mirror, though unwillingly, knowing that was where all of my ghosts would collect. They were calling for me to look upon them. They were crowded there, a horrific mess of limbs and eyes and teeth.

We'll go to your scryer, they teased, their voices piercing. *We'll show her the truth about you.*

"No! Don't show her!" I cried. "You've already shown her enough!"

The images started to disintegrate before my eyes, their features separating as though wisps of smoke. Marianna emerged from the dark center of the mirror, and the sight of her face filled me with dread. I fell to my knees upon the stone floor.

You made a promise to me, she said. Her voice penetrated like a blade.

"I haven't forgotten my promise, I haven't forgotten, I haven't forgotten."

Then you will keep her safe? Like you promised me?

"I wanted to keep you safe!" I cried, reaching out to the mirror, but Marianna's face collapsed upon itself, broken into a thousand shards. I fell forward upon the cold stone floor, my body racked with sobs. If only I had known then what Sinestra had taught me—

if only I could have taught Marianna how to be safe, then she would still be with me, alive.

Sinestra's voice returned to me: *You made a promise to keep the girl safe, and you could do it.*

"I could teach Snow," I murmured. Sitting up from the floor, I noticed the Bible lying open on the table before the mirror.

You are all-powerful here, he reminded me, his words echoing in the cavernous silence that the ghosts had left behind. *In this castle, you are God.*

I stood and moved closer to the Bible, the mirror watching my every move. I lifted it before my face, my vision still swimming. The story was Genesis. My eyes fell instantly to the lines he wanted me to read:

God created man in his own image . . .

I had created heaven and hell. I had granted life or death to those who worshiped me. It was too late to help Marianna. It was not too late to help Snow.

Your greatest act against God. Sinestra's voice rumbled like a coming storm. *To corrupt the most innocent of his followers.*

His voice roared through my body like a crash of thunder. I stood and leaned back, as I had that night in the dungeon. I leaned back, my arms spread like wings, and let his dark laughter wash over me. Then suddenly the room was silent; I was alone. I was standing before the mirror, looking at my own face. Beyond the wall, in the chamber next door, Snow was praying: I could hear her voice like an unbroken current, a stream of frantic words pouring from her mouth, in fear.

God is not listening to you, I thought, looking at myself in the mirror, *but I am.*

My laughter broke through the silence like the shattering of glass.

Late the next afternoon I heard footsteps on the stairs to the tower. Snow stood in the doorway.

"You've slept late, are you quite well?" I asked her. Snow shuffled into the room and sat heavily upon the couch, but her spine remained rigid, her eyes fixed on nothing. I wondered for a moment if she was sleepwalking.

"Snow? Are you all right?"

"I had a vision," she told me, her voice flat. I shivered involuntarily.

"What did you see?" I asked lightly.

"It was a real vision," she said, as if to correct me. "I had it last night and I can still see it in my head. A girl dies here."

"You've already told me that this castle is full of ghosts, Snow. What makes this vision different?"

"I don't know if it's happened yet," she told me, her voice hoarse with fear. "I think it's about to happen, but it hasn't yet."

My lips parted to speak, but I thought better of it. I sat still and quiet, waiting for her words.

"She was in this room. Her head and arms were upon that table and she couldn't stand. Then I saw her on the floor, dropped like a rag doll. There was a woman in the room, but it was as if she didn't see her. She kept walking past, her gown brushing against the dead girl's face."

"How does she die, Snow?"

"I don't know—all I know is that she was drained of life. She had no life left in her. That's what the voices told me—the voices crying." She slumped forward suddenly, her neck limp. She held her head in her open hands. I rushed forward and bent beside her.

"I've never had such a vision before." Her voice cracked with weariness. "It was so clear, so powerful."

"I've heard of such powerful visions, Snow." I put my hand on her arm, reassuringly. "I think this was more than just a vision—I think it was a warning."

"A warning," she said flatly, and her eyes met mine. "What do you mean?"

"Have you ever considered that the girl in the vision could be you?"

The fire snapped. The wind blew. The blood coursed through my veins.

"Yes; yes, I did. But I didn't see her face," she murmured.

"You've never seen your own face," I reminded gently.

She stood and stepped toward my dressing table, lit with candles, her eyes still unfocused.

"But why? Why would the vision be of me?"

"Be honest with me, Snow," I said, grasping both her shoulders in my hands. "Be honest with yourself. You've been living under a curse all your life. Don't you think God wants some retribution?"

"For what? For what I did when I was born?"

I stared into her eyes and said nothing. She looked back at me, unblinking. She knew what my answer was.

"Did my mother ever use this mirror?" she asked, her throat scratchy and dry.

"Yes, she used this one more than any other." I pulled the chair out before the table and urged her to sit. "A mirror always remembers what it sees."

I detected the barely perceptible flutter of her eyelids as she looked into the glass, then a slight gasp and pulling back, as though in fear. After a moment of staring at the pale face before her she leaned forward, gently touching a fingertip to the mirror's surface.

"I've told you that you're beautiful. Don't look so surprised about it now."

"I don't know if it was me," she said, her fever-bright eyes welling with tears. "I couldn't really see her face—I saw it but I can't remember it. It seemed to change."

"Don't worry, child," I said, sitting in a chair beside her.

"You don't understand—you don't understand what I've seen." She shook her head vehemently. "You're right—I do fear death. I've seen the dead, all my life, and they are full of anger and bitterness and fear. Death is damnation, I can feel it. It will mean damnation for me." Her words made me warm to her; we were even more alike than I suspected.

"You can escape the vision," I began.

"There is no escaping it," she cried.

"Oh, that's not true. I'm still here, aren't I?"

I looked at her face and considered it for a moment, then moved over to my jewelry chest and pulled a piece of parchment out of hiding.

"This was the vision they saw about me, on the day of my birth," I said. I watched as she made out the words, slowly, haltingly.

"An angel and a demon," she repeated, and looked at me, her eyes full of questions.

"I'm older than you think." I smiled.

She looked back at her reflection in the mirror, amazed and horrified, as if she had seen a beautiful ghost.

"But how did you do it? How did you escape?"

"Don't worry, child." I smoothed her hair with my hand. "I'll teach you."

The next day I gathered Mary, Althea, Sarah, and Elizabeth to my side. They each recognized the look in my eyes and followed without question. I took them to the kitchen granary, the sunshine warm upon our heads as we walked. Once we were inside, I pointed to a pulley system that had been constructed to hold the body of a large buck, already eviscerated and strung by its ankles to bleed dry.

"We will need this in the dungeon below the tower," I told them. "Take the buck down and reassemble the pulley down there." I turned to look at them once I was done speaking; somehow discussing these things in daylight had the strange effect of increasing their terror, making it even more vividly real.

"It will need to be strong enough," I cautioned them, "in order to hold her weight." I delighted in the understanding I saw dawning in all of their eyes.

"The dinner will take place in one week, and I will require your assistance." They all nodded in acquiescence, and I left them in the granary to their task.

I had no concerns that they would release Dariah from her chains in the dungeon. They were smart girls; they knew that one of them would take her place if the victim were to escape.

At midnight the night before the blood party I took Snow to the garden, clasped our hands, and taught her how to spin. I had never heard her laugh before, and even she seemed surprised at the sound bubbling up from her throat. I spun her so fast that her feet no longer touched the ground and she was floating in a wide arch, her cape spread out like dark wings.

It was a warm night, though the summer was slowly coming to an end. The roses had grown heavy and wilted upon their black vines, but we plucked them anyway and set them in crowns upon our heads.

"Did you ever do this with my mother?" she asked.

"Yes, we did, many times."

"Tell me her name," she demanded. "My father would never say it aloud."

"Marianna," I said in a low voice, afraid of what ghosts may overhear.

"It's such a beautiful name."

A warm wind blew against my face, and with it came the smell of rain. My vision blurred for a moment, veiled by memory; it was in late summer and it was raining, the night that Marianna died. That was years ago, but the memory of it clenched my heart in its icy grip. Eleven years—Snow was eleven years old.

"Look, Snow, this was our favorite sculpture," I said, climbing on to Athenus's marble pedestal.

"He is very handsome," Snow remarked. Looking at her face in the moonlight, I could easily detect the change that had taken place over that summer: she was teetering on the brink of time, between childhood and womanhood.

I was saving her just in time.

XLVII

Snow slept late the next day. I tried to rest, but was too excited. I sought solitude in my bedchamber. I was inspecting a gold silk gown before the mirror when Rowena entered suddenly. Seeing her face reflected behind me in the mirror reminded me of so many years before, when she had tended to all of my childish needs. It made me warm to her for a moment, until I saw her expression: her eyes wide with fear and accusation.

"I must speak to you, Erzebet," she began timidly, a threat embedded in her trembling voice. "I'm concerned about Snow."

"She's a troubled child, admittedly. I worry about her myself."

"Do not play games with me!" Rowena shrieked, beads of moisture forming on her forehead, despite the cold of the room. "What are you planning to do to her, Erzebet? Will you use her like the others?"

"These others you refer to, have they issued any complaint regarding their treatment?"

"You know what I mean, Erzebet. Snow is only a child—she's Marianna's child."

I lifted my eyes to the mirror and locked my gaze with hers.

"I know it as well as you do, Erzebet; do not attempt to deny it." She sighed, but her breath was shaky and raspy. "Are you going to use her, in your way, because of who she is?"

"I will not use her like the others, Rowena, because of who she is," I stated coldly.

"I could take her away from here," she hissed. "I don't trust you. I don't want her to trust you."

"Where would you take her, Rowena, without risking her life? You're both lucky to be here."

"To be safe so that you can kill us?"

"I have no intention of killing you," I said, as if this were a ridiculous notion. She wiped hastily at her tears, suddenly ashamed.

"How can I trust you, Erzebet?"

"I made a promise long ago, to Snow's mother," I told her. "I made a promise that I would take care of her. Do you think I would deny that promise?"

"No," she muttered, still wary, "I don't suppose you would."

"Besides," I said, and suddenly turned. In one swift motion I lunged forward and grasped her neck in my hand. She gasped desperately, her knees buckling under her. "Besides," I began again, "you should know better than to cross me. I will not hesitate to harm you if you dare to cross me."

She struggled, but could not speak. My fingers gripped her neck tighter as I pushed my face close to hers.

"Whatever you do, do not put yourself between me and the girl. You will only cause more hardship if you do. Do you understand me?"

Rowena's eyes streamed with tears; she only gurgled in response.

"What happens was meant to happen," I told her. "This is the only place the girl is safe. If you choose to leave on your own accord, then so be it, but the girl remains here."

I released her suddenly and she scrambled to the door.

Snow visited the tower later that afternoon, with her embroidery hoop and a fistful of threads. I could tell she was still distracted by her vision; even after days spent with needle and thread, the roses upon her vine did not seem to bloom. When I looked over at her she was gazing out the narrow window, or into the fire, her eyes glassy and distant. But the silence between us was generally restful; I tried to conceal from her my anxious excitement.

"There is to be a party tonight, Snow, and you are invited."

"A party? Where?"

"Here, of course. We will take our meal in the dining hall, then adjourn to the tower for music and dancing."

I burrowed deep into a chest in the corner as she lay back upon the couch, the embroidered linen upon her lap. When I pulled the white gown free from hiding, a faint scent of lavender rushed up to greet me. The scent was overpowering; I pressed my hands to my warm cheeks to calm myself.

"What's that?" she asked. Instantly I regretted opening the door to this memory. What had I been thinking? This was too much to share, even with Snow. But it was too late, she was already staring at me. It was important to pull her into my confidence, now more than ever.

"This was your mother's favorite gown, Snow." I stood and shook the gown out before me, its delicate lace folded and creased like a worn piece of parchment. "She wore this on her wedding day."

As Snow stood from the couch the embroidery hoop slipped, unnoticed, to the floor.

"It's beautiful," she said, fingering the delicate pearls embedded in the lace.

"You could try it on—here," and I began efficiently to help her from her gown. Usually so modest, she did not struggle this time. Once the dress was secured, I steered her over to the mirror. The gown sagged over the top of her narrow body, so I cinched a handful of extra fabric and pinned it close to her, the lace hugging her narrow shoulders. When I was done, the effect was remarkable: the lace and her fair skin shimmered like moonlight upon fresh white snow. I stood in the shadow of her brightness.

This is what it's like to have a daughter, I realized. I had never really wondered about it before. I lifted a silver comb from the dressing table and affixed it in her smooth black hair.

"It looks lovely with your fair skin and dark hair, just as it did on your mother. I can have it tailored to fit you." I watched her face closely, aware of a perceptible change. Her eyes were wet and her lips softly parted. Vanity bloomed inside of her, for the first time—I could see it reflected in her eyes.

"There is one thing you need, in order to look perfect." I moved over to a gold silk satchel lying on the dressing table and removed a small pot of paint. The red paint glistened like the skin of a ripe, red apple. Her eyes grew wide at the sight.

"Imagine this color upon your lips."

"It's perfect," she murmured, "like roses."

I put a bit of the stain on my fingertip.

"Do you know what it's made of?" I asked.

"No," she said, staring at the contrast of the red upon my pale finger.

"It contains the blood of a beautiful young virgin." I turned to look directly at her face. Her eyes were still transfixed upon my finger for a moment, and then she looked at me, a crease forming between her brows.

"No," she said, shaking her head, "I can't. Blood is holy."

"Indeed it is. I offer you the holiest, the most powerful, of all sacraments. It can protect you. Do you consider yourself safe enough to refuse?"

"This is a sin," she informed me, but watched carefully as I painted my own mouth red. I was still pleased with the effect of the stain, and my lips curved into a smooth smile in the mirror before us.

"Don't you fear God's judgments?" she asked.

"I did, but now I make my own judgments. God is not always fair with His. He was not kind to your mother, or to me. Or to you."

She lowered her head for a moment, her shoulders slack. I pressed my hand upon her arm.

"You don't want to be weak in this world, Snow, I warn you. If you are weak, this world will crush you. God will crush you. It doesn't matter what you do."

I moved to the dressing table for a small Bible, which I pressed into her palm.

"Here," I told her. "Now that Pugrue has taught you to read, I want you to read the passages I have marked for you."

She sat abruptly and opened the book to the appointed page. I listened intently as she struggled over the words.

"'The life of the flesh is in the blood . . .'" It was intoxicating to hear the words spoken in her voice. She lifted her eyes to mine.

"I've heard this passage before," she told me.

"I want you to read it, Snow, and think about it. Someone very important to me shared it with me, when I most needed it. And now I'm sharing it with you."

She cast her eyes back to the page and touched each word tenderly with her fingertip.

"Remember, Snow. No one should be alone in this world."

That night I held a blood party for Dariah's death. It was also for the death of two other girls whom I had chosen that day for their innocent beauty—Anna and Celia—though they didn't know it yet. And neither did Snow, sitting at the table in a dark blue gown, smiling over mouthfuls of roasted fowl and beef stew.

Even in the company of others, Snow couldn't hide her preoccupation with food. Since the previous winter when she had first come to live with me, I had watched as the vices she had given up during her life of asceticism gained a stronghold upon her. She was becoming enamored with her appearance, and before the dinner that evening had spent hours in front of the mirror in her bedchamber rearranging her hair and devouring the sight of her own reflection. I had procured a new corset for her, and earlier that evening she had encouraged me to tie it as tightly as possible: she liked the effect of her minuscule waist encased in the smooth blue silk of her gown.

Likewise with food; that which she had somehow sustained herself without for so long was now a matter of constant concern. She seemed always to be in the midst of eating, or planning what to eat. When the doors connecting the kitchen to the dining hall opened and the platters of food began to stream in, her eyes grew wide and bright. She clearly still took Rowena's initial encouragement to get some meat on her bones to heart, for she did not hesitate to fill her plate with second and third helpings. With childish abandon, Snow eagerly sank her teeth into the bright red apple of greed and gluttony.

Seated at the table with Anna and Celia and myself, Snow was quiet but flushed, taking generous gulps of wine between mouthfuls while listening to the bawdy rhymes of the assembled minstrels I had chosen to entertain us. But I was far more entertained watching Snow. Though she was engrossed in the food, wine, and music, I noticed that her eyes not infrequently bounced to the faces of her companions. I knew that look well: the art of envy at its finest. I could see her deconstructing them in her head, comparing their own beauties with her own. I smiled at the thought of what would happen to them later that night—fodder for my midnight bloodbath. I wondered if someday she would be able to smile at this thought as well. That night she seemed to be so much like me, as if she were my daughter, and no one else's.

Snow enjoyed the dining and the music, and she enjoyed the dancing and the sweetmeats in the tower all the more. All three of the girls had long, dark hair that swayed freely as they danced, their dark eyes sparkling in the candlelight. Snow joined hands with Celia and Anna and they all danced in a circle, a sort of loose dance that seemed somehow dire, urgent in its joy. But perhaps that was because of what I knew, and what they did not know. I asked the minstrels I had invited to the tower to play louder, to drown out the distant howling of Dariah, still chained in the dungeon and awaiting her death.

Snow was put to bed once the revelry in the tower chamber was drawing to a close. I saw to it myself that she was safe under the covers and fast asleep before returning to the tower room for the culmination of the celebration, when I would lead Celia and Anna on their descent into hell.

"There is more dancing to be done below the depths," I told them, smiling, lifting a glass of red wine in toast. They laughed at me and followed me down the stairs, nearly stumbling over themselves in their drunkenness. The girls' laughter was deafening in the narrow stairwell, then grew to an echoing crescendo as we entered the dungeon.

They are here to be punished for their sins, Sinestra murmured, his voice in my head. The girls were still glowing from the delights of the tower chamber above: greed, sloth, vanity, and pride indulged by the warm glow of the fire. In the main chamber they continued their dance without benefit of music, spinning madly, their laughter reverberating off the stone walls.

It was only natural that after such indulgence, there was a steady descent: wasn't this what they'd been taught in church, all their lives? Harsh punishment should be expected after an excess of sin. Here, in the light of vivid flames, in a cavern beneath the earth, they would face my judgment. I saw this realization dawning on each girl's face as soon as she saw Dariah, already chained in the corner. I saw the animal-like urge to run flash across their faces, but where would they run to? My assistants emerged from the shadows, their faces cold as stone. Kyzoni, too, emerged, growling, baring his teeth. I called to him and he sidled up beside me, licking my hand affectionately as I scratched his neck.

"I will take your beauty into me, assimilate your beauty through your blood," I told the girls. I thought they deserved an explanation.

I chose Dariah to bleed first. If I had left her much longer she would have died of cold or hunger, and I would have been robbed of witnessing her death. I inflicted the initial wounds as soon as she was unchained, then my blood girls moved forward to do their work.

The pulley system had been reconstructed in the dungeon chamber, just as it had been set up to bleed the deer dry. The tub was placed beneath the pulley, and the grate was removed. While Dariah was dying, the girls bound her feet with rope. She was strung up by the pulley, suspended over the tub. I administered the fatal wound, slipping the blade easily between her ribs.

Sarah moved forward to help me quickly undress. I lay down in the tub beneath the dying girl, her blood flowing directly from her body onto my skin. The sight of it mesmerized me: this was my greatest triumph, drawing one life directly into my own.

"Look at me," I demanded of Dariah, suspended from ropes above me. I had to raise my voice to be heard over the wailing of the other girls. Dariah was silent; I knew her life was nearly drained. I reached up and pulled her hair to force her neck to arch. She looked at me with wide, blank eyes.

In the darkness of those eyes, I faced both life and death, and took it all into myself, fearlessly. This was what Sinestra had been telling me about all along: the final act, the ultimate break from God. This was power and control as I had never experienced it before. As the girl was slowly drained of life, I felt myself consuming her power until I had been infused with the entire breadth of her beauty and her life. I closed my eyes and saw visions of pastures, sunrises, houses, faces that I had never seen before in my own life—I was taking all of it into me. It made me love the girls, almost as much as I had envied them. It made me love them for the power they had given me.

I remained in the tub, covered in blood, as the other two girls were dragged over to me. They pushed Celia close to me, holding her still as I plunged the knife into her belly. Then they strung her up to be bled, and Anna after her. It made me proud as I watched my girls do this; they had helped me achieve my greatest victory in the face of God.

Dariah, Anna, and Celia had no choice but to submit. They offered me their death, and their beauty, and their power. When I was done, I was more than human. I had become immortal; I had never been more certain of it. The new knowledge and feeling of safety shone from my eyes.

I looked up to the corpse hanging above me, her dark hair dangling close to my chest. As she rocked gently upon her rope, I caught a glimpse of her face, her still-open eyes staring blankly through her strands of dark hair. For one moment I thought I saw Snow's face looking back at me. I blinked rapidly and the vision disappeared.

XLVIII

Late-night murmurs, fires dying in the hearth. I remembered from my youth how to walk soundlessly. I prowled the hallways listening, drinking in the sounds. I could be aware, this way, of what everyone was doing at all times. The servants were slowly readying themselves for bed, others up late darning their stockings, nodding off by the fire. The blood gave me enough energy that I did not need sleep. The mere thought of sleep had begun to frighten me: lying in bed, motionless, as though dead. Time could not find me in such a state of weakness. I had best be on my guard.

Snow was generally in the tower room or in her bedchamber. It was important to know what she was doing. I often watched her from the shadows.

"Just like you watched me, when I was her age," I told Sinestra. He did not answer, but I knew he lingered close by in the cover of darkness. I wondered if she could feel my eyes upon her, as I often could feel Sinestra's—wary for the mysterious stranger to visit, afraid and hopeful. I thought for a moment of all he taught me, how afraid I had been but how grateful to have someone to understand. I would be there for Snow, in a way that no one else would.

One night, in search of Snow, I passed a sitting room and heard low voices muttering, sitting in the light of a dying fire.

"I don't want to have visions anymore," Snow stated. "I'm tired of listening to the demands of the dead. I think it was a demon who gave me these visions."

"Hush, Snow, don't say such things!" Rowena pleaded.

Snow stood before the mirror, twisting languidly, then stroking the smooth nap of her velvet gown with the flat palm of her hand.

"I had a vision that frightened me," she told Rowena, still staring at her own face in the mirror. "That a girl would die in the tower room. I still think that girl is me."

"We can't predict our fates, Snow," Rowena offered. "We must trust God's design for our lives." She had stood from her chair and approached Snow; there was something more she wanted to tell her, and I knew well what it was.

"Why should I trust God?" Snow whined. "What has He done to give me any reason to trust Him?"

Rowena held back at the sound of this, and my chest filled with pride at the sound of Snow's voice. I reveled in the nervous silence that followed, then slipped into the doorway like a dagger into its sheath.

"You're still awake, Snow?" I asked. She turned from the mirror to look at me, her dark eyes gleaming. Rowena immediately stepped away from her as I entered the room.

"It's late, you must be tired." I held out my hand to her. "I'll take you to my tower and care for you myself."

A special silence followed these words, and I witnessed the meaning of what I had said register in Rowena's wide eyes.

In the tower room, Mary, Elizabeth, Althea, and Sarah were already assembled. I invited Snow to join them at my dressing table, trying on different jewels and posing before the glass. I poured a glass of wine for Snow and relaxed in my chair, watching them. The candles in the chamber were lit, and the room glowed with a warm, golden brilliance. An additional chair had been pushed up to the wooden table in the center of the room.

When the time was right, I called all of the girls to sit at the table. Snow sat quietly, listening intently as the four girls offered their confessions to me, their heads bent piously. Tonight it was Sarah's turn for bleeding. She placed the bowl dutifully beneath her arm and waited, patiently, for the slice of my blade. Snow jumped a bit in her seat at the sight of the blood.

"Blood is the most important sacrament, Snow. I've already told you."

"It was her blood that you meant?" she asked, her voice very small.

"Her blood, or the blood of another girl," I said, and smiled at the girls seated before me.

"And this is how it's done," Snow murmured, leaning closer to watch.

When the bleeding was done, I thanked the girls and bid them good night, nestling a gold hairpin into Sarah's palm. She smiled and bowed briefly, never looking at the bowl of blood before she turned and left. Snow and I sat across from each other at the table. Her eyes were transfixed on the bowl of blood before her, watching the way the candlelight flickered golden upon its surface. I watched the same flickering dance in her eyes.

"Do you remember the Bible passage you read? The life of the flesh is in the blood. This is what will keep us safe."

"Do you drink it?" she asked.

"Sometimes," I conceded, putting a few drops into my goblet and swirling its contents.

I drank first, then handed her the cup. She looked at it, but would not extend her hand.

"I don't want to have visions anymore," she told me, her voice trembling.

"But it's more than that, isn't it? You don't want the vision you saw to be about you. You deserve some protection, just as I did."

"This is what I need to do, to be safe?"

"This is how I am safe," I told her, and rested my hand upon hers. "I would have done this for your mother, if I could have. I wish I could have, but I didn't know enough then. Now I want to do this for you."

"Safe from death," she murmured, her eyes darting from mine to the goblet of wine. "And you will let me stay with you?" she asked suddenly.

"Of course I will," I told her. "We will be always be together. We are more alike than your mother and I ever were."

Her eyes grew wide at this, with both fear and greed. She took the goblet and drank, slowly. When she lowered it, her eyes were different. I turned to the mirror and saw our faces, reflected side by side.

This mirror remembers everything it sees.

Day twenty-one, night

I've just learned that the year has turned to 1600, and I didn't even realize or feel any change. The world was destroyed in one moment, at midnight, then born again the same as it was yesterday. We are deep into this seemingly endless winter. After weeks of waiting I'm still here, in this tower. At least I don't have to worry about the passage of time.

"Has anyone been to see me?" I ask the meek girl. She arrives before the rest, and her presence calms me. "Any visitors?"

"Not that I'm aware of, my lady. But I'm sure Prince Stephan will be here soon."

This troubles me, but I watch as the girl sits on the couch and begins her sewing, moving the shining needle in and out of the hem of an apron. I like the look of her fresh skin in this light.

"And what of the trial?" I ask, leaning against my dressing table. "I'm sure you know more than I do. Please tell me."

"All I know is that the executions are scheduled for today, my lady."

"Executions?" I repeat the word aloud. The sound of it fills me with dread, but for a moment its meaning is intangible, as though I have never heard it before. The servant gasps at the look in my eyes.

"I'm sorry, my lady. I thought that you were already aware."

"Who is being executed?"

"Your servants, my lady." Her eyes flutter nervously over my face. "They testified against you. They're being put to death for their part in the crimes."

"Mary, Elizabeth, Sarah, Althea." It takes me a moment before I realize I have said their names out loud.

"How?" I ask, because I can't stop myself.

"They will be hanged, my lady."

"A peasant's execution," I murmur; I am not surprised by the method. But for a moment I swoon as though I might faint; the servant rushes toward me and helps me to the couch.

"Is there anything I can get for you, my lady?"

"No, no. You've been a good girl. You're the only one who has told me the truth."

As my breath slowly calms, the girl sits beside me on the couch and pulls her sewing back to her lap. I reach out a hand and touch her gently on the wrist.

"You're a sweet child to sit with me, when I feel so alone." I smile, and she smiles back.

Peasants are the disposable living meat of this country, but if you kill enough of them you're bound to get some attention. It was not uncommon that a parent would arrive at the front gate, demanding to see me and learn the whereabouts of his or her beloved daughter, sister, niece. I chose a different story for each: illness, perhaps, or kidnapped by the Turks, or simply ran away. Often I paid the parents for their troubles, knowing this was the easiest way to be rid of them. They wouldn't have been pleased to find their loved one stacked as she was in the box of dead girls. My stories and my money were far more comforting than the truth.

This time it was a father at the door, and I recognized him instantly.

"Konrad," I said, approaching him at the kitchen entrance. "It's a surprise to see you. It's been many years."

"Yes, indeed it has," he said, bending in an awkward bow. It pained him to be standing in Castle Bizecka; I could see it in the crease of his eyes. The years had left him looking old and ragged.

"I'm sorry to bother you, Countess." He straightened, suddenly formal. "But I'm concerned about the whereabouts of my daughter, Snow."

"I'm sorry to hear that, Konrad. How long has she been gone?"

"Nearly a year now, but I did not learn about it until recently. I was traveling and she was—well, I did not see her often."

"I see. And you think that I can help you?"

"I think maybe you already have," he said. "I was told that you took her when the villagers had turned against her. Is that true?"

"I'm afraid I can't help you, Konrad," I said sadly; it was a little sad, after all. "Your daughter isn't here. I don't know where she is."

And this wasn't actually a lie. The child he had left behind in that ruined hut was not the same young girl who lived under my care. It was best for Konrad—for both of them—if he not learn just how much she had changed.

"I'm sorry, Konrad." I grasped his hand briefly in mine. "I wish you luck in your search," I said, before bidding him farewell.

Snow had blossomed. I had seen it with my own eyes. Every night in the weeks previous to Konrad's visit, she had been present during the midnight blood rituals in the tower chamber. At first she was a hesitant onlooker, lingering in the golden shadows of the tower room, but after a few nights she became more curious about our circle at the candlelit table: perhaps it reminded her of her own candlelit table of the year before. But instead of a mirror in the center of this table, there was a bowl full of blood. She stood silhouetted by the fire in her dark green gown, peering over Althea's shoulder to get a closer look at her white arm held over the wooden bowl.

As Althea bled, I stood quietly and moved another chair to the table; Snow sat upon it, wordless. Her presence at the table caused a perceptible shift; the girls carefully measured their somber expressions, but I saw their eyes flash at Snow's face. She was still young, so young, but the bloom of new womanhood had begun to alter her childish face. Small breasts now filled out the bodice of her new gown; I was both fascinated and envious at the prospect of saving her before her monthly blood would arrive. Her large eyes glittered like jet against her pale skin; I saw the flames of the candles wavering within their dark centers as she stared, in awe, at the wound on Althea's arm. She leaned forward to take a closer look at the blood pooling in the bowl; her black hair gleamed like satin in the low light.

When the girls stood to leave, Snow rose from her chair to follow them as she had on all the previous nights, leaving me to my own private portion of the ritual. On this night, I touched her hand as she stood. She was startled by my touch, and opened her mouth as she turned to look at me. When her eyes met mine I felt she understood.

"Good night, girls," I said as the others departed. They each turned slightly, casting one last wary look upon the room, realizing that Snow was not coming with them.

I moved the extra chairs from the table, leaving only two. Snow sat across from me and watched as I bathed my face in the blood. She watched in silence. When I was done, patting my face dry with a fresh cloth, I lifted my eyes to meet hers. I could see the new freshness of my face reflected in her stare.

"You will live forever?" she whispered, the candles trembling with her breath.

"Yes," I told her, "and so can you."

I touched a clean fingertip to the blood in the bowl; it was still warm. I reached up tentatively to touch Snow's cheek, but she recoiled at the sight of my bloody fingertip. I sat back in my chair, and she pulled the bowl closer. She stared at the blood for a moment, and I heard her repeat the words from Leviticus beneath her breath, like a prayer. Taking a deep breath, she pushed the bowl back toward me and closed her eyes. This time she did not flinch. She sat patiently, quietly, holding her breath as I painted her face with the blood.

"Blood given, blood taken," I murmured soothingly, my voice like a lullaby.

When we were done, our faces freshly washed, reflected side by side in the mirror, I asked her how it had felt. Her red mouth curved in a slow smile.

"Powerful," she told me, her breath shuddering in her chest.

Snow slept soundly all that night; I know because I watched her. I walked the halls of the castle in the hope of distracting vagrant ghosts from her dreams. It had been an important night for Snow. I did not want a host of nightmares to mar the memory of it when she woke. Meanwhile, in the shadows of her bedchamber, I was overwhelmed with alternating waves of pride and envy at the sight of her perfect face.

"Don't worry," Sinestra murmured, sidling up close to me in the darkness. "You will always be my love. You don't need to worry about that."

I turned and kissed him in the hallway, ghosts flitting in cold rushes by my face.

"I'm envious of you," Snow told me the next day in the tower, a few hours before the next blood ritual was to begin.

"Why is that?" I asked, meeting her eyes in the mirror. *Because you are so beautiful,* I yearned to hear her say, but she did not.

"Because of the way they look at you," she told me, smiling. "The girls, during the ritual."

"That is power, Snow," I told her. "They could look at you in that way, too."

"Do you think I'm ready?" she asked quietly.

"Of course I do." I smiled. I set the bowl and blade upon the table. "You crave this feeling of power. I think you are ready." I turned to the mirror and painted my lips perfectly with red lip stain. Snow stood from her chair to watch me do this.

"The question is"—I posed, admiring my full red lips—"which girl will you choose? You've thought of that, haven't you?"

Snow's cheeks turned pale, and her eyes watered slightly.

"Envy is dangerous, Snow," I told her, but laughed at the look on her face.

"I choose the one I envy the most," she murmured, but her words were cut short by the sound of footsteps up the stairs.

At the table, once confession had been complete, I paused for a moment with the blade in my hand. I caught Snow's eyes with my gaze and settled the handle of the blade in Snow's open palm.

"Elizabeth," she said, and held out her hand for Elizabeth's arm. I felt my own surge of power from this: Snow suffered envy, too. I was delighted at the thought that Elizabeth's languid grace and curvaceous body had haunted Snow with all the traits she did not possess herself.

Elizabeth held her arm steadily over the wooden bowl. The knife seemed suddenly enormous in Snow's small hands, and I wondered for a moment if she would be able to wield it. But after a moment she became used to the weight and feel of the blade. When she was ready, she sliced a thin line down Elizabeth's arm. Snow stared for a moment, the knife still in her hand, captivated by the contrast of the red blood against white flesh.

XLIX

Sinestra lay in bed with me—his touch kept the voices of all the ghosts at bay. But in the midst of his kisses I was distracted, and not by the screams of angry ghosts.

"What was that?" I whispered, breaking away from his kiss.

"Did you hear that?" I asked again as he kissed my neck. I was sure of it: human voices sliced through the darkness; the sound of mortality seemed to shimmer in the air before me, like a polished silver blade.

"I have to go see what it is," I said regretfully, pulling from his warm embrace.

"I'll see you again, soon enough," he promised, with a smile.

I wrapped myself in a velvet robe and hurried down the stairs in search of the sound.

I followed the hollering to the dining hall, where the maids tended to a young girl lying on the floor.

"Snow?" I asked, and a pale man in a dark cloak walked toward me, bowing hastily. He began to cough, his shoulders trembling.

"Erzebet, I apologize," he said, once he had recovered. "We had nowhere else to go. I am Charles, a cousin of your father's—I was sorry to hear of his passing." He bent double and began coughing again. I motioned to the servants to tend to him. They pushed a goblet to his lips and he drank greedily.

"We were on our way to Emperor Rudolf," he said, smiling in spite of his pallor. "My daughter, Helena, is to wed Rudolf's cousin, but the harsh weather has made our journey very dangerous. I beg you to pardon our intrusion."

"Of course," I said, looking over at a girl, huddled in heavy blankets by the fire. She struggled to stand, but her legs buckled beneath her. I lifted my hand, motioning for her to sit.

"You need to rest. You may remain here for as long as necessary."

Then the Bizeckas would be connected to the Habsburg line, after all. The count would have been so pleased—though displeased that it was his cousin's doing, and not his own. Indeed, this Helena was important to the Bizecka name, to regain our stronghold in Hungary and respect in the Viennese court. We would, of course, show our guest the finest hospitality.

The next day I met Snow, wan and pale, late in the evening. The midnight blood rituals had taken a toll on her sleeping pattern, and she often was not fully awake until the moon had risen. I informed her that we had a guest staying with us, and she brightened instantly.

"I will wear the white gown you tailored for me," she announced; the prospect of a new guest meant a reason for her to wear her finest clothing, particularly a guest ready to wed into the emperor's family.

When she emerged from her chamber that night she did indeed look resplendent, as well as anxious: she looked at me warily, as if in my face she saw something that was both familiar and horrifying. I suppose she wondered about my plans for the evening. I smiled and led her to the dining hall.

I had the hall prepared as would be fitting for guests of noble blood: the fire was high to ward off the wintry chill, the air was sweet with soothing incense, great glass carafes gleamed with red wine and a rich meal was spread out before us. Helena appeared in the entrance to the hall and bowed awkwardly. I saw her eyes flicker over Snow's face; I detected a vague flinch, her cheeks turned pale.

"I'm afraid my father is not quite well enough to join us," she stammered, taking her place at the table. "I apologize for being late—I needed to check on him."

"No apologies are necessary, Helena." I smiled and poured for her a glass of wine. "I'm glad that you're able to join us. Are you feeling well?"

"Yes, I am indeed—I'm afraid I slept the whole day." Her eyes flickered to Snow again, but she looked quickly away. "I can't tell you how nice it is to have this respite from traveling. We do appreciate your kindness."

"I'm glad to be of service to you, as well as Emperor Rudolf—not to mention your bridegroom."

At these words she blushed, and took a great gulp from her glass.

Even in the golden light of the fire, Helena's skin seemed sallow. Her cheeks were soft and round, like the face of a child, and her nose was a touch too wide. As far as I could tell, her hair was her only claim to true beauty: honey-colored and elegantly styled. I introduced her to Snow and the two nodded in greeting. Helena's eyelids fluttered; I could easily perceive the blooming of jealousy in another woman, like a poisonous flower. Out of the corner of my eye I looked at Snow, to appraise her beauty in the warm glow of the fire.

"Are you prepared for the impending royal wedding?" I asked as Helena began to feast heartily on the food spread out before her. I doubted she would have eaten so well had her father been seated at her side.

"I suppose I must be," she said, between mouthfuls. "It's nearly here now, as soon as we are able to travel again."

"Have you met the prince yet? He's a bit older than you, I believe."

"Yes, he is much older. We haven't met, but my father assured me there would be plenty of time for that, after the wedding." She attempted to laugh at this, but the laugh faltered. She bit hard into a hunk of bread.

"Well, until then you must relax. Your father may need time to recuperate."

"We are both very thankful for you, indeed," she assured me, her eyes glistening, vaguely unfocused in the soft light. I offered her more of the roasted lamb and she accepted it eagerly. As she ate, I softened to the young creature. She was, I realized, the daughter that the count had always hoped I would be: demure, obedient, and willing to be married off for a chance at power.

Snow was quiet all through dinner, but ate heartily, as usual. I savored a bite of pheasant while chatting with Helena, thinking how remarkable it was to meet a young woman so attached to this earth, so unwary of what fate might have in store for her.

"What did you think of our dinner guest?" I asked Snow after dinner, in the tower.

"She seems to have quite a future ahead of her," Snow sighed, a bit enviously. "A powerful husband, a life of royalty. It's really quite exciting."

"And all thanks to her father for arranging it. He seems particularly devoted to his young daughter." I knew this comment would cut deep, and it did; Snow wrinkled her brow as though in pain.

"But did she look familiar to you, at all—do you think she could be the girl in your vision, who dies in this chamber?"

"No," she told me, shaking her head with certainty, "it's not her. I can feel it about her—she isn't the one doomed to die."

"Yes, I agree," I said, and leaned forward. "I think that she's destined to live a long and happy life, with her royal husband and many children. You could scry her future and see for yourself."

"The mirror tells me nothing but my own face; you know that," she said accusingly. "Besides, I don't see how that would change anything. She wasn't the girl in the vision."

"But she could be," I told her. "Then the vision would be complete, and you would not be harmed."

She turned to look at me, her expression accusatory but also curious.

"What are you suggesting that I do?" she asked, daring me to say it.

I gripped my gown to hide my trembling fingers. It was late, close to midnight.

"You can make her the girl in the vision—you can give her your death," I told her, "and then you would be safe."

Her eyes met mine, peering through the black silk veil of her hair. I glanced to the corner of the tower, where the bath still stood. I went to poke the flames in the hearth, making them rise, as if they might consume the room itself and both of us in it. I turned from the flames and laid the silver blade upon the table.

"We had best act quickly," I said.

Day twenty-eight, night

"Have any of you heard about the trial?" I ask when all of the servants are assembled. Most of them nod reluctantly.

"We've heard a bit, my lady," the round-cheeked girl tells me.

"Have they made any other arrests?" I am anxious at not having seen Sinestra—I have to know if he has been captured. Though even if Sinestra was caught, he would be able to escape the ultimate punishment they could offer.

"I've heard of no other arrests, my lady."

"No other accomplices were mentioned?" They flinch awkwardly at this admittance. "Surely the servants mentioned someone—a young man? They've seen him, I'm sure."

"No, my lady. I heard their testimony, and they said you did the killings alone, with their assistance."

"His name is Sinestra—I can tell you because I'm sure he'll be safe. A tall young man, with very striking dark eyes. Have you heard of him?"

"No, my lady," the meek girl answers, confused and almost concerned. "There has been no one mentioned by that name, or that description."

I'm about to insist that they are wrong when I see it—Sinestra's face appears, only for a moment, in my mirror. It has been so long since I noticed how much he looks like Athenus, the sculpture in my garden. I smile at him and I'm about to say something when his image seems to shimmer.

His features slowly dissolve into my own face.

"Where are you going?" I demand. "Why are you leaving me?"

"We're not leaving you, Countess," the meek servant says.

"Don't leave me—after all that has happened, you can't leave me!"

I have no reason to stay with you. *His voice rumbles loudly in my ears.* **I have already given you everything. Now you must live with what you've done.**

"Live with what I've done?" I ask, and he answers with a laugh. His image moves like smoke across the surface of the glass, but as I watch it take shape it changes before my eyes: slowly turning to stone, just like Athenus, his hair encrusted with snow.

It was so easy to know what form I should take to approach you. You told me the first time we met.

"But you were real," I insist. "You were real then, and now you are only a shadow."

I was only ever a shadow, but I was real for you. I'm real for many people. I become exactly what they want me to be; then I make them exactly what I want them to be.

"What about eternity?" I ask, but his laughter nearly deafens me. I cover my ears from the sound but it doesn't help; his laughter is stuck inside my head.

"You . . . you lied to me," I utter, shocked, before he has the chance to vanish completely. "Everything you told me was a lie."

What is true doesn't really matter.

"Don't tell me that! I believed you. I believed everything that you said."

It was what you wanted to hear. Think of all that I did for you. I fell from the sky to be with you.

I see it streak through my vision: the falling star on the day of my birth, burning a white line of fire through the black night sky, rendering my life in its fiery wake.

"Did you give me the prophecy? Did you make that up, too?" I cry.

I wasn't the scryer, *he murmurs.* **I was the star.**

Jesus saw Satan fall like lightning from heaven. . . . *Suddenly I feel as though I'm being flung from a black sky, stars cascading through the air around me. I'm falling so far and so fast that I don't know where I'll end up, I don't know when the falling will end. The tower chamber melts away and the cold winter wind rushes by me as I fall.*

"This is what is to become of me?" I ask him. "You'll just leave me here?"

I'll never truly leave you, *he says consolingly.* **I created you in my own image. I know where we will meet again. Remember what I told you.**

"What should I remember? Of all the things you told me?"

No one knows power until they've witnessed the glory of hell.

With a loud crash I find myself on the floor of the tower chamber, gasping, the circular room spinning around me, the pale faces of servants merely blurs across my vision. I stumble forward to the mirror.

"Then I'm still human, after everything I've done?" I ask him. "I'm human, and mortal?" But his face does not appear in the glass, and there is only silence in answer. The rich, deep voice does not echo in my ear. The silence overwhelms me as I slump to the floor, stuck in the vortex of the spinning. Once the spinning ceases and only the silence is left, I realize that Sinestra has left me forever. What has taken his place is far more terrifying: God is staring down upon me as I sit here on the floor. I can feel His judgment setting fire to my mortal flesh.

When I look up, the servants are all staring at me. I feel naked, suddenly, exposed. I look down to make sure I'm still dressed. I notice that my hands are shaking.

I suppose any life is an eternity if you live it completely alone.

Just before midnight, I startled Helena in her bedchamber, twisting nervously before the mirror. She jumped at the sight of me.

"Oh, Erzebet," she said, smoothing her palms efficiently against the satin folds of her gown. "I'm sorry."

"You look lovely, Helena," I told her, and grasped her hand. "You will make a very elegant bride."

She blushed bashfully, her smile awkward.

"I'm not surprised to find you awake," I remarked. "You're a young girl with many things on your mind."

"I suppose so. I doubt that I will sleep at all."

"I would like to invite you to my tower chamber, to help calm your nerves. I know a variety of treatments that will leave you feeling refreshed, ready for your adventure."

"Treatments?" she asked, one eyebrow lifting sharply.

"Beauty treatments," I told her, "to enhance your complexion and smooth your skin."

From the look in her eyes I knew that I had hit a nerve: her bridegroom had yet to meet his bride, after all. If she were to be found wanting in any way, her entire family would bear the humiliation. If Rudolf's brother was fickle, she could easily be cast aside for a more attractive match. Her eyes seemed to glisten in the firelight.

I held out my hand. Her palm was warm and moist in my own.

"I must thank you again for your kindness," she murmured, and lifted her skirt as we ascended the stairs to the tower.

When we opened the door, the room was warm from the raging fire, and the kettle was already bubbling over the flames. The room was lit with dozens of candles. Seeing Snow standing in the corner reminded me for a moment of her candlelit hut, the pentagrams, the circle of protection drawn around her in the dirt.

"Oh, it's so lovely," Helena breathed, twirling around to inspect the circular chamber. She flinched, surprised, when she saw Snow, and seemed suddenly embarrassed. Snow stood beside a tub with a black grate over the top of it.

"We've prepared a steam treatment for you," I explained, pointing out the grate that she would lie upon. "It will restore your skin."

"Will it make my skin look as perfect as hers?" she asked, her face and neck red with envy. I lifted a finger and touched her cheek tenderly.

"Don't worry, darling. You will be lovely."

Snow remained in the corner as I helped Helena undress. When she stood naked in the firelight a harsh wind began to blow, making the tower seem to sway. She grasped my arm with sudden wariness, then laughed self-consciously. Her arms turned prickly when exposed to the cold air.

"You'll feel better once you lie down," I assured her, and helped her into the tub. "Close your eyes," I said, striving to keep my voice even, measured. The moment Helena lay down, bright flashes of Ursula sliced through my vision, even with my eyes open. This time I could not push the visions away.

"I can see her, too," Snow murmured, moving closer to me.

"Who?"

"I can see all of your other girls." She stared at me with wide eyes. I looked into the mirror and I could see them, too: Anastasia with her golden hair and Ursula soaked in blood. Others emerged behind them, crowding into the mirror's surface. The three most recent kills fought their way to the front, their dark eyes burning in their milk-white faces.

"I see them all the time," I told her.

"You've done this before?" she asked, but did not seem surprised.

"I thought you would have known that by now."

I heard Helena sigh deeply, adjusting her body on the wire grate. Her eyes were already closed. I handed Snow the blade; her small fingers curled tightly around the silver handle.

"I think I did know," she said, looking up at me. "I didn't want to believe it."

"We all do things we may regret, in order to save ourselves. Don't you agree?"

Snow held the blade in her hand, gazing down at Helena in the tub. For a moment I feared that she wouldn't go through with it. Sinestra appeared from the shadows behind her suddenly, and smiled at me. I basked in the pride of his smile.

"Please help me," I murmured.

"You don't need my help," he said. "You're not alone."

"What did you say?" Snow looked up at me, her eyes questioning.

"I don't want to lose you, Snow. I don't want to lose you, the way I lost your mother." As I said it, I realized it was more than that.

Snow reached out and held Helena's hand, lifting her arm gently from the side of the tub. Her arm was pale as the belly of a fish. The sharp edge of the blade glinted for a moment, then in one swift motion she sliced Helena's arm with a graceful sweep across her flesh. Like an expert. Like a woman.

Helena's eyes flew open and she cried out in pain and fear. When she saw the blood upon her arm, her eyes glazed over in shock. She did not scream again.

"One of us has to die," Snow explained, startling Helena from the sight of her own bleeding arm.

"No, Snow, don't—"

"You will be safe in the eyes of God, I promise you—but I won't. It can't be me." With these words the blade came down again, cutting faster and deeper with each pass across Helena's skin. Despite Snow's small hands, she wielded the blade with surprising force. I watched Helena writhe and thrash angrily in the tub, blood splattering onto the floor. For a moment I thought to stop Snow, but slowly Helena's struggling ceased and she turned heavy and limp. I did not stop Snow. I only watched.

It was breathtaking.

When Snow turned to me, her white gown was wet with blood. Her chest was heaving.

"And now I am free," she breathed, standing before the tub, but there was still a question in her voice.

"God could not have predicted this," I assured her. "You are freed from the whims of fate. What happens is your decision alone."

I bent to her level and looked directly into her eyes, resting my hand upon her face.

"I am God, here, in this castle. I have created heaven and hell. And I have created you in my image."

The steadiness of Snow's cold gaze faltered when there was a sudden commotion on the stairs. The blade dropped to the ground with a splintering crack. The door flew open and the girls rushed in: Mary, Elizabeth, Althea, and Sarah. They took in the scene before them quickly, not pausing to decipher what had taken place.

"They're coming," Althea blurted out, slamming the door behind her. "They know something's wrong and they're coming."

They held the door fast, all four of them pressing against it with all of their strength. Mary cast a pleading glance in my direction, needing both strength and approval. I smiled at them, but felt somehow removed from the scene. After all, this kill was not mine. Snow stood before the tub, motionless, her bloody hands trembling at her sides. I watched the scene progress as if it were all a dream.

The door gave way, and the girls were thrown to the floor. Konrad was the first to enter, followed by Pugrue and Rowena. They stopped short at the sight of the blood upon Snow's white gown.

"Snow?" Konrad asked; I knew he was uncertain, and that uncertainty stung Snow like a needle in her heart. He moved forward, panting, to look at her bloodstained face. Pugrue's rheumy eyes seemed to melt at the sight before him. I expected someone to scream, but they only stared, their faces white as parchment. I think I've never stood in so silent a room. I looked at Snow and saw the fear return to her face. She clenched her bloodstained hands into fists.

"What has she done to you, Snow?" Rowena cried, then turned to me. "What have you done!"

"We can't let you harm this child, Erzebet," Pugrue told me, his voice old and weak. "I can't let you kill such an innocent young girl. Not when it can still be stopped—and it looks as if we are just in time. Are you all right, Snow?"

"Snow? Speak to me, please," Konrad pleaded, his dark eyes glistening, feverish in the firelight.

"I'm afraid you misunderstand this innocent girl," I informed them. "Just as you've always misunderstood me."

Rowena walked over and pulled Snow into her arms, but the embrace did not seem to register on Snow's blank face. She could not touch Rowena with her quaking hands.

"Snow, did she hurt you? You're bleeding! How has she hurt you?"

But as she pulled Snow forward, the tub was revealed. Helena's head was limp against the side of the tub, her honey-colored hair falling over the edge. Rowena's eyes turned again to me.

"What did you do?"

"I didn't do anything," I assured her. "The girl is dead, isn't she, Snow?"

Pugrue crossed himself and moved closer to Helena, her white skin mottled and grotesque with blood. At Pugrue's tentative touch, a spasm shook through Helena's body. Helena lifted her hand from the edge of the tub. I heard Rowena shriek in fear; Pugrue stood as if carved from stone. Helena lifted her hand, and pointed to Snow. Her head rolled against the edge of the tub, her eyes, barely open, gleamed in the firelight.

"You did this," she said, her voice high and thin. "You will burn for this."

When her hand dropped heavily against the tub, Pugrue rushed to her side.

"No!" Rowena cried, her hand grappling onto Pugrue's arm like a claw. Rowena's liquid eyes pleaded with him, her other arm still tight around Snow. The blood on Snow's hands finally registered on Pugrue's face.

"It's too late for her," Rowena hissed over the sound of Helena's labored breathing. "We can only save one of them—we can only save Snow."

Helena's breath rattled thickly, her eyes nearly shut. My girls lay huddled together on the floor, uncertain whether to focus on Helena, or on my face. Pugrue, Konrad, and Rowena stood in dumb silence, watching Helena die. When she gasped her last breath, I could not help but laugh. Rowena turned her coal-bright eyes to me.

"How could you?" she asked, horror and shame vivid upon her face.

"No, Rowena, how could you? What kind of beast are you? You could have saved her"—I pointed at Helena's corpse—"but you made your choice to save her killer instead."

I looked at Snow, her eyes wide and glassy, her bloody hands still trembling. When she looked at me, I smiled. I knelt beside her and lifted the bloody blade from the floor. I cast it upon the table before me, where it clattered loudly. They all flinched at the sight of it. Only the corpse of Helena remained still. Rowena began to gasp through her tears, but no one else in the room dared make a sound.

"We are as God made us," I told them.

Part Four

THE BLOOD CONFESSION

And always, night and day, he was in the mountains, and in the tombs, crying, and cutting himself with stones.

But when he saw Jesus afar off, he ran and worshipped him. . . . [Jesus] said unto him, Come out of the man, thou unclean spirit.

And he asked him, What is thy name? And he answered, saying, My name is Legion: for we are many.

MARK 5:5–9

LI

Day twenty-nine, night

They're all angry at me for what I did to the girl. Tried to do, more like it, and failed. Just one meek young girl. Just one drop of blood, pulled out of her soft flesh with a needle—not my weapon of choice. But they all pounced upon me the moment they saw the needle in my hand. Then they even scolded her for trusting me too much, for not getting up from the couch when I sat down beside her.

"One of you left that needle behind. Does that make this your fault?" I asked the round-cheeked girl.

I don't see how it matters now.

Day thirty, day

After countless days of waiting here, Stephan has finally arrived. Even though I've waited so long, I can't help but feel startled. His satin robes glitter like sapphires in the bleak candlelight. The servants hastily fall to their knees upon his entry. I, too, kneel, warily. He steps forward and helps me to my feet.

"Erzebet," he says, "I'm sorry for my delay. Please understand. I'm here to protect the family name."

"Of course," I begin, but he cuts me off before I can continue.

"The noble blood of Hungary can't bear this . . . impurity. You do understand, don't you?" His eyes flicker for a moment upon mine.

"You need my confession," I state carefully. I glance at the Bible, pages filled with the words needed to explain.

"No," he says suddenly, "you are a Bizecka, daughter of the count. You will not stand trial, and you will not confess anything. I have devised a better solution."

He grasps my hands in his and presses them to his dry lips.

"May God have mercy on your soul," he whispers, and turns to the door. The priest who arrived with him hastily presses a Bible into my hands, all the while nodding and praying a stream of benedictions beneath his breath.

As Stephan and the priest sweep from the room, I notice that my servants follow meekly. When I move to follow them, the door to the chamber is closed in front of my face. I hear the sound of the latch being nailed to the door, the iron bolt dropped into place. Still listening, I hear muffled voices, the grunting of men. The sound of stone scraping against stone, just beyond the door.

"What's happening?" I ask the door, banging my fists against the wood. "What are you doing?"

The door only shudders in response.

"Don't speak to her," I hear a voice say from the other side. The men only grunt, the stones continue to scrape and shift.

I stare at the door, then continue to plead, more loudly. After a while my questions make no sound, but merely echo loudly in the confines of my skull: What are you doing to me? *The sound of the moving stones grows louder, harsher. I listen to it all.*

In time, even these noises cease. I'm alone in this chamber, surrounded by silence: it presses upon me like a thousand grasping hands, suffocating, as I realize what has happened.

This chamber is my tomb.

No one ever understands the evil queen in any of the fairy stories you've been told—they think her heart is full of hate. But beneath that evil there is a lover of beauty, of all things beautiful. For this love I became a slave. If I could have taken one girl's charming smile and another's lustrous eyes, her delicate hands, her voice, the way she walked, the way she laughed, her silhouette in the moonlight, the shape of her lips, the sun on her hair. If I could take all of these things that captivated me and make them a part of me, I would be all things young and beautiful. I would have nothing left to envy, or fear.

Not one person in this world believes that they are truly good enough as they are: good enough to be admired, to be respected, to be loved. Only I am willing to admit this.

In the village, fables grow. The people stay indoors when the moon is full, string their windows with garlic and herbs, throw salt over one shoulder, and never whistle in the dark. They revel in the safety of superstition and bury their true fear deep in the sediment of their souls. They pretend to feel protected, but I am their truest, deepest fear: the fear that I am not a witch, or a monster, that I am merely human. I am no different from their mothers and sisters and daughters and wives. And humanity will eternally bear the sin of my existence, like a scar upon the flesh.

I sit here with this Bible and I wonder. If the faithful are right, and all of our actions are preordained by God, then how can I be guilty of anything? God sacrifices us for the sake of evil, and we are powerless against Him. I have been entombed here for my sins, and for His.

I wait all night for Marianna to appear in this mirror. When she appears, I shrink from her gaze, afraid of what she sees when she looks at me.

"I've offered you my confession, Marianna." I wonder if she will answer. I think of my mother for a moment, and her madness. Love is immune to madness—Marianna must understand this, as well as I.

I'm here, Erzebet, *she tells me; her voice undulates like water.* I'm standing here in the chambers of your heart. *The distance in her voice makes me shiver with fear.*

"Please, Marianna, please. You must forgive me. Snow came to no harm, in the end."

But do you admit that you have done wrong? Do you repent for your sins?

"I've told you everything," I utter. "There is nothing left to tell."

But would you have done things differently if you could do them again? *Her reflection ripples over the words.*

"All I ever wanted was not to be alone! Things would be different if you had stayed with me."

You can't blame this on me, Erzebet. You can't blame this on God, or on Snow. Or on Sinestra—you were the one to follow, to listen. If you don't repent, there is no room for forgiveness.

"I've confessed all my sins," I tell her, my palm pressed against the heat in my head. "I can't deny what God has made of me."

God is the judge in the end, Erzebet. He will judge what you have made of yourself.

"Then tell me what I should do, Marianna—tell me what to say, how to say it."

I cannot teach you to feel remorse; it is something you must find in yourself. I'm standing here in the chambers of your heart. . . .

"You know my heart, Marianna." My voice trembles, my vision blurring. "You know my heart better than anyone."

I did love you, Erzebet, and I still do. But you have changed beyond recognition, and I cannot save you. I'm standing here in the chambers of your heart. There are rooms here I no longer recognize. The corridors are lined with ice.

She blinks slowly. For a moment her skin seems to shimmer like crystal, like snow.

Erzebet, it is so cold in here. *Then she turns and walks away.*

"Please, Marianna! Don't leave me here, please!"

The room is silent. The mirror is dim, and only a mirror. It shows me only my own face. It's only glass, this mirror, reflective glass made of science and not magic. As I look, my reflection begins to change: my blush fades and my complexion turns sallow, dark circles emerge from beneath my eyes, and deep lines crease the skin of my cheeks. Strands of my hair turn white and wiry, as if covered in frost. It does not matter what is true, but what is believed. Now that all of my beliefs are gone, this mirror shows me the truth. It has nothing else to show.

I grasp a goblet from the table and smash it into the mirror's silver surface, splintering my own reflection. A shard of glass slices my palm.

Blood of my blood, flesh of my flesh . . . my hand slices just like mortal flesh. Like the flesh of all those peasant girls I bled, limp white arms held over a wooden bowl. The blood glimmers in the light of my last candles. I can't stop myself: I press it to my lips. The taste is bitter, metallic.

At least no one will watch me grow old.

We will watch you, *the ghosts croon, in unison.* We will never leave you. *Their voices turn my blood to ice. I whip around at the sound, but I see nothing.*

We will watch you grow old.

No one ever understands the evil queen within us all. They deny her existence, but that doesn't mean she isn't there. We are all hungry, every one of us hungry: to be desired, to be loved, to never be alone.

Laughter ripples along the walls. I turn at the sound and see blood dripping from the stone walls, on the floor, on my gown, my pale hands. I look in the mirror and see blood splattered upon my face. I reach up a trembling hand to touch it; the laughter returns, this time shrieking laughter, too loud for my head to contain. I stumble back against the wall in fear.

We will never leave you. You will never be alone.

I press myself against the wall, but there is nowhere to hide. When I open my eyes, I see pale arms and legs and hands emerging from the walls.

"Anastasia, Ursula, Therese . . . Elizabeth, Mary, Sarah, Althea . . ." I chant their names as they climb out of the walls, walking toward me. I call their names loudly, my voice pulling from me as if by forces outside myself, pulling the names out louder and louder, as if a desperate prayer. They smile at the sound of their own names and repeat them, until the tower is shaking with the cacophony of their cries.

"Katarina, Susannah, Josephine . . . Anna, Celia . . . Helena . . ."

I can barely hear my own voice; their screaming fills my head. My mind is like a chamber, no way out and no way in. Their cold fingers burn my flesh: winter is inside of me.

It is so cold in here.

Acknowledgments

I couldn't have completed this novel without a lot of support.
My heartfelt thanks go out to . . .

Amanda Holman, who handed me the business card of a literary agent she had just met.

My agent, Esmond Harmsworth, for taking a chance on a new writer and helping to shape the bloody mess of a first draft I sent him into something that sounded like a young adult novel.

To Professors Susan Bloom and Anita Silvey at Simmons College for their enthusiasm and words of encouragement throughout my editing adventure.

To the staff of the Interlibrary Loan Department at Simmons College, who fulfilled my numerous book requests.

To Mark McVeigh at Dutton Children's Books, for not being scared away by the dark subject matter, and for his enduring patience throughout the course of editing.

To my sisters Marcie, Valerie, and Susan and to my Grandma Sunny for their patience with me as I devoted my time, energy, and the vast majority of my brain power to this novel.

To friend and poet Lesley Jenike, for long chats about the Countess that stirred up my inspiration and excitement to start those first, rough drafts.

To all of my friends who have been eager to hear about my progress.

To my mother, Bernice Moskowitz, for her superhuman patience, unending support, and knowing when to tell me to get back to work.

To my husband, Thomas Libby, who contributed to lengthy, enlightening discussions about the nature of good and evil, and has learned more about young adult fiction and a certain sixteenth-century countess than he ever imagined possible.

All of your help has been immeasurable; I simply cannot thank you enough.